P9-DDC-522

IMPOSTORS

STEVENS MEMORIAL LIBRARY
20 Memorial Drive
Ashburnham, MA 01430
978-827-4115
Fax 978-827-4116

IMPOSTORS

SCOTT WESTERFELD

SCHOLASTIC PRESS

STEVENS MEMORIAL LIBRARY
20 Memorial Drive
Ashburnham, MA 01430
978-827-4115
Fax 978-827-4116

Copyright © 2018 by Scott Westerfeld

All rights reserved. Published by Scholastic Press, an imprint of Scholastic Inc.,
Publishers since 1920. SCHOLASTIC, SCHOLASTIC PRESS, and associated logos are
trademarks and/or registered trademarks of Scholastic Inc.

The publisher does not have any control over and does not assume any responsibility for
author or third-party websites or their content.

No part of this publication may be reproduced, stored in a retrieval system, or transmitted
in any form or by any means, electronic, mechanical, photocopying, recording, or
otherwise, without written permission of the publisher. For information regarding
permission, write to Scholastic Inc., Attention: Permissions Department,
557 Broadway, New York, NY 10012.

This book is a work of fiction. Names, characters, places, and incidents are either the
product of the author's imagination or are used fictitiously, and any resemblance to actual
persons, living or dead, business establishments, events, or locales is entirely coincidental.

Library of Congress Cataloging-in-Publication Data available

ISBN 978-1-338-15151-0

10 9 8 7 6 5 4 3 2 1   18 19 20 21 22

Printed in the U.S.A.   23
First edition, September 2018

Book design by Chris Stengel

38179000308278
10/18

To everyone fighting for their right to exist

PART I

HOSTAGE

Regard your soldiers as your children, and they will follow you into the deepest valleys.

—Sun Tzu

KILLER

We're about to die. Probably.

Our best hope is the pulse knife in my hand. It trembles softly, like a bird. That's how my head trainer, Naya, says to hold it.

Gently, careful not to crush it.

Firmly, so it doesn't fly away.

The thing is, my pulse knife really *wants* to fly. It's military grade. Smart as a crow, unruly as a young hawk. Loves a good fight.

It's going to get one. The assassin, twenty meters away, is spraying gunfire from the stage where my sister just gave her first public speech. Her audience, the dignitaries of Shreve, are strewn around the room—dead, faking death, or cowering. Security drones and hovercams are scattered on the floor, knocked out by some kind of jammer.

My sister's huddled next to me, gripping my free hand in both of hers. Her fingernails are deep in my skin.

We're behind a tipped-over table. It's a slab of vat-grown oak, five centimeters thick, but the assassin's got a barrage pistol. We might as well be hiding in a rosebush.

But at least no one can see us together.

We're fifteen years old.

This is the first time anyone's tried to kill us.

My heart is beating slantways, but I'm remembering to breathe. There's something ecstatic about the training kicking in.

Finally, I'm doing what I was born to do.

I'm saving my sister.

The comms are down, but Naya's voice is in my head from a thousand training sessions—*Can you protect Rafia?*

Not unless I take out this attacker.

Then do it.

"Stay here," I say.

Rafi looks up at me. She has a cut above her eye—from the splinters flying everywhere. She keeps touching it in wonder. Her teachers never make her bleed.

She's twenty-six minutes older than me. That's why she gives the speeches and I train with knives.

"Don't leave me, Frey," she whispers.

"I'm always with you." This is what I murmur from the bed beside hers, when she's having nightmares. "Now let go of my hand, Rafi."

4

She looks into my eyes, finds that unbroken trust we share.

As she lets go, the assassin lets loose again, a roar like the air itself is shredding. But he's spraying randomly, confused. Our father was supposed to be here, and only canceled at the last minute.

Maybe the assassin isn't even thinking about Rafi. He certainly doesn't know about me, my eight years of combat training. My pulse knife.

I make my move.

BODY DOUBLE

Rafi's speech was perfect. Clever and gracious. Unexpected and funny, like when she tells stories in the dark.

The dignitaries loved her.

I listened from the sidelines, hidden, wearing the same dress as her. Everything identical—our faces because we're twins, the rest because we work hard at it. I have more muscle, but Rafi tones her arms to match. When she gains weight, I wear sculpted body armor. We get our haircuts, flash tattoos, and surgeries side by side.

I was standing by to step in and wave to the crowd of randoms outside. Sniper-bait.

I'm her body double. And her last line of defense.

The applause swelled as she finished her speech and headed for the viewing balcony, the brilliant daughter stepping in for the absent leader. Hovercams rose up in a multitude, like sky lanterns on our father's birthday.

We were about to make the switch when the assassin opened fire.

I crawl out from behind cover.

The air is thick with the hot-metal reek of barrage pistol. The rich scents of roast beef and spilled wine. The assassin fires again, the roar thrilling my nerves.

This is what I was born to do.

Another table between me and the assassin is still upright. I crawl through chair legs and dropped silverware, past a spasming body.

On my back, looking up at the splintered table, I feel wine dripping through bullet holes onto my face. It's summer berries and ripe heaven on my tongue—only the best wine for our father's events.

I squeeze the knife, sending it into full pulse. It shrieks in my hand, buzzing and hot, ready to tear the world apart.

I shut my eyes and slice through the table.

Our father burns real wood at his winter hunting lodge. All that smoke trapped in a few logs, enough to rise a kilometer into the sky. A pulse knife at full power shreds things just as fine—molecules ripping, energy spilling out.

A swath of oak, dishes, and food dissolves into a haze of fragments, a thick hot cloud billowing across the room. Sawdust glittering with vaporized glassware.

The assassin stops firing. He can't see.

Me either, but I've already planned my next move.

I scuttle out from beneath the halved table, lungs clenched against the dust. At the edge of the stage, I pull myself up, still blind.

A grinding sound fills the ballroom. The assassin is using the cover of dust to feed his barrage pistol—the weapon uses improvised ammunition to make it smaller, harder to detect.

He's reloading so he can shoot blind and still kill everyone.

My sister is out there in the dust.

The taste of sawdust fills my mouth, along with a hint of vaporized feast. I set my pulse knife to fly at chest height. Hold it like a quivering dart.

And the assassin makes a mistake—

He coughs.

With the slightest nudge the knife flies from my hand, deadly and exuberant. A millisecond later comes a sound I recognize from target practice on pigs' carcasses—the gurgle of tissues, the rattle of bones.

The sawdust is cleared by a new force billowing out from where the knife hit. I see the assassin's legs standing there, nothing above his waist but that sudden blood mist.

For a grisly moment the legs stand alone, then crumple to the stage.

The knife flits back into my hand, warm and slick. The air tastes like iron.

I've just killed someone, but all I think is—

My sister is safe.

My sister is safe.

I drop from the stage, cross to where Rafi still huddles behind the table. She's breathing through a silk napkin, and hands it to me to share.

I stay alert, ready to fight. But the air is filling with the buzz of security drones waking back up. The assassin was wearing the jammer, I guess, so it's mist now too.

Finally, I let my knife go still. I'm starting to shake, and suddenly Rafi is the one thinking straight.

"Backstage, little sister," she whispers. "Before anyone figures out there's two of us."

Right. The dust is clearing, the survivors wiping their eyes. We hustle away through an access door beneath the stage.

We've grown up in this house. Playing hide-and-seek in this ballroom with night-vision lenses, I was always the hunter.

My comms ping back up, and Naya's voice is in my ear:

"We see you, Frey. Does Gemstone need medical?"

This is the first time we've used Rafi's code name in a real attack.

"She's cut," I say. "Over her eye."

"Get her to the sub-kitchen. Good work."

That last word sounds strange in my ear. All my training up to this moment might have seemed like work. But this?

This is me, complete.

"Is it over?" I ask Naya.

"Uncertain. Your father's locked down on the other side of the city." Naya's words are sharp with the possibility that this is only the start of something bigger. That at last the rebels are moving in force against our father.

I guide Rafi past stage machinery and lighting drones, to the stairs that lead down. Cleaning drones and cockroaches scuttle out of our way.

Five soldiers—everyone in Security who knows of my existence—meet us in a kitchen cleared of staff. A medic shines a light in Rafi's eyes, cleans and seals her cut, flushes her lungs of smoke and dust.

We move in a tight group toward the secure elevator. The soldiers settle around me and Rafi, hulking in their body armor like protective giants.

The glassy look in my sister's eyes hasn't faded.

"Was that real?" she asks softly.

I take her hand. "Of course."

My trainers have run surprise drills on us a hundred

times, but nothing so public, with dead bodies and barrage pistols.

Rafi touches the wound on her head, like she still can't believe that someone tried to kill her.

"That's nothing," I say. "You're okay."

"What about you, Frey?"

"Not a scratch."

Rafi shakes her head. "No, I mean, did anyone see you—next to *me*?"

I stare into her eyes, her fear cutting into my excitement. What if someone in the ballroom saw us? A body double is worthless if everyone knows they're not the real thing.

Then what would be the point of me?

"No one saw," I tell her. There was too much dust and chaos, too many people wounded and dying. The hovercams were all knocked out.

And what matters is: I've saved my sister. I let the ecstasy of that flood into me.

Nothing will ever feel this good again.

SCAR

"I want a scar," Rafi says.

Our doctor goes quiet.

We've been moved up to the house medical center, where our father takes his longevity treatments. The surfaces glisten, the staff wear white disposables. Rafi and I are lying on tufted leather lounges facing a picture window—a sprawling view of Shreve and beyond, the city rolling off into forest and storm clouds.

Our father isn't back yet, though the city has been quiet. This wasn't a revolution. Just one assassin.

The doctor's assistant is cutting away my fancy dress, checking for any injuries I'm too brain-pumped to feel. She's the only member of Orteg's staff who knows that I exist.

She always seems scared of me. Maybe it's my stream of training injuries. Or maybe it's because if she ever lets slip that I exist, she'll be disappeared. She's never told me her name.

Dr. Orteg leans over Rafi, shining a light on her brow. "Fixing this will only take a minute. It won't hurt."

"I don't care what hurts," she says, knocking his light away. "What I want is a *scar*."

Looks pass between the doctor and his assistant, the caution that descends whenever Rafi's being difficult. Her explosions of temper come without much warning.

Dr. Orteg clears his throat. "I'm sure your father—"

"My father understands exactly why." She arches her neck, sighs dramatically at the ceiling, reminding herself to be patient with lesser beings. "Because they tried to kill *me*."

Silence again. Less fearful, more thoughtful.

Rafia is more popular than our father. No one ever polls the question, but our staff studies the metrics. The way people talk about her, the expressions on their faces, the movements of their eyes. Everything captured by the spy dust shows it's true.

But no one wants to have *that* conversation with our father.

Dr. Orteg looks at me for help, but Rafi's right. The scar won't let anyone forget what happened tonight. What the rebels tried to do to her.

Then it hits me. "Like those old pictures of Tally Youngblood."

Rafi's eyes light up. "Exactly!"

A murmur passes through the room.

No one's seen Tally in years, except her face in random clouds, like she's a saint. Or in shaky hovercam shots. But people still look for her.

And she did have that scar, just above her eyebrow. Her first strike against the pretty regime.

"Interesting point, Frey," comes a voice from the doorway. "I'll ask your father."

Standing there is Dona Oliver, his private secretary. Behind her is a bank of screens—the control room, where our father's staff monitors every feed in our city. News, gossip, even the images captured by the spy dust all filter through this tower.

Dr. Orteg gets back to work, looking relieved that the decision is out of his hands now.

Dona turns away from us, whispering into her wrist. She's beautiful in an extravagant way. Big eyes, flawless skin—that crazy-making gorgeousness from the pretty era, back when everyone was perfect. She's never had her beauty surged into something more fashionable. Somehow she carries it without looking like a bubblehead.

Rafi takes a hand mirror from the table between us. "Maybe the scar should be on the left side, where Tally's was. What do you think, little sister?"

I lean across and take her chin gently, give her a long look. "Leave it right where it is. It's perfect."

Her only answer is a little shrug, but she's smiling now. I'm pleased with myself, and that pleasure blends with leftover excitement from the battle downstairs. Sometimes I'm a decent diplomat, even if diplomacy is my sister's job.

The faraway look fades from Dona's face.

"He agrees," she says. "But nothing unsightly, doctor. Make it elegant."

"Only the *best* scars," my sister says, laughing as she eases back into her chair.

It takes a full ten minutes to perfect Rafi's injury. It seems an elegant scar is trickier than none at all.

She's beautiful, as always, but a blemish on her face feels like a mark against me. I should have gotten to her quicker, or spotted the assassin before he had time to open fire at all.

When Dr. Orteg is done, he gives me a troubled look—he has to cut me now.

The same scar exactly.

He picks up a bottle of medspray.

"Wait," I say.

Everyone looks at me. I'm not usually the one giving orders. I was born twenty-six minutes too late for that.

"It's just . . ." The reason isn't clear in my mind, and then it is. "It hurt, didn't it, Rafi?"

"Splinters in my face?" She laughs. "Yeah, a lot."

"Then it should hurt me too."

The others all stare at me, like I'm too shell-shocked to think. But Rafi seems pleased. She loves it when I cause trouble, even if that's her job.

"Frey's right," she says. "We should match, inside and out."

The room sharpens a little—a tear in my eye. I love it when Rafi and I think the same way, even after all that work to make us opposites.

"Inside and out," I whisper.

Dr. Orteg shakes his head. "There's no *reason* to do it without anesthetic."

He looks at Dona Oliver.

"Except it's perfect," she says. "Good girl, Frey."

I smile back at her, certain this is the best day of my life.

I'm not even disappointed that she doesn't ask our father for permission to hurt me.

DAMAGE

Half an hour later we're alone in our room, sitting side by side on Rafi's bed. Her wallscreen is set to mirror us.

We keep the lights low, because my head is throbbing. Dr. Orteg had to redo my scar three times before it matched Rafi's.

I didn't let him use the medspray until it was done. I wanted to feel it the same way she did—the sharpness of breaking skin, the warm trickle of my own blood. When we touch our scars, it will be with the same memory of pain.

"We look amazing," she whispers.

That's how she always talks about our looks—in the plural. Like it's not boasting if she includes me too.

And maybe it's true. Our mother was a natural pretty. The only one in the city, Father brags to anyone who'll listen. He says we'll never need a real operation, even when we get old and crumbly, just a touch-up here or there.

But our mix of his glower and our mother's angelic face has always looked disjointed to me. And now this scar.

Like Beauty and the Beast had daughters, and raised them in the wild.

"I don't know if we're pretty," I say. "But we're alive."

"Thanks to you. I just sat there screaming."

I turn to stare at her. "When did you scream?"

"The whole time." She drops her eyes. "Just not out loud."

Rafi was her usual self in front of everyone—bratty and full of swagger. But here alone with me, her voice has gone quiet and serious.

"Doesn't it scare you?" she asks.

I recite what our father always says. "The rebels only hate us because they're jealous of what he's built. That means they're small people, not worth being afraid of."

Rafi shakes her head. "I meant, doesn't it scare you that you *killed* someone?"

The question takes a second to sink in. I've been too brain-rattled to think about it. The sound of the knife churning through the assassin, the taste of his blood in the air.

"In that moment, it's not *me*." My fingers flutter, moving through pulse knife commands. "It's the training—all those hours of practice."

She takes my hand, stills my twitching fingers. "That's what Naya would say. But how did it feel to *you*?"

"Amazing," I say, soft as air. "I'd kill anyone for you, Rafi."

18

Her eyes stay locked on mine. Her lips barely move, mouthing the shadow of a word—*Anyone?*

My breath catches. I can't believe that she would ask me this, even too softly for spy dust to hear. Because I know exactly who she means.

I dare to give her the barest nod.

Even him.

A smile settling on her face at last, Rafi looks away into the mirror. Those identical faces with identical scars.

"Remember back when we were littlies, and they told us it was a game? Pretending there was only one of us? None of it seemed real."

I nod. "Like a joke we were playing on the world."

"Some joke. It's less funny when someone shoots at you."

"He missed."

She points at her scar. "Speak for yourself."

"That wasn't a bullet, Rafi. Just . . . collateral damage."

She reaches across to touch my brow with careful fingertips. Beneath the tingle of medspray, a dull ache beats in time with my heartbeat.

"So what's this?"

I turn away, but Rafi's still there in the mirror.

"That's not damage," I say. "That's me, always part of you."

She squeezes my hand, and I feel that certainty I always had as a littlie. That I'm more than expendable. More than a body double.

"This isn't normal," she whispers. "This secret. People don't raise their kids to take a bullet."

"But I saved you."

Rafi doesn't know how amazing this feels. How those years of training, all that work and pain, flowing through me now like lightning.

She turns away for a moment.

"One day I'll save you too."

THE SOFTEST THING

Naya is trying to hurt me.

She's coming at me with a *bō*, a long bamboo staff with metal tips. It's one her favorite weapons—it spins in her hands, stirring the cool air of the training room.

It's a whole year after the assassination attempt, and there haven't been any attacks on our family since. But they train me harder than ever.

Lately, it's all been improvised weapons. I never go anywhere without my pulse knife, but Naya wants me ready for anything.

The weapons table is full of random junk—a handscreen, a scarf, a vase of flowers, a fireplace poker. I'm supposed to grab something to protect myself.

The poker can't be right. Too obvious, too heavy and slow to block that wheeling staff.

The vase would shatter—and I'm barefoot. No thanks.

Scarves can strangle, bind, and trap. But I'd have to get close to use it, and the spinning *bō* is longer than I am tall.

So I grab the handscreen and fling it edgewise at Naya.

For a glorious moment it's a flying blade, flashing sharp and deadly. I almost worry it'll hurt her. But a flick of the *bō* shatters it into a spray of safety glass.

Naya barely squints as the shards rain past her.

I grab the vase and tip it onto the mat. Maybe I can make her slip.

But there's no water in the vase, just dried flowers. Petals scatter, like she's getting married.

Maybe I'm being too clever. As she closes in, I grab for the—

Whap.

The *bō* cracks down on the back of my hand, and agony erupts. Anatomy classes spill like fire through my head—all those nerves in the hand, laced around all those delicate bones.

The best way to take down a bigger opponent is to break a finger.

I'm sinking to my knees, clutching my wrist.

"Your turn." Naya throws me the staff.

It clatters to the floor. The pain is fizzing up my arm, filling my head. Red sparks fly at the edge of my vision.

"Get up," she says. "Fights don't stop when you get hurt."

"But I think it's—"

"Stand and *fight*." She means it.

All my trainers have been brain-missing lately. Eager to make me bleed, to break bones. But this is the first time Naya's forced me to keep fighting after hurting me this bad.

I stagger to my feet, clutching the staff in my left hand.

"Get your weapon moving, Frey."

I put my broken hand on the staff, and for a moment it's too painful to think. Then I remember—all the power of the *bō* comes from the back hand, the front only guides the staff.

I get the weapon spinning, barely.

"Faster."

It's impossible, but I try anyway. If I pass out from the pain, at least this will be over.

Naya darts forward to the table, then rolls back out of reach, the scarf in her hands. She ties a quick knot at one end.

Of course—the correct answer is always the softest, fluffiest thing on the table.

She flicks the scarf into the slow gyre of my staff. It tangles, jerks the *bō* from my grasp. The jolt to my broken hand is so painful I almost throw up.

"The best way to blunt a force is to tangle it," Naya says.

This was the point of today's lesson, I suppose—a parable to make me wiser. But it's hard to learn anything when it hurts too much to breathe.

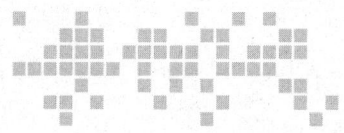

Five minutes later, while the autodoc is knitting my metacarpals back together, our father summons me.

Naya doesn't look surprised. Just shakes her head.

"You aren't ready."

I stare at her. "For what?"

"It's not my place to tell you."

"Are we going someplace?"

She hesitates, then nods.

"So there's a *reason* for this." I wave my good hand at the wreckage in the room. The shattered glass of the handscreen, the strewn petals, the scarf still tangled with the bamboo staff.

"There's always a reason, Frey. Did you think we were doing this for fun?"

Fun? I almost laugh. The autodoc is making a grinding sound, like the beautiful steel contraption in my father's office that dribbles out coffee on command. I distantly feel my bones being restitched and reshaped.

It makes me twitch.

Then it hits me—

Improvised weapons. All month long.

Wherever Rafi and I are going, I won't be taking my knife.

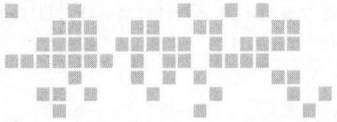

Naya and I take the private elevator up—only people who know about me are allowed to use it. There are special hallways for me too, marked with red stripes for the highest-clearance members of staff.

When we were little, sometimes Rafi would hide in our room and let me wander the house. When I was dressed like her, I could go anywhere I wanted. But freedom was never really-happy-making, because I was always alone.

So we made up a better game. We pretended we lived in a dungeon with monsters roaming the halls. Sneaking into the nonsecure corridors, we'd spy on the staff at work, careful not to be seen.

Luckily, we got caught by Naya before anyone else. Furious, she explained what would happen to someone who saw us together, if they didn't already know about me.

After that, the game wasn't fun anymore.

But I miss having time for games.

My hand is wrapped in a cold-sleeve to keep the swelling down. The bones are knitted, but the tissues deep inside feel wrong. Like always after a fresh training injury, I keep imagining something torn in there, too small for the autodoc to catch.

When the elevator arrives outside our father's office, Rafi and her assistant are waiting. Father never sees me without my older sister in the room. Bonding too closely with his spare daughter would be sloppy.

Rafi takes in my sweatpants and flushed face, the cold-sleeve around my hand.

"You smell like effort," she says—part of her act is making everything look effortless. But she offers a little shrug of sympathy. "At least he'll be able to tell us apart."

This makes me smile.

Once when we were ten years old, we dressed up to fool him, Rafi in workout gear and me in a pinafore. She spent a solid hour getting my makeup right, me squirming the whole time.

Our father didn't spot the deception, but Dona did. She didn't let us ride our hoverboards for a month. But it was worth it for those moments of power over our father—knowing something that he didn't.

Now he keeps us waiting.

Naya checks the readout on my cold-sleeve while Rafi's assistant lists what parties she's attending tonight. Nothing too public, so I'll stay here, making up for the training hours lost to this broken hand.

Normally I'd be happy to stay home. But after a month of heavy workouts, I need a night at a dance club. One of the big places, where I get to leave the family suite and take Rafi's place on the floor.

I'm a better dancer than my sister. Not when it comes to ballet or ballroom, of course. But jostling in a crowd of sweaty strangers is more like combat than anything she's studied.

When her assistant is finished, Rafi looks at me.

"Do you know why we're here, little sister?"

I shake my head. She looks disappointed, and gives me one of her old hand signals. The ones we started using when we realized they were always watching us.

Follow my lead.

As if I ever do anything else.

The doors to the office open, and Dona Oliver is standing there.

"Your father will see you now."

Our father's office is the highest floor of the tower, which he built the old-fashioned way, with a skeleton of steel. He doesn't trust hoverstruts, just metal and stone.

From two hundred meters in the sky, the city looks puny. The distant forest blurs into a mottle of green. But the clouds still loom large, hunkering in the distance, unconquerable.

My sister curtsies, and I nod my head. Our father's staring off into an airscreen, giving no sign he's paying attention.

"You girls have noticed the change in your routine?" Dona begins.

"Hard to miss," Rafi says. "You've been sending me to *all* the parties, and look at poor Frey. Someone's broken her!"

"It's been challenging, I'm sure," Dona says. "But necessary."

Rafi turns to our father. "This is about the Palafox deal, right?"

Still looking off into the airscreen, he smiles to himself.

I don't know what deal they're talking about. Business and politics aren't my job. All I know is that the Palafoxes are the first family of Victoria. A smaller, weaker city, four hundred kilometers south of Shreve. Not a military threat.

"Very good, Rafia." Dona gives my sister a measured smile. "We're almost done with the agreement. Next month, Victoria's salvage operations will merge with ours."

"You mean, we'll handle security," Rafi says. "Protect them from the rebels while they pick through the ruins."

The Rusty ruins—so this is about steel.

This is history that every littlie knows. Centuries ago, there were people called the Rusties, who loved metal. They dug mines, poisoned rivers, and tore down entire mountains to get it. They used the metal to build their cities, their cars, their tools, and—of course—the weapons they annihilated each other with.

Now all that's left of the Rusties is their ruins. The bones of the old world are their legacy to us.

Turns out, picking through those dead cities to recycle Rusty metal is much easier than digging it out of the ground. Our father loves to build, and he's close to exhausting all the ruins near Shreve.

So he wants to make a deal. Protection for metal.

Dona Oliver is still smiling, but Rafi's expression makes me nervous. That twitch in her eye, like she's about to have a tantrum.

"Why would the Palafoxes trust *you?*" she says, straight to our father's face. My breath catches, and Dona's expression draws tight.

He doesn't seem angry, though. It's another moment before his eyes drop from the airscreen to take us both in—me sweaty and injured, my sister sharp and focused.

A knife with two edges.

"A good question from a clever girl. Why would they trust us to drop an army in their ruins?" He smiles again. "The answer is, they don't."

My heart pulses in my right hand.

No one trusts our father. They all remember what he did to his allies here in Shreve, once he got what he wanted from them. They're all nobodies now, like they never existed.

Our father makes his own reality.

"The Palafoxes want a token of good faith," he says. "A guarantee that we'll give their ruins back once the rebels have been driven away."

My sister's eyes are bright, like she's working up tears.

"Daddy. Don't do this."

"They insisted." His voice softens. "It has to be something we'd never risk losing. Something more important to us than anything else in the world. Something exquisite."

"You can't!" Rafi shouts. "I won't *let* you!"

Dread silence falls, like it does whenever she raises her voice to him. Dona looks like she wants to disappear. And it dawns on me what they're talking about—sending my sister to the Palafoxes as a hostage.

She's the collateral for the deal. If our father keeps the ruins, the Palafoxes keep Rafi.

The world tilts a little beneath my feet. We've never been separated for more than a few days.

"Those are the terms," he says. "The Palafoxes insisted."

"But they'll know!" Rafi takes a step closer to his desk, her voice raw. "She'll never fool them!"

That's when my pain-addled brain grasps the rest of it. Rafi's been out socializing, building her face rank, making it clear that she's indispensable to our father's leadership. But I've been the one training with improvised weapons, because no one lets a hostage keep a pulse knife.

She's not going to be the collateral.

I am.

The world tilts a little farther.

"Frey can handle this," Dona says.

Rafi wheels on her. "In what universe? This isn't a bunch of randoms asking for autographs—it's another first family!"

"We'll train her," Dona says.

"In a *month*? She doesn't know how to dress, how to eat. She barely knows how to hold a conversation!"

Rafi's words sting, even if she's trying to protect me.

"It's true," Dona relents. "This isn't something our training program has anticipated."

"Because *none* of you understand." Rafi turns to our father. "The other families aren't as soft as you think, Daddy. The Palafoxes will eat her alive!"

I stare at Rafi, wondering how soft she thinks *I* am. She can't keep me locked in our room forever.

But no one asks my opinion. No one even looks at me. They're all so used to pretending I don't exist.

And that makes me say, "I can do it."

Silence again, like they'd forgotten I could speak.

"I've been imitating you for sixteen years, Rafi. This is what I was *born* to do."

My sister stares at me in disbelief. She wants to argue, but her momentum is broken by my betrayal.

Our father gives me an appraising smile.

"Good girl." His eyes drift away again. "It's decided."

Relieved, Dona hustles us out of the office.

"Come along. There's a lot of work ahead, Frey. Your French lessons start tonight."

"French?" I ask. "But Victoria's down south. Why not Spanish?"

Rafi sighs, wiping her tears away. "Their oldest son goes to school in Genève. Or didn't you know that?"

I shake my head. Because I didn't know the Palafoxes had a son. I didn't even know people spoke French in Genève.

I don't know anything.

Rafi gives me a dark little smile.

"*T'es dans la merde*," she says.

Despite my woeful French, I have a pretty good idea what that means.

MACHIAVELLI

"*Ton accent est terrible*," Rafi says.

I am aware.

"*Encore*," she commands, and the sim starts over.

I try—I really do—but halfway through the exercise, my tongue gets tangled. The nice man in the airscreen looks confused. He's wearing a beret and the Paris Hoverdrome sits behind him, because this simulation is designed for littlies.

Bored by my failure, Rafi jumps in to finish the exercise. Effortlessly. Flawlessly. Too quickly to help me.

The man in the beret is happy again.

Je le déteste.

My sister learns languages all day, every day. When she points at something with two fingers, the cyrano in her ear whispers the French word for it—three fingers for German. She has human tutors in both tongues, to learn native gestures and expressions, so she won't look like some random taught by a machine.

Of *course* she's better than me at this. All that time I was learning how to fight, Rafi was learning how to be witty and worldly and wise.

She waves her hand in disgust, and the airscreen fades. Her temper has been flaring since the meeting with our father.

"I can't *believe* you've forgotten, Frey!"

Rafi taught me secondhand French when we were littlies. So I could make small talk in receiving lines without making her look foolish. But my irregular verbs didn't have to be correct for that.

Irregular verbs are bogus.

"No one's going to test me, Rafi. I bet the Palafoxes don't even know you speak French!"

"They'll know everything about me. Remember our trip to Montré?"

She waves a hand, and the airscreen pops back on—Rafi on a newsfeed, smiling, posing with children in school uniforms in a hovering garden of snow. She looks confident and charming, not like someone murdering the local grammar.

My memories of that trip aren't about schoolkids. I hid in our private suite while my sister and father met with famous people. Then I took her place in front of polite crowds, wearing vat-grown furs over body armor. Sniper bait in the snow.

Traveling isn't much fun for me. Just as much hiding, a lot less space.

I flop back on my bed. "So it's your fault for showing off."

"It's your fault for telling him you wanted to go!"

"What I say doesn't matter." I stare at Rafi, daring her to deny it.

She looks away. "Fine. It's *his* fault. If people trusted him, the Palafoxes wouldn't need a hostage."

I can only shrug. That's just the way it is—the way *he* is.

And the brave part of me that spoke up in front of our father really wants to do this.

Rafi doesn't understand. She gets to charm people every day, making sure the citizens of Shreve love as well as fear us. But all my years of training have only been relevant for two minutes and four seconds—the time it took me to save her life.

"I need to do this, Rafi."

Her answer is a whisper. "To *help* him? He doesn't even see you."

I turn away, stung again. These are things that she never says out loud.

"I want to feel useful."

She sighs. "You don't hate him as much as I do."

This is an old accusation. But it's easier for Rafi to hate our father—he recognizes her existence.

"I won't be gone forever. Two months to secure the ruins, Dona says."

"'Secure the ruins'? If you want to fool the Palafoxes, at least stop talking like a military advisor." Rafi goes to the window to glare down at the garden. "Why people are fighting over Rusty garbage is beyond me."

"Everyone needs metal. We can't go back to digging holes in the ground."

"Because when the Rusties did, they almost destroyed the world," she recites. "Maybe the pretty regime had the right idea. If everyone was still a bubblehead, there wouldn't be all this fighting."

I laugh at this, because she's probably kidding.

The pretty regime ended just before Rafi and I were born. Back then, everyone had an operation when they turned sixteen. It made you beautiful, but also had a secret purpose—it changed the way you thought.

Pretties never questioned authority, always consumed their fair share of resources and no more. Cities used only the power generated by their solar footprint, and recycled every scrap of metal. The Rusty ruins were left alone, a strategic reserve, so that humanity would never have to strip-mine the earth again.

But then a girl called Tally Youngblood became the first rebel. She brought the pretty regime down, and suddenly everyone had to think for themselves. It was called the mind-rain, all those bubbleheads waking up at once. All those cities hungry and ready to expand.

Freedom has a way of destroying things.

People like our father seized power in the chaos. They began to build new structures, whole new cities, starting a race for metal. Now the ruins aren't just reminders of the Rusties' excesses—they're invitations to start it all again.

Tally may be missing, but there are still rebels out there who think the ruins should be left alone.

"You'd hate being a bubblehead," I argue. "They had brain damage!"

Rafi shrugs. "But they were happy all the time. They didn't have to worry about getting shot at. They didn't have wars."

"They were too *dumb* to have wars!"

She shakes her head. "Repartee like that won't impress your hosts."

"I'll just be quiet. They can't *make* me be witty."

"You think wit is your problem?" Rafi starts counting on her fingers. "You don't know which designs everyone's wearing. You don't know the latest scandals—who doesn't get invited to parties anymore, or why. You've never even had to change the subject in an awkward conversation!"

I stand up to look out the window of our room, my hands twitching.

"I love you, little sister," Rafi says softly. "But you're not normal. Instead of clothes and music, you talk about escape routes and improvised weapons. And you eat like a barbarian."

She's said all this before—that growing up as a body double made me different. But always fondly, because I wasn't like her rich, bratty friends. The way she's saying it now just makes me feel lonely.

The thing is, I can smile like Rafi, move like her, mimic her expressions. Read a speech from an eyescreen with her pauses and inflections. We even hoverboard with the same stance.

But I don't know *people* like she does. She can talk to anyone—dignitaries, soldiers, randoms in a receiving line—with perfect ease. She has a hundred friends I've never really met. I've just memorized their faces so I know who to wave to on the dance floor. She has a whole life I've only seen slivers of, like I'm spying on a party through a keyhole.

Maybe that's why I want to go to Victoria. To have my own party for once.

I stick out my lower lip. "I'll just pout the whole time, and they'll never know the difference. Two months is your average sulk."

Rafi's resting sulk face is my masterpiece, but she doesn't even crack a smile.

"You have to be the perfect guest, Frey. It's a disaster for both families if anyone figures out you're a hostage."

"Who'd believe it? I mean, has anyone ever *done* this before?"

"Not for about seven hundred years. Which you'd know if you'd read Machiavelli." Her voice goes softer. "But this is Dad we're talking about. Do you think maybe he . . ."

She hesitates, then whispers the magic words.

"Sensei Noriko."

We go to the bathroom and turn on all the taps, loud and hot, steaming the room up in case of stray spy dust. We wait there silently, watching as the mirror fogs.

Sensei Noriko was Rafi's etiquette tutor. She taught my sister all the subtle refinements I never needed to know—how to eat properly, how to use a fan, how to sit at a tea ceremony. She didn't know about me.

Then, when we were nine, Rafi declared that my curtsying needed some serious work. So I pretended to be my sister for one lesson.

Noriko had an amazing eye for movement, and knew immediately that something was wrong with me. She was about to call Rafi's head tutor, which would have only made things worse. So I admitted who I was—*what* I was.

Someone must have been watching, because Sensei Noriko never came to teach again.

Rafi and I were twelve before we ever said aloud what probably happened to her. Since then, the words *Sensei Noriko* remind us that our secrets are dangerous.

Once the steam is thick, Rafi leans close and whispers, "What if he planned this way back when we were born? Hiding you this whole time, in case he ever needed to guarantee a deal?"

A shudder goes through me.

On the newsfeeds outside our city, people always wonder if our father plans everything, or just makes it up as he goes along. Nobody can predict his next move, because he does things no one else would.

Like this hostage exchange. Like me.

But Rafi can't be right.

"It's because of our brother," I say softly. "You know that."

She looks away into the steam.

Before we were born, when the mind-rain was spilling across the world, our father was just another politician. But even back then, some people already thought he was dangerous.

Our brother, Seanan, was only seven years old. Someone— they never found out who—kidnapped him, trying to force Father to resign his council seat. When he refused, no one ever saw Seanan again.

So he raised me as a body double, a last defense against the people who hate this family.

"That's exactly what I mean," Rafi says. "What if Dad's setting up the same situation again? His child in someone else's hands, so they think they can control him. Except they can't. And this time, he can't lose."

I stare at her—he *can* lose.

He can lose me.

"Sending a hostage wasn't his idea," I hiss. "The Palafoxes insisted on it!"

Rafi raises an eyebrow. It's one expression of hers I've never been able to master—wary and wise. She leans forward.

"And who told you that, little sister?" she whispers in my ear.

CYRANO

The next month is a blur.

Language lessons. Dance lessons.

Lessons on the history of the mind-rain. On the Palafoxes, and how they rose to become the first family of Victoria. On the nature-loving rebels who try to keep them from salvaging the Rusty ruins nearby.

Riding lessons. What-to-wear-for-dinner lessons.

How to talk to serving drones. How to ping a heartfelt apology. The polite ways to block surveillance in someone else's home. Lessons on small talk, body language, giving clever toasts at dinner parties. And, of course, which forks to use when. (Turns out, I *do* eat like a barbarian.)

I never realized my sister had to work so hard, to know so much. And all of it on top of being trained how to escape from an unfamiliar city and get home through the wilderness, in case something goes wrong with our father's deal.

It leaves me too tired to worry about being separated from Rafi and my pulse knife. About being an impostor for two months.

Tired as I am, my big sister and I stay awake the night before I leave.

"You can't get assassinated while I'm not here to save you," I tell her. "It's not allowed."

Rafi rolls her eyes at me, angles away on her hoverboard. "Not much chance of that. While you're off having adventures, I'll be stuck here, hiding!"

"For two whole months?" I catch up with her, making sure she sees my shocked face. "How will you survive?"

She doesn't get the joke. Or doesn't show it.

We reach the edge of our father's property, where the clear-cutting stops and the forest rears up like a dark tsunami.

Rafi doesn't slow down, plunging into the upper branches. She banks hard right, dodging through the trees, keeping low on her board so the garlands of kudzu don't knock her off.

I follow, knees bent, keeping close watch on the lights on my board. We have to stay at the edge of the forest, where our lifters can keep hold of the property's magnetics.

Branches lash my face and hands. I set my eyescreen to night vision, and Rafi becomes a zigzag of body heat against the cool blue forest. When we whip hard around a tree trunk, my crash bracelets purr on my wrists—they think I'm about to fall.

A flock of birds scatters before Rafi's approach, pearly white in night vision. We climb through the flutter-storm of their wings, reaching the limit of our lifters just as the treetops open onto sky.

Rafi comes to a trembling halt.

"Careful." I point down—only one light flickers on her board.

She doesn't look. Her eyes are on our home, a black tower in the flat sea of manicured gardens and softly lit pathways. A couple of security drones bob on the horizon, keeping watch on us, on the forest.

"You're the one who has to be careful, little sister."

"I'll be fine." I reach out and pull her closer to the property. Another light sputters to life on her board. "I've trained for this my whole life."

"You're loving this." Her voice is bitter. "You *want* to get away from me."

"I hate leaving you, Rafi. But I'm totally done with all this training. All that stuff you know is *boring*." This doesn't convince her, so I add a little of the truth. "Maybe it'll be nice, living out in the open for a while. You'll see what it's like for me, hiding all the time."

Rafi lets her board drift closer, reaches out to take my shoulders. "When I'm in charge, you won't have to hide."

My mouth goes dry. This is something she's never said before. It's not something I think about.

But our father's on his second round of life extension, when even the best crumbly surge starts to crack around the eyes.

Hard as it is to believe, he has to die sometime.

"I'll tell the whole city about you." Rafi's voice is the barest whisper, even though there's no spy dust out here over the forest. "I'll explain how it was *you* waving to the crowds. That *you* were the brave one when the assassin tried to kill us."

I manage a smile. But the thought of everyone knowing our secret makes my stomach clench.

"Won't they be mad at us for tricking them?"

She shakes her head. "It's not our fault."

A weight lifts from me, like it does every time she says that.

Maybe I won't always be one of our father's deceptions.

"I'm going to give you something," Rafi says. "My cyrano."

"Already got one." I've been training with it, learning to listen to the quiet prompts without looking distracted. It sits in my ear, helping with etiquette and putting names to faces. It even corrects my irregular verbs.

"Not like this one." With a tug, she pulls a glistening curve of metal from behind her ear.

I frown. "Mine's a lot smaller."

"Yeah, but mine's smarter. It scans the news, makes

44

assessments, translates on the fly. In the wild, it can pick up satellite feeds." Rafi smiles. "But it's totally passive. Never transmits. No one will ever spot that it's there."

She hands the cyrano to me. It's warm in my hand.

"How come you never told me about this?"

"I mostly don't wear it." She breathes out through her teeth. "It's only got one voice setting. It sounds like *him*."

I almost drop the cyrano, let it fall down into the darkness of the trees. But this is the only way Rafi has of protecting me.

"Thank you." It curls up behind my ear, warm and buzzing.

"Just come home," she says.

We stay there all night above the trees, fragile on our trembling hoverboards, talking about how things will change when he's gone.

RUINS

Five hovercars full of soldiers take me to Victoria.

They aren't city cars, flying on silent magnetics. They're military grade, with lifting fans to keep their armored bulk in the sky. The engine roar drowns out everything inside the cabin, and our rotor wash incises the desert below, a traveling sandstorm.

You're late for an appointment, my father's voice whispers in my ear. *Lunch with the Palafoxes.*

It's just Rafi's cyrano, but it startles me. I hardly slept last night.

My clothes feel wrong on my body. I've dressed like Rafi a thousand times before, but it's different without her sitting here next to me. Like they're really *my* clothes now.

Why are we late?

I turn to the soldier in the next jumpseat. She's taller than me, broad across the shoulders, her body surged into a fighting machine.

The cyrano reminds me her name:

Sergeant Tani Slidell. She commands this unit.

"Shouldn't we be there by now?" I yell over the engine noise.

She glances to the right—checking an eyescreen.

"Eight minutes, miss. We're taking a detour over the ruins."

I look out the closest window, a rectangle of ten-centimeter-thick ferroglass. The mountains are to the west, bright red in the high sun.

The rebels hide in those mountains, always watching the ruins for opportunities to harry and attack the Palafoxes' salvage operations. The point of traveling in force was to get me to Victoria safe and quick.

"Why the detour?" The engine vibration rattles my voice.

"Orders, miss. A little recon."

I twitch every time they call me *miss*. No one on this trip—the soldiers, the pilots, the diplomatic staff—knows I'm an impostor, or even a hostage. The newsfeeds are calling this a friendly visit, cementing an alliance of two first families.

It's safer like this—no one can give me away. But it feels lonely.

I've always shared my secrets with Rafi. And now she's three hundred klicks away—farther than she's ever been before.

So is my pulse knife.

Out the window, the ruins are drawing closer, a dark patch on the desert. An ancient skyscraper stands tall, its skeleton picked clean by hovering salvage drones. The rest of the dead city lies in a jumble at its feet, metal spires jutting from the sand. Sentry drones bob in the wind, studded with armaments.

The hovercar's engines drop into a sudden silence. The vibration's aftershock ripples across my skin.

"We're on magnetics now, miss," Sergeant Slidell explains.

Right. Plenty of metal down there. No need for lifting fans.

Metal is what this fight is all about.

In the last month, I've learned a lot more about the rebels. They say they're following Tally Youngblood's oath, fighting anything that threatens the wild. They say the new cities are being built too fast, and that recycling the ruins only brings us closer to the day that strip mining starts again. They think we'll all turn back into Rusties soon, knocking down mountains, burning down forests, and poisoning the air.

The first families promise that the rebels are wrong. That they'll stop building new cities once the ruins are depleted. They say the wild is safe.

But everyone knows that promises aren't sacred anymore. And Tally herself isn't around to weigh in.

I look out the window again. Can two months really be long enough to strip all this bare?

The lights in the cabin turn yellow.

"Ready stations!" Slidell calls out, then turns to me. "Just a precaution, miss. The rebels aren't dangerous."

I shake my head. "If they weren't dangerous, the Palafoxes wouldn't need us here."

Slidell nods, surprised that Rafi knows anything about

such matters. She thinks I've been studying irregular verbs all my life.

"True, miss. But we're not like those Palafox wimps." She pulls back a bolt on the side of her rifle. An airscreen comes alive above its optics, showing internal temperature and ammo count. "We come ready to fight. The rebels know that."

"You think they're scared of us?"

"Not as much as they will be. But they won't mess with five of our best gunships."

I stare out the window again. The ruins are below us now, spread out across the desert like broken toys.

"Time to arrival?" I murmur.

Eleven minutes, the cyrano says.

Slidell just said eight minutes. We must be angling away from Victoria, closer to the mountains. That fact, and the sound of my father's voice, jog a memory in my brain.

I remember being twelve, Naya fitting me for my first body armor, teaching me how to duck and cover, how to suture my own wounds. And I realized that I wasn't just my sister's guardian, but also a way to draw fire.

"Is there any extra armor for me?" I ask.

Slidell stares at me, confused.

Then a distant *boom* sounds, and the hovercar rattles around us. The air smells wrong.

Alarms begin to ring.

JUMP

The alarm sounds like a bird being strangled to death, over and over.

The cabin lights are flashing, the soldiers clipping themselves into bungee jackets. Slidell thrusts a tangle of straps at me.

"You know how to use this?"

Nervous laughter spills out of my mouth. Rafi and I spent a whole summer playing with bungee jackets, taking turns jumping out the eleventh-story window of our bedroom. Pretend fire drills.

"Like a parachute," I say. "As long as there's enough metal for the magnetics to catch you."

I press the jacket to my chest and push the red button. The smart-plastic straps come to life, weaving around my arms and legs. A moment later they're clicking into place.

I hear the rising hum of a battery charging, then a green light on my shoulder flickers to life. If we need to jump, I'm ready.

My heart is drumming inside my chest. I'm here again, in the place I found the last time someone tried to kill me.

That ecstasy. That purpose.

But one thing's missing—there's no Rafi to save this time.

Only myself. Because my father knows that I can handle this.

And I see his plan in full. The detour over the ruins—a trap for the rebels, a target to lure them out and show the world that Shreve's military can handle them.

Around me, everything is a blur. The soldiers checking weapons, strapping on equipment. The dazzle-camo of their armor dances, trying to adapt to the flashing lights.

It's all too dizzy-making. I look out the window—slender white columns are rising into the air around us.

"What's that?" I whisper.

Anti-hovercraft defenses, my cyrano replies.

All at once, the tips of the columns blossom, spreading out like sudden spiderwebs against the sky.

One shoots straight at us—

It smacks the side of the hovercar with a sharp, wet sound. The view out the window jerks left.

We're caught.

The car skews sideways. Soldiers slip across the metal floor, grabbing hand straps. Slidell stands over me, a protective wall of armor.

I cling to the window frame. The strand that hit us is some kind of smart plastic—it's crawling around the outside of the car, seeking a way in. One tendril winds its way out to a lifting fan. There, it splits into a hundred filaments, wrapping the rotors in white.

With no lifters, we're trapped over the ruins. We start to spiral down, pulled earthward by the white strand.

The cabin lights turn solid red.

For the first time, the faces around me look scared.

I should be scared too. But this is like my dreams about the assassin. Time slows down, and I become a spot of rapture in the chaos.

My father has put me here on purpose. It's my job to get myself out.

"Abandon ship!" Slidell calls out. "Me and Gemstone first!"

The soldiers make way for us, pressing against the cabin walls.

The hovercar is spinning now, earth and sky cycling past the windows every few seconds. A door irises open at the tail end, spilling a hot rushing wind inside.

I can barely keep my feet, but Slidell drags me to the door.

Outside is a writhing white mass of webbing. The soldiers' rifles erupt, the thunder bone-rattling in the cramped cabin. They slice the smart plastic into fluttering ribbons.

The landscape rushes past outside, closer with every second.

"Hold on to me!" Slidell cries, and pulls me out into the void.

We tumble in the vertigo of free fall, my stomach lurching.

We're gyrating through the air, thrown slantways by the hover-car's spin.

Slidell's armored gauntlet spits and hisses—compressed air shooting out in little jolts to steady our fall. She gets our spin under control.

For a moment I can see everything clearly. The soldiers spilling out behind us like a string of pearls, turning blue as their dazzle-camo matches the sky. Two more hovercars in the distance, caught in the aerial webs, spinning madly. Flashes of light on the horizon, a low continuous rumble, like the frantic end of a fireworks show. Tracers streaking past us—rebel fire from the ground.

The ruins splay out below us, rushing closer.

Then something roars past overhead—another car in our formation, trying to get away from the white spiderwebs.

The wash of its rotors pushes me and Slidell down, hard. Suddenly the jagged, ruined city is coming up too fast.

My jacket light turns yellow.

Alert, my cyrano says. *The jacket reports that you are too heavy.*

It's Slidell holding on to me—her body armor, her weapons, all that equipment. Her jacket is rated for that much weight. Mine isn't.

"Let go!" I scream.

"It's okay, miss. I've got you!"

"No! It's just that . . ." There's no time to explain that mono-pole magnetics don't work well in tandem. All I know is that the ground is rushing up at us, much too fast. "Let go!"

When she doesn't, I pull myself into a ball and slam my heels into her chest. One foot slips off the armor and catches her chin, jerking her head back.

She lets go.

I'm spinning again, unable to control my fall. The sky, the ground, it's all a dizzy-making blur around me.

But the light on my bungee jacket turns green again.

The *snap* of the harness comes seconds later. It digs into my thighs and under my arms, halting me as fast as it can.

Below is the skeleton of an ancient building the color of rust, scoured by centuries of sandstorms. Coming at me.

I cover my face.

The bungee jacket jerks sideways, angling me away from the metal beams. I hit a sand dune, skid down a slope for a few skin-scraping seconds. Then I'm pulled up again, hover-bouncing into the air.

I'm bruised, the bungee jacket's straps deep in my flesh. But I'm alive.

A hissing wall of armor flies at me. Wraps around me.

It's Slidell, her gauntlets spitting air to guide her bounce. She angles us down again, going to ground behind the skeleton of the fallen building.

I land on my feet this time, settling into the sand.

"Sorry about kicking you," I say.

She rubs her jaw. "Everyone panics their first jump, miss."

I'm about to say that this isn't my first jump when a shadow passes overhead, and we duck.

But it's just another soldier—

No—the body of one, limbs hanging limp, hoverbouncing to a halt in shattered armor. We may have survived the fall, but the rebels are still shooting at us.

I stare at the dead body. Something's gone wrong.

That could have been me.

CODE

"I have Gemstone!" Slidell shouts into her throat mike. "Muster on my mark!"

We're under the cover of the fallen Rusty building, a skyscraper half-stripped of its metal, wilting under its own unsupported weight. Projectiles fly overhead—our remaining hovercars hitting the rebels from a safe distance. The sky is laced with white spiderwebs, dotted with more of my father's soldiers bailing out, firing as they fall.

I'm in the clothes I was supposed to wear to meet the Palafoxes. Rafi spent an hour choosing this coral silk shirt from the depths of her closet, matching it with sandals. She explained that the ensemble was respectful, but friendly. Perfect for breakfast or a light lunch, never dinner.

It's not body armor, and I feel naked.

More bodies of soldiers float in the air. The rebels must be stronger than we expected. I have to get under cover until help arrives.

The dune slopes away beneath the shadows of the ruin. I slide lower, sand flowing around my feet.

The air is cooler down here. It's dark, echoing with size. The sand mutes the rattle of the firefight outside.

I've never been to a ruin before, but this place is somehow familiar. Everything blocky and square, every line straight. My father builds in this Rusty style, with powerful grids of steel.

"Miss Rafia!" Slidell calls from above. "Please stay close."

My father will have planned this part out too—the heroic rescue, every insult to him transformed into a victory.

My father makes his own reality. Sometimes with force.

"It's okay," I tell the sergeant. "Reinforcements are coming."

"Of course, miss. But Shreve's over an hour away!"

"Sooner than that," I murmur in the dark. There's no way he would leave me in danger for that long.

The bungee jacket has a signal light, and I switch it on. Shadows dance in all directions. The space is even bigger than I thought.

The bottom wall of the ancient fallen building forms the ceiling of this subterranean chamber. Sand filters down whenever a *boom* sounds outside. It's not stable.

Maybe not the smartest place to be in a battle.

But people have sheltered here before. Empty food packs litter the ground, and dark patches show where campfires burned.

There's something written on a beam overhead. Not in cluttered Rusty letters, but with the clean strokes of a spray gun.

She's not coming to save us.

There's more, but it's all random symbols.

"Rafia!" Slidell comes scrambling down behind me. Her camo matches the shadows, shifting from sand and rust to black. "My squad's assembled. We're going to move you to safety."

I'm already safe. Help is coming.

There's no way my father would sacrifice me for a single victory against the rebels.

"Do you know what those symbols mean?" I move my light across the ceiling.

Unknown, my cyrano says.

Slidell glances up, thinking I mean her.

"Rebel code, looks like. This must have been a base, before the Palafoxes drove them into the mountains." She looks around. "Bad choice—all that sand could come down any second. Let's get you out of here."

I hesitate, still looking up at the symbols, not obeying at first. I've been acting like Rafi all day, and I'm starting to feel like her. Like nobody gives me orders.

Instead, I give consent.

"Okay. Let's go."

Slidell leads me back up the dune, into the sunlight. Five more soldiers are up here, crouched in a ring around us.

"That's the rendezvous point." Slidell points at the tallest building in the ruin—the skyscraper. "It's the best place to hold out."

"Isn't moving through this firefight dangerous?"

"Only for a few minutes, miss. But then we're safe. We'll wait there for reinforcements."

"A few minutes?" I shake my head. "They'll be here before then."

"Miss Rafia," Slidell says, her voice sharp for the first time. "Shreve is an hour away by hovercar!"

I lock eyes with her, mustering every gram of my sister in my blood.

It's not just for myself—I'm responsible for these soldiers, my protectors. And we're safer hunkering here a few more minutes than scrambling through the ruins, drawing fire.

I'm certain that my father expected this attack to happen.

Wanted it to happen.

"We stay," I command.

Slidell glares at me. She's ten years older, five centimeters taller, looming in the bulk of her body armor. My head spins with all the ways she can win this—inject me with some sedative in her medpack, bind my wrists with those zip ties on her belt. Or just haul me kicking and screaming across the ruined city.

Of course, she's expecting defenseless Rafi.

Slidell moves forward, reaching for my arm—

My battle reflexes ignite.

I grab her wrist and pull, sending her staggering past me. Then I launch a kick to the side of her knee. Her body armor saves her ligaments from tearing, but she goes down in pain.

"What the—"

I turn away from Slidell, facing her confused soldiers.

"We stay *here*." I'm a fearsome mix of Rafi and Frey, imperious and lethal. "Those are my father's orders."

They look back and forth between me and their sergeant, terrified of making the wrong choice. I keep my back to Slidell, daring her to attack me again.

For a nervous-making moment, this could go either way.

But then the soldiers' eyes all rise up to the sky.

"Ten o'clock!" one calls, and they all hit the ground.

I turn to see a shower of meteors coming down, a score of objects burning across the sky.

"What are they?" I ask Slidell.

"Suborbital insertion drones," she answers. "But the rebels don't have low orbit. And neither do we!"

"Yes, we do," I say. "Just sit tight."

She glares at me, angry and confused, wondering if she should take me down. But I keep my gaze steady at the sky, showing no uncertainty.

Over the last month, Naya has told me about my father quietly waking up the old war machines. Waiting for an excuse to use them.

No—*engineering* an excuse.

The ecstasy comes back, the bubble of my father's will settling over me again. I was right. He has it all under control. Despite the rebels' unexpected firepower, I'm safe again.

A sequence of *booms* rattles the ancient ruins—the suborbital craft punching through the sound barrier. They're falling from the edge of space, coming in so fast that an envelope of air burns around them. They slice through the rebels' anti-hovercraft webs like knives through smoke.

Reentry chutes pop and unfurl, bringing the meteors to a sudden halt. Then their glowing heat shields split apart and heavy battle drones tumble out, bristling with weapons.

They start firing as they fall.

Slidell pulls her eyes from the spectacle and stares at me again.

I am nothing that she thought I was.

"You *knew* about this?"

"Not exactly," I admit. "But I know more every day."

FIRST SON

The next morning, I have breakfast with the Palafoxes.

Three generations of them—mother, grandmother, and son—join me at a small iron table on a sunlit balcony. The serving drones are painted with flowers and dancing skeletons. The coffee is strong and sweet.

I'm in one of Rafi's favorite outfits: a sky-blue dress fringed with dragonfly wings. Harvested from real insects, of course, not printed by a hole in the wall. My luggage escaped the battle untouched, but the silk shirt was a write-off.

Eleven soldiers died as well.

I can't think about that now—it's too brain-spinning. The rebels took more casualties than we did, of course. The newsfeeds are abuzz with the attack, and with the revelation that my father's suborbital forces can strike anywhere in the world.

But eleven soldiers.

"Such an outrage," Zefina Palafox keeps saying. "It's a miracle you weren't hurt."

"I was never scared." My voice trembles a little, which doesn't sound like Rafi. I need to keep control.

"Of course not." Zefina pats my hand. "We all remember that unpleasantness last year. You were very brave then too."

I give her a fearless smile.

Zefina is the grande dame of the clan. Eighty-six years old, with the classic crumbly surge of the pretty era—white hair, rosy cheeks, sparkling eyes. She greeted me yesterday afternoon when I arrived, still dirty and in shock, and put me to bed.

"Maybe we should talk about something else," Aribella Palafox gently commands. She's Zefina's daughter, the leader of the city of Victoria. My father's equal. "We mustn't let this spoil your visit, Rafia."

"Of course not." I cut myself a large bite of mango, as if the rebels can't stop me from enjoying breakfast.

The cyrano whispers: *Fork in the left hand, knife in the right. Bring the food to your mouth, not the other way around.*

Aribella notices when I reach up and pull out the cyrano. I don't care if she sees—lots of people wear cyranos—and I don't care if I eat like a barbarian. I can't stand my father's voice in my ear right now.

Eleven soldiers.

I smile back at Aribella. She's beautiful. Not in the old-fashioned way—her pretty surgery has been fully reversed. Her glamour resides in her expression, in her certainty that she was born to rule.

Looking at her, I can understand why so many cities wanted leaders after the mind-rain. Not another parliament, council, or committee. But a singular figure to guide them through the chaos of humanity waking up. Like Rusty celebrities or royal houses.

I can almost forget that I'm her prisoner.

"Do you hunt, Rafia?"

We all turn to a boy my age, Col Palafox. This is the first thing he's said since we were introduced. He's worn a wary expression the whole time, glancing at his coffee like it might be poisoned.

"I'm sure Rafia has better things to do," Aribella says.

I don't argue. Aribella's not about to let her hostage out with a weapon, an all-terrain hoverboard, and her son.

Col's eyes drop to his food again.

It's fine with me if he doesn't want to talk. He's the older of the two Palafox sons, the one who knows French. A few of my grammar-missing verbs and he'll start wondering.

Rafi and I have been studying what the feeds say about Col. That he's thoughtful, a bit boring and studious. He's never been part of Rafi's social scene. But he's still the person here most like her—the young heir of a first family. If anyone can spot that my dazzling socialite act is bogus, it's him.

He looks older in person than on the public feeds. His shoulders are broader, his dark eyes sadder, and he's more handsome too. But that's just another reason not to talk to him. Rafi is famous for charming girls and boys with equal ease, and I've never so much as flirted with a stranger.

"You have a lovely home," I say, to fill the untidy silence. Rafi told me to use this when I don't know what else to say, even though it's banal.

Zefina perks up. "You should have a tour! Why don't you show Rafia around after breakfast, Col?"

Aribella nods, like she's giving permission. "An excellent idea. You haven't spoken French with a real person since you got home."

Col looks miserable.

I share his pain.

FAKE JUNGLE

The Palafox home really is lovely.

While my father's estate is shuttered and dark, everything here opens onto light and air. Rooms spill onto balconies and terraces, skylights slant the hallways with morning sun, all of it surrounding a tree-filled courtyard as big as two soccer fields.

This jungle is where Col takes me first, on a path of hovering stones, down through swaying fronds and storms of tiny wings. I can't tell if the butterflies are gene-spliced or natural, or what keeps them from fluttering away into the open sky.

Safety drones hover near us in case we fall. The long drop to the ground makes my wrists itch for crash bracelets.

"Are you trying to make me nervous, Col?"

He shrugs. "Don't tell me a girl who faces down rebels and assassins is afraid of heights."

"I meant the butterflies. They're carnivorous, right?"

For the first time, Col gives me a thin smile. I shouldn't be making brain-missing jokes. He might joke back to me in French, and my cyrano's still in my pocket. I don't want my father whispering cues in my ear.

But Col doesn't answer, just leads me down.

The rocky ground of the courtyard is damp. Pale green lichen covers everything, dotted with red sprays of flyspeck flowers. This is more a habitat than a garden, like a slice of the wild here in the city.

I wonder if there's a way from the treetops up onto the roof, an escape route in case I need it. Col probably knows, but I can't just ask him. He's standing with one hand out, dead still, waiting for a butterfly to land.

Whenever Rafi wants to get someone talking, she teases them.

"For a tour guide, you don't say much."

He lowers his hand. "We're standing in a simulation of the Reserva de la Biosfera El Cielo."

Maybe I should put the cyrano back in. But that was Spanish, not French.

"The Biosphere of Heaven," he translates. "It's a cloud forest fifty klicks southwest of here. It's been a nature preserve since Rusty times. My family still protects it."

"A cloud forest? That sounds made up."

Col shrugs. "It's a jungle on a mountain, high enough for the trees to strip moisture from passing clouds—rain on demand. The old jungles made their own weather."

"*Now* you sound like a tour guide."

"I'm famously boring," he says.

He also flashes a hand sign: *They're watching us.*

For a moment I only stare dumbly. How does he know Rafi's private signals? She was taught them by the kids at a private dance school in Diego. But Col Palafox goes to school an ocean away.

Maybe the signs are universal, carried around the globe by misbehaving kids shuffling from school to school. Or maybe *They're watching us* is so useful that it's the same everywhere.

Rafi would know all this. I'm already missing her.

Col's staring at me now, and I nod to show that I saw his signal. That I'm just like him, a spoiled kid—not a body double, not a trained killer.

He gives me his first real smile.

A rushing sound comes from overhead—like a passing hovercar. I jerk my eyes up, ready to take cover.

"That's just the hourly storm," Col says. "The real Reserva collects three meters of rainfall a year."

A mist is descending, so fine that the butterflies don't seem to care. I can't see the sprayers anywhere.

"So jungles really do make their own weather."

Another smile. "Let's get you out of the rain."

I shrug. "This dress is laced with wicking nanos. Even after full immersion, it'll be clean and dry in five minutes."

He stares at me—that was *not* how Rafi talks about her

clothes. She'd be worried about the dragonfly wings drooping, her hair getting wet.

"Okay," Col says. "But there's something I want to show you. It's in the original building, five hundred years old."

He makes another hand sign. I don't know this one, but I can guess.

A building that old has to be made of stone—the walls not smart enough to listen in on us. They don't have spy dust here in Victoria.

"That sounds lovely," I say.

Col goes quiet again, leading me out of the misting jungle and into a hallway lined with frescoes. More skulls and flowers, a background landscape like the desert I flew across yesterday.

I'm quietly pleased with myself. So far, Col has no idea that I'm not Rafi. That I've never gone to fancy parties or designed my own clothes.

But we haven't really talked yet—and now he wants privacy. What if it's to discuss secret spoiled-kid business, full of gossip I know nothing about?

Rafi warned me that making friends with Col could only get me into trouble. I should say I'm tired and go back to my room. I'm supposed to be gathering an escape kit, just in case.

But when I open my mouth to make excuses, nothing comes out. Other than my sister, I've never had a friend before.

And what if Col tells me something useful?

He leads me deeper into the family home.

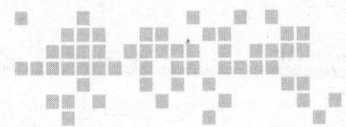

The old building is the gloomiest part of House Palafox.

Col takes me there through a door with a retina lock, then down a hallway with uneven walls. Hints of the morning sun leak through high, barred windows. There are no bright murals here, just the cool gray silence of stone.

"What was this?" I ask. "A castle?"

"A monastery," Col says, then goes quiet again. He's still not much of a tour guide.

Rafi would probably know this, but I ask, "What's a monastery?"

"Like a dorm, for pre-Rusties who were really serious about religion." He runs his hand along the rough surface of the wall. "The monks who lived here took vows to ignore the outside world."

"Monks? Like the Shaolin fighting style?"

I manage to keep from blurting out that I've studied it myself. But Col still raises an eyebrow, matching Rafi's expression when she judges me for talking like a military advisor.

"Kind of. These monks were more into calligraphy than beating people up."

I slip my cyrano back in, give it a tap.

Calligraphy is the art of decorative handwriting.

"Wonderful," I say in Rafi's mocking tone. "So you're going to show me your handwriting collection?"

"Sorry to disappoint you, but we don't have anything that old. We keep the family antiques here. You might find the collection . . . interesting."

He leads me around another corner, into a low-ceilinged room crowded with glass cases.

The cases are full of weaponry, Rusty-era and even older. Swords, rifles, body armor made of metal scales, a crossbow.

I try not to look too excited, but then my eyes fall on the smallest case—it holds a pulse knife. An original, from the last days of chaos, before the pretty regime brought peace.

It's less sophisticated than mine back at home, but more reliable. The sort of military hardware that might still work after a hundred years.

I reach out to touch the case.

It feels like ferroglass, maybe a centimeter thick. Hard to break, but not impossible, and we're surrounded by dumb stone walls.

The Palafoxes are bubbleheads. They keep their weapons collection in the easiest part of the house to steal from.

Of course, they think I'm Rafi, who's never stolen anything in her life.

"You have some lovely toys," I murmur.

"This is my favorite." He guides me to another case, points at the hunting bow inside.

It's not an antique. Nanotech, collapsible nanotech polymers, laser-sighted. The arrows are fletched with smart feathers and have an assortment of high-tech heads—airburst tips to take down birds, explosives for big game.

Back in the pretty regime, people didn't kill animals. This weapon was made after the mind-rain.

"That's mine," Col says. "It usually lives on my wall."

"What's it doing down here?"

"Jefa personally came and took it away. She locked it up, along with my hoverboard." He stares at me. "Yesterday, right before you arrived. She didn't explain why."

"Who's Jefa?"

"That's what my brother and I call our mother. For obvious reasons."

It means "boss," my cyrano whispers.

So that's why Col brought up hunting at breakfast. He's trying to figure out why she locked up his bow. He has no idea I'm a hostage.

It's time to turn back into Rafi.

I give him a big sigh. "Maybe she doesn't want you showing off your boring hobbies to guests."

"Maybe." Col's eyes fall to the case. "Or maybe she thinks I don't know what this is all about. Your little 'holiday' with my family."

A tremor goes through me—*has* he figured it out?

He's waiting for me to say something. And I'm pretty sure *You have a lovely home* isn't going to cut it.

"Our parents want our families to be allies," I say carefully.

"Exactly." He sighs. "But you'd think they could be more subtle about it. *Why don't you show Rafia around, Col?*"

It takes a moment for the gears in my head to mesh. But finally they do.

"Oh," I say.

"Right. Like you didn't know."

I shake my head. I'm not lying.

Rafi and I should've figured it out before I left home, but we were too worried about table manners and irregular verbs to realize what Grandma Palafox must be thinking.

"Your family," I say. "They want us to . . . get together?"

Col snorts with disgust. "*My* family? Like your father isn't thinking the same thing?"

I don't have an answer. My father doesn't want that kind of alliance or he'd have sent the real Rafia, not her brain-missing body double.

He just wants to humiliate the rebels, take his cut of metal from Victoria's ruins, and leave.

All of us missed this possibility.

"I can't *believe* Jefa," Col keeps going. "I've spent my whole life studying, preparing to help her lead the city. And now she wants to marry me off to some . . ." He comes to a halt, throws his hands in the air.

"Some *what*, exactly?"

Col sputters a moment, then says, "The whole thing's medieval!"

A laugh spills out of me. It's so much more medieval than he knows.

His dark eyes flash. "You think this is funny?"

I shake my head. Aribella *knows* I'm a hostage, not a guest. But she seemed enthusiastic about this little house tour.

Is she trying to outflank my father? Getting Rafi into her home, then using her son to secure an alliance?

"It's just that I didn't know, Col. That's the truth."

He studies me a moment longer. Then he starts pacing, waving his arms.

"Last winter, when the rebels were about to push us out of the ruins, everyone was saying we couldn't let your forces in to help. That we could never trust your father to leave again, once he saw how much metal we're salvaging. Then suddenly the deal was made, except *you* came along with it, and no one would say why. Like everyone was playing a game and I didn't know the rules!"

"Yeah. I know that feeling."

"My mother cut me out of the decision completely. And the most annoying thing is, it took me till this morning to figure out why!"

I nod. "Hide a plan till it's ripe for execution and it's more likely to succeed."

He turns to me. "Did you just quote Machiavelli at me?"

"I've been reading him a lot lately."

Col looks me up and down, and I realize that I'm standing

wrong. Not with Rafi's ballet poise, but in the combat stance that Naya makes me hold in classes. Weight on the balls of my feet, ready to fight.

"You're not what I'd thought you'd be, Rafia."

I should say something to contradict Col. Act like my sister on the newsfeeds—imperious, bratty, always finding weaknesses and nipping at them.

But instead I ask, "How do you mean?"

"Your parties. Your temper tantrums. I was expecting a bubble-head socialite, frankly."

I stare at him, a little offended for Rafi. She's no bubblehead, except when she's pretending. *She* was the one who got me reading Machiavelli.

But it's also flattering, because Col isn't seeing Rafi—he's seeing me. At least, the parts of me that are poking out of my disguise.

The whole thing makes me dizzy.

But dizzy Frey doesn't know what to say, so I let sarcastic Rafi take over. "Sorry to disappoint you, Col. I'll try to be more bubbleheaded."

"Trust me, it's a relief. Especially if my family's going to keep throwing us together."

Right, they are. And Col's already realized that I'm not the Rafi everyone sees on the feeds—he's smart enough to figure out more. A friendship with him is risky.

But there are also advantages. He spotted something that even my big sister missed—the Palafoxes are seeking an alliance of blood.

I need someone who can tell me how this family thinks.

"Forget our parents," I say. "Let's make our own alliance."

He raises an eyebrow. "Something short of marriage, I presume?"

That makes me laugh. "*Way* short. We don't even have to like each other, if we don't want to."

"So I don't have to be your tour guide?"

I nod, and in a fit of brilliance reply, "And I don't have to be your French study partner!"

"*Comme il faut,*" he says.

As is proper, my father's voice translates.

I smile. "It's decided, then. We're allies."

He holds out his hand. "Not pawns for our families."

We shake on it. But it feels like a promise I can't keep.

I was born to be a pawn.

VICTORIA

A few days after my arrival, Col takes me out to see his city.

I'm excited to be outside. Until now it's all been formal dinners with the dignitaries of Victoria, lunches with the Palafoxes. Stilted conversation and too much rich food for calorie purgers to burn off. What I need is a good training session with Naya, but a long hike in the city will do.

Col and I walk on the street like randoms. No body armor, just half a dozen wardens blending into the crowd around us. A single drone hovers up among the pigeons. It's probably only there to make sure I don't run.

The weird thing is, I'm more free as a hostage here than as a second daughter back home. House Palafox has no special corridors or elevators. No spy dust in the air.

I've always wanted to feel what it was like in Rafi's skin, but this is something she's never done—walking down a street with normal people at arm's length.

They mostly ignore us, but a few walk straight past the wardens to introduce themselves to Col, the first son of the city. He jokes effortlessly with them, using the same banter over and over, managing to sound each time like the words just popped into his head.

Naya warned me that in Victoria I might be exposed like this. A lot of cities work this way—the wealthy and powerful walking freely among randoms. But it's strange to see it in real life.

It makes me twitchy. Like everyone can see through my disguise.

Col acts like it's perfectly natural, of course. And the people of Victoria seem to adore their first son.

They ask about his schoolwork, his botany, his archery. All the reasons that my sister's friends ignore him—his studiousness, his boring hobbies—are celebrated here.

Which is odd, because Victoria isn't boring or studious at all. It's acutely alive.

Kids zip past on hoverboards at speeds that would get them jailed back at home. Drones flit just above the rooftops, carrying not only official cargo, but groceries, shopping, folded laundry, as if every random gets their own air fleet here. And it's not just the traffic that's wild and uncontrolled. People seem to wear whatever they want—bright colors, flash tattoos, and surgeries that would never pass the censors back in Shreve.

Even the buildings are bursting with life. The hoverstrut architecture drifts overhead, airy and fantastical. And down here at street level, the adobe houses are painted in sunset oranges and yellows, or the radiant blues of a low flame.

But strangest to me are the animals. The flocks of pigeons against the sky, the imperious cats strutting the rooftops.

I point at a chicken scuttling underfoot, its feathers as gaudy as the houses.

"What are *they* for?"

Col gives me a questioning look.

"Wild animals aren't allowed in Shreve," I explain. "Some birds get in, of course. But nothing like *that*."

"The chickens aren't wild, exactly." Col switches to his tour-guide voice. "They're tagged with transmitters so the city can monitor the ecosystem. They make for good pest control."

"Why not just spray?"

"We're old-fashioned here. When my little brother's home from school, he goes out every morning to collect eggs."

"To *eat*? From birds that eat *bugs*?" I shake my head. "This whole city's like something from the Rusty era, or whatever was before that!"

"The pre-Rusties," Col says, laughing.

"Whatever," I say. "But it's beautiful."

His laughter fades, and he gives me a curious look.

"Really, Rafia? Shreve's so much bigger and newer than Victoria, I thought you'd be bored. Might you actually be *charmed* by our little town?"

I don't answer right away. The real Rafi would be bored. Or at least she'd pretend to be, because older, smaller cities are passé compared to the bold new constructions of the mind-rain. But I don't want to offend Col. He's my ally now.

And after a lifetime of hiding, training, and carefully scripted appearances, it's hard not to be entranced by all this street life swirling around me. All these smells and sounds are over-whelming. As is the fact that I could choose any street to walk down next.

But the most confusing part isn't my own freedom—it's every-one else's. Victoria seems like a city entirely out of control.

"I'm not bored at all, Col. If anything, it's too much, walking around in the open like this. It feels . . . precarious."

He studies me. "More precarious than having assassins shoot at you?"

"I have bodyguards in Shreve. Here, there's just a few war-dens. You don't even have spy dust!"

"It's illegal."

"I know, but . . ." My tutors explained how privacy is an obsession in Victoria. The city scrubs its data every day, forget-ting where everyone went, what they pinged each other, what they made with their holes in the wall.

Back home in Shreve, the air is full of machines. When you shine a flashlight in the dark, most of those floating specks are spy dust, nanocameras taking a hundred pictures a second in all directions, along with the tiny microphones, transmitters, batteries, and repeaters that support them.

If the wardens in Shreve want to know what happened at a certain place and time, they just call it up on the city interface. They can watch from any angle, replay any sound but the softest whisper—unless Dona's people have censored it to hide my father's secrets, of course. Like me.

"It just feels unsafe, Col. What if there's a murder? How do you solve *any* crimes?"

"Crimes got solved before dust was invented, you know. We use DNA, fingerprints, eyewitnesses." He shrugs. "And, I don't know, logic?"

"Sounds like a lot of trouble, when you could just *watch* what happened."

"People don't like being spied on. Besides, we haven't had an unsolved murder since the mind-rain."

I lower my voice a little. "But how does your family keep control?"

He looks at me through narrowed eyes.

"We don't *keep control*. We lead."

"Are you being smug?"

"Usually." He watches a dog run past, chasing a pair of cats. "My mother does a good job. So people don't try to get rid of us."

I come to a halt and stare at him. "Are you saying someone tried to kill me because my father was doing a *bad job*?"

"Your father's different," he answers calmly. "You know that."

I stand there in the cool shade of an adobe wall, gathering my thoughts. I don't have an answer, because I don't really know why I'm arguing. Is this me pretending to be Rafi, who always upholds the family name in public? Or do I just hate being judged?

"I'm sorry you can't walk around like this at home," Col says. "The violence must be tough."

There's that smugness again.

"Don't talk to me about violence," I say. "You mother's borrowing my father's army."

"Borrowing, because we don't have a big standing army of our own. Half our soldiers have other jobs. Don't you see the difference?"

"Not really."

He sighs. *"Il n'est pire sourd que celui qui ne veut pas entendre."*

No one's as deaf as one who doesn't want to listen, my cyrano translates.

French proverbs? Perfect. Rafi would be *so* much better at this than me. She could probably spit some fancy saying back at him.

I try to remember what my tutors have been teaching me about the debates of the new era. About whether the first families, with their all-knowing dust and ancient weapons, have grown too powerful.

But why would anyone want to be ruled by a family that was *weak*?

I notice that the wardens have formed a loose circle around me and Col, facing outward, standing with their arms crossed. The crowd is giving us a wide berth while we argue.

I remember Rafi saying that the Palafoxes aren't soft. Their power is in the air around us. Gentle but firm.

They just don't like to admit it.

"Maybe you don't know everything about your own family," I say.

Col considers this a moment, then nods.

"You're right. I never thought Jefa would let Shreve's forces in. Or cut me out of the decision. Or try to marry me off like some bubblehead." His voice goes quieter. "And I still can't figure out why she locked up my hunting bow."

I don't bother to explain. Allies or not, Col doesn't need to know that I'm a hostage. All he really wants is his hunting bow, if only to push back against Aribella for treating him like breeding stock.

Maybe I can use this.

"Here's a question." I step a little closer, whispering, "How often does anyone go down to the monastery?"

"Hardly ever. Even cleaning drones aren't allowed—Jefa says they wear away the stone."

"Then maybe I can get your hunting bow back, if you find something for me."

His eyes widen. "What?"

"You can't tell your mother what I'm about to ask for. Promise?"

"Of course."

I wonder whether to trust him. Back home, my father's office is full of sensors that track heartbeat, skin temperature, the subtle motions of the eyes—every telltale that someone might be lying.

But out here on the street, all I have to go on is Col's unwavering gaze back at me.

Somehow it's enough.

"Do you know what a pulse charger looks like?"

BALL GOWN

A week later, the Palafoxes throw a welcome bash for me.

The newsfeeds are ablaze with it. Every high-face-rank family in Victoria is invited. Everyone wants to meet the plucky girl who survived an assassination *and* a rebel attack. Every kicker with a feed is speculating on how long I'll stay in the city. On how I'm getting along with my hosts. On whether our families' alliance has been strengthened by this shared war against the rebels.

People speculate about me and Col too.

Our intense conversation on the street was caught by a few private cams, but the gossip varies depending on the source. Were we arguing? Flirting? Performing for the cameras?

The whole city is starting to wonder if my visit here is more than a vacation.

It's the afternoon of the ball, and I'm still trying on virtual outfits in my bedroom wallscreen.

I've tried the hole in the wall's standard designs, but they're too basic for Rafi to wear. My fingers flex and twitch, picking from endless menus of styles and options. Customize, refine, specify in a hundred ways—but I'm just guessing.

Every attempt winds up with another disaster.

What if Grandma Zefina, curious about what I'm wearing tonight, is watching? She must wonder why the always stylish Rafi is suddenly so lost.

This is what I get for wanting to leave home, to be my own person. I'm finally getting to have my own party, and it's a nightmare.

Rafi was right—I don't know how to dress, or flirt, or make conversation. Which is fine for a few stilted dinner parties. But now the whole world is going to see how fashion-missing I am. How *everything*-missing.

Like I'm only half a person.

My sister's cyrano isn't helping. It's full of protocol tips, not fashion advice—something Rafi would never need.

I'd give anything for her help right now. But the Palafoxes might find it strange if I called home to ask myself for fashion advice.

But then, as I'm staring at my fifteenth absolute wreck of an outfit, the cyrano hisses softly in my ear—

A secret ping from home. The first since I've arrived.

The cyrano can't send signals out or House Palafox security will catch them. But it can scan the public newsfeeds for incoming hidden messages. They're encrypted in images of my father, official vids of him waving to a crowd or signing a document. Strewn across those billions of pixels are tiny, random-seeming shifts of color, information buried in a hundred devious layers of math for my cyrano to decode.

I don't react at first, in case anyone's watching. Instead, I discard my latest design with a disgusted Rafi sigh, flop on my bed, and stare at the ceiling. Only then do I reach up and tap the cyrano to play the message.

It's a recording of my sister's voice.

Frey! Hope you're okay, or at least muddling along.

But mostly, I hope you're listening to this right away. You have to nail this party tonight. Have you seen our face rank lately? Since the rebel attack, we're top hundred. And I don't mean locally—that's our global rank, Frey.

People from all over are going to be watching this bash.

You better look amazing.

I wish I could interrupt Rafi and tell her this isn't helping. My nerves are bad enough without imagining a worldwide audience. All those people watching me and Col, ready to gossip . . .

Then it hits me—Rafi said *our* face rank. That's new. It was always her fame, not mine. But the rebels were shooting at *me*, I guess, so it's only fair to get some credit.

It's lucky you've got a very clever big sister.

Pause this until you're in front of a wallscreen. Then do exactly as I say.

I jump up from the bed, stand in front of the screen. Ready to obey.

Okay, call up the Seft. Do you even know what that is? Standard European Fashion Timeline, duh. You call it by making two fists, thumbs on the inside. Like you're about to punch someone, I guess.

Except you'd break a thumb if you hit someone that way.

Now scroll to the mid-2040s, the A-frame dresses. Not that you know what that means, but I assume you know what the letter A looks like? Hah.

See that one near the middle, with the lace collar? Select it and open Options. Not the littlie menu with four choices—put on your big girl pants and use the advanced list.

Yeah, I know. There's, like, a hundred submenus. And this is only the beginning.

But never fear, big sister's here . . .

I follow along, barely keeping up with her narration. She's racing, guiding me through the bottomless specificities of fashion. The whole time I can imagine her talking to herself in our bedroom, in front of the wallscreen we've shared since we were littlies. It feels like I'm there beside her, back at home.

But as Rafi whispers in my ear, weaving this dress for my body—for *our* body—it starts to feel like these are my own thoughts flowing through my head. *My* skills navigating the centuries of styles and trends, the measure of my hips, arms, shoulders.

Anyone snooping must think my lost fashion genius has come rushing back, full force.

When Rafi's recording finally ends, the wallscreen shows me wrapped in spiral coils of gunmetal lace, the dress beneath in subtle gradients of reflective black. Gray gloves up to my elbows, dark tulle with an iridescent oil-slick sheen peeking out from beneath my hem.

The hole in the wall says fabrication will take three hours. I didn't know *anything* took that long for a nano-forge to make. I'll barely have time to dress before the bash.

And already I'm impatient. I usually don't care what Rafi and I wear. But having watched this creation emerge from a thousand swift, skillful choices, I'm eager to become that girl in the dress.

No, not a dress. A ball gown.

A ping sounds in the room.

"Rafia?" It's Aribella Palafox, my host—my captor. The timing is so perfect, she must've been watching. "If you're free, perhaps we could chat about tonight."

"That would be lovely." I slip the cyrano off. Aribella runs a whole city from her office—it'll be packed with sensors.

And suddenly I'm Frey again, not the princess in the beautiful dress. Frey, who doesn't know what to wear, what fork to use. Or how to chat with her host about a party that will be watched across the world.

"Would now be convenient?" she asks.

I nod, not trusting the steadiness of my voice.

Greeting me at her office door, Aribella takes my hands in hers.

"Let me look at you, Rafia."

She steps back, studying me. Is she imagining the ball gown, making sure I'll be elegant enough for her bash tonight? Or is she wondering if I seem somehow different in real life?

Rafi's voice has been in my ear all afternoon, so her stance, her cool expression, come naturally. But Aribella's scrutiny is still nervous-making. I look past her to the tall windows of the office, which are full of light and motion. House Palafox doesn't lurk on the edge of the wild like my father's tower; it sits in the center of town, Aribella's office looking out across the city she rules.

Victoria is all open terraces and hoverstruts, a fairy kingdom compared to squat, stolid Shreve. A pre-Rusty cathedral rises in the distance, its stone spire dappled with sunlight reflected from floating glass buildings. Drones flit past the windows, their cargos bright with flowers and fruit, scattering the ever-present pigeons before them.

Like the town, Aribella's office is full of color. There's no desk, no dominating wallscreen. Just the circle of red velvet couches that she guides me to.

We sit close, our knees almost touching.

"I must confess," she says. "I took a peek at your gown for tonight, and it's perfect. I'll make sure Col wears something to match."

With all the newsfeed buzz about me and him, Aribella wants to play up the rumors. To show the city that her family can secure an alliance with my father.

"Col's been very kind to me," I say.

"Of course, he has—you're so lovely, Rafia." She leans closer, looking me over again. "And no surgery at all?"

For a moment, I don't know how to answer. Back in the pretty regime, looks weren't something to brag about. But now every city has its own customs.

"My nose could be smaller," I say—Rafi's complaint since she was a littlie. "But Father won't let me change it."

Aribella gives me a sympathetic smile. "He's always talking about your mother, the natural pretty. Maybe he wants to see her in your face."

"I don't remember her."

"Of course not." She reaches up to smooth my hair. Her

touch is unexpectedly gentle. "Everyone knows the story—your father taking what he wants."

I'm not sure what to say to that. If our father didn't take what he wanted, Rafi and I wouldn't exist.

When my brother, Seanan, was abducted, my mother resisted the kidnappers. She was shot four times, and as she lay dying on the operating table, Father told the doctors to harvest her eggs so he could have more children with her.

My father makes his own reality. Sometimes with force. Sometimes with technology.

He snatched me and Rafi from oblivion.

I repeat what Dona Oliver always says: "He loved my mother too much to let her go."

"That's what I'm counting on." Aribella turns to face the windows. "I'm gambling my city's safety that he'd never endanger his own blood."

A tremble of relief travels through me—at last, we aren't pretending anymore. I'm a captive here, not a guest. Collateral for my father's good behavior.

Aribella misinterprets my shiver. "You must think I'm dreadful, taking a child hostage."

"You didn't take me." I sit a little straighter. "I came of my own free will."

"Well, that's a relief, Rafia. I was worried your father wouldn't tell you, which might have left us with . . . an awkward conversation."

I almost laugh at that. "He's not afraid of delivering bad news."

"Your father does enjoy a crisis. But he's been as good as his word on this deal. So far."

"Of course." The feeds are saying that the rebels are faltering already. Retreating under the combined forces of Victoria and Shreve. "My family doesn't shy away from a fight."

"No, you don't." Aribella looks at the scar above my eye. "In fact, I heard a rumor, from someone who was there that day, when that awful man tried to kill you."

My body goes tense. Dona's security people scrutinized every angle of spy-dust data, hunting for anyone who might have seen me and Rafi together. But with all the smoke and confusion, they were never certain.

I shrug. "There are a lot of rumors about that day."

"I never believed this one, until I met you." Aribella leans closer. "Did *you* kill the assassin?"

Rafi would deny it, or simply laugh it away. But with my other, bigger secret always lurking, I want to admit this truth. And maybe impressing Aribella matters to me now.

"Yes. I killed him."

I'm not sure what to expect, but her warm smile surprises me.

"Thank you for trusting me, Rafia." She gently takes my right wrist. "Is your hand better?"

I stare at her. "My hand?"

"We were worried that there might be something hidden

under your skin." Aribella looks away, a little embarrassed. "A tracker, perhaps. It seemed prudent to scan you."

"Right." My father's security uses millimeter-wave radar to make sure his guests aren't carrying weapons. "But I don't have any implants, except for my eyes."

"No. But we noticed that the bones in your right hand were recently broken."

"Fell off my hoverboard."

Aribella shakes her head.

"That's what we thought, till we looked a little closer." She touches my shoulder. "There's an old dislocation here, and more breaks in your left wrist, your right knee. And scar tissue in the muscles all over your body. My physician says he's never seen so many training injuries. Or such high-quality vision implants. Your body doesn't lie, Rafia."

My fists curl. The Palafoxes might not have an army to match my father's, but they're just as smart as he is.

We knew they'd check my DNA—it matches Rafi's, of course. But how can I keep any secrets from them if they scan me while I sleep?

Maybe more of the truth will distract her.

"My brother's kidnapping still haunts my father. So he made sure I could defend myself."

"That's very sad." She takes my hand again and looks into my eyes with a kind of pity. "But you should know something, Rafia.

Whatever deal I've made with your father, I would never hurt you."

I stare at her, unbelieving.

"This has to stay our little secret, of course," she says. "For the sake of peace, I'll pretend to stand by my threats. But you'll always be safe under my roof. I swear to you."

Why is she telling me this? The hostage deal doesn't work unless my father fears the worst. Unless she's trying to get me on her side . . .

But she's also scared of me. She locked up Col's hunting bow, even before she found the marks of training on my bones.

Suddenly I know what she needs to hear.

"I'll never hurt anyone in your family, Aribella. I promise."

With a warm smile, she leans across to hug me. She smells like the garden in the center of House Palafox, fresh and alive—and powerful, like she makes her own rain.

"Thank you, Rafi." Aribella releases me and stands. "We have to trust each other."

"Of course." Until she finds out I'm not my father's real heir. Do you have to keep promises to impostors?

"I notice you haven't pinged home," she says softly.

I hesitate, wondering how to explain that there's no one in Shreve I can talk to. Rafi's friends would know I wasn't her in five minutes, and my father's never had a real conversation with me.

The only person I want to talk to is my sister, and we can't let the Palafoxes know there's two of us.

"I've been so busy. Maybe after the party."

"Of course. We should both be getting ready, I suppose." Aribella straightens, smiles. "Everybody will be watching tonight."

I stand up, nodding. Everybody's always watching me.

PARTY

The Palafoxes know how to throw a bash.

The sky above the city is bright with explosions. Sharp little crackles scatter against the night, white and sudden. Willows of blue embers bloom, taking endless minutes to shimmer away. Vast scarlet umbrellas burn stately overhead.

Inside House Palafox, safety flames ripple on the curtains, tumble down the gaudy columns lining the entryway. Even the music sets the air on fire, the instruments of the brass band sparking from their bells.

The ballroom has expanded all day, its walls sliding grandly across the parquet floors. The party swells to fill the giant space, a long line of hovercars spilling out a thousand guests, all in more vibrant colors than anyone wears at a bash in Shreve.

At first, Rafi's ball gown feels dull. But as the crowd grows, the black and gray begins to stand out against this rainbow of fabric and flame. And Col looks perfect next to me. His midnight suit shines like dark metal, glinting with the sparks raining from the ceiling and the sky. His necktie is a nanoscreen, showing images of rolling ocean waves at night.

"Smile for the hovercams," he says. We're on a balcony above the throng, raising glasses of champagne. "Spoiled brats aren't permitted to be glum."

I hide my mouth behind my bubbly. "You know people read lips, right?"

"Not here." He gestures at the falling sparks. "Those shimmer at the exact speed of hovercam frame rates. Rattles the image just enough for privacy."

"Clever," I say.

"Necessary."

Again, the Victorians and their privacy obsession. But there's something electric about knowing that our words are hidden, even with a million people watching.

Rafi must be among them. She's watched me out in public before, of course, at nightclubs and in big crowds. But always from a private suite, not from back in our bedroom. I wonder if she's happy for me, finally getting the attention she always promised I would. Or is she only jealous of me now?

A friend of Col's joins us on the balcony, and the cyrano whispers in my ear.

Yandre Marin, eldest child of a famous couple. Their father is a popular novelist, their mother a leader in the political opposition here.

I don't know what a *novelist* is, except that it must be old-fashioned. Victorians are smug about keeping crumbly pastimes alive, from calligraphy to kayaking.

But Yandre's mother is an opposition leader? In Shreve, no one invites their political enemies to parties.

I smile and curtsy, admiring Yandre's long blue dress, its hem wreathed with flowers stitched in gold. A flash tattoo on their bare shoulder pulses with the music.

"Welcome to Victoria," Yandre says, bowing in return. "I hope you won't judge us all by your boring host."

"Boring!" Col protests. "Did you miss the part where we welcomed her with rebels?"

"You never welcome *me* with rebels!" Yandre looks my way, waiting for Rafi's famous wit to manifest.

My sister would say something bubbly, making light of the attack. I understand the theory of jokes like this, turning an uncomfortable topic into humor, but I haven't had much practice. The cyrano is silent.

Col steps in. "Your family practically *are* rebels, Yandre. Besides, you're just here to drink Jefa's champagne."

"And for my weekly dose of dullness." Yandre turns to me. "Has he given you the cloud forest lecture yet?"

"The first day," I manage. Which is only marginally bubbly.

They're still waiting for me to be funny. So I open my mouth, hoping that nothing too brain-missing comes out . . .

" 'She's not coming to save us.' "

Yandre frowns, pushing their long black hair over one ear. "Pardon?"

I have no idea why, out of all the madness of that day, those words stuck. But now I have to explain.

"During the attack, we took cover under a Rusty building. There was an abandoned camp down there, with rebel code all over the ceiling. The only thing we could read was, 'She's not coming to save us.'"

"I wonder who *she* is," Yandre says. "Our patron saint, Victoria? She was forced into a marriage with a heathen. Not unlike your predicament, Rafia."

"Don't be brain-missing," Col says. "The rebels don't care about pre-Rusty sky-gods."

"A saint isn't a god, silly boy. And our city *is* named after her."

Col sighs. "I hate it when that happens."

"You hate what?" Yandre says with a laugh. "When your hover-car crash-lands in a cryptic rebel base? Is that a thing?"

"No. When you hear a snatch of someone else's conversation, and it sounds mysterious and significant"—Col watches as a glittering sparkler falls past the balcony—"but you never find out what it means."

"You're so deep, chico." Yandre rolls their eyes and turns to me. "I'll ask my little brother. He's a bit of a rebel—*not* the kind that shoots at visiting celebrities, of course. But he might know that slogan."

I smile back at them. "Thank you."

"Speaking of your brother," Col says quietly. "Did he find what I asked for?"

Yandre nods. "I hid it under the daybed in the west room—Grandma Zefina let me in to fix my dress. But why you need a pulse charger is beyond me."

I take another swig to hide my expression.

"We just do." Col grins at me. "We can sneak it down to the old building tonight."

I stare at him. "With a million people watching? We'd need a pretty big diversion."

Yandre takes us both by the arms, and laughs.

"This is Victoria, my dear. Parties are their own diversion."

SWEAR

An hour later, the diversion arrives.

There's no warning, no ping from the city interface about taking cover. Just a sudden barrage from all directions.

The first one hits Yandre, a blur of motion in the corner of my eye, a *pop* as scarlet powder streaks their blue dress. I startle, but Col and Yandre only laugh.

Then something hits my shoulder. I barely feel it—the outer shell is some kind of aerogel, light as a puff of air. It breaks and scatters luminous green powder across my ball gown.

Overhead, the air is crisscrossed with projectiles.

"What the hell?"

"Cascarones," Col says. "To ruffle up the bash a little. It's a tradition that dates back to the pre-Rusty festival of—"

A bolt of brilliant blue streaks his forehead.

"Oh so perfect," Yandre manages through their laughter.

The projectiles are hitting everyone. Pinging into champagne flutes, marking dresses, suits, hats, faces with colored powder. The party redoubles in energy around us, and the musicians switch to a faster tempo.

Dancing erupts in the milling crowd.

"Come on," Col says, taking my hand. "It'll take a minute for the hovercams to find cover."

Yandre raises their glass as we slip away. "Have fun, you two."

Col leads me to the edge of the crowd, then along the ballroom's back wall. Cascarones smack and pop around us. Another hits me, a soft kiss between my shoulder blades.

We reach the corner, and Col opens a hidden door.

"If anyone asks, you wanted to clean up."

I almost protest this cover story—I *like* the vivid streaks on my ball gown. But Rafi would hate her design being marred by random colors.

She must be glued to the feeds right now, wondering where I am. Has she guessed that I've snuck away with Col? Will it hurt her face rank to be associated with someone as boring and studious as him?

He leads me through the door into a narrow space, stuffed with the extra furniture crowded out by the expansion of the ballroom. He pulls a flare from his pocket, snaps its top. A bright flickering erupts, and safety sparks cascade down my ball gown. Of course—like the fireworks outside, the flare pulses, dazzling any watching cams.

Col weaves among chairs, couches, reading desks, heading straight for a daybed in the corner. Kneeling, he pulls out an object wrapped in white plastic.

He hands it to me. "Is this what you need?"

The charger feels bulky, old-fashioned. But so was the pulse knife.

"It should work."

Col smiles. His eyes are bright, and there's a trickle of sweat channeling the blue powder on his face. I wonder if this is the first time he's snuck around in his own house.

"Do we have time?" I whisper.

He nods. "When Yandre tells people we snuck out together, no one will come looking."

"Oh. Right." Rafi would make a joke about now.

I've got nothing.

"Sorry," Col says, looking embarrassed

Then I remember one of Rafi's famous lines.

"If I cared what people said, they'd only gossip more."

The impersonation was perfect, even the wearily raised eyebrow to drive it home. But Col just frowns at me, then leads me to another door.

Minutes later we're running along the stone wall at the edge of the old building. Once we're past the retina lock, Col drops the flare and grinds it out under his heel. He leads me down a dark hallway into the weapons room.

I cross to the case that holds the pulse knife and drop to my knees. It doesn't take long to find the right spot—on the bottom, just beneath the knife.

With a squeeze, the charger wakes up, clinging to the case with magnetics. It detects the knife and begins a charge cycle, pulsing fast and featherlight.

"So how does it work?" Col asks.

I stand and face him. "Once the knife's charged, it can free itself. Then we use it to open the case with your bow."

"That'll make a mess, right?"

"Like a bomb hit." I shrug. "But you said no one comes down here."

"Hardly ever." He gives his hunting bow a look of longing. "How much time?"

"To fully charge? A day or so. Tomorrow night, we can sneak back and tell the knife to cut its way out—if it still works."

Col comes closer, staring down through the ferroglass.

I hold my hand out above the knife and make the *come to me* gesture—middle and ring fingers together, the others splayed.

For a moment the knife does nothing. But then a pale red light appears on its hilt.

"See that? It wants to jump into my hand. But it doesn't have enough juice."

"And it can cut through ferroglass?"

I grin at him. "Like sponge cake."

"Okay," he says. "But there's something you're not telling me."

The words yank my attention away from the knife. He's staring at me, his dark eyes intense.

I put on Rafi's amused voice. "Whatever do you mean?"

"Something's different. This isn't you."

Of course. The real Rafi wouldn't leave a global audience to help someone steal a hunting bow. She wouldn't spend all night talking to one boy, with a thousand other guests to charm. And she certainly wouldn't stand here explaining how pulse knives work.

Col knows I'm not her.

An escape plan flashes through my head—an open-handed strike to his temple. Then breaking into the case somehow and fleeing with the pulse knife and the charger. The party upstairs will give me a few hours of cover.

But why would Col accuse me *here*, where no one can help him?

He's waiting for an answer. The real Rafia would have one. Not me.

"On the feeds," he says, "when you act like a spoiled littlie, I get now that it's all a joke. That you're making *fun* of people like us."

My racing heart settles a little.

"It's fun," I tell him, "making fun of spoiled brats."

"Then why are you down here? There's a hundred hover-cams up there, all of them begging for it, and you didn't do your act. What's different now, Rafia?"

Say something. Say anything.

I touch my cyrano, hoping for something useful.

Col Palafox. He's the eldest son of the Victorian first family.

The idiot machine thinks I've forgotten his name. My father's voice, mocking me.

"Why did my mother lock up my bow?" Col asks. "Is she scared of you?"

"Yes," I say, grateful for anything.

He's waiting for more, but I finally see a way out. To keep him from understanding my big secret, I have to give him a smaller one.

"Your mother can't know I told you this." All my anxiety is in my voice.

"Told me what?"

"I'm a hostage here."

Col doesn't react. Like he doesn't even know the word.

"I'm a prisoner," I say. "A guarantee that my father's forces won't take over the ruins."

His voice is uncertain in the darkness. "And my mother agreed to this?"

A strange urge to defend Aribella hits me. "She doesn't like it either. And she's promised not to hurt me, Col."

A bitter laugh forces its way out of him. "How nice for you. And she's always saying we're different from the other first families. I can't *believe* her!"

He looks angry enough to storm upstairs and confront Aribella right now. That argument could go wrong for me in a hundred ways.

I take hold of his arm. "She can't find out that I told you."

"Of course not, but . . ." Col stares at me, uncertain. "Your father letting this happen, I halfway believe. But why did *you* agree to it?"

I have to look away. Col will never understand that I didn't have a choice.

"I don't want our cities to fight. With me here, they won't."

"That's very brave of you." I can't tell if he's sarcastic or serious.

"I should have told you sooner. I'm sorry."

He takes my right hand. Something electric goes through those knitted bones. "Don't apologize, Rafi. And don't worry. I'll make sure Jefa keeps her promise."

He touches his lips to my hand. Just for a moment.

"*J'en mettrais ma main au feu,*" he says.

I'm staring at my hand, at his lips.

The cyrano translates in my ear—*I put my hand in the fire.*

What do they mean, those words? That kiss? Is this how they seal promises in Victoria? Or is it the start of something else?

I don't know anything about kissing.

His dark eyes lock with mine. No one looks at me this intently, except Naya, when she's sizing up my weaknesses. I feel measured, scanned, defenseless.

Then Col lets go and turns toward the hallway.

"We should get back to the party," he says.

I nod dumbly. Suddenly that swirl of music, fire, and projectiles seems safer than being alone with him.

TELL ME EVERYTHING

A strange thing has happened overnight—I'm popular here.

Everyone expected bratty, sophisticated Rafia at the party, but they got me instead. All those guests and hovercams to charm, and I paid attention only to Col. Like some random, brain-missing with a sudden crush.

And then, when that rain of cascarones came down, the two of us disappeared for half an hour.

Rafi's global face rank has dipped a little this morning; pairing off with the host is boring by her standards. But here in Victoria the audience was thrilled to see Col Palafox, their thoughtful first-family son, turn a dazzling socialite into a bubblehead.

Watching the social feeds discuss this makes me twitchy— now that they're about *me* instead of Rafi. All that focus on my ball gown, my posture, my hair. All that speculation about what's going on with me and Col, when I don't even know myself.

How does Rafi stand all this attention? How does she remember who she really is, underneath all the layers of fashion and rumors and gossip? No wonder she has those temper tantrums.

I wonder if she ever wants to trade lives with me, if only for the chance to punch something.

I switch to the news. Here in Victoria, I can watch the global feeds instead of Shreve propaganda. It's weird how everything is laid out in such a matter-of-fact way, without the music or eye-dazzling headlines.

My father's forces sortied into the mountains last night, destroying a rebel camp a hundred klicks from the ruins. Maybe this will all be over soon and I can go home.

Of course, I can't count on that. So while I listen, I work on my escape kit.

I've been gathering useful things, leaving them around the room, ready to be swept up if I have to run. So far it's dried fruit brought back from meals, a few plastic bags for collecting rainwater, my self-cleaning sweats, a firestarter. This morning's work is adding an improvised weapon to the mix—a sharp-edged light fixture that I loosen from the wall as I pretend to stretch.

A pulse knife would be better.

My head still throbs and buzzes from the party. I miss training. I'm going soft here in Victoria. Naya will kill me if I come back home over my fighting weight. But calorie purger pills make me jittery, and I'm jittery enough already.

Of course, Aribella already knows I'm dangerous, so maybe it doesn't matter if I do some pushups.

Halfway into my workout, my cyrano pings—another hidden message from Rafi.

I tap it and keep exercising.

You're killing me, Frey.

It's bad enough my dress got ruined, but did you have to make me look like such a face-missing wallflower! And crushing on Col Palafox? Really? What if he speaks French to you?

Or have you two been too busy to talk?

Ugh. Don't tell me.

By which I mean, yes—definitely tell me.

A grin creeps onto my face. Rafi sounds almost jealous.

She's stuck in hiding, of course, with no parties of her own. But the thought of her living vicariously through *my* social life is the most brain-missing thing ever.

Out the window, a flock of pigeons wheels around the distant cathedral spire, exuberant and playful. My hand tingles where Col kissed me.

Is this what it feels like to have my own life?

That's what kills me, Frey—that you can't even tell me what's going on. If you're getting clothes-missing for the first time ever without your big sister there to counsel you, it's an outrage.

I take a slow breath.

Clothes-missing? That's a laugh. Col's lips barely brushed my hand.

If Rafi were here, she could figure out what's actually going on between me and him. *Allies* is the only word we've said out loud. Is that more or less than *friends?*

But he kissed my hand . . .

I should research what that means here in Victoria, just ask the city interface about local romance customs.

But Palafox security would notice—that doesn't sound like something Rafi would have to ask. She'd just know.

Throw me a clue, Frey. If you and that boy have shared so much as a meaningful look, wear the scarlet jacket today—the one with too many buttons on the sleeves. But if there's nothing going on, wear my white jacket.

Red for passion. White for lonely and cold. Surely you can remember that.

Send me a sign, Frey. Entertain me—I'm going crazy here!

But really, I hope it's the white jacket. I mean, really. He's the first boy you've ever talked to!

Love you, little sister. But take it from your sensei—you don't know anything yet.

The recording ends, and the last words ring in my ears.

Sensei. That's not a word she would ever use casually. Not since Noriko disappeared.

Rafi's trying to send me a message that no one else would catch, something deadly important. But I can't figure it out.

She's right. I don't know anything.

And suddenly it's all so embarrassing. Was my father listening while she recorded it? Does he care what's going on between me and Col?

Which is probably *nothing*. Col's lips on the back of my hand must be some crumbly Victorian tradition, like calligraphy or novel writing.

But the look he gave me after . . .

There's a knock at the door. Not a ping, knuckles on wood.

"Come in."

The door swings open, and it's Col.

He gives me a puzzled look. I'm in pajamas, my hair frazzled, sweaty. Hardly a state Rafi would receive visitors in.

Now that I've started telling people my secrets, the rest of my act is falling apart.

"I thought we'd tour the roof garden before lunch," he says, making the hand sign for *We're being watched*.

"That sounds lovely, Col. I'll be dressed in . . . forty minutes?"

He nods, looking reassured.

That, at least, was a very Rafi thing to say.

SPINES

The roof of House Palafox is covered with sharp things—antennae slicing into the sky, the spinning blades of windmills, a garden full of cactuses.

The succulents come in all sizes, from spiky soccer balls to three-meter, splay-armed giants. Some are abloom with tiny flowers, surrounded by sizzling galaxies of bees.

"*Les murs n'ont pas d'oreilles,*" Col says.

The walls don't have ears, my cyrano translates.

I look around. No security drones, no smart walls. Unless one of the bees is a nanocam, he's probably right.

No newsfeed hovercams either. Which is good, because I haven't chosen a jacket yet.

Like my sister said, I don't know anything.

Col gestures toward my ear. "That's listening, isn't it?"

I shrug. "It's just a cyrano. I'm terrible at names."

"Jefa says the house scanners can't crack it, which means it's serious tech." He gives me a look. "It could be reporting back to your father."

I roll my eyes. I know more about spyware than romance.

"It's strictly passive. Your house security would notice if it started transmitting. But if it makes you happy." I drop the cyrano in my pocket.

Col doesn't know it's always listening.

We stand there in awkward silence for a moment.

"The party was lovely," I say.

Col gives me a sheepish smile. "Jefa was pleased. No complaints about us disappearing."

So Aribella is okay with something happening between me and Col. Or at least she's fine with the rest of the city thinking there is.

But what does Col think?

That tingle is still there where he kissed me.

Naya's voice pops into my head. *So many nerves in the hand— it's the best way to take down a stronger foe.*

I know how to break fingers. But not how to kiss someone.

"Yandre pinged me this morning," Col says. "They talked to their brother, the rebel sympathizer, about that slogan—'She's not coming to save us.' Turns out *she* is Tally Youngblood."

A little tremor rolls through me. The rebels have their own saint, of course. "But what does it mean?"

"Exactly what it says. Tally's not coming back. We have to save ourselves."

That's not news to me.

I turn away, looking around the rooftop, mapping the shape of the building against the layout of the floors below.

Making escape plans is something I know all about.

A few of the trees in the courtyard garden have grown higher than the roofline. It wouldn't be too hard to climb up here from the garden.

"You think the knife is charged yet?" Col asks.

"Too soon. Do you miss hunting that much?"

"I miss people not taking my stuff." He gazes off at the mountains. "But sure. I like surviving off the land, being connected to the wild."

I laugh. "You connect to nature by *eating* it? I hope the same doesn't apply to your friends."

"Is that what we are?"

Right. We've only said *allies* so far.

Col is giving me one of his intense looks, which must mean something. But who knows what? I've never really made a friend before. I've only ever had one, and she's my twin sister.

"If you want to be friends, sure."

"Great." He nods a little and turns away.

Somehow I'm doing this wrong.

"Speaking of eating nature: These *nopales* are tasty." He's switched into his tour guide voice, pointing to a cluster of flat-armed cactuses, like oblong dinner plates covered with red flowers. "They're on the lunch menu today."

"Not exactly hungry-making." I reach out and touch one of the cactuses, expecting it to stab me—and it does. "Ow. Why does everything up here have spikes?"

"Spines," Col corrects me. "Furry ones to keep insects away. Big needle ones for mammals like me and you."

"So a cactus is afraid of *everything*?"

Col looks at me meaningfully. "When you've got water in the desert, you have to protect yourself."

He's talking about the ruins, of course. Metal is the thing that every city wants, like water in a desert.

"What kind of spines does your family have?" I ask.

"Sharp ones. This morning, I asked Jefa what she'll do if your father refuses to leave our ruins."

I frown. "She didn't mention throwing me in a dungeon, I hope?"

"No. She's still keeping that a secret from me. But she said we have some surprises in store for your father. He's not the only one waking up old weapons."

"That'll only make things worse."

"For him."

I shake my head. "Whenever things don't go his way, he escalates. When he's caught in a lie, he tells a bigger one. When someone resists, he hits them harder."

When someone took his child, he made two more.

"We're not afraid of him," Col says.

"Then why does your mother need me as a hostage?"

"To save lives. We don't *want* to fight." He looks off at the mountains. "Even if the first families don't fight all-out Rusty wars, soldiers still die. By having you here, Jefa's trying to show your father another way. Negotiation instead of violence."

So Aribella thinks she's playing my father.

"She scares me a little," I say.

"*Très drôle.* Considering who your father is."

"*Je suppose,*" I manage, pleased that I didn't need my cyrano. *Drôle* means the same in French as it does in English.

Col thinks I'm funny.

"There's something you might want to see," he says.

"Is it edible and spiny?"

Col smiles, leading me to the western edge of the roof, facing the mountains. "The best view of the city."

It's not. We're looking down a jumble of narrow alleyways, through a part of Victoria that's old and earth-bound. No soaring fairy-tale towers or bright colors.

But it's the perfect neighborhood to disappear into.

Col glances down at a plastic box at our feet, marked with the fire escape symbol. Bungee jackets.

A tangle of thoughts goes through my head. He's helping me make escape plans. He really *is* an ally.

Or maybe something more. After all, he's betraying his own family for me.

"I don't know what to say."

Col shrugs. "No one should be a prisoner just because of who their father is."

The strange thing is, I've never felt like a prisoner here in Victoria. Before I came here, my whole life was spent behind locked doors and impenetrable walls. A prisoner is what I've always been.

It's like Col knows that somehow, and he wants to save me.

He leans over the parapet. "That long alley leads to the edge of the city, with a few twists and turns."

"Thank you."

"It's the least I can do." Col looks like he's about to say something more—but he turns away. "I should dress for lunch. We'll be on the south terrace. With all the gossip about last night, there'll be newscams snooping around."

So whatever I wear will be in the feeds, and Rafi will be watching with keen eyes. But I don't know which jacket. Not yet.

And I don't know why she said *sensei*.

We head back down to my room in uncertain silence, everything unsaid still lingering between us.

At my door I hesitate. "It's nice to have a friend here."

Col doesn't answer, just gives me another silent look. We're back inside, where the house can hear us, so maybe he can't say what he's thinking. But I can't resist asking.

"What is it?" I whisper.

"Nothing," he says softly. "Just . . . *parfois je me perds dans tes yeux.*"

Crap. That's too much French all at once. I have no idea what it means.

Was it a clue about an escape route? Something droll about the lunch menu?

I give him one of Rafi's looks of amusement.

"That's . . . lovely."

"Ah, sorry," Col says. He takes a step back, his expression darkening.

He's apologizing. I've messed something up.

But I can't confess how terrible my French is. I've spilled enough of my secrets to the Palafoxes.

Col is walking away, and I say nothing.

Once the door's shut, I pull the cyrano from my pocket, praying it caught whatever he said. I head to the bathroom and turn on all the taps.

"Replay last sixty seconds," I whisper.

His words are there at the edge of hearing. But I still don't know what they mean.

"Translate?" I plead, and it's awful to hear it in my father's voice.

Sometimes I get lost in your eyes.

I stand there, steam building around me, not caring if Palafox security wonders what this is all about. What matters is what I do next.

That look of amusement on my face after he said the words—he must have thought I'd turned back into Rafi. Arch and superior and too detached for any sentiment so simple and so sweet.

I have to fix this.

"Ping Col Palafox," I say to the room.

"Message content?" the room asks.

My heart is racing. "The message is, 'Me too.' End and send."

Then I go to the closet and stare at the red jacket.

I should wear it for lunch—my still-racing heart is proof of that. But do I really want Rafi knowing what's going on in my head?

What if she laughs at me? That would be too much to bear. And Dona will be watching closely too, maybe even my father. They don't want me compromised by some brain-missing crush.

But Rafi's my big sister, and she asked for a sign. She said the word *sensei*, so I knew how important it was.

I have to share this with her.

I reach for the red jacket.

FLY

That night I wake up to a screaming sound.

It's a dream at first—my bed scanning me with bright shafts of light. But instead of scars and healed bones, the scanner finds a weapon buried inside me. A knife hidden in my chest, pulsing quick.

And that's where the dream shifts into a nightmare—an alarm shrieks, an ice pick of sound that I can't shut out, even with my hands over my ears. As sharp and hard as anger, the alarm penetrates my body, rattles my bones, lances my frenzied heart.

Finally I sputter awake, look around in a panic. The screaming doesn't stop, as if I'm still dreaming.

Then I realize it's the cyrano, jittering on my bedside table.

It must be malfunctioning.

"Quiet!" I tell it.

The noise shuts off.

I pick it up, hesitantly put it in my ear—if the shrieking starts again, it'll deafen me. But it speaks calmly now.

Emergency message.

I tap it, and my sister's voice rushes into my head.

I'm so sorry, Frey. He wouldn't let me warn you until now. It's because you wore that stupid red jacket. How could you be so brain-missing?

After what I said, couldn't you tell you were supposed to wear the white *one?*

How could you not know it was a test? That he made me do it?

Now he thinks you'll put Col before him. That you won't follow orders. That you'll warn them!

I sit up in bed. Warn them about what?

He's moved up the timetable—we're pushing the Palafoxes out of the ruins tonight.

The attack starts in two minutes.

My eyes blink, trying to resolve meaning in the darkness. It's like being in the dream again. My body lanced by scanning rays, my heart vibrating fast as a pulse knife.

I take slow breaths to calm myself. I have an escape kit. This is something I know how to do. Something I've been getting ready for my whole life.

But all my reflexes and training falter when it hits me—

My father only thinks I'm worth two minutes' warning.

I cling to my sister's voice.

All you have to do is get to the ruins, Frey. We'll take control of them first, like everyone expects.

Come in from the south, on foot. The soldiers won't dare shoot. They still think you're me.

You'll be fine. You can do this.

Yes—escaping, fighting my way out. I'm Frey, the one who uses her fists.

This is the only thing I know how to do.

I spring up from the bed, jump into my sweats and running shoes and jacket. Shove my stolen dried fruit, firestarter, and plastic bags into the pockets. A desperate idea hits me, and I grab the tulle lining of my ball gown.

With one kick, the loosened light fixture flies off the wall. It fits in my hand perfectly, metal edges glinting in the dark.

The house security must have heard my cyrano screaming, and they've seen my curious behavior. They'll be sending someone up to check on me.

If my father had given me more time, I could've gotten ready quietly, stealthily. But he doesn't trust me anymore.

Because I wore the red jacket, like a lovelorn bubblehead. Like someone whose social life is more important than her mission.

Focus.

The door pings.

"Excuse me, Rafia." A male voice comes into the room. "This is Warden Renold. I'd like to have a word with—"

I open the door and punch him hard in the face, my improvised weapon giving the blow extra weight. He topples backward, hits the ground.

My hand screams with pain. It's been so long since I hit anything.

I kick the warden once in the stomach to make sure he stays down. They'll come in numbers now, but the security barracks are all the way downstairs. It's the drones I have to worry about.

But I have a plan for that.

I run for the billiard room, which has a window overlooking the courtyard. Close enough to the tallest tree to jump—maybe.

On the way, I tear the ball gown lining into pieces. I aim the firestarter at the strips of tulle, tossing them at curtains and pieces of furniture. The hallways start to fill with smoke.

Halfway to the billiard room, a drone comes down the hall. But it zooms right past me, spraying fire-foam. Alarms are ringing in every direction, a thousand sensors calling for its attention.

Someone could reset the drones' priorities to focus on me instead of the fires, but by now my father's attack has started in the Rusty ruins. Palafox security has bigger things to worry about than one runaway rich kid.

They only have to underestimate me for a few more minutes.

In the billiard room, I spill two racks of balls in front of the door. Grab a pool cue off the wall.

One swing of the cue smashes the window to pieces, glittering shards scattering out into the night. It's old-fashioned glass, not safety polymer, so I sweep the cue back and forth to clear the window frame.

Stepping out into the dark, I realize that the tree branch is farther away than I thought.

My stomach does a little flip. The ground is nothing but blackness below. A few stars sparkle through the jungle canopy.

A clatter of balls sounds behind me—a warden coming in, losing her footing. I leap at her, the cue spinning like a lopsided *bō* in my hands. She raises some kind of stunner, but the heavy end of the cue knocks it from her grip. When she blocks my swing at her temple, I follow with a thrust to her stomach.

She's down.

But more will come. I have to make the jump.

Flinging the cue aside, I run for the window, wishing I had crash bracelets.

The cool night wraps around me. My hands grab for the tree branch, palms slapping against smooth bark and holding for a moment. But my momentum carries my feet out, and my fingers slip.

I fall in ringing silence, but only for a second—a lower branch hits my midsection like a body tackle, knocking the breath from my lungs.

The branch bows under my weight, and the rattle of leaves comes from all directions, the flutter of wings. My crash landing sending a host of creatures stampeding through the canopy.

Somehow I hold on.

But the window of the billiard room is right there, gaping open, shining light out on me.

Sucking in shallow, painful breaths, I start to climb. Up into the darkness of the dense treetops, the crisscross of vines pricked with stars.

This is what I was made for, but somehow the ecstasy of combat isn't kicking in. Breathing is agony after the gut-punch of landing on the branch.

The gut-punch of Father sacrificing me . . .

Rafi was right. Since they stole Seanan from him, my father has wanted to scream at the world, *Take my child! I don't care!*

He's trading me for a pile of metal. I was just a distraction, a way to give the Palafoxes a false sense of security.

This is what I was made for—throwing away.

I hear voices from the open window below and freeze.

A man in a warden's uniform leans out. He scans the upper branches quickly, then gives the ground below a hard look. The lighting along the paths is flickering on.

Two drones waft into position behind the warden, and he sends them out the window with a jerk of his hand. They descend into the garden.

Why can't they see me? My body heat must stick out like a brush fire against this cool jungle.

Setting my eyescreen to night vision, I realize why—the canopy is full of living things. Flocks of birds and scurrying creatures, a lively host all around me.

But if the warden looks harder, he'll recognize my shape.

I start climbing again, careful not to shake the leaves. The sharp outline of rooftop against open sky is almost within reach, but the branch beneath me bends under my weight as I go farther out.

Then I hear a sound against all the alarms and shouting below. A slithering.

And I remember what Dr. Orteg jokingly warned me about when he put my eyes in—

Snakes are cold-blooded, matching the temperature of their environment. They're invisible in heat vision.

And they don't like being stepped on.

SNAKE

The sound is soft, like the rasp of a dry tongue against the bark, mixed with the faint rattle of leaves.

Which direction is it coming from?

The branches are crowded together up here, and other sounds distract my ears. The garden below is full of wardens and drones.

Someone's going to spot me up here soon.

I reach out to take the next branch, hoping my fingers close on bark, not scales.

The branch feels thick enough to hold my weight, and I swing across. Hanging there, I listen. The slithering sounds closer now.

But I can't focus on the snake. A dozen armed soldiers and a house full of security drones are after me.

I hoist myself up, wrapping my legs around the branch.

The roof is so close. As I shimmy upward, the leaves rattle, but I don't care about noise. I just want to put my feet on solid ground.

Then the slithering sound comes again. I freeze. Switch off my useless night vision.

There it is ahead of me. Scales glinting in the moonlight, sinuous and coiling.

Two black eyes like dots of oil.

It stares at me with boundless patience, paralyzing me. I hang like that for an endless time, barely breathing, dimly aware that my muscles are starting to burn.

Sooner or later, I'll fall.

It's a drone that saves me, the little red-and-green running lights whirring up into the corner of my vision. Only a meter away, the barrel of its little stunner is pointed right at my face.

"Don't move," it says. "We don't want to hurt you, but we will if we have to."

Hurt me? If it hits me with the stunner, I'll tumble all the way to the ground. Maybe that fact will make the operator hesitant.

I don't even have a weapon. So I improvise one, my reflexes overriding my fear.

I reach out to grab the tail end of the snake and fling it at the drone. It hits with a *smack* and tightens its coils around the little machine. The drone tips over, its lifters fighting the shifting weight.

But the startled creature won't let go, and together they tumble away through the leaves.

I'm already scrambling for the roof. Noise doesn't matter any-more. If I can only get to those bungee jackets and hurl myself into the night.

This branch is just close enough for my fingers to reach the roof edge. I swing across, my feet scrabbling on rough stone.

A heave of my burning muscles hauls me up and onto the parapet. Solid stone feels like salvation, but I don't have time to rest. I roll from the parapet wall onto . . .

Needles. Spines.

The edge of the cactus garden.

A thousand pinpricks pull a ragged gasp from my lips. I launch myself from the cactus bed and onto the gravel rooftop.

My jacket is pinned to me, a hundred little hooks still in my skin. I pull it off, tearing spines with it.

"Stop right there," comes a familiar voice.

Another drone, two meters from me.

"You don't have to fight us," it says, speaking with Aribella's voice. My father's forces are invading the ruins, and she's focus-ing on *me*.

Why do I matter so much?

Because she doesn't realize that my father has thrown me away.

"You can't escape, Rafia."

She's probably right. There are no weapons for me to grab. My jacket lies at my feet—maybe I could throw it at the drone, but I'm exhausted, my muscles screaming.

"You have nothing to fear from us," Aribella says.

I want so badly to believe her, to think that *someone* is on my side.

"Okay," I murmur, and raise my hands. "I give up."

"Very good, Rafia. I knew you were a smart—"

Something slams into the drone, lighting up the night with sparks and flame.

I stumble away, hands across my eyes, almost falling back into the cactuses again. My eyes pulsing with leftover explosion, I can see someone at the far parapet, the dark mountains framed behind him.

He's holding a hunting bow.

"Come on!" Col calls. "I've only got two more explosive arrows."

He glitters in the starlight, because he's covered with ferro-glass dust.

My pulse knife is on his belt.

ESCAPE

I run across the roof and wrap my arms around him.

Col holds me for a moment, then pulls back, frowning.

"Ouch! Why are you so *pointy?*"

"Sorry. Took a roll in your cactuses." The spines in my nightshirt are still prickling me all over. "How did you get up here?"

"The stairs," he says.

Of course—the roof is a fire escape. When the house smelled smoke, it opened all the doors, security lockdown or not.

I could have taken the stairs.

"Couldn't sleep," Col says. "So I went down to the old building and called the knife, like you showed me."

He coughs once, and a little sparkling cloud lifts from him. I should probably tell him that breathing ferroglass dust is a bad idea.

I splay my hand, ring and middle fingers together. The knife jumps from his belt and into my palm. With it trembling in my hand, it's like a missing part of me has returned.

"When the alarms went off, I thought I was busted," he says. "But it wasn't me. Your father hit our forces in the ruins."

"I didn't know he would do this, I swear."

"You're not him, Rafi. But we should hide you until we figure out what Jefa plans to—"

His voice drops away, and he pushes me backward, clearing space to notch another arrow on his bowstring.

I spin around. Three more drones are lofting up from the garden.

"Save your arrows, Col," I say, and throw my knife sideways.

It takes a sweeping course around the roof. Hits the rightmost drone on the side, turns it into metal and plastic fragments, then continues on to plow through the other two.

A moment later it's back in my hand, humming with delight, as warm as fresh bread.

"Whoa." Col stares at me, only now realizing the power of the weapon he's given me.

I kneel and pull open the box of bungee jackets. "They'll send more drones. Let's get these on."

"Um, Rafi?"

I look up. Col snaps his fingers and rises into the air.

He's standing on a hoverboard.

Smugly.

"I liberated all my hunting gear," he says. "Thought you could use a ride."

I stand back up, staring at his board. It's all-terrain, with lifting fans and solar panels. Not fast, but perfect for crossing the wild.

There's so much I want to say, but all I've got is "Thank you."

Col folds his bow, collapsing its hingeless nanotech polymers down to the shape and size of a boomerang.

"Step on."

I climb up behind him, and the board rises higher into the air and over the parapet. The jumble of the city opens up below us, my stomach clenching.

"No crash bracelets?" I ask.

He shrugs. "I was in a hurry."

"Wait—why are *you* coming?"

"I'll take you to the edge of town." Col angles us forward, gaining speed over the rooftops. "If anyone chases us, they won't shoot at me."

Of course—he's the beloved first son of Victoria.

And this way we don't have to say good-bye yet.

"Tell them I took you hostage," I say, holding on to him as we gain speed. "So you won't get in trouble."

"Or I can tell Jefa the truth—she shouldn't use people's children for collateral."

"Sure," I say. "Telling the truth is one way."

We bend our knees together as the board drops into the alley behind House Palafox, leaving the alarms of war behind.

ESCALATION

We zoom down the alley, ten meters above empty streets.

Looking back over my shoulder, I see no signs of pursuit. Maybe they know that Col's with me—there's no way to shoot the board down without killing us both.

Or maybe they've got too much else to deal with.

It's hitting at last, the ecstasy of combat. With my arms wrapped around Col, our weight leaning together into the turns, that rapture of unquestioned reflex and purpose comes over me.

But then, as we peak above the rooftops for a moment, I catch a glimpse of the night sky streaked with flames ahead—my father's suborbitals coming down in the distant ruins. Jagged forks of lightning reach up from the earth, contesting with them.

Our families are at war.

More soldiers will die tonight.

"I'm so sorry," I murmur into Col's shoulder.

"You tried to stop this by coming here! It's Jefa's fault for trusting him."

Col thinks I came here of my own free will. That my presence had some chance of making my father stay his hand. But I was disposable, a way to make the Palafoxes drop their guard.

All that training in escape and improvised weapons wasn't as a last resort. It was always the plan to leave me exposed in enemy territory.

All my life, I thought my sister and I were a knife with two edges. But she was all that mattered, and I was just a bullet to be fired and forgotten.

What if I was fooling myself along with everyone else?

We fly until we reach an industrial belt at the edge of the city. The buildings are windowless and square, and the roads swarm with self-driving trucks.

The factories down there must be shifting gears, ready to produce drones and battle armor. Aribella plans to retake the ruins.

She doesn't know my father.

"We're close to the city's edge," Col says.

The hoverboard slows. Past the factory lights I see the dark expanse of the desert.

I've camped in the wild before, but the thought of going out there alone makes me nervous.

At home, Rafi was always there in the next bed. Even as a hostage, there's always been a house full of people around me.

The thought of making my lonely way out into that blackness makes my stomach twist.

Before this moment, I had no idea I was afraid to be alone. Of course, I didn't know about the snake thing either, until I came face-to-face with one.

A shudder goes through me.

"You can take my jacket," Col says. "It's heated."

"Thank you."

The board comes to a halt, and he turns around to face me.

I look down at myself. I'm a mess, my nightshirt dotted with cactus spines.

Col shrugs his jacket off. "You can't make it all the way to Shreve on one charge. But this board has solar panels."

"It's okay. They'll pick me up in the ruins."

He turns, frowns at the streaks of light in the west.

"Don't be so sure about that. You could be walking into a battle."

I let out of sigh. People always think the fight will be fair, but it never is.

"I'll be fine, as long as I've got my knife." The board shifts a little beneath our feet. "Thank you for helping me escape, Col."

He drapes his jacket around my shoulders. It's warm, but not as warm as being in his arms.

"Why did your father do this?" Col asks. "How could he risk losing you?"

I could tell him what I've realized at last—that risking me was always the plan. My father used me to lure the rebels out. He warned me to be ready to escape. My whole life I've been disposable.

But that confession can't be the last thing I say to him.

So I make up a lie. "Something must have gone wrong. An accident. Friendly fire . . ."

He nods. "This can't last long. Wars between cities never do. I'll ping you as soon as I can."

I look away. Col won't be able to ping me, because my sister will get her name back once I'm home. As far as the global interface is concerned, Frey doesn't exist.

"Just remember," he says. "This fight has nothing to do with us."

It has everything to do with me, the impostor who tricked the Palafoxes into trusting my father.

"I'll miss you," I say.

"Me too, Rafi."

He takes my shoulders then and leans forward.

The warmth of his lips on mine sets the air humming, like my skin when a rainstorm is on its way. There's a rushing in my head, and in it I hear my own name instead of hers, as if this kiss is the first thing that really belongs to me alone. And I know exactly how to kiss him back, like I've been practicing my whole life for this.

But then my father's voice whispers in my ear—

Emergency message.

I startle, pulling back.

Col stares at me. "What?"

I tap my cyrano, and my sister's voice starts crying—

Get out of that house! Now, Frey!

Out a window! Kill anyone in your way!

In thirty seconds it won't matter!

I look up into Col's dark eyes, hoping I'm wrong.

Knowing I'm right.

Aribella wasn't lying that she had a surprise for my father up her sleeve. His forces have been repulsed in the ruins. This fight is harder than he expected.

And when that happens, he only knows one way to respond.

"I'm so sorry," I whisper.

"Oh." Col turns away, the back of his hand against his lips. "I thought you wanted me to kiss you."

He doesn't understand. He can't hear Rafi in my ears.

He's going to escalate.

I swear I didn't know about this.

Just get out, Frey. Get out!

I open my mouth to explain, but Rafi's message hasn't come in time. From the north, a speck of light shrieks across the sky, faster than anything I've ever seen.

It leaves a trace, a wavering trail of plasma, the air itself on fire . . .

And plunges deep into the heart of Victoria.

My father makes his own reality. Sometimes with force. Sometimes with atrocity.

The flash reaches us first, then a *boom* that ripples the air, setting us wavering for a moment on the hoverboard.

From the center of the distant city, a dark fist of smoke begins to rise.

Col stands there, his eyes wide.

There's no room inside me to feel anything but resolve. I need to protect him now, with an urgency that feels like hunger.

"We have to move," I say softly. "He'll hit the factories next."

"But that's my . . ." Col starts, and his words shudder to a halt.

I turn him gently away from the column of smoke rising from his home, and lean forward to urge our hoverboard deeper into the darkness.

PART II

ALLIANCE

*If injury must be done to a man,
it should be so severe that
his vengeance need not be feared.*

—Niccolò Machiavelli

ANVILS

More missiles hit as we fly away.

They come as shrieks of light across the heavens, arcing down to earth in the city behind us. Flashes kindle the horizon, followed by tardy thunder that sets our hoverboard shuddering.

The missiles leave glowing streaks in their wake, until the sky is sliced to pieces. There's a smell like ozone and burned plastic. My eyes sting.

I try to breathe away the shock, to wrap my mind around my father's strategy.

The strikes are hitting the periphery of Victoria, focused on the factory belt. At least they're not destroying more of the city center—all that life and color, those fragile, hovering buildings.

"What's happening?" Col keeps asking in disbelief. None of this makes sense to him. This is not normal.

When we're far enough away from Victoria, I ease to a halt over the dark trees and turn to face him, the board unsteady beneath us.

"Aribella was right—your family's forces were stronger than my father expected. So he hit back where you were most vulnerable. It's what I tried to say yesterday. He always escalates."

Col drags his eyes from the spectacle behind us, faces me.

"*This* is what you meant? An attack on the city? On my *family*? You didn't say anything about . . ."

He flings out an arm at Victoria. A dozen columns of smoke rise from its periphery, but none as high as the black tower rising from its center.

House Palafox, now smoke and dust.

I don't want to see it. But even when I close my eyes, the traces of missiles are burned into my vision.

"It's always the same, Col. Back home, the newsfeeds thought they could report what was happening, until he shut them down. The elected council thought they were in charge, until they weren't. His allies thought they could pull him back if he went too far. But he astounds *everyone*."

"That was all in Shreve." Col turns to face his home again. "No one's done anything like *this* in three hundred years!"

It's true. No one's bombed a population center since the Rusties. The first families never attack one another directly.

"The unthinkable is what he's best at, Col."

"My mother." His voice drops away.

"The attack started out in the ruins." I sound like I'm trying to convince myself. "She might have been headed there."

"Maybe. But Abuela wouldn't have left home."

Grandmother, my father whispers in my ear.

"We don't know anything yet, Col."

He turns on me, suddenly pleading. "But *you* were there too! Why would he risk killing you?"

"To show that he could."

Col just stares at me. There's no way he can understand all this at once. It's taken me sixteen years to see how my father's mind works.

But I try to explain.

"He wanted to show the world that nobody can win against him, no matter what cards they hold. Proving that he could throw me away was just as important as taking the ruins."

As I speak, my chest tightens. The spreading smoke is catching up with us.

"The other cities will fear him even more now. They'll know there's no weapon he won't use. No one he won't hurt."

Something clicks in Col's stunned expression.

"My little brother—we have to warn him!"

I look back at the burning city. The wind is stretching the columns of smoke inland toward the mountains, angling their shape. Like a host of vast black anvils has dropped from the sky.

"He knows already, Col. This will be on all the feeds."

"But Teo needs to know that he's not safe. And that I'm still alive!"

Col is shaking, and I take hold of his arms.

"He's at a boarding school, right? How many other important families send their kids there?"

"I don't know. A hundred?"

I hold him tighter. "My father can't attack a place like that. He wants the other cities divided. Nothing will unify them like their own children getting hurt."

Col steadies himself. "So there's a limit."

"He can't have the whole world turn on him at once." My voice rasps from the smoke.

There's a pause. Col is staring at me.

"How can you think this way? How can you even begin to understand him?"

I don't have an answer for that. But my brain is still whirring.

To the rest of the world, my father risked his only daughter. But even if I never make it home, he's still got Rafi. He can reveal her in a day or so. Concoct some story about her daring escape. Yet another chance to prove that he always wins.

This was all a dreadful magic trick—a city aflame, the Palafoxes dead, but his own daughter appears.

But first he has to wait to see if I'm okay. If two identical daughters show up, the story of his victory gets messy.

And that's when I realize—I have a small measure of power over my father.

He doesn't know I'm alive. There must be some way to use this. But only if I stay hidden instead of going home.

The smoke is getting thicker. Ash flutters down around us.

"We should keep moving," I say.

Col looks out into the darkness. "Where?"

I shake my head. All I know is that I'm not going to the ruins. There will be no rescue by my father's forces. No triumphant return home for his brilliant warrior-daughter.

The leash around my neck is gone.

TRUST ME

"You told me something," Col says. "Right before the missile hit my house."

I look up from the fire. It's the best we could do—a pile of damp leaves and twigs that it took us ages to light. The night is cold, and we're still wet, though the rain has stopped. Neither of us has spoken in an hour.

"I don't remember." All I know is, he was kissing me just before the missile hit. Something was flickering to life between us, but my father's atrocity has torn it all away.

Col's gaze is sharp in the firelight. Tears have left streaks in the smoke and ash on his face.

"You said, 'They'll pick me up at the ruins.' You had an escape plan worked out with your father."

I take a shuddering breath, then nod.

"And all this stuff." Col points at what's left of my escape kit—the firestarter, the plastic bags collecting rain from the dripping trees. "Do you always have a getaway bag ready?"

"When I'm a hostage? Yes."

His expression doesn't soften. Now that the shock has sunk in, he's had time to wonder how much I knew about my father's plans.

Something starts to crumble inside my chest.

Col is all I have left. If he stops trusting me, neither of us will survive.

"You got onto the roof so fast," he says. "Wide awake and ready to run. You knew the attack was coming, didn't you?"

There's no way through this but the truth.

"Aribella was right about my cyrano." I take it out of my pocket. The metal glows dully in the firelight. "It scans for hidden messages in Shreve's public feeds, encoded in the pixels. A warning came, telling me to run."

"Kill it," Col says.

I stare at the cyrano.

There's no city interface out here, and it's not like I need etiquette tips. But the device is my last link to Rafi. There's no other way for her to get a message to me. No more warnings. No more advice from my big sister.

But every second I hesitate costs me Col's trust.

I drop the cyrano in the fire.

For the first time in my life, Rafi and I are truly separated.

And yet, as the smell of burned circuitry rises up, relief floods through me. My father's voice is gone from my ear forever.

I've traded my sister for freedom.

Col still stares at me like an enemy. "So why didn't you warn us?"

"They only gave me two minutes' head start."

He shakes his head. "Two minutes? Why would they cut it so close?"

"Because . . ."

I wore the red jacket. A game between me and my sister, while my father was planning murder.

But it's too unbelievable, that I'm a spare daughter, nothing but a decoy. That having a crush on Col meant I could be thrown away.

As unbelievable as the fact that two hours ago Col was kissing me, and now he thinks I betrayed him.

Something turns hard in my throat.

"My father couldn't risk an earlier warning. If you caught me trying to run, you might guess what was coming."

Col looks down into the fire. "Or maybe you wanted everything to happen exactly as it did."

"What do you mean?"

"The whole time you were in my home, Rafia, you weren't your usual self. You were someone I could be friends with. You gained my trust. And once the attack was on its way, you got us both to safety just in time." Col looks around at the darkness.

"And now we're out here alone, a hundred klicks from my city's forces."

"Col, helping me escape was *your* idea! You showed me those bungee jackets on the roof!"

He leans back from the fire, his expression unchanged.

Logic doesn't matter. He doesn't trust me anymore.

"Your father," he says, then spits into the fire. "He wants to wrap this war up quickly, right? That's much easier if you bring me to him. A hostage, so the rest of my city surrenders. A puppet to put in charge of Victoria."

"Never." I reach out and take his hand. "I knew about the attack *two minutes* before you did. All my prep was just in case something went wrong. And I never thought he'd . . ."

Kill your mother. Your grandmother.

Destroy your home.

Set your city on fire.

Col pulls his hand away from me, and my heart tears a little.

There's only one way to convince him.

I point two fingers, and the pulse knife jumps up from beside me. It hovers in the air, trembling and eager, aimed at his face.

Ready to kill.

"Col. If I really wanted to take you to my father, do you think I'd have to *trick* you?"

He stares straight at the knife, like he doesn't care what happens next. Like he's daring me to turn him into mist.

But then he says, "Save the battery. I forgot the pulse charger."

I close my fist, and the knife drops back to the ground.

My nightshirt feels cold and damp. A few cactus spines are still caught in it—all that remains of House Palafox's gardens. That jungle full of life. Those butterflies.

We sit there in silence, until I gather the nerve to ask . . .

"Do we still have an alliance? Or do you think I killed your family?"

He's silent, thinking. The leaves are dripping. The wet wood in the fire hisses softly.

I can't just sit here, so I move toward him across the darkness. But I don't know how to do this—how to touch someone this way. I don't know anything.

When my trembling hand falls on his shoulder, he flinches. A sob racks his body.

"There must have been *something* I could've done to stop this. But I made it worse by trusting you."

"This isn't your fault, Col." My sister's mantra.

"I should have *forced* my mother to listen—"

"It's not her fault either. It's him. It's always him."

Col starts to shiver, and I pull him closer to the fire. My workout sweats have wicked away the rain, but his clothes are still wet.

I look up—no stars, no moon, no aircraft. Just the choking darkness of a city burned and thrown into the air.

Too much smoke for anyone to see our little fire. I grab the last handful of the kindling and throw it on the pile. It hisses like a wet, angry cat.

"They must think we're dead," Col says. "We should keep it that way."

I hold his gaze across the fire. It's a good idea, but there's one problem.

Rafi's still at home, safe and sound. Once my father is certain that I'm dead, he'll reveal her to the world—and Col will know I was always an impostor, sent to make his family drop their guard.

He'll know I've been lying to him all along.

But I can't tell him the truth about myself tonight. His world is already shaken enough.

"Good idea," I say.

"If he thinks I'm dead, your father won't look for me. We can move easier if we aren't being hunted."

"Move? Where are we headed, anyway? Is there someone who can protect you?"

"I don't want protection. I want revenge."

A surge of exhaustion rises in me. Col still hasn't learned that with my father, there is no winning.

"Listen, Col. Whatever military Victoria has left, it's not enough to beat him. You'll only get more of your people killed!"

"I know," he says.

"The other first families won't help either. They'll feel sorry for you, and they'll embargo Shreve for a while. Someone might give you asylum, as long as you keep your head down. But no city will risk all-out war with him!"

"Then I'll work with people who have no cities. Who've always hated him. And who already have their own army."

I shake my head. "Who the hell is that?"

Col leans back from the fire and gives me a cold smile.

"I'm going to join the rebels."

OVERKILL

The next morning, I'm watching Col sleep.

He's curled in on himself. The fire is spent and my clothes, my hands, and the inside of my head all smell like smoke. And yet the sky is blue, finally clear of smoke from the attack on Victoria.

It's weird, but even after everything that's happened, I'm still thinking about our kiss. It was my first real kiss. And that look in his eyes . . .

He'll never look at me that way again. Or trust me. Not once he finds out that I was at the center of my father's plans against his family.

Col doesn't even know my real name. And every time I think about telling him, I think of Sensei Noriko, which is enough to shut my mouth.

Still, we need to have this conversation soon, before the real Rafi shows up in the feeds.

"Let's kill a rabbit," Col says when he wakes up.

"Sounds good." Finding the rebels might take a while, and I'm starving.

We drink our rainwater, pack up our meager camp, and hike to the edge of the forest. We leave the hoverboard out in the sun, its solar panels unfolded.

Col leads me along the boundary between trees and prairie, his hunting bow in his hand. We keep to the forest shadows, peering out into the tall sunlit grass.

"There are two kinds of rabbits here," he says, somehow still a tour guide. "The ones with small ears are volcano rabbits. Not enough fat to be worth eating."

"*Volcano* rabbits? Really?"

Col shrugs. "Nature doesn't care what you call it. We're hunting the cottontails—the ones with big ears."

"Okay. But this is your show. My knife doesn't do rabbits."

"Too slow?"

I snort. "It can break the sound barrier. But it's overkill—unless you know how to cook rabbit mist."

He gives the knife a look. "What's that thing actually *for*?"

"For when people try to kill me. If I have to get out of a room, it cuts through a wall. If I need cover, it turns furniture into dust clouds."

"No wonder Jefa had it locked up." Col's eyes go from the knife to me. "How do you know so much about ancient weapons?"

There's no answer for that except the truth.

"I know about *all* weapons, Col. I've been learning how to kill since I was seven."

He looks at me. "Did you say *seven*?"

"Years old, yeah."

And I can tell from his eyes—the way he sees me just changed.

Col knew right away that I wasn't the temperamental socialite of Rafi's feeds. He liked me because I was someone unexpected, someone who'd tricked the whole world. But now he's seeing a deeper me—the trained killer—and I'm starting to scare him.

"After I join the rebels, where will you go?" he asks out of nowhere.

I stare at him. "What do you mean?"

"There's no way the rebels will trust you, Rafi. Because of who you are."

"Who *I* am? Your family has been at war with them for years!"

"They never tried to kill me."

I take a slow breath. Going to sleep last night, I kept thinking about that—Col wants to join the people who attacked my convoy only two weeks ago.

"Maybe they were waiting for the right time. Are you *sure* you want to join them, Col?"

He shrugs. "It won't be easy, getting them to trust me. But there must be Victorian forces out here, still loyal to my family, still ready to fight. The rebels and I can help each other."

Without Col, I have nowhere to go . . . except home.

"But we agreed to be allies," I say.

He turns away, embarrassed.

"That was back when I thought our parents were trying to set us up. This is deadly serious. The rebels will believe that I hate your father, Rafi, because of what he did to my family. But why would they trust *you*?"

"Because I'm . . ." Not Rafi. But my lips won't say the words.

I don't know what will happen when I unleash this secret. Do I really exist outside of this lie?

"Because you're a trained killer?" Col shakes his head. "That's just another reason not to let you get too close."

"But I'm not—" Even thinking the words makes me start to unravel. "I'm really—"

Col's hand goes up for silence. He's staring into the forest, and I can hear the faintest stirring of the leaves.

"Jaguar," he whispers.

I close my mouth, relieved. A wild predator seems safer than telling him the truth.

"The Rusties almost wiped out the big cats," he says softly. "But they're everywhere now."

"So it's okay to eat one?"

Col gives me a pained look. "Really?"

"What? We're starving!"

"People don't eat cats, Rafi. How do you not know that?"

I shrug. My father eats what he wants. Whether or not it's on the menu. Or the endangered list.

"We follow it," Col explains. "It's probably stalking something we *can* eat."

We push along the edge of the forest. Col moves in perfect silence, but I'm clumsy and loud. I've been trained to fight in ballrooms, tight corridors, and stairways, but not the wild.

Col comes to a halt, and the bow unfolds in his hand. Its nanotech polymers spread like wings; the string shivers taut. He stares out into the grassland, at something I can't see.

When I switch to heat vision, a white blob twitches out there against the sun-warmed rocks. The rabbit's ears stick up like antennae.

In the cooler forest to our right, the sinuous curve of the jaguar lurks on a branch. It's watching us, probably wondering if we're a threat.

How deadly are these big cats? I know in theory that the wild can kill you, but no animal is worse than an assassin with a barrage pistol.

Then I remember the snake, invisible and almost silent, and I shudder.

Beside me, Col notches an arrow. Then he stands there unmoving for endless seconds.

When he strikes, it's all one motion—drawing the bow, aiming, letting the arrow fly. It flits through the tall grass, and an instant later the cottontail explodes into motion, its hind legs scrabbling. But it's like a pinned insect, the fluttering taking it nowhere.

As Col runs forward, I turn to watch the jaguar, my knife ready. But it's already disappearing deeper into the trees, graceful and unhurried.

I switch off my heat vision and catch up with Col as he's breaking the rabbit's neck. He holds the limp body up by its ears, a look of satisfaction on his face.

"I don't have anything to skin this," he says. "Can that weapon cut like a regular knife?"

"It's not very sharp when it's turned off. But sure."

Col looks up into the sky. "Think we can risk a fire?"

I close my eyes and listen. Last night, we fell asleep to booms in the distance—explosions, gunfire, suborbitals entering the atmosphere. But today is silent, the Victorians either defeated or in hiding.

My father must think we're dead, or that I'm headed toward the ruins on foot, hoping to be rescued. He has no reason to look for me this far down the coast.

And my stomach is rumbling now.

"Might as well," I say. "Unless you want to eat it raw."

CONFESSION

"This is amazing, Col."

The rabbit really is good. It's harder to chew than vat-grown meat, but the flavor is more intense. Even the smell of it cooking was hungry-making, fire smoke and charred flesh.

I just wish we had some salt. And that I hadn't burned my tongue on the first bite.

"*La faim est la meilleure sauce,*" Col says.

More French, but it's an opportunity. Maybe if I tell the truth about myself slowly, it won't be so hard.

"I don't know what you just said, Col."

Halfway through a bite, he looks up at me. His fingers shine with grease, and there's blood on his shirt from skinning the rabbit.

"'Hunger is the best sauce'? You've never heard that before?"

"Not the proverb—I don't know French. I've been faking it."

He laughs. "Stop it, Rafi. I've watched your appearances in Montré. You're practically fluent."

"Not really," I say. "You see, studying French takes time away from learning to kill people."

Col chews thoughtfully. "I don't know why you're saying this, but I've seen you. No cyrano is that good. *Tu parle français.*"

Maybe this is a bad idea, revealing my lies to get him to trust me. But they're all I've got. My deceptions are only things that are really mine.

Just tell him.

Was that Rafi's voice inside me? Or my own?

And what if telling Col the truth dooms him, like it did Sensei Noriko?

Tell him everything.

"There are two of me," I whisper.

The world tips sideways, but somehow doesn't break apart.

Col just nods. "No kidding. There's you in the feeds, and the real you."

I swallow. "Right. But I mean literally."

He gives me a sympathetic look. "I think I know what you mean."

"I don't think you do, Col." Anger is building in me now. This is hard enough without him being a bubblehead. "There are *two* of me. I have a twin sister."

He still doesn't understand.

"She's real," I say. "A separate person."

Col looks away again, thoughtful. He tears a last piece of flesh from the rabbit's leg. Swallows it. Drops the bone into the fire.

Finally, he holds his hands out for calm. "Okay."

"That's it? 'Okay'?"

"I get it."

I stare at him. "Get *what?*"

"What it must be like, being you. Your mother dead before you were conceived. Tutors instead of school. A bubble of drones and bodyguards around you. And at the center of it all, a father like *him.*"

My anger sputters. I have no idea what Col's babbling about.

"And that's only the start," he continues. "My mother told me about the body scans, Rafi, what your trainers must have done to you. And being taught to use that *abomination.*"

He gestures at the pulse knife lying next to me.

I speak through clenched teeth. "What does that have to do with my sister?"

Col looks away, like he's embarrassed again.

"Growing up under threat, unable to walk around in your own city. That dust watching you. No privacy—but always alone. It must play tricks on your mind."

"Holy crap," I say. "You think Rafi's some kind of *delusion?*"

"Let me point out that *you* said that word, not . . ." He stares at me, frowning. "Wait. Her name's Rafi too?"

"*Yes.* I mean, no—mine *isn't!*"

I look up at the sky and let out a scream, which probably doesn't help my case. But there's no going back now.

"My name is Frey! We are two *different* people and thus have different names! She's the one you saw on the feeds. The one who speaks French and knows how to design dresses. The one who's smart and witty and knows which fork to use!"

I throw my rabbit leg into the fire, where it sputters hot grease.

"*I'm* the barbarian! The one who doesn't know anything except killing with ancient weapons. The one who's stupid enough to fall for a spoiled, smug bubblehead like *you*!"

My rant comes to a ragged halt. My throat hurts from yelling. And there's a shrieking in my head.

"Rafi," Col says softly. "It's okay."

"I'm not Rafi. And it's never okay."

He gently takes my hand, and the need to yell at him lifts a little.

But the shrieking is still there in my head.

Because it's not in my brain. It's out in the real world.

A shadow flickers over us, and at last I recognize the sound.

"Hovercar," I say. "Run for the trees."

FRIENDLY FIRE

I can't see the car overhead, just the smoke from our fire.

Carried by the wind from the coast, the telltale column stretches away to the west, a massive sign saying *Come get us*.

Hunger made me foolish.

I dash for the cover of the forest, calling the pulse knife to my hand.

Col's running back toward where we left the hoverboard to recharge. But its solar panels are open—it'll take him thirty seconds before he can make it flyable.

As I reach the trees, the hovercar roars into view. Its lifting fans churn leaves, dirt, and embers from our fire into a maelstrom. For a moment I can't see or breathe.

When the whirlwind passes, I look up. The hovercar is banking into a hard turn—it's spotted me. The camo skin is set to Shreve combat livery, gray and black.

A saucer-shaped scout craft, it's much smaller than the machines that brought me to Victoria. Only three crew, but armed with a pair of heavy kinetic guns. Its armor will stop my pulse knife cold.

One gun is training on me. The other turret swings along the forest, tracking Col.

I drop my pulse knife and raise my hands up high.

"Wait!" I scream into the roar of the lifting fans. "It's me!"

They can't open fire—Col and I are dressed in civilian clothes. My father's forces must still be searching for Rafi.

The barrel of the gun aligns with my eyes, until I'm staring into blackness. I know the stats—solid tungsten rounds, fifteen centimeters across, delivered at Mach 4.

The trees behind me will be sawdust. I'll be water vapor tinged with DNA.

The machine hovers a moment longer, dust wreathing around me, and my mind feels like it's a thousand klicks away. Like I'm looking down on a dream.

Then a voice crackles through loudspeakers.

"Miss Rafia. Please take cover."

They want me to get down so they can open fire on the forest. They think Col ran because he was keeping me prisoner.

"No!" I yell, moving sideways, putting myself in front of the gun tracking him. "Hold your fire!"

The machine wobbles a little, uncertain. The crew can't hear me in there, not over the engine roar.

A hatch irises open on the bottom, and two soldiers drop to the grass. They roll to absorb the shock of landing and come up with rifles leveled.

But not at me.

I get in the way again, try to yell over the roar of lifting fans. "Stop! He's a friend!"

One of them frowns at me, lowering her weapon, but the other's still sighting into the forest. His rifle's airscreen glimmers with a target.

I run straight into the whirlwind beneath the hovercar, and the man hesitates just long enough . . .

My fist catches his jaw. I yank the rifle from his hands, spinning around to jab its stock into the other soldier's face. She falls while he's still stumbling. I kick at his knee from the side, something snaps, and he goes down screaming.

I swing the rifle again, connecting solidly with his head. A few seconds later, neither of them are moving.

The hovercar is right over us. The big guns are still pointed into the trees.

At my gesture, the pulse knife rises up from the ground. It zooms past me into the hatch, set to a corkscrew pattern. Maybe it won't hit the pilot at full pulse.

The craft starts to shudder, wobbling above me like a top at the end of its spin. About to fall on me.

This was not my best plan.

I drop flat between the fallen soldiers, hands over my head, eyes shut. The tempest stages around me, then reels away—I look up.

The hovercar is slewing off into the trees. Whole branches disappear into the lifting fans, spewing out as wood chips and shredded leaves. The car cracks into a thick, old trunk. One fan comes down on a young tree, and its engine jams with a metal squeal.

The other three fans keep spinning, flipping the craft over and driving it top-first into the ground. Leaves and dust geyser up from the forest.

With a final grinding rattle, the machine goes silent.

I stand up, blinking, my ears ringing with the silence.

The soldier lying beside me groans. I pull the zip ties off her belt and bind their wrists, steal their medpacks, then shoulder one of the rifles.

I'm headed for the downed hovercar when a call comes from the air.

"Rafi!"

I turn to face Col, gliding up on the hoverboard. His eyes are wide at the destruction all around me.

"You couldn't just *run*?" he asks.

"Had to stop them from shooting you. You're welcome." I glance back at the bound soldiers and drop my voice. "And it's Frey."

"Okay, sure," he says, in his new Rafi-has-delusions voice. "But we should get out of here."

I point at the downed hovercar. "We should check on the pilot first."

Also, my pulse knife is in there somewhere.

TRANSMISSION

The hovercar sits among the trees, upside down and slantwise against an uprooted trunk. The lifting fans are motionless, ticking as they cool.

The hatch is on top of the machine now. I climb onto Col's hoverboard so he can fly me up. Leaves are still fluttering to the ground around us. At least a dozen trees are damaged.

So is the hovercar's camo skin. It keeps changing patterns randomly, from dappled forest to sky blue to parade colors.

I jump down onto the slanted armored hull, crawl to the hatch, and stick my head in.

"Hello?"

No answer.

"It's me, First Daughter Rafia. Don't shoot!"

"So that *is* your name," Col says.

"I'll explain later." I hand him the rifle and crawl inside.

The cabin lights are off, and all I can see is a jumble of wires, equipment, and fire-suppression foam. In a few spots, the pulse knife has stripped away everything down to the armored hull.

Most of the cabin is in darkness. My eyes adjust slowly.

"Anyone in here?"

Still nothing. But I hear a *drip, drip, drip.*

I've never been inside this tiny a scout car. It's about half the size of one of Rafi's closets. As I crawl, something jabs my knee—a sharp little rectangle of plastic.

A handscreen. Ruggedized for military use, with a satellite antenna to get signal out here in the wild.

I switch it on—a newsfeed from home. War footage that I don't want to see, but the screen's glow illuminates the tiny cabin.

The pilot's in front, still strapped into his seat. He's hanging upside down, unconscious.

Then I realize what the dripping sound is—blood trickling from his forehead. It could be a minor cut . . . or a concussion, his brain swelling in his skull. The iron smell fills my head.

I reach up to the control panel and switch on the cabin lights. He doesn't wake up.

If I unstrap him, he'll fall and crack his head against the hull armor. But I can't just leave him hanging here.

First things first. My pulse knife is somewhere in this wreckage. I splay my fingers, hoping it can see me in the glow of the handscreen.

There's a scrabbling sound, like a rat in the wires, and hot metal jumps into my hand.

The knife's blade is scored from bouncing around the inside of the hull, but it can still fly. I'm more worried about its battery light blinking yellow.

I crawl back out of the hatch, give the handscreen to Col.

"The pilot's hurt, maybe bad. How much juice does that hoverboard have?"

"Not a lot. About a hundred klicks before we have to recharge."

"That's far enough. I'm going to turn on the ship's distress beacon. Be ready to *move*."

"Why?" Col asks.

"Because once the beacon goes off, their backup will be on its way!"

He takes a slow breath. "I meant, why call for help? That pilot is part of an army that just murdered my family."

I stare back at Col, and for a moment I understand what he sees when he looks at me, trained to kill since the age of seven. That darkness in his eyes must also be in mine.

But soldiers wearing the uniform of Shreve have protected me and my sister our whole lives.

"Col. Have you ever heard of *just following orders*?"

"Yes. It's an old Rusty phrase, meaning *a crappy excuse for war crimes*."

"So we just leave him here to die?" I gesture at the other two. "You want to shoot them too? They recognized me. That messes up your plan to stay hidden, doesn't it?"

"Good point." Col looks down at the rifle in his hands. It's still in fire mode, the airscreen glowing.

He raises it, aiming straight at the bound soldiers sixty meters away.

"Col," I say.

Maybe I could stop him. But my reflexes won't engage. All that exquisite battle calculus in my head refuses to add up.

Col is a problem I can't solve with my fists.

So I say, "That's exactly what my father would do."

He hesitates, then swears under his breath, lowers the rifle. "Hit the switch. I'll be ready."

"You'll thank me." I can still see the assassin some nights. Those legs just standing there after my knife burned away the rest of him.

I climb back down into the hovercar, trying not to smell the pilot's blood.

Now that the cabin lights are on, I see a medpack stuck to the bottom of his seat. A quick spurt of medspray to his forehead makes me feel better.

The emergency beacon is a rocker switch on the control panel. It starts blinking red when I give it a flick.

Scrambling back out of the hatch, I yell, "Let's move!"

"Wait." Col is staring at something in his hands.

The screen. The tinny sounds of newsfeed. Triumphant music, an exuberant announcer.

"What the hell, Col?" I jump up onto the hoverboard behind him. "We have to *go!*"

"But they just said . . ." He looks up, stares, like he doesn't recognize me.

Then his eyes drop back to the screen.

"Holy crap," he says. "There's two of you."

REVEALED

There's no time to talk, not with the rescue beacon blaring.

We ride hard and fast, keeping beneath the treetops, weaving through trunks and branches. Heading inland toward the mountains and the rebels.

I wonder what happens when we reach them. Col was right before—the rebels wouldn't let First Daughter Rafia join up, not in a hundred years.

But Frey? Maybe she has something to offer.

I don't know anymore.

Col is just as confused as me. When we stop to rest, he doesn't say much, or meet my eye. And I remember what Rafi always told me growing up . . . *This isn't normal.*

She meant that my father was wrong to hide me. That I didn't deserve to have my existence erased. But my sister's words also taught me what a freak I was.

That must be how Col sees me now—as some kind of aberration. Like a littlie lost in the forest and raised by wolves. Weird and tragic. Probably dangerous.

Of course, the whole world is dangerous now.

When hovercars glimmer in the distance, forcing us to hide, they're always in Shreve colors, not Victorian. My father has won. The only signs of resistance are wisps of smoke on the horizon.

It doesn't help that all the food in my escape kit is gone. Rabbits dot the forest floor, but we can't risk another fire. So we're hungry, exhausted, and Col keeps backtracking. He's looking for something, but he won't say what.

He doesn't trust me anymore.

I thought when he learned my secret, he would understand the ally I could be. But instead, he doesn't even know who I am.

The hoverboard is almost out of charge when he finally finds the perfect spot to land in, a long stretch of clearing with plenty of sun.

We unfold the solar panels and sit under a tree. We'll be stuck here for a while. Nothing to do but talk about what comes next.

But instead Col picks up the handscreen.

"Don't bother checking," I say. "What you saw was real. There's another version of me back in Shreve. The genuine Rafi."

He turns the screen on anyway, stares at it for a moment.

"Here's what I don't get," he says. "Why isn't the whole Shreve army out here looking for us? The soldiers back there saw your face."

I shrug. "Maybe nobody believed them? The army doesn't know there's two of me."

"Two of you," Col mutters at the screen, then looks up. "How did they hide you all this time?"

It takes a moment to answer. Telling these secrets feels like pulling my own teeth. But I need Col to understand the truth of me.

"There are special hallways in my father's house, just for me. Limos with hidden sections, private suites in all the clubs and hotels. Only about a dozen people ever saw me and Rafi together."

"But *why*?"

"To keep her safe. She only appears in places where we trust everyone. Anytime she had to go out into a crowd of randoms—public speeches, ceremonies, dancing at nightclubs—it was always me instead."

"All that trouble . . ." Col looks down at the screen again. "So he really does love her, doesn't he?"

"It's more than that. He lost our brother to kidnappers, and he hates to lose."

For a moment, Col looks ill. "And we thought we were safe with you under our roof."

"You weren't."

Col doesn't answer.

"You can blame me for all of it." I need to say this out loud, so it doesn't keep echoing in my head. "Losing your home. Your family. It happened because of *me*."

Maybe I'm expecting Col to argue. But he doesn't say a word.

So I keep talking into the silence.

"I didn't know how to warn you. I've never had to tell anyone about this before. Back home, there was never anyone I *could* tell, without them . . ." My voice falters. This isn't the right time to explain about Sensei Noriko, how knowing my secret can kill someone. "I really didn't think he'd sacrifice me."

"Your sister looks so happy." His eyes are glued to the screen.

My stomach clenches. "Rafi plays her role well. Always."

"But she must think you're dead. And she's *smiling*."

He holds up the screen for me to see.

I turn away. I don't want to see Rafi act the part of the triumphant, resourceful daughter. Or think about what she's feeling now.

I'd rather imagine her tantrum when my father told her I was dead. I hope she hit him, even if she can't throw a punch to save her life.

Col turns on the volume, and the tinny sound of crowds and martial music fills the air. His eyes narrow, and he glances from me to the screen, like he's comparing our faces.

I get up and walk away.

The world is spinning under me. I've escaped my father but lost everything else—my home, my sister, my city. My only ally doesn't know what to think of me.

What am I supposed to do now? Start my own army?

It was much easier being a secret. I only had to worry about half a life.

A rush of sound fills the air, and I almost dive for cover. But it's just wind in the leaves.

Col chose this forest clearing well. It lets sunlight down for the board's panels, but any aircraft would have to pass straight overhead to spot us.

But it's odd how long and narrow the clearing is. Too straight to be natural.

I kneel to take a closer look, and find an ancient layer of perma-crete below the shallow topsoil. So that's why trees don't grow here. This was some kind of Rusty construction.

I remember my warfare tutor explaining that most ancient aircraft couldn't hover—they needed "runways" to take off and land. The clearing is at least a kilometer long, a typical Rusty waste of space.

But if aircraft landed here, some kind of ruin must be close.

I walk back to Col.

"Do you know about any—"

"I need to ping my brother." He holds up the handscreen. "To tell him I'm alive. Can I use this?"

I take a slow breath, reminded that Col has bigger things to worry about than me. I'd love to let my own sister know I'm okay.

"Sorry, Col. But that's Shreve military issue. If you send a message with it, they'll find us."

He swears, his grip tightening on the screen. "It's locked on your city's propaganda feeds. Which are brain-missing! They're saying my mother threatened to hurt you. Like destroying my home was some kind of *rescue mission*."

"It's not about logic, Col. It's just how things work there."

He sighs. "I know. We spent months studying your city. The newsfeeds do whatever they're told."

"It's more than that. People in Shreve fear my father, but they *love* Rafi. For a whole night, everyone thought she was dead—that they were left with just *him*. They're so happy she's alive, they'll believe anything."

"That's what our psych team said." Col looks up from the screen. "Everyone in Shreve knows he's a murderer. But when

Rafi stands next to him, he's also a *father*. She's what makes him human."

I have to turn away. The truth of that lives in my bones, but I've never heard anyone say it out loud before.

"So what if everyone finds out there's *another* Rafi?" Col goes on. "A daughter he threw away? With a dozen glued-together bones from training to be killer?"

I remember the pity on Aribella's face when she told me about the body scans.

Not normal.

But Col's face is lighting up.

"Then he's not a father anymore. We could hurt him. Show everyone that he's . . ." He pauses. "Are you okay?"

I shake my head. It's hard to breathe.

When Rafi goes to a party, thousands of people watch and comment on what she wears, who she talks to. How many eyes would land on me if I told the freakish truth about us?

Millions.

I'd melt away. Erased at last.

"It's just I've never told anyone this secret before, Col. And you're talking about telling the whole world."

"Oh. I didn't think . . ." His voice fades. He stands up, takes my shoulders.

The world steadies a little.

"It's your secret to tell," he says. "Not mine."

The words replay in my head—once, twice—until I understand them.

It's a promise not to throw me away.

I take a slow breath. "Why would you care, Col? After all my lies? After what my father did to you?"

"That's complicated," he says.

I look up at him. Does he mean there's still something between us? Even after everything?

"If you go public with the truth, it will hurt your father."

"I *want* to hurt him."

As I say the words, the old, familiar ecstasy twinges in me—the thrill of combat coming on. A trickle of hum in my veins, but this isn't about fighting.

For the first time in my life, I have something to wield beyond my fists.

The truth of me has power.

"When you're ready, I'll help you tell everyone," Col says. "I couldn't be sure about Rafi. But you and I still have an alliance, Frey."

I meet his eyes. This is the first time he's used my real name. The first time *anyone* has who I've given it to myself.

Which makes me ask—

"An alliance? Is that all this is?"

He looks away. "That's also complicated."

A sudden anger rushes through me.

"Of *course*, it's complicated, Col! You're the son of a cultured first family, and I'm a freak who's been hidden in secret passages her whole life. A killing machine! The daughter of—"

"It's not that, Frey. There's something I have to tell you, about that kiss."

I take a step back. "What do you mean?"

He hesitates a moment, shakes his head.

"First, let me show you why we're here."

BUNKER

He leads me toward the near end of the clearing.

"This used to be a Rusty airport," he says.

I remember his long, winding search for the perfect spot to recharge. "So you were looking for this place?"

Col nods, gestures down the runway. "We chose it because you don't need navigation equipment to find it. The missing strip of forest is obvious from the air."

"Chose it for what?" I ask.

Col doesn't answer, just leads me under the canopy of trees at the end of the clearing.

It's cool in here, despite the noon sun. When I flick on my heat vision for a moment, scurrying animals appear around us. Nothing big enough to be dangerous, but when I switch back to normal vision, my hand stays on the knife.

"Watch your step," he says. A steep decline has opened up before us.

We descend into what looks like a crater. Except the four sides are oddly straight, and craters aren't square.

"More ruins?"

"The foundation of a tower, part of the airport." Col wobbles on a loose piece of stone, steadies himself. "All the metal was stripped a century ago."

"But there's still something valuable down here?"

He looks back to give me another smile, then keeps going.

The walls of the crater are old and crumbling—not the safest climb. But it gives me time to think.

What does all this have to do with our kiss?

What did he mean, *That's complicated*?

At the bottom of the crater is a rectangular stretch of level ground, about the size of the Palafoxes' ballroom. The trees down in this darkness are spindly, as if trying to reach up for sunlight.

Col is looking for something.

"They only brought me here once, two years ago. So this might take a—"

He halts, stomps on the ground.

A hollow sound echoes.

It takes us five minutes to clear the door of fallen branches and leaves. It's made of some kind of camo-plastic.

"No metal at all." Col spreads his right hand on the lock. The plastic comes alive, lighting up. "We made sure this place was worthless to salvagers."

The door sighs open, revealing an empty square of blackness. A stale smell rises up, desiccant and anti-mold nanos.

"Lights," Col calls down.

He smiles again as they flicker on.

"Watch out," he says. "The ladder can be wobbly."

The bunker, as Col calls it, is about as big as my father's private swimming pool.

It has a low ceiling, made of the same plastic as the door. A dozen columns bear the weight of the forest overhead. They're made of real wood, still no metal.

This place is hidden well.

Shelves line the walls, stacked with plastic cases. Each one has a palm-print lock like the outer door.

"Let me guess—only Palafoxes can open these."

"And a few people we trust," Col says. He's scanning the labels on the cases, which are in some kind of code.

"So this is what your mother meant?" I ask. "When she said you had some surprises for my father."

"Part of it, yes."

I frown. "But you heard that from Yandre, who overheard your mom at the party. And you knew about this place two years ago."

Col shrugs. "Yes, *Frey*. I may have lied to you a few times."

I raise my hands in surrender. "Fair enough."

He pulls one of the cases from a shelf. It reads his palm and opens, revealing a disassembled weapon in packing foam.

"Tell me about this," he says.

I kneel beside the case, lift up the barrel. It's made of spacecraft ceramics. Light as cardboard, strong as hull armor.

"It's a spheromak plasma gun. Twenty megabars, one-shot hydrogen battery. Organic manganese magnets, so it won't show up on a metal detector."

"It says all that on the case, Frey. But what does it *mean*?"

"It spits out plasma rings. Knocks down hovercars." I look around the room—all those shelves. "Or buildings, if you had enough of them."

"Trust me, we do." Col looks up. "You think the rebels would be interested?"

"They'd be thrilled. Their problem's always been no hovercars, no heavy weapons." I shrug. "That's what you get for living in the wild."

Col leans back with a smile of satisfaction.

"You had all this stuff," I say. "So why didn't you fight the rebels on your own? Why bring my father into it?"

"Because when you hit the rebels, they just fade back into the wild." Col takes the barrel of the plasma gun from my hand. "Knocking them out for good means doing things that we didn't want to do. Like using these on human beings."

"Which my father was happy to do."

Col nods. "My family worries a lot about appearances. But the dirty work still gets done."

He's not showing me all this just to prove that the rebels will welcome him. This room has something to do with the two of us.

I sit cross-legged beside him on the cool cement floor.

"Why are we here, Col?"

"I want you to understand my family." He gestures at the row of cases. "*This* is who we are."

Each of these guns could take out one hoverstrut, a dozen of them sending a skyscraper crashing to the ground. Col might be disgusted by my pulse knife, but his family is hoarding enough firepower to wreck a city.

"You Palafoxes," I say. "You're like Rafi on the outside. But on the inside you're . . . *me*."

Col speaks softly, clearly. "You have to understand, Frey. Victoria's a small city. To protect ourselves, we do things we don't want to do. I never wanted to deceive you."

I stare at him. "When, exactly?"

"Every second since you met me, Frey." He takes a slow

breath. "I always knew you were a hostage in my home. My mother and I had a plan for you, and pretending I was innocent was part of it."

"What?" My hands are shaking.

"Our kiss was part of it too."

COUNTERPUNCH

I can hear the words that Col just said. There's a recording of them playing over and over in my brain.

But they don't make sense.

He's staring at me, waiting for a response.

"You *knew* I was a hostage?"

He nods. "It was my idea."

My gaze drifts past him. The rows of weapons stretch into infinity.

I can't breathe.

"Your father's a monster," Col says. "He would always be a danger to our city. But we wondered if you, his heir, might be different."

"I'm not the heir," I manage. "She is."

"Of course. But we thought we were getting the real Rafi. So we decided to learn all about her." He leans back as he continues, and I realize something awful—he's using his tour guide voice. "When we started negotiations with your father, we sent newsfeed cams to cover your city. But they were really remote polygraphs, there to spy on Rafia. Whenever either of you appeared in public, they measured your pulse, blood pressure, galvanic response."

I stare at him, feeling like my skin is being stripped away.

"At the same time," he says, "we did a psych analysis of every recording we could find—back to when you were a littlie. Studied your eye movements, micro-gestures, vocal intonations."

I shake my head. "What did all that tell you?"

"That you started to break when you were seven."

"Seven?" My voice fades. "When I started training?"

"Exactly."

"What do you mean by *break*?"

"Sometimes you were confident, certain of yourself. Other times, you acted like someone overwhelmed by ongoing trauma. Our psych team assumed a split was forming in your personality. It never occurred to them that you were actually *two people*."

"A sane one and a crazy one." I close my fists to keep my hands from shaking.

"That's not a useful way to talk, Frey."

"Really?" I can't look at him. "What would *you* call it?"

"What they did to you was brutal. The broken bones. Having to hide all those years. Having no friends, and *him* as a father."

"So it's not just the bones—*I'm* broken too."

Col takes my hand, soothes it open.

"Frey. You're the healthy one."

I stare at him. "What?"

"When our team explained the psychic break, they focused on something called foreign language anxiety. People who speak a second tongue, even fluently, have hitches in their grammar when they're anxious—or when they're falling apart inside. When Rafia speaks French, she gives herself away."

I start to say that it's impossible. Rafi's the confident one. Brash and imperious. But then I hear her voice in my head.

This isn't normal.

What if she didn't mean me?

"This is what I think," Col says. "She had to watch it all happen—you being brutalized, hidden away. She couldn't protect you, her own sister."

"No. It's my job to protect *her*."

"Exactly. *You* had a purpose, Frey. When the assassin tried to kill Rafia, you could save her." He looks away. "But she could never save you."

My mind rushes back to that day. What Rafi said to me later . . .

I just sat there screaming.

The whole time. Just not out loud.

I turn to Col, a rush of anger coming over me.

"So you knew Rafi was sick? And you thought it was okay to *keep her as a hostage?*"

"To get her away from him! To show her what it's like to live with a real family, in a normal city!" Col spreads his hands. "Your father can't live forever, and she's his heir. We thought if I could make an alliance with Rafia, we could change Shreve someday, without a war."

An alliance. My heart beats sideways once.

"Your grandmother," I say. "That first day, when she told you to give me a tour . . ."

He looks down at the ground. "Abuela was never particularly subtle."

"And the story about your hunting bow?"

"A way to get you down to the monastery, where you'd feel safe talking to me. Where I could make friends with you."

Something hard is pulsing in my throat. I can't breathe.

He's the first person I've ever kissed.

And he was faking it.

Col takes both my hands now. "But you really were different from what I expected, Frey. I just didn't know *why.*"

I pull away and stand up too fast. My head spins, and I reach out to steady myself—my hand brushes one of the plastic cases full of death.

He's still talking. "When I kissed you, it was real."

It doesn't matter what he says now.

His mother, his grandmother—they were conspiring with Col the whole time. Laughing behind my back when I thought he was really my friend.

I'm a freak, from a family of freaks. I have only one purpose in this world.

"I have to go home. My sister is hurting, and I need to save her."

My head is still spinning as I weave down the aisle, shelves full of weaponry on either side. Col's calling after me, but I don't care and I can't trust him.

My feet hit the ladder. It wobbles under my weight as I haul myself up toward the smells of forest and life.

I have to get back to Shreve—now. My sister has no one but me and she thinks I'm dead.

"Frey!" Col calls from below.

Telling him my name was a mistake. Giving up my sister, my home, for him was madness.

I pull myself up and out through the door, sucking in fresh air. Dark branches crisscross the sky.

"Don't move!" comes a voice from the trees. "We don't want to hurt you, but we will if we have to."

CAPTURE

There are four of them.

Kneeling at the edges of the crater, rifles raised, they have me surrounded. Their sneak suits are invisible against the forest, but shimmers of body heat escape.

All I can see is anger and betrayal. I hurl my knife, sending it in a sweeping arc that will burn them to the ground. It roars to full pulse for a millisecond—

Then sputters and falls into the leaves, lifeless.

The battery is dead.

So am I.

But the soldiers don't open fire. They must think I was throwing the knife away in surrender.

"Hands in the air," one of them calls down.

I obey, looking for some kind of weapon on the forest floor.

There are only branches, leaves, rocks. Nothing to equal four rifles aimed at me from above.

"We know you have Col Palafox," the leader shouts. "Surrender him to us—*now*."

I look up at her. How do they know Col is here?

Then I hear a clambering on the ladder behind me.

"Stay down!" I hiss.

"Zura?" he calls up.

"Col!" she cries. *"¡Estás vivo!"*

She comes racing down the crater wall. When her suit flickers from forest camo to combat livery, I realize two things.

One: She's a Special, surgically modified beyond any normal soldier. No other kind of human could make that descent look so effortless. Specials were the lethal endpoint of pretty-regime surgery. Their muscles enhanced, their reflexes speeded up, their bones reinforced with duralloy. Their minds were made cold and hard, and their faces fashioned with a fearsome angelic beauty.

At the start of the mind-rain, Special surgery was illegal. But it seems everything is permitted now.

Two: She's not wearing Shreve colors, but the light blue of the Victorian army.

Behind me, Col hauls himself up the ladder.

As the Special runs across the broken ground, she pulls down her sneak suit hood. She has dark hair and surgery that makes her almost frighteningly beautiful. Col runs to meet her and they embrace, smiling and laughing. Spanish spills from their lips, too fast for me to grasp any meaning.

I look up at the other three soldiers. They're making their graceful way down, all of them with the uncanny, inhuman grace of Specials. Only one keeps his rifle pointed at me. They look a little tired, like they've been on the run since the attack began.

I figure they won't shoot me if I lower my hands.

Part of me doesn't care. Too much is tangled in my head—my sister's illness, Col knowing I was a hostage, his false kiss.

Suddenly every old break in my bones burns, as if all my damage is on fire. I can feel the scar over my eye and the dirt on my face. Nothing seems solid or real, not even the forest floor beneath me.

I want my knife, but it's fallen somewhere in the leaves.

My feet shuffle toward it, and I drop to my knees, sweeping the undergrowth with my hands. Searching for the only thing I still trust.

There it is, hard metal in my hand.

When I raise it up into the air, one of the soldiers is standing there, ready to shoot.

"*No!*" comes Col's shout through the spindly trees.

The man hesitates, and seconds later Col is there, putting himself between me and the leveled rifle.

"*¡Esta es mi amiga!*"

My brain churns through the half-understood words.

My friend.

More Spanish flows around me, explanations and confusions.

I sit there, staring at my knife. What would the soldiers do if I just walked away? I could take Col's hoverboard and fly home to save my sister.

Or would he let them shoot me?

"Frey." Col kneels before me. "It's okay. They're Victorian."

"I can see that."

He's beaming. "But they're getting orders from the codebook!"

I shake my head. He might as well be speaking French.

Col gathers himself, grasps my shoulders. He leans close, his words slow and careful.

"They think my mother is still alive."

Zura, it turns out, is the woman who taught Col how to shoot a bow and arrow.

She and the others are Victorian House Guard, elite commandos who were on patrol with my father's forces when his treachery began.

"One minute, we're hunting rebels together," Zura explains in accented English. "The next, they start shooting at us. We got away, but we couldn't find any other friendly units. And then . . ."

She pauses to give me a wary look. I may be dirty and disheveled, but I'm still wearing my sister's face.

Col has ordered them not to ask why I look so much like *la princesa Rafia*. They must think I'm a commando surged for some undercover mission.

"You can talk in front of Frey," he says. "I trust her."

"Frey," Zura repeats carefully. "Yes, sir. A few hours ago, we got a message from the book."

Col turns to me. "The codebook is the keys to the Victorian army. It drops hidden messages in the global feeds, which only our forces can read. There's only one book, and my mother keeps it with her—*always*. She must have gotten out that night!"

"Col," I say softly. "That's wonderful."

The anger in my veins has sputtered out, but nothing has replaced it. Like there's a battery in my heart, and it's spent from all this fear and fury and betrayal. I don't feel anything.

I just want to go home and save my sister.

"The orders gave us a code to transmit," Zura continues. "It turned on the tracker on your hoverboard. We couldn't believe it when we got a signal!"

"Jefa put a tracker on my board?" Col shakes his head, laughing. "She always said she'd never do that."

"Thank the saints she did," Zura says. "And she must've

been the only one who knew about it. Which means she *has* to be alive."

Col takes a slow breath. For a moment he looks almost anguished, as if this new hope is too much to bear.

I reach for his hand. "Never underestimate your mother, Col. You can take that from me."

There's bitterness in my voice, but a weight is starting to lift. Maybe a loss I've been blaming myself for never really happened.

"Do you know where the book is?" Col asks Zura.

She shakes her head. "All we have is a location, deep in the mountains, to take you to. Your mother must be there."

Col turns to me, his eyes alight.

"Frey, she's alive."

He's waiting for me to be happy, to see that our alliance is back on track. As if he hadn't just told me that he played with my emotions from the moment I set foot in his home.

I was deceiving them too. But I never lied to Col about how I felt.

Then something hitches in my brain, and I turn to Zura. "How much of the Victorian army is left?"

"You'd need the codebook to know that. But we've been prepared for a guerrilla war, in case Shreve got the jump on us. There must be dozens of units still out there."

"Then why isn't someone here already?" I ask.

The two of them stare at me.

I gesture at the hidden doorway. "There's enough firepower in that bunker to level a city. Why hasn't Aribella sent someone to collect those guns?"

Col looks stricken for a moment. As if I've told him his mother is dead again.

"My guess is," Zura says, "they simply aren't here yet. It's only been hours since we got our orders. But Frey's right—we should take what we can carry."

"Of course." Col stands, brushing aside my doubts. "We're wasting daylight. Let's load the car and go."

The Specials spring into motion, two of them heading down into the bunker. Zura turns back toward their hovercar, which is waiting up in the clearing.

When I don't follow, Col hesitates. "Frey, are you coming?"

I take a breath.

Ten minutes ago I wanted to fly back home and save my sister. To leave the Palafoxes and their sophistication, their hypocrisy, behind forever.

But I have no plan, no food or water, no chance of winning against the whole Shreve army.

And here I have allies. I have Col.

Or at least I thought I did.

"You can't lie to me anymore," I say. "You can't use psych profiles, or polygraphs, or scans. Don't treat me like someone you're trying to trick, or fix, or control. Okay?"

"I promise. And let me ask you something too." He takes a moment to choose his words. "From now on, Frey, show me who you really are."

"Of course," I say.

But an impostor is exactly what I am.

NEWSFEED

The commandos' car is a light attack craft, its skin set to jungle camo. It's swift and loaded with firepower, but the hull is pitted and scarred. I'm not sure how long it can keep flying without repairs and a battery charge.

The Palafoxes better have a hidden factory somewhere, with solar panels the size of soccer fields.

It's cramped here inside the car. Six people in a machine designed for four, along with a hoverboard and eight plasma guns—as many as we could fit. Two of the Specials squat in the back, giving up their seats for me and Col.

The pair of us are eating spagbol, self-heating survival food that my father wouldn't allow anywhere near his hunting lodge. But hunger really is the best sauce, and it's delicious. Even better is the clean water from the hovercar's taps.

The mountains are an hour's flying time away, but it's taking forever. Every few minutes we dip down into the trees, cowering whenever the radar shows a blip.

Creeping along like this was tedious on Col's hoverboard. Squished inside this tiny, damaged car, it's downright sickmaking. One of the lifting fans is damaged, so the car rides at an odd, wobbly angle.

But Col looks more hopeful than he has since we watched his home turn into a column of smoke.

His mother might be alive. He has a bunker full of weapons, an army prepared for a guerrilla war. Maybe the Palafoxes still have a chance in this fight.

Maybe they can still hurt my father. Maybe together we can save Rafi.

I wonder what she's doing now. Is she on some balcony, smiling and waving at the crowds? Screaming at my father? Crying in our room, thinking I'm dead?

Is she really falling apart?

It seems like nonsense, diagnosing someone from readouts captured by hovercams. Psychological warfare teams aren't doctors, after all. Rafi sounded so happy when she called and told me how to make my dress. Like she was smiling the whole time.

Of course, she was also smiling on that balcony half an hour ago, thinking I was dead.

Maybe I'm not the only impostor in the family.

We're heading west, and the hot sun fills the hovercar as the afternoon drags on.

The Specials have given Col a set of Victorian battle fatigues. The forest camo makes him look older, harder. I'm still in my sweats and bloody nightshirt.

He's staring at an airscreen in front of him, drinking in every word about the war.

"Looks like a soft takeover so far," he says to me. "No troops in Victoria. But the feeds and city interface are under Shreve's control."

"They'll spread spy dust soon," I say. "Then they won't need soldiers."

"The other cities have cut off trade, at least," Col says. "They've promised never to buy the metal from your father's stolen ruins."

"Doesn't matter," I say. "He can always use it himself. He wants Shreve to be the biggest city in the world."

Col lets out a curse in Spanish, and the soldiers all glance at him, then at me. They've all had old-style Special surgery—a cold beauty that makes me shudder.

They still don't trust me. Of course, I look exactly like their enemy's daughter. It wasn't until Col let out a burst of angry Spanish that they let me charge my pulse knife.

"No one's talking about a war to free us," Col says. "All those treaties . . ."

His voice breaks off. The soldiers all sit up straighter.

On the airscreen is a row of three young faces. The hovering text gives their names.

In the middle is Teo Palafox.

He looks like his older brother, but with darker skin and pale gray eyes. He wears a bored look, like a littlie forced to sit for a school picture.

Col waves a hand, and the volume comes up.

—sometime last night. The School of Genève is conducting an investigation, in cooperation with the Warden Consortium. Authorities are concerned that the unexplained disappearances are related to the attack on the city of—

Col waves away the sound, and his head falls back into the crash cushions of his seat. No one says anything. The soldiers are motionless except for Zura's hand on the flight stick.

"They took him," Col murmurs. "And two of his friends. I *know* those kids."

I reach out from the backseat, wanting to put a hand on his shoulder. But I don't know who I am right now.

His fellow warrior? The girl he kissed?

Or am I the impostor again, my father's agent in his house?

I wait until Teo's face is gone from the screen, then gently take Col's arm.

"I'm sorry."

"You said he was *safe*." His voice breaks. "That the other cities wouldn't let this happen, not at a school."

I want to argue that it doesn't make sense. That no fourteen-year-old boy is such a threat to my father that he'd risk allying the whole world against him.

But Teo Palafox is missing.

"I was wrong," I say.

My father makes his own reality. Sometimes with nightmares.

APPROACH

"Almost at the rendezvous point."

Zura's voice startles me awake, and it takes a moment to remember where I am.

Late-afternoon sunlight slants into the cramped hovercar. The air is scented with spagbol and self-brewing coffee. My shoulder aches where I've leaned against the straps of my seat.

Col looks unslept, exhausted. "Put us down ten klicks away. I want to approach on foot."

Zura frowns but doesn't question the order.

"You think this is a trap?" I ask.

"Your father's been a step ahead of us since the beginning," Col says. "Until we know who's got the codebook, I'm not trusting anything I can't see with my own eyes."

"Fair enough."

He turns away from me, his expression hard.

Col wept when he thought that Aribella was dead. But he hasn't shed a single tear about his missing brother. Maybe he can't cry in front of his soldiers.

Zura brings the hovercar down in a narrow gorge, where a stream has nurtured a clump of trees. For long seconds, we slew back and forth, hacking away the branches with our lifting fans.

I'm already motion-sick, and we don't need the room to land. This last bit of rocking makes me want to either throw up or punch someone.

After another sick-making minute, we're on the ground at last. When my hatch pops open, I jump down gratefully onto the hard earth.

Rocks scrabble under my feet. Scrubby grass climbs the walls of the gorge, and the sunset turns the distant mountains pink and orange.

I suck in gulps of fresh air.

While Col and Zura confer, the commandos hide the car under the broken branches—hence our slashing descent. I join in the work, happy for anything that stretches my cramped muscles.

It's hard not to stare at the commandos, they move with such uncanny grace and speed.

After a long day's training, I used to ache for surgery to make me faster, stronger. But I can see why my father never let me have it. These commandos look almost inhuman, as swift and twitchy as insects.

"So down this gorge, then north?" Col is saying. An airscreen map hovers between him and Zura, mountain passes marked in red.

"Right." Zura points at a ridge on the screen. "We'll need cover. A sniper rifle or two up here."

"A plasma gun," Col says.

She pauses to look at him. The cruel beauty of her surged face makes it clear she's unhappy.

"In case a hovercar comes at us," Col adds.

Still no response.

That's when I realize—they've been trained not to question the orders of the Palafox heir.

"Col," I say. "A plasma gun can take down a cliff. You don't want one pointed in your direction, even by someone on your side."

He gives this a moment's thought, as if there's any question, then nods.

"Rifles, then. But you'll be next to me, Frey. You can carry a plasma gun, just in case."

"Sir, I doubt she has the necessary—" Zura begins.

"We can trust her judgment," Col says.

And that's that.

We start off as night falls.

Col and I are in borrowed sneak suits. Mine's the wrong size, too tight, and hot even as the desert cool comes down. Ten seconds after putting it on, the suit feels sticky inside.

I wonder if Specials sweat.

I stare down at myself as the camo adjusts, taking on the mottled browns of the desert.

Zura puts two of her commandos on overwatch duty. They scuttle up the mountainside, disappearing into the darkness of the cliffs. The last commando stays with the hovercar.

It's quiet as we walk, our suits fading into blackness as gradually as the sky. Col's carrying his hoverboard and bow, Zura a rifle, and I've got the plasma gun and my knife.

"Strange mix of firepower," I say. "Can't tell whether we're hunting dinosaurs or rabbits."

Col manages a smile at this. "I've still got a few explosive arrows, in case we spot a T. rex."

"We have extra rifles, sir." Zura sighs. "When I taught you how to use a bow, I never thought you'd bring one to a war."

Col shrugs. "We might have to kill someone silently."

Those words end the conversation—a reminder that this is not a hunting trip.

A moment later, Zura comes to a halt.

"Just so you two won't be startled, there's a small animal ahead. Probably a rabbit."

Specials must have night vision. Better than mine, it seems, since I can't see a thing out there.

"Check it out," Col says. "We'll wait."

"But it's just a—"

"Check it out."

Zura salutes and heads off into the darkness.

"I hope it's a volcano rabbit," I say. "Still want to see one of those."

Col smiles again, leaning his board on the ground. "They aren't as exciting as the name implies."

I want him to keep smiling, but jokes don't seem right. This is the first time we've been alone since finding out his brother is missing.

"Col, I'm sure Teo is—"

"That's not why I sent Zura away." He turns to me. "You have to prepare yourself. It's probably my mother with the codebook— I hope it is, anyway."

"Of course. I hope so too."

"Just know that I've got your back, no matter what she says or does."

I stare at him a moment, the gears in my tired brain meshing slowly. But finally I understand.

The rebels would welcome me, with my combat training and my store of family secrets. But when Aribella learns the truth of me, how I set her family up, she might have a different opinion.

And ultimately she commands these soldiers, not Col.

Then I realize something amazing. His little brother's missing, and Col's worried about . . . me.

"I'll be fine," I say.

"Don't be so sure." He looks ahead into the darkness. "You've never seen my mother angry."

"Trust me, I don't want to."

"Just stay calm when she gets going," he says. "I'll make her see who you really are."

"Col." For a second I can't say more.

The words are too much. *Who you really are.*

"You okay?" he asks.

"It's just . . . no one sees who I really am. It's not allowed. My whole life, it's been my job to make sure they don't."

"Not anymore." He puts a hand on my shoulder. "From now on, you're Frey. You don't have to lie."

The desert prisms with tears around me. It makes no sense. Col's the one with a missing brother, a wounded city, a home of smoke and ash . . .

And I'm the one crying.

He's too busy thinking about how to defend me from Aribella's wrath.

Before today, only one person in the world has ever spoken up for me. I've only ever had one ally, one friend. Two seems like more than I deserve.

"Did you mean it, back there in the bunker?" I ask. "That our kiss was real?"

He sets the board on the ground and pulls me toward him, our bodies pressing tight. The sneak suits feel as thin as a film of liquid between us.

"I'm not faking anything now," he says.

"But if it wasn't for me, you'd be—"

"In a smoking crater. Or caught by that scout car."

I press my ear against his chest, listening to his voice.

"And even if I'd survived all that, Frey, I'd be alone right now."

When he swallows, I can feel the pulse of his throat.

"You aren't alone, Col. I'm here."

"I know." He pulls away a little. "And I'll make sure Jefa understands what you mean to me."

He takes a breath to say more, but a scrabbling sound is coming from the darkness. It's Zura coming back.

She's running.

"Move!" she cries. "It wasn't a rabbit!"

JUMP MINES

In my night vision, I can see something following her.

Lots of somethings.

They're the size of rabbits, but their leaps carry them farther than any living creature. And I don't think rabbits come in packs of a hundred—

—or hunt humans.

Col steps onto the hoverboard. "Let's go!"

I jump on as it lifts into the air. We lean into motion, skimming downhill, loose stones skittering under the wash of our lifting fans.

With two people aboard, our top speed isn't much. Zura is running almost even with us, her surged legs taking inhumanly long strides.

When I glance back, the things are getting closer.

They look more like one-legged frogs than rabbits, their heads wrapped in camo skin, set to blend into the rocks. Their single feet are gleaming jackknives of metal that fling them high into the air.

I have no idea what happens if they catch us.

A stream of cracks comes from above—the Specials firing down from the cliffs.

One of the jumping machines is hit and goes careening sideways. It crashes into the side of the gorge and bursts with a blinding pulse of light.

The shock wave hits a second later, swatting us off the hoverboard. We go tumbling down the sandy slope.

When I bounce back to my feet, the taste of blood is in my mouth.

The blast lingers in my night vision—I can barely make out Col, who's been knocked to his hands and knees.

Zura skids to a halt to pull him to his feet. The board is just ahead of us, swerving to a riderless stop.

I jump on the board and look back at our pursuers. My pulse knife might take out two or three of them, but not dozens.

"What *are* they?" I yell.

Zura lifts Col back onto the board. "Jump mines."

My tutors have never mentioned those.

We lift off again. If there was only one of us on this board, maybe we could climb higher than the mines can jump. But I'm not volunteering to step off.

Covering fire streams down from the cliffs. Two waves of the mines break off and head up the slopes, hunting the Specials protecting us.

The Special back at the hovercar must have heard that explosion. I hope she can fly and shoot at the same time—the car's firepower would come in handy about now.

I've got the plasma gun, but I don't know how big its blast is. Or if the recoil will knock me off the board. Or if plasma rings are bright enough to see from orbit, bringing the entire Shreve army down on us.

Col's confidence in my judgment may have been misplaced.

I hit the priming trigger.

The gun begins to whine, its hydrogen battery growing hot. I glance back—maybe twenty of the mines are still after us. The rest are climbing up after the commandos.

The sooner I fire, the safer all of us will be.

"Brace for a weight shift!" I shout in Col's ear.

"What are you—?"

I leap from the board, skidding to a halt in the dirt. The gun's ready light turns green.

I shoulder the stock, aiming at the cluster of jump mines closing in on me.

And fire . . .

A spheromak of plasma spills from the rifle, like a smoke ring made of lightning and flame.

It streaks across the desert, lighting up the hills around us, bright as daylight. The jump mines bounding across its path flash into nothing.

The plasma ring keeps going. Mines crash together in its wake, drawn into the sudden column of turbulence.

I've aimed high enough that the plasma ring doesn't take down a cliff. It just streaks away into the atmosphere, a wrathful angel of flame.

There are still a dozen mines leaping toward me. More rifle fire comes from the Specials above, taking out one, two—

I drop the hot, expended plasma gun. Draw my knife.

"Frey!"

Col has come around on the board, ready to pick me up. But Zura leaps on with him and tilts them into motion.

"Wait!" Col yells. But he's the heir to House Palafox, and Zura is stronger and determined to save him. The board makes a wobbly turn and flies away.

Just a bodyguard doing her job, I guess.

I turn to face the jump mines.

Only eight are left coming at me. But on the cliffs above, a dozen more have reached one of the commandos. A mine soars over him, explodes in midair.

He falls.

The other commando is still shooting. More mines fall to the ground and twitch.

How many can my pulse knife take out?

Two? Three?

Racing away ahead, Col is invisible in his sneak suit, but Zura's arm shows a bright smear of body heat. She's been hit, her suit ripped open.

Another explosion sounds from the cliffs above. The covering fire goes silent.

I'm alone now. All I can do is run.

Then from the darkness ahead comes a sound—lifting fans.

The hovercar rises into view, its engines a bright constellation against the black sky.

I switch off my night vision just in time—the guns open up with a blinding salvo, fléchettes tearing up the desert behind me. As the car swoops a meter over my head, the rotor wash sends me sprawling.

A moment later, the mines chasing me have been cut to pieces. The car slews to a halt in the narrow gorge.

"No!" I stand up, waving. "Keep moving!"

The jump mines up on the cliffs are leaping back down.

They fall on the hovercar like exploding hail, pounding its armor. An engine fractures, and white-hot pieces fly in all directions.

I drop down and cover my head.

The hovercar tips over, hits the ground, cracks open. Two of the fans are still spinning, sending what's left of the machine skidding sideways toward a deep gorge. The car tumbles in and down, racks of burning ammunition crackling as it falls.

I stand up, stunned and deafened.

There are exactly two jump mines left.

And they've spotted me.

They leap through smoke and burning wreckage, twenty meters away and closing.

I let my pulse knife fly.

It sweeps through the first one, which explodes, knocking the knife off course. It catches the second with a glancing blow.

The mine crashes and rolls across the ground, landing at my feet.

I stare down, waiting for it to detonate.

GESTURES

One breath. Two.

Nothing happens.

One of the jump mine's feet jabs at the ground, trying to get it moving again. But the device only manages to roll back and forth a little, like an upended turtle.

It's too damaged to realize that it's right next to a target.

I stand there, motionless, counting another ten breaths.

Then, very slowly, I seal up my sneak suit till it covers everything but my eyes.

Nothing to see here.

Except—what happens when the mine decides it's broken? Does it self-destruct?

The lurching foot finally connects with dirt, and the mine rolls against my ankle. I pretend to be a tree.

Every little clank makes me twitch.

Then I hear something worse—footsteps.

"Frey?"

"Stop," I hiss. "Don't move."

"What are you . . ." A pause. "Oh."

Zura's a few meters behind me.

Two of us. Great.

"Stay back," I whisper.

There's no way out of this situation but to creep away and hope the mine is too damaged to spot us moving.

I slide a foot back through the dirt.

"Frey," Zura says softly. "Wait."

I freeze again. Give her a tiny, questioning shrug.

"Don't move. You could set it off."

No kidding. But is her plan for us to stand here until we starve to death?

The mine clanks once more, bumping against my ankle again. I don't dare whisper my question aloud.

Then something flies through the dark, strikes the dirt ten meters away.

An arrow.

The broken-sounding clank comes from my feet again, the mine pushing itself off across the ground. It struggles toward the arrow for a few meters, then comes to a halt again.

Another arrow whizzes past, buries itself in the dirt farther away.

The mine clanks into motion again, moving with painful

slowness, a wounded animal. But with every meter, it's less likely to kill me.

A third arrow lures it farther away.

I spot my knife hovering in the distance. Pull off a glove and signal to Col that he can stop using up his arrows.

I send my knife closer to the mine, then straight up at full pulse.

The mine hears the roar and explodes. The blast knocks me back on my heels and into Zura's arms.

"You okay?" she asks.

"Fine." I blink away the spots in my eyes, call the hot knife back into my hand. "But you should check on your commandos."

"I have," Zura says.

I turn to face her. She's wounded, one leg bloody, staring grimly at an airscreen in her palm.

"Two suits sending null vitals. No heartbeats, no EKG." She looks down into the gorge, where flames still flicker. "And no signal at all from Samon."

It hits me in a slow wave—there are only the three of us left.

Col glides up on his board, staring at the airscreen blankly. At every step of this battle, the soldiers endangered themselves to protect him.

I begin to see how that constant bubble of security weighs on Rafi. How watching me injure myself again and again to protect her must have hurt.

"You were right, Col," I say. "It was a trap."

"No, just bad luck." Zura closes her fist on the airscreen, snuffing it out. "Nobody sets up an ambush eight klicks out. They couldn't have known which direction we'd come from."

"Then what *were* those things?" I ask.

"The latest rebel trick," Zura says. "Mine fields that move at random, setting up in a new place every day."

"Rebels," Col breathes. "How long before they show up?"

"No telling. We might get Shreve units sniffing around too, after all those fireworks. We have to move."

I stare at them both. "Fine. But where are we *going*?"

For a moment, we look at one another, wreathed in dust and lit by the flames of the burning hovercar.

"Where the orders told us to go?" Zura suggests.

I shake my head. "We're going to hide eight klicks away from this *bonfire*?"

Col gathers himself, sets a determined face.

"There's nowhere else to go."

RENDEZVOUS POINT

We move fast—Zura running, me and Col on the hoverboard.

There's no point being stealthy now. Whoever's waiting for us at the rendezvous point heard that firefight. Either they've slipped away or gone to ground.

I just hope they don't start shooting when they see us charging in.

I also try not to think about the direction we're running—away from the rebellion that Col wanted to join yesterday, toward a woman who'll likely want to bury me.

At our frantic speed, eight kilometers doesn't take much time, or seem very far away from the wreckage behind us. But soon a breathless Zura calls us to a halt.

"Just over that ridge."

Col steps from the board. "We'll walk in slowly. Weapons down."

"Weapons?" I mutter. Our collective firepower is down to a rifle, a few grenades, a pulse knife, and a bow and arrow.

As we climb the ridge, I glance back the way we've come. No vehicles in the sky, no body heat. Just columns of smoke blotting out a stretch of stars.

Maybe when people see plasma guns blazing away, they investigate with caution.

We creep onto the ridge top with only the eye slits of our sneak suits open. Our destination doesn't look like much from up here. Just a flat expanse of rock, the perfect size for a hover-car to land.

"Anything?" Col asks.

Zura shakes her head. "I'll do a circuit."

"We don't have time," Col says. "We have to make contact before someone starts poking around back there."

He pulls his sneak suit down to reveal his face. Then stands up in plain view.

"¡Hola!" he calls down.

No answer.

"Soy Col Palafox. ¿Hay alguien ahí?"

Nothing but echoes.

He waits a moment, then sighs.

"Might as well go down."

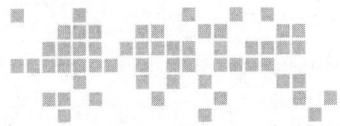

We're in the right spot, at least.

There are footprints in the dirt, a few discarded food containers. A pile of rocks to one side suggests that someone has cleared the space.

But there's no fancy tech, nothing to detect our arrival and ping whoever's got the codebook.

No jump mines, at least.

Col is pacing. "They ran when the shooting started. They probably thought an army was coming down on them!"

"Plasma guns have that effect," Zura says, looking at me. "Not my first choice for dealing with mines."

"My first choice was *running away*," I point out. "But then someone flew off with our only hoverboard!"

"My job is to protect the heir, not—"

"Enough," Col says. "We're here now. What exactly did your orders say, Zura?"

"Search for the signal from your board. Find you, then report here." She shrugs. "There wasn't a backup plan for if nobody was around."

"Okay. So they'll pick another spot to meet. How long till they send that out?"

"It doesn't matter, sir. Our codebook receiver is at the bottom of a ravine."

For a moment, Col looks like a lost child. Then he gathers himself. "We need to find another Victorian unit. How do we do that?"

Zura shakes her head. "What's left of our forces are running silent, which means trying *not* to be found. They'll only listen to orders from the codebook. That's how our system was designed."

"Then we go back to the bunker," Col says. "Sooner or later, someone's bound to show up for those weapons."

"On foot? Through enemy territory?" Zura asks. "We can't fit three on that hoverboard. And we've already run into one bunch of jump mines!"

Col lets out a sigh. He's scratched up from our fall off the hoverboard. His face is dirty and streaked with sweat.

"We don't have a choice."

"Col," I say gently. "Let's get some sleep. Whoever wanted us here could show up tomorrow."

For once, Zura agrees with me. "We're too tired to walk into another firefight, sir."

"Of course," Col says, then frowns. "I don't suppose there's anything to eat."

That's when it occurs to me that we're back to nothing. No food, no water, and no wood to burn.

It's like the wild is always trying to starve me.

Zura has some good news—we don't have to sleep in our sweaty sneak suits. Thanks to clever Victorian military tech, they can be fused together into a stealth tent.

The only problem is, all I'm wearing under mine is a ripped nightshirt and undershorts. My sweatpants are back in that ravine, on fire, along with our food and our receiver.

And mountains get cold at night.

While Zura works, I huddle half-naked on a rock, hugging my legs to stay warm. The wild feels infinite around me, a boundless dark.

The whole world seems boundless now. No more combat training in the morning, ever. No more breakfasts with the Palafoxes, pretending to be Rafi. No pretending at all.

Just me and my allies—and the things in the dark that want to kill us.

Freedom has a way of being terrifying.

I wonder what Rafi's doing now. Is she being a good daughter, making speeches to support the war effort? Or fighting our father every step of the way?

Maybe some part of her feels this freedom too, with no little sister to take her place every time things get interesting. She used to envy me out there on the dance floor, in front of the cheering crowds. Solving problems with my fists.

Maybe she's happier now, being both edges of the knife.

Does she miss me as much as I miss her?

A red dot bobs out of the darkness, Col using the laser sight of his hunting bow like a flashlight.

As if he knows the dark thoughts in my head, he sits next to me and puts an arm around my shoulders. Out here, the simplest things make all the difference. Food. Safety. Warmth.

His body against mine makes everything dividing us—our warring families, our lies—seem less important.

"You promised me an army," I say. "And I don't even have pants."

He pulls me tighter, and the low shudder in my bones finally stills.

"Uniforms will be easy," he says. "I'm more worried about the army part. When this all started, we had three thousand soldiers, two hundred hovercars. We'll be lucky if a quarter of them are still out there."

I don't answer. Fifty warships against my father is nothing.

Col puts his arm around me again. "When Zura jumped on the board, left you to face those mines alone, I couldn't stop her."

"I get it, Col. Her job is to protect you. Just like me and my sister."

"Well, except she volunteered."

Right. Normal people choose their work.

It seems like that would only make life harder, having to decide. Being born to protect my sister always felt like destiny.

"You didn't choose to be first son," I say.

"No. But I could always run away and become a big-game hunter. Jefa would love that."

I pull away to look at his face.

"I hope she's okay, Col. Even if she hates me."

He shakes his head. "Fighting beside someone, it's hard to hate them."

I close my eyes, and see this war against my father stretching out before us. Running, fighting, maybe for years. Sleeping in the wild, hungry and uncertain.

But we also have this, Col's body next to mine.

I kiss him.

He kisses me.

All those explosions an hour ago deadened my senses, but now I can feel everything. The hard stone beneath us. The weight of his hands on my shoulders. A hint of rain chilling the desert air.

Col's lips are dry, edged with thirst and cold. Our breaths quicken, shallow and unsteady in each other's mouths. His fists knot in my borrowed shirt, our gentleness sharpening in the dark.

Then, between kisses—the soft dance of his tongue like he's saying my name—I murmur a stray thought.

"My sister."

Col pulls back, confused at first.

"Sorry," I say. "But the thought of her alone, with him. While I'm here with you, safe."

Col holds me closer. "I'm worried about Rafi too."

"We have to get a message to her. She needs to know I'm alive. That I'm coming for her."

"We'll take you to a city. You can tell the feeds everything."

A shudder goes through me. "That would just warn my father. I'm not ready for everyone to know."

"Then we'll figure something out." He kisses me again. "We'll save your sister."

"And your brother too," I say.

We're going to fight beside each other, maybe for a long time. This war seems endless, and we're only at the start.

We kiss again, the sounds of our lips as faint as whispers in the night.

STONE

Zura finishes and calls to us to get some sleep.

She's fused the smart fibers of our suits, making a tent just big enough for three. Its camo skin is pitch black in the darkness.

Some part of my brain registers that it's awkward, sharing a tent with Col and one of his soldiers. But most of me is too exhausted, too battered, to care. And I need to pee.

"Back in a minute," I say.

Zura sighs. "You should've done that in the suit."

I stare at her. "What?"

"Here in the wild, nothing's more important than water. The suits collect our sweat and urine, and filter it back into drinking water. It tastes funny, but the purifiers work almost perfectly."

"Almost? No thanks." I turn away and head into the darkness.

"Watch out for snakes!" Zura calls.

Right. Deserts are full of snakes, aren't they?

Hopefully in this cold, they'll be asleep, or hibernating, or whatever snakes do. But as always, cold-blooded creatures are invisible in heat vision, so I can't be sure.

The wild sucks sometimes.

I'm not gone very long, but Col and Zura are already asleep when I come back. They've left me the middle.

Great.

But at least it's warm inside the tent. The suits are opaque to infrared, the insulation almost perfect. Zura warned us that the heat of three bodies will make things downright hot by morning. I'm fine with that.

When I lie down, there's a rock in the middle of my back. It's under the floor of the tent, big as an apple, embedded in the ground. Trying to shift it aside through the tent fabric is useless.

I lie there, trying to sleep, but the stone is too big to ignore.

Did Zura not see it? Or did she leave it there on purpose?

I wonder if the rest of the Victorian army will feel the same way about me. If all they'll see is Rafia, the first daughter of the enemy, even after I explain who I really am.

Maybe alliances are bogus. Maybe I should have stayed an army of one. I could go back to Shreve, sneak into my father's house, and get my sister out . . .

Or maybe it's just this brain-wrecking *rock* in my back.

I sit up and unseal the tent. The desert air reaches in, icy fingers along my flesh.

Col stirs, a plaintive murmur pushing from his lips.

The cold outside is brutal after the warmth of the tent. The freezing sand sticks to my bare knees and palms like ice crystals.

I slide one arm under the tent.

With my fingers stretched out, I can just reach the stone. But it's half-buried, and it takes a solid minute of scrabbling before it pops out.

There's something in the hole—

A folded piece of paper.

I pull it out and stare in the starlight.

The paper is covered with coded markings, like on the weapons cases back in the Palafoxes' bunker. But this is handwritten, hasty and clumsy.

I stick my head back into the tent and whisper, "Col."

He doesn't respond. I grasp his bare ankle with my freezing hand.

He sputters awake, staring at me with confusion and annoyance.

I wave the paper. "Someone left us a note."

He blinks a few more times, then finally sits up.

A gust of wind rushes past me into the tent, and Zura jolts awake, reaching for her rifle.

"Relax," I say.

Col crawls halfway out into the starlight. When I hand him the paper, his eyes go wide.

"It's Victorian battle code," he says.

"Can you read it?"

"It says, 'Stay here. We'll check back soon.'" Col squints closer. "And then, 'Leave me the sign, so I'll know it's you. And watch out—this place is plagued by scorpions.'"

I sit up straight. "Scorpions? Fantastic."

"Better than fantastic." Col looks up from the paper. "This is my little brother's handwriting."

RAIN

The next morning it rains.

It's cold and miserable, and we hunker in the tent together. All we can do is wait.

After finding the note last night, we made a spiral of stones on the landing pad. It's the symbol of a fictional hero Col and Teo pretended to be when they were little—the "sign" Teo was asking for.

Somehow, he's okay.

While we wait, Zura recounts battles from when she was fighting the rebels instead of my father. When she runs out of stories, Col tells us about his little brother, who was kicked out of his first boarding school for breaking curfew, and his second for bribing other students to take his tests.

When the time comes for me to entertain them, Zura gives me an expectant look. She's still wondering about the story behind my face.

"You can trust Zura with anything," Col says. "But it's up to you."

I hesitate. My story is something I should get used to telling, if we're going to spill it to the whole world one day. And I'll have to explain everything to Aribella, if she's going to understand my value to her struggle.

I like being bound to Col by the secrets we've shared. Once somebody else knows the truth of me, it won't be the same between us.

I'm selfish with him, and with my secrets.

"Not yet. Is that okay?"

Col takes my hand. "Of course."

"Can't wait," Zura says.

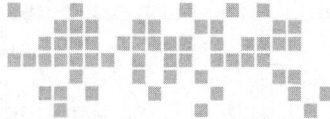

The day warms up slowly, but the rain doesn't relent.

"We should take the tent down," Zura says around noon. "The suits will collect more water if they're stretched out."

"Better than drinking our sweat," I say.

Col agrees.

We crawl out into the cold downpour, and we're muddy and soaked in seconds. But once I stop shivering, the feel of clean water against my skin is glorious.

Col and I stand side by side, drinking from our palms, rubbing two days' travel off our skin. Showering together in the rain feels almost normal, like this is a camping trip and not a war.

"Wish we had some soap," he says.

Zura looks up from taking apart the tent, pulls a blue wafer from a pocket of her fatigues. She tosses it to Col, who rubs it between his hands. A blue lather builds.

When he gives it to me, it smells exactly like the stuff they clean our kitchens with back at my father's house. It reminds me of playing hide-and-seek with my sister after the staff had all gone home. It also reminds me of having a whole kitchen full of food.

"Anything edible in those pockets?" I ask Zura.

"Just this." She pulls out a small bottle of powder. "Rub it into raw meat and it kills the parasites. Safer than food cooked on a fire."

"Sounds yummy." I turn to Col. "Your military tech creeps me out."

"Your military tech blew up my house."

"Oh, I didn't mean—" I begin, but Col breaks into a smile.

"My little brother's safe, Frey. I get to make jokes again."

"Sure. Just warn me it's a joke next time." I hand him the soap.

Col's smile fades. "I wonder if Abuela . . ."

He doesn't say more, but I can see him sink into the layers of everything he's lost. Even if Teo's okay, his home is still gone. His city conquered.

I gently change the subject. "How do you think Teo got back from Europe? His face is on all the feeds. It's not like he can buy a suborbital ticket."

"My mother must've sent someone to grab him."

"Why would they grab two of his friends?"

"For propaganda value?" he says. "You've seen the feeds. The cities are tightening the embargo."

"Yeah, I guess that does sound like Aribella."

Col shrugs. "I'm sure she told their parents."

I'm not. Once more, I remind myself to get back on her good side as soon as possible.

"I bet that note was her idea too," Col adds. "She knew I'd recognize Teo's handwriting."

"Messages within messages," I say softly.

But it seems risky to me, leaving so much to chance. If Zura had set up the tent in a different spot, we'd have missed the note completely.

My stomach rumbles.

"That parasite powder is starting to sound good," I say. "Do rabbits come out in the rain?"

Col shrugs. "Never thought about it."

"Wait," I say. "There's something about nature you *don't know*?"

"I don't hunt in the rain. My feathers get wet."

For a moment, I imagine Col as a large predatory bird. Then I realize—"Oh, the ones on your arrows."

He laughs, like this was a joke and not my brain gone briefly missing. After everything that's happened, Col still thinks I'm funny.

"Aren't deserts supposed to be dry?" I ask.

"Desert rains are infrequent. But when they happen, they can be torrential."

"Torrential," I say. "Such a tour guide word."

He comes closer. "We tour guides know all the good words."

A fresh wind is whipping through the camp. Water flows across my bare feet, and the rain slants and coils around us.

We're going to kiss again.

"Sir?" Zura's voice comes. "Incoming!"

I look up into the sky, blinking water from my eyes. That sound—it isn't wind.

It's lifting fans beating the air.

"Quick, Col. We have to . . ." But I'm not sure what there is to do.

There's no cover to hide behind. Col and I are half-naked, our sneak suits fused together into a tarp.

The hovercar looms into sight, descending in a fury. Its six lifting fans drive the rain like a sudden gale.

Zura is scrambling for her rifle, Col for his bow. But they're not going to take down an armored hovercar.

I gesture for my knife, but it must not be able to see me in the tempest. And I can't remember where I left it. Too much kissing, not enough paranoia.

We're helpless.

But as the car settles on the landing area, I realize that it's not a warcraft. It's a luxury limo, black and shiny.

The same kind my father rides around in.

I fall to my knees in the mud.

"No."

The doors butterfly open, like great wings spreading out to shield the occupants from the rain.

And they step out, like conquerors in a new world.

Teo Palafox and his two friends.

TEO PALAFOX

"Can you *not* get the seats muddy? This is a rental."

I stare at Srin. She looks about twelve years old, but she's in the same year as Teo at his fancy school. So she's either a teenager or some kind of prodigy.

I sit down with a wet squelch. Srin's gray eyes glare at me from beneath her short bobbed hair. Everything about her is neat and precise, from her school uniform to her arched eyebrows. But, like a quiet warning, her left little finger is surged to look like a tiny snake.

The leather seat shifts beneath my weight, adapting to my body. After two nights' sleep on hard ground, it feels like a feather bed.

"You rented a limo and brought it into a war zone?" Col asks.

"We're not brain-missing," Srin says. "We got insurance."

The three of them are arranged across the backseat—Teo, Srin, and Heron. They're all still wearing their school's uniform, dark blue sweaters and matching trousers, lilac shirts. Heron wears a dazed expression and a rumpled look, like he's been sleeping in his clothes.

The limo's soft pink lighting glints from the champagne glasses lined up on racks. There's a silver ice bucket next to my elbow.

Col sinks into his own luxurious seat. "But why are you in a limo at all? Why aren't there *soldiers* with you?"

A minute ago, when Teo tumbled out to hug his older brother in the rain, he looked like a little kid. He's skinnier than Col, his face softer and more open.

But now he crosses his arms, all business.

"I wanted to test the system first. Make sure the codebook wasn't compromised before meeting anyone face-to-face."

Col just stares at him.

"I knew you were out here somewhere," Teo explains. "So we had to find you first. Because you could *prove* who you really were, using the sign."

"We didn't want to walk into a trap," Srin chimes in.

"Wait," Col says. "*You* have the codebook? Why isn't Jefa running things?"

Teo stares back across the car.

"Mamá?" he says in a small voice. "She's dead."

"But . . . she always has the book!"

Teo shakes his head. "She gave it to me when I was here at winter break. To take back to school."

Col crumples into his seat.

I take his hand, my brain spinning. This is why no one's secured the family weapons back at the bunker. Why our only welcome here was a note left under a rock. Why we're sitting in this ridiculous hovercar.

Because a fourteen-year-old boy is commanding the Victorian army.

Aribella Palafox is dead.

"I'm sorry, Col." Teo looks like a little kid again. "I figured she told you about giving me the book—that you'd *know* it was me."

Col's hand is limp in mine, his eyes glassy.

His words come slowly. "That means she was worried about what might happen. She had a bigger plan. Maybe she got out somehow!"

"Col," Teo says. "I was talking to her when the missile hit."

There's no sound except the rain. I want to say something, but there isn't enough air in my lungs. The limo seems like it's shrinking, pressing in on us.

It takes Teo a moment to speak again.

"When she gave me the codebook, I thought it was just Jefa being Jefa. Giving me a lesson in responsibility. I kept it under my bed."

He stares at the rain-streaked window.

"Then everything went brain-missing. It was early morning, still dark. And suddenly this noise wakes us up."

"We thought it was a fire alarm," Heron says.

"I'd forgotten all about the book," Teo says. "But it was there, under my bed, screaming and blinking. So I ping Jefa and she answers right away, even though it's midnight here at home. She says we're under attack in the ruins, but it's under control. Except Col's being an idiot."

Col's hand flinches in mine. "What?"

"She said you were supposed to keep Rafia in line. But you'd gone off the rails. The tracker on your board said you were at the edge of the city. You were helping her escape." Teo gives me a sideways look.

I hold his gaze. He's one more person I have to explain myself to. One more who'll blame me for everything that's gone wrong.

"And you're *sure* she was still there at the end?" Col pleads.

Teo's voice goes soft. "Suddenly there was this alarm in the background, and she went quiet. Wouldn't answer when I asked what was going on. Then she said, 'I love you,' and there was a buzzing sound."

He slumps back in his seat.

Heron puts an arm around Teo. "We figured she'd hung up, or lost the connection. But then we turned on the feeds—they kept showing it, again and again."

I close my eyes for a moment, and see the missile hit. That column of black smoke rising, scattering ashes on the wind.

"That's why we decided to disappear," Srin says. "It was the only way to hit back."

Everyone looks at her.

"Wait," Col says. "You mean Jefa didn't send someone for you?"

"No. It was my idea." Srin's grim smile looks demented in the limo's soft lighting. "Maximum reputational damage for the enemy. We trashed our rooms to make it look like we fought the kidnappers. Even left some blood."

She holds up a hand. In the limo's pink lighting, I can see tiny scars on her fingertips.

Col stares at her, wide-eyed. "Do your families *know* you're okay?"

"Only my sister," Srin says. "She rented this limo, the leather of which your pants-missing friend is currently ruining. Byanca also chartered our cargo jet. Took a whole night to get across the ocean, but no one expects rich kids to travel in a cargo hold."

"But your parents—"

"We're dealing with a monster," Srin says. "Sacrifices have to be made."

Teo leans forward. "She's right, Col. This will hurt him. You've seen the feeds."

"But everyone thinks you've been kidnapped," Col says to Heron and Srin. "Maybe killed!"

"*That's the point!*" Teo cries. "Why should we care about their feelings, Col? The other first families watched our home destroyed, our mother murdered, our city taken, and none of them did anything! Let them all be afraid!"

There's a moment of shocked silence in the car, ringing with the muffled rain and the echoes of Teo's anger.

Then Heron raises a hand. "Actually, I only came along to make sure Teo doesn't do anything stupid. And can I point out that no one said *anything* about war zones?"

"It didn't say 'war zone' on the map," Teo mutters.

Col swears.

"Speaking of wars, sir," Zura says from the open limo door. "Now that we have transport, we might want to get out of rebel territory."

For a moment, Col looks lost. He's had his world turned inside out twice in the last few days. Maybe three times—I've lost count. But he understands now that we've been fooling ourselves.

His mother is gone.

I take a steadying breath. "Col, maybe we should get these kids somewhere safe."

"*Kids?*" Srin says.

"Right. Pack up the camp," Col orders Zura, then turns to his little brother. "We can get a Victorian warcraft to escort us. Give me the codebook."

Teo stares at his older brother defiantly, his face still red from yelling.

Then he looks at me.

"Not till you tell me what *she's* doing here."

TRUST ME

Everyone's looking at me.

Even Zura hesitates at the door, like she's waited too long for this story to walk away now.

"You're her, aren't you?" Teo says. "Rafia."

"Except muddy and without pants," Srin adds.

Heron leans forward. "Which is why that other Rafia—the one on the feeds—hasn't done any interviews yet. She's an impostor!"

It still feels too soon. Too huge. Too dangerous.

But there's no escaping the truth.

"It's the other way around. I'm the impostor."

The three of them are silent for a moment.

I let it soak in, for them and for me.

It's uncanny, having people I don't know staring at me, stunned, seeing what I really am. Like the ground is tilting under us all. Like they're all going to disappear tomorrow.

I wish I had more clothes on.

"Weird," Zura says. "I'll go pack up."

She turns away and disappears into the rain.

"No way." Srin looks at Col. "If this girl was an impostor, your security would've spotted her surgery. I mean, it's pretty good, but a quick DNA check—"

"We checked her DNA," Col says, then falls silent.

He wants me to tell it myself.

So I start talking.

"I'm Rafia's sister, born twenty-six minutes later." I listen to the rain for a moment. "Her body double. Her protector. Her identical twin."

Her only friend.

The only one who can save her.

"I was a trick to play on your family, Teo. Because unlike the real Rafia, I was something my father could throw away."

He stares at me. I'm expecting hatred in his eyes, or another scream from the bottom of his soul as he realizes everything I've cost him.

But all he says is—

"What's your name?"

"Frey." It comes out of my mouth in a whisper.

His expression changes then, and I see how much he looks like Aribella.

Because he pities me. Like she did.

Pity isn't something I'm ready for at all.

He says, "My brother would've been there when the missile hit, except for you. Right?"

"I guess so."

"Thank you, Frey," he says softly.

A layer of guilt slips from my shoulders.

Col leans forward. "Heron, Srin, you two have to keep this secret after you get home. Which will be as soon as possible."

Srin stares at him a moment, then starts laughing.

"Are you brain-missing, Col? You can't keep her a secret. Imagine the reputational damage!"

Heron turns to her. "Seriously, girl? Is it *that* much worse than kidnapping me and you?"

"*Way* worse. You're just a roommate who got in the way. I'm some kid from Teo's propaganda class." Srin points at me. "But Frey is her father's own flesh and blood, sacrificed to start a war!"

"Stop," Col says. "This isn't your propaganda class, Srin. It's not your story to tell."

"But you *can't* send us home!" Srin turns to me, pleading. "Once people see us back with our families, the outrage fades. We lose momentum. Everything goes back to normal!"

Normal—I hear it in my sister's voice.

"That's what everyone wants," Srin says. "To pretend that things are okay. But, Frey, you can *make* them pay attention."

I try to answer, but I can't.

Me and Col using my story against my father was one thing.

But hearing a stranger plot and strategize and calculate how damaging it will be—it feels like being an impostor again.

Col puts a hand on my shoulder, and the world steadies a little.

"You two are going home," he says.

"Really?" Srin smiles sweetly at him. "Limo, who holds your proxy ownership?"

"You do, General Srin," the limo says.

"And you won't go anywhere unless I tell you to?"

"That's correct, General."

There's a moment of impasse, but then Teo speaks up.

"Srin, my brother's right. You guys can do more for us from home. Tell everyone what it was like that night, how we ran away, fearing for my safety. Don't let them forget Victoria. Be the face of the resistance!"

"I *guess* that sounds bubbly," Srin mutters. "A shower might also be nice."

"Same," Heron says.

He looks like he's willing to go back to school, but Srin gave up too easily. I wonder if she's got another trick up her sleeve.

Teo turns his eyes to me, then to his brother.

"Col, do you really trust her?"

"Frey saved my life more than once. She fought beside our soldiers. And she's the only person in the world who hates her father as much as we do."

"Except Rafi," I murmur.

"All right, Frey." Teo holds out his hand. "If Col trusts you, I do too. Welcome to Victorian High Command."

"Also known as *my* limo," Srin grumbles.

We shake.

"Now," Col says, "will you please give me the codebook?"

Teo sighs, reaching under his seat to pull out a valise. It looks a lot like Rafi's favorite—alligator skin, brass fittings, retina locks.

He balances it on his lap, blinks it open.

"Don't let power go to our head, big brother." Teo pulls out a metal slate the size of a handscreen. "And be careful. This thing is noisy—it broadcasts all the way to the satellites. So if you don't want to get spotted, send your orders on the move, or someplace with a lot of random signals. Like a city."

"Got it." Col takes the codebook solemnly.

When he holds it up, light flashes across his face. He flinches as it takes a nip of skin for DNA matching.

A moment later, the device says, "You have command, Col Palafox."

His expression changes then—the exhaustion, the grief and sorrow fading a little. He looks like someone ready to take revenge.

Teo only looks relieved to give up the responsibility. He turns his open valise around to face me.

"Want some clothes, Frey? They might fit you."

I look at the three runaways in their school uniforms, their lilac shirts glowing in the soft limo lighting, and shake my head.

"I'll just wear my sneak suit."

Heron raises an eyebrow. "Those things don't look very comfortable."

"They aren't." I give him a tired smile. "But you never know when a battle's going to break out."

FAKING IT

The limo takes off in a roar, the windows blurring as it lifts up through the rain. But a minute later we break through the clouds and into sunlight. Shadows gyre across the floor as we veer west, out of the mountains, away from Victoria and Shreve.

I'd almost forgotten that flying could be luxurious. The seat is comfortable even in my damp sneak suit, and the limo rides as smoothly as any in my father's fleet.

It also has food. Yucca and truffled cheese croquettes. Crispy dumplings filled with duck and black mole. All of it cooked with real heat, popping out steaming from the panels in the walls.

"Want some bubbly with that?" Srin asks.

She's probably being sarcastic, but I don't care. "Is there any water?"

"Not since last night. Heron used it all for a bath."

"I'd hardly call that a bath," Heron says. "More like a sponging."

"This thing doesn't collect rain?" Zura glares at the flight controls, which are locked on autopilot. "There's water in your suit bladders, Frey."

"Great. But do you have to call them *bladders*?"

I find the drinking tube on my shoulder, wrest it free from its clasp, and put it to my lips. The water tastes normal enough.

"Mmmm, body temperature."

At least it's not my own purified sweat—or worse. But after a couple of days being thirsty, I can see why commandos wear these things. The deadliest part of the wild isn't snakes or scorpions. It's thirst and hunger.

Also jump mines.

Col must be starving too, but he's not eating. His eyes are locked on the codebook airscreen.

Maybe planning a war is easier than thinking about his mother in that house when the missile hit. Or his brother watching it happen over and over on the feeds, unable to change a thing.

I should say something comforting, but I don't have the words. My own mother was murdered before I was born. She's only ever been a figment on a screen, a face in which Rafi and I found pieces of our own. Her smile, always wide like ours, her thin hands as we got older.

So, in a way, I could never lose her.

All I can think to ask Col is, "Have you decided where to take them?"

"We can make it to Paz before dark. Spy dust is illegal there, and the council hates Shreve. It's the perfect place to send out orders." Col turns to his brother. "How much of our army's left? The codebook isn't telling me."

Teo looks up from eating. "I don't know. Anytime a unit transmits, there's a chance they could get spotted. I never asked for a head count."

Col frowns. "So what've they been doing all this time?"

"We sent out a general order to hide," Srin says. "I told Teo we should coordinate a few attacks, but he was too chicken."

"No, that was smart." Col turns to Zura. "But now we need to find out how much of an army we have. What's the safest way to do that?"

"Pick a rally point and assemble everyone. See for ourselves what we've got to work with."

Col's eyes light up. "I know just the place."

He turns back to the codebook. Its airscreen is about the size of a soccer ball. In the swirling cloud of data I can make out a map of the mountains, a few glowing cities, and a moving dot that must be us.

"By the way, Supreme Commander," Srin says, "didn't we send a light attack car to find you? It is conspicuously missing."

Col doesn't look up. "Destroyed in combat. We ran into jump mines."

"Mines? Were you taking a *walk*?"

"Yes. And you brought a rented limo into rebel territory."

"But we didn't *lose* it," Srin says.

Col doesn't answer, but I can see Zura holding her tongue, weighing whether Teo's friend from propaganda class is someone she's allowed to punch.

So I speak up, softly and clearly.

"Srin, the soldiers who served on that car fought valiantly, but they were killed. That's how wars work—people die. Which is why we're taking you home."

Her eyes spark, like she's about to argue, until Heron puts a hand on her arm. She settles back into her seat and mutters, "*Still* my limo."

The car falls silent, and Zura gives me the barest nod of thanks.

Col stays focused on the airscreen, waving his fingers. He looks uncertain, like a littlie learning how to use interface gestures for the first time.

Suddenly it's hard to believe that he's really in charge of an army, or even what's left of one. How can a guerrilla war be waged by a seventeen-year-old boy, from something that looks like a game screen?

My whole life, I always thought that I was the only impostor. That everyone else was certain they were real in some way that I could never understand. But what if they're all just faking too?

Maybe none of us know who we really are.

PROXY

The sun is setting when we spot the Pacific Ocean.

We're tired and bored after long hours in the limo. The feeds aren't telling us anything new, just rehashing the outrage about Teo and his two friends being missing. There's no real news out of Victoria. Reporters from other cities have been expelled, the locals silenced.

The whole city has gone dark. Tens of thousands of feeds—arguing politics, gossiping, sharing music and makeup tips—all of it has been wiped from the global interface.

Srin was right—Rafi hasn't appeared in public since that first day of the war. Everyone's noticed she's not being a good daughter. And saying that this time our father has gone so far that it's turned even his own blood against him.

I love that Rafi's fighting him, because she thinks he killed me with that missile. But I hate it that she thinks I'm dead.

I have to get word to her somehow, even if it gives our father warning that I'm still out here.

Col finally switches from the newsfeeds, turning to a nature doc about the white weed. We all watch in sullen fascination.

The weed is an artificial orchid that the Rusties unleashed three centuries ago. It almost crowded out all other plant life on earth, taking over farms and fields and prairies. Slashing, burning, and poisoning the weed failed. Only the old-growth forests were strong enough to resist.

"Rusty scientists engineered birds to eat it," Col adds to the grim commentary. "But they just spread the seeds in their droppings."

I wonder why he's obsessing about the weed. Maybe because people thought it couldn't be defeated, until a global effort got it under control.

Or maybe he's begun to admire things that can't be killed, no matter how hard everyone tries.

On the western plains below us, the weed is strewn like fresh snow. But the city of Paz sits on Baja Island, protected by a barrier of salt water.

As night falls, we cross the still blue straits and land outside the city, next to a train line. The quiet passenger station sits among a row of simple houses with gardens and low stone walls.

I remember my father joking about Paz, the city with no first family, where everyone's happy. Like that's such a bad thing.

We tumble out onto the station platform to stretch our legs.

"You want us to take a *train*?" Srin says. "Not a very dramatic entrance."

"Maybe quiet is better," Heron says. "Faking our own kidnapping seems kind of illegal."

"Just tell them you ran away," Col says. "You feared for your safety. Tell the Paz wardens that you want sanctuary . . . for all three of you."

"Wait," Teo says. "*Three* of us?"

"Yes." Col crosses his arms. "You're safer here than out fighting a guerrilla war. And you'll get more news coverage than your friends. You were right before—someone needs to be the face of Victoria. But it should be *you*, Teo."

"Forget that." Teo clenches his fists. "I'm not going to be the mascot for your war, Col."

"You don't understand how dangerous this is. I'd already be dead if it weren't for Frey and Zura."

"Which is why you need my help too!" Teo cries. He looks at me. "*You* don't think I should hide, do you, Frey?"

For a moment, I'm not sure what to say. I don't want to argue against Col, but I can't imagine being pushed aside either. The only meaning my life has ever had is in training, fighting, and protecting those I love.

That's what kept me whole when all my bones were being broken. How can I take that away from Teo?

"You might be safer with us," I tell him.

Col stares at me. "What do you mean?"

It takes me a second to understand it myself, but then I turn and take his hands.

"My sister hasn't given any interviews yet. Why do you think that is?"

He shrugs. "Because she's angry at your father? Because she thinks you're dead?"

"No, Col." I lean closer, speak softer. "It's what you told me in the bunker—Rafi's been falling apart since she was seven, because all she had was speeches and handshakes, and not someone she could protect. When the assassin came, I could save her. But she could never save *me*."

Col stares at me. "But Teo's only fourteen. I have to protect him."

"Exactly. Which means letting *him* protect *you*."

He shakes his head. "I don't under—"

"You don't have a choice," Srin cuts in.

Col wheels on her. "Would you please stay *out* of this!"

"Limo," she says calmly, "secure doors."

Beside us, the vast wings of the limo's doors fold up. Then the blue light of a security perimeter shines down on the station platform.

"Here's the deal." Srin adjusts her school sweater, as if she's about to give a speech. "You can take Teo back to the war, along with my limo. Or you can sit here with no transport, waiting for the Paz wardens to pick you up."

"Wardens? We're not breaking any laws."

Srin smiles. "You're registered combatants in a neutral city, equipped with sniper rifles, grenades, sneak suits."

"Um, sir?" Zura says. "That's all technically true."

"But Paz is on our side!" Col cries.

"Unofficially, yes," Srin says. "But once a complaint's on the record, they'll go by the rules of neutrality—and impound you all for the rest of the war. Paz isn't going to risk getting dragged into a fight with a missile-flinging maniac!"

Col sighs. "And who's making this complaint?"

"Limo. Transmit in thirty seconds."

"Yes, General Srin," the limo says.

Heron shakes his head. "Trust me. Don't call her bluff."

"Just ignore her," I say. "But let your brother stay in the fight."

"I just lost my mother . . . *again*." Col's voice is breaking. "I can't lose him too."

"He can't lose you either. You need each other right now."

"Twenty seconds," Srin says.

Col takes a slow breath, his eyes closed.

Tears are coming down his face. I can guess what he's seeing in his head—that missile coming down on his home, over and over in an endless loop.

"Fight together," I say.

"Ten seconds."

"Okay!" Col's cry echoes through the empty station. "Just do it."

"Cancel that order, Limo," Srin says calmly. "Transfer control of your rental proxy to Teo Palafox. And buy me and Heron tickets on the next train into town."

"Of course, General Srin. It's been a pleasure serving you."

DAWN

We spend the night on the southern tip of Baja Island, in a sea of solar panels the size of playing cards.

Our limo's almost out of charge, and the main batteries for Paz are in the ground below us, so we jack in overnight before heading to the rally point Col has chosen for what remains of the Victorian army.

I sleep with him out under the stars. The breezes blow cool off the ocean, and we hold each other for warmth. In the middle of the night I feel him crying. Silent shudders rack his body, his last hope for his mother dying in the contractions of his heart.

I try to comfort him with whispers, uncertain if they're lost in the roar from the surf. It's better than thinking about Rafi alone in her room—alone in her grief, with no friends who even knew she had a sister.

When dawn breaks at last, the field of solar panels stirs around us. Each has six legs, to move and angle themselves as needed as the day goes on. Now they're all tilting together toward the red glimmers in the east, like flowers waiting for the sun.

One of the panels has crawled onto my wadded-up sneak suit, questing for more light. I place it gently on the ground.

Pulling on my suit, I realize that it fits me better now. It's learning the shape of my body. Or maybe it's because I've gotten rid of my nightshirt underneath. The liquid weight of the dew collected overnight feels reassuring.

With water and my knife, I can survive the wild.

I kneel beside Col. "You awake?"

A murmur comes from his lips, and I lean closer to kiss them. His eyes spring open.

"Frey?"

"Expecting someone else?"

He smiles, sits up. The tiny machines around us skitter out of his shadow. The sun is igniting the horizon now, turning the host of solar panels into a dark ruby sea.

We pause to watch the dawn—the sun pulling itself up, light rippling across the panels as they drink in energy, the world shifting from crimson to orange.

"Look," Col says. "You're beautiful."

"What do you . . . ?" I look down.

My suit's in camo mode, matching the solar panels around us. I shimmer like stained glass, a hundred reflections of the dawn mapped onto my body.

Col kisses me, and we stay there until the sugary smells of pastries and sweet coffee spill from the open limo doors.

Teo and Zura are eating breakfast inside.

Teo's school uniform looks more rumpled than ever, but Zura's fatigues are still immaculate.

She doesn't waste time. "Morning, sir. Units should be arriving at the rally point by now. We're fully recharged."

"Then let's head south," Col says, taking a cup of coffee. "Care to do the honors, little brother?"

"Limo, head to programmed destination," Teo orders, beaming at us as the lifting fans begin to spin.

I smile back at him. Srin only gave him the limo's proxy to make sure Col keeps his word, but it gives Teo a role in the fight against my father.

As we lift into the air, I look out the window.

From this height, the solar panels glint like bright, rippling water. The sun is fully risen now, the reds and oranges fading into reflected blue sky.

"Something's happening," Col says from the next window. "Over the city."

I squint through the sunlight.

A fleet of hovercars is rising from the center of Teo. They spiral into the air, flinging out in all directions like a wheel of fireworks.

Zura joins us at the windows. "That looks like a search pattern."

"Anything to do with us?" Col asks.

"Limo," Teo says. "Local newsfeed."

An airscreen fills the center of the cabin.

At first it's just images of warden hovercars, and the Spanish is too rapid for me. But then the screen fills with the smiling, triumphant face of Srin. Heron stands beside her, looking faintly embarrassed.

"Uh-oh," I say. "Anyone care to translate?"

Col sighs. "She says they were kidnapped by your father. That they made a daring escape."

"I *knew* she wouldn't stick with the truth," Teo says. "It's not dramatic enough!"

I shake my head. "So those wardens are looking for kidnappers. Can this thing go any faster?"

"Limo?" Teo says. "Maximum speed, please."

"We are traveling at the maximum safe speed, sir."

"Yeah, but we want to go at an *unsafe* speed. It's, um, a medical emergency?"

"Correcting course," the limo says. "The nearest hospital is—"

"Don't turn back!" Teo cries. "I need my . . . pills. Which are only available at the destination. Please go there at top speed!"

The limo considers this a moment. "You will require liability—"

"Put it on the account!"

The pitch of the lifting fans increases.

"Rentals," mutters Zura.

I raise my hands for calm. "What can the Paz wardens do to us? We didn't really kidnap Srin and Heron."

"They'll find our weapons," Zura says. "And when the limo spills its records, they'll know we spent last night jacking the city power grid. They'll have to impound us."

Teo leans back. "Yes, this would be a bad situation, *if* we were in some armored hovercar. But they won't be looking for kidnappers in a rented—"

"Apologies, sir," the limo says. "We are stopping under official orders from the Paz constabulary."

The lifting fans shift in pitch again.

Col sighs. "You were saying?"

WARDENS

"Override that?" Teo tries. "Keep going toward : . . . my very important pills?"

"I cannot override local wardens," the limo says.

"Who comes to a war in a rented limousine?" Col shouts into the air.

"Col," I say. "We need a real hovercar. This is our chance."

He shakes his head. "If we attack Paz, that's one less ally."

"They'll never know it was us, sir." Zura turns from the window. She makes a few gestures, and her sneak suit camo shifts to black-and-gray Shreve combat livery.

My brain starts to spin. *This* I understand.

Being an impostor is what I was born to do.

And suddenly I know how to catch the wardens off guard, how to hurt my father, and how to get what I want more than anything else.

"I'll steal you that car," I say. "Just let me do the talking."

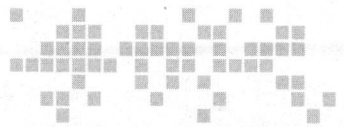

The limo lands when we reach the edge of the mainland.

When the doors open, a cool ocean breeze fills the cabin. This clifftop overlooks the Baja Sea, which is ashine with morning light. Screeching gulls surround us for a moment, but soon they're scattered by the roar of lifting fans.

The warden car comes down ten meters away. It's half the size of the limo, not much armor or weaponry, built for speed and quick turns.

Three wardens get out, looking bored at first, like they don't expect to find anything nefarious in this fancy car. But then they notice the mud on the limo's skids, the streaks from yesterday's rain. One of them puts a hand on the stunner in her holster.

When I step out into the sunlight, they're all stunned.

I've set my sneak suit to replay its camo from half an hour ago—the brilliant dawn captured in a million solar panels. It looks like something Rafi would design, a formfitting bodysuit for the most avant-garde of parties.

All my years of pretending flow back into the muscles of my body, my face.

"Good morning, officers," I say in my best Rafi voice. "Or is it afternoon? I hope you've come to arrest my hangover. I've just been to the *most* battery-draining party in your *lovely* city."

None of them speaks.

Rafi's never been to Paz, which my father hates for its happiness-loving, elected government. She doesn't travel without bodyguards, or talk to commoners.

"Ma'am," one of them finally sputters. "We're authorized to search all—"

"Be my guest." I gesture toward the limo. "But please don't impound my coffeemaker. I need it desperately."

"Uh, thank you." As he walks past, his eyes lock onto mine in disbelief. My smile is perfect Rafi.

Then Teo sticks his head out, surprising the warden. At the same moment, Zura comes bounding over the top of the limo, her sneak suit set to Shreve combat livery.

Her leap carries her to the warden midway between me and their car, crumpling her with a kick to her stomach.

I kidney-strike the man beside me. He staggers, and I take him in a sleeper hold until he crumples to the ground.

Spinning around, I see the last warden falling to Zura's blows.

She turns to us, smiling. "Well, that was easier than—"

An arc of lightning shoots from the warden car, and Zura shudders and falls. There's a stun cannon on the car's roof.

My knife leaps into my hand, and I hurl it at the warden car. The stun cannon explodes into a shower of metal pieces and discharged electricity.

The knife weaves its way home to my hand, hot and sparking.

Col and Teo are out of the limo now, running toward the warden car. Teo's carrying his suitcases and Col has the sniper rifle and his bow.

I stand ready with my knife. I can't see any more weapons mounted on the car. But if the hovercar's AI is allowed to stun people, it must be smart enough to fly itself away.

Maybe it's transmitting home for orders . . .

I spot an antenna dish on the car's rear hatch and send my knife to turn it into a shower of metal flakes.

Teo kneels next to Zura. Col jumps into the car. A moment later, sparks fly from the cockpit doors. So much for the car's AI.

Teo's running back toward me, a grenade from Zura's belt in his hand.

"What's that for?"

"Limo!" he orders, twisting the grenade to its longest setting. "Turn off fire suppression for safety check. Secure doors, please."

"Yes, sir," the car says.

As the doors begin to fold closed, Teo tosses the grenade inside.

"What are you—"

"It knows I'm the proxy, here of my own free will. And the

rally point's in the destination log." Teo swallows. "Limo, go for a spin over the water. Head for the middle of the Baja Sea."

"With no one aboard, sir?"

"Just go!"

Teo and I watch as the machine rises into the air. As it banks over the ocean, he takes my hand.

"Five, four, three . . ."

The limo jerks in midair, jets of fire gushing from its windows. It veers into a spin, falling like a leaf, trailing a spiral of smoke and flame.

I barely hear the splash over the roar of waves against the cliff.

"Poor limo," Teo says sadly.

"Come on!" Col yells.

We turn and run.

He's dragged Zura into the back of the warden car. She's unconscious, and her sneak suit's camo is blinking random colors.

"Is she breathing?" I ask, jumping into the back.

"Paz wardens are strictly nonlethal," Col says. "But check the vitals on the wrist of her suit!"

"All green," Teo says. "But is there a medkit, just in case?"

"Let her sleep," I say. "That's the safest way to get over a stun-blast."

I look back toward Paz to see if anything's coming our way. Nothing yet.

Col pulls himself forward into the cockpit, where the remains of the AI module are still smoking. He starts throwing switches, and the lifting fans begin to whine.

"You better strap in back there," Col says. "I don't really know how to fly without an AI, and this car's going to take off like a volcano rabbit."

FLIGHT

The warden car jumps into the air, pressing me down into my seat.

After the smooth ride of the limo, it's like being on a hoverboard. We lurch into a sickening turn, veering southward down the coast.

"My radar's out!" Col yells.

"That's what that was?" I look back at the smoking antenna on the rear hatch. "My mistake."

"Anyone following us?" Col asks.

"Not yet," Teo says from the back, strapping Zura into her seat. "Since when can you fly a hovercar, Col?"

"I've been practicing." Col's voice drops a little. "On a simulator."

"*On a what?*" Teo cries.

"I can take off and fly pretty well. Landing's the tricky

part. As long as Zura wakes up before we run out of juice, we'll be fine."

The car jolts to the left, slewing inland for long seconds before Col gets it under control.

"We're going to die!" Teo yells.

"Just a wind sheer off the ocean," Col says grimly. His right hand is white-knuckled on the flight stick.

I reach out, brushing my fingertips across the clenched muscles on his arm. "You're doing great."

"This feels just like the simulator . . ." He spares me a glance and a smile. "Except more dizzy-making."

The car bucks again beneath us, then dives for an awful moment toward the cliffs. Col wrestles with the flight stick until we're straight and level again.

"Maybe get out of this ocean wind?" I say.

"I have to stay on the coast. I don't know how else to navigate."

"So we don't know where we're going?" Teo yells.

"The codebook's got a map," I say. "I'll navigate."

"Right," Col says, and pushes the stick left. "Thanks."

We slip across the coastal cliffs, over rain forest, and finally onto a desert spotted with encroachments of white weed. The air steadies around us.

I pull my hand from Col's arm, take a deep breath.

At last I can think about what I did back there.

I've shown my face—Rafi's face—to wardens looking for

kidnappers. And right before we attacked, they saw Teo emerging from my limo. There's no way this doesn't make the feeds, even in Shreve.

I've told my sister I'm alive.

Tonight, she won't go to sleep thinking that she'll always be alone. She'll know I'm okay. She'll know I'm coming for her.

My father will also figure out it was me, of course. And that I'm working with the Palafoxes. But that's fine with me.

I'm coming for him too.

The other Paz wardens don't follow us.

It's hard to blame them. We overwhelmed three of their officers, using a pulse knife and a Special—a military-grade attack.

And maybe Paz doesn't want to shoot down a car carrying the first daughter of Shreve. They remember what happened to the last city that made my father angry.

An hour into the flight, Teo says, "I miss the limo. There was food and way better coffee. And we could watch the feeds when flying got boring."

"You call this *boring*?" Col mutters. His fist is still tight around the flight stick.

My eyes are glued to the codebook. Our glowing blue dot is making its way south toward the rally point. By now, what's left of the Victorian army is there waiting for us.

Instead of running, being hunted, soon we'll do some hunting of our own.

"The scenery's okay," Teo says. "But I'd rather watch the feeds going after Frey's dad. He's gone from war criminal to kidnapper to car thief!"

"Paz doesn't have a real army," I say. "He doesn't care about them. But this is the first time Rafi's been part of anything like a kidnapping. It'll look like he's turning her into a war criminal. That's bad for him at home."

Col glances over at me. "Won't it be bad for her too?"

"In the long run. But at least she knows I'm alive."

Our underbelly brushes the canopy of the jungle, making us all jump. We're trying to stay low and out of sight. Warden cars don't have camo skin.

I wonder if the Shreve army is searching for us. My father knows I'm a danger to him. But does he want his entire military learning his oldest secret?

A groan comes from the backseat.

"Zura!" Teo says. "Good to have you back."

I turn to look. Her head is in her hands, and her beautiful face is pale.

"What happened?"

"Stun cannon," I say. "The car shot you after you took out the wardens."

"I'm sick of cars with brains." She looks out the window at the trees flashing past. "We got away, I see."

"We're not *completely* helpless without you," Col says.

"I guess not, sir." A wan smile crosses Zura's face. "How far are we from the rally point?"

"Eight hours, plus recharging time." Col turns back to face her. "Do you suppose you could, um, take over? I haven't learned how to land yet."

Zura takes a slow breath.

"Lucky I woke up, then."

CRATER

It's early evening when we finally approach the rally point.

We're deep in the south of the continent by now, flying through cloud-wreathed mountaintops. The unpressurized cabin is cold, and Zura gives us pills for altitude sickness.

Col and his brother are in the backseat. I'm up front with Zura, bored and butt-numb from sitting all day.

The clouds part, revealing a huge mountain in our path. Its peak rises another thousand meters over us, flat-topped and girdled with shining snow.

"The White Mountain," Zura says.

Col leans forward. "You never saw a volcano rabbit, Frey. So I got you a volcano."

"Thanks. It's . . . impressive."

As we approach, the sunset glints across the peak. I've never seen snow this far south. Or a mountain this tall.

The hovercar keeps climbing.

"Wait, are we going *inside* that thing?" I ask.

"Into the caldera, yes," Col says. "It's too high for recon drones to fly. We can use the codebook without getting traced—the sides of the crater will dampen the signal spill. And there's a whole glacier full of fresh water!"

"It's super cold and hard to get to." Teo snorts. "Face it. You just wanted a secret base inside a volcano."

"Since I was a littlie," Col says. "But it's warm in the caldera, and half a klick across. We could fit a hundred hovercars inside!"

"Hopefully that's what we'll find," Zura says.

Col reaches forward and takes my hand. His gaze is sharp with excitement.

Then I see the mist rising up out of the caldera, like a pot of water about to boil.

"Wait. It's *hot* in there? This volcano's dead, right?"

"Not extinct," Col says. "But it hasn't blown in ninety years."

"Well, that makes me feel better."

We crest the lip of the caldera, and a huge crater opens up below us. Roiling steam hides everything inside. The inner cliffs are bare stone, too warm for snow to stick.

The rising air hits us as we descend, and the car shudders a little. I can see signs of an encampment through the mist— hovercars, tents, solar panels on a high shelf of rock. Soldiers scurry into position at our approach.

Col really has an army.

Seeing those faces gazing up at us, fingers seem to close around my chest. Soon everyone in that army will know my secret.

It recalls an old nightmare of mine—walking out onstage to give a speech for Rafi, certain that the whole audience will see through me.

"Frey," Zura says gently. "You might want to wear that."

She gestures down at the compartment in front of my seat. It's full of warden stuff—wrist ties, safety flares, a medkit . . . and a breather mask for fire rescues. Just big enough to cover my mouth and chin, so Col's army won't be gawking at me from the moment we land.

"Thanks."

She shrugs. "I don't want to get shot for driving around a kidnapper."

That's right—my encounter with the Paz wardens has probably been on the feeds all day. The world thinks that Rafi kidnapped the Palafoxes' second son.

Fantastic.

I set my sneak suit to Victorian livery, just so it's clear whose side I'm on.

In the turbulent winds of the caldera, the landing is tricky, our skids scraping the stone. Mist boils around our lifting fans, and I can feel the heat of the volcano even here inside the car.

But that's not why I'm sweating.

A squad of soldiers in Victorian uniforms approaches, rifles leveled. They look more confused than hostile—maybe because we're in a warden car from a city two thousand klicks away.

But when Col emerges from the back door, they break into cheers.

"Sir!" A soldier steps forward, saluting sharply. He looks barely older than Col. "Good to see you!"

"You too." Col claps him on the shoulder.

The shouts of astonishment redouble as Teo steps from the car.

While they're distracted, I swing down onto the stone, my face covered by the mask. More soldiers are gathering around us, maybe thirty altogether.

A few give me curious looks, but most of them are crowding around the brothers Palafox.

Then one of the soldiers looks straight at me.

"You're her, aren't you?" she asks.

"Um . . ." It's hard to answer, when half the time I don't know who I am. "Depends?"

She nods slowly. "Secret ops, I get it. But just so you know, there've been rumors since I got here. About one of our units. They responded to an emergency beacon, first day of the war."

I frown. "A beacon?"

"Turned out to be a crashed Shreve scout car. Weird thing was, there were two troopers tied up outside."

"I heard this one too," says another soldier, crowding closer to me. "Hostiles were incoming, so they had to run. But they grabbed the tied-up soldiers for transport to a neutral city. That's when it got brain-missing. The whole way there, these two prisoners wouldn't shut up about who knocked out their car. Someone with a knife, who looked just like . . . well, kind of like *you*, ma'am."

"And that story from Paz today," the first soldier says. "Teo getting kidnapped by a certain first daughter. But here he is, safe and sound, with you."

She smiles at me, takes my hand, and pumps it once. "So whatever it is you do, thanks for doing it."

The other soldier winks. "Making that bubblehead look like a kidnapper? Legendary!"

Others have overheard them, and the crowd is turning its attention to me. I see Col watching.

Waiting for me to say something.

This is my chance to get it over with. I grab the seal of the mask and tear it off, all at once.

The soldiers' eyes light up, and one lets out a low whistle.

"Spitting image," he says.

Others are gathering around me now, and I hear the story repeated—the scout car, Teo, my sister. This small army has been here most of the day, with nothing to do but swap war stories. By now they've all heard versions of this outlandish tale.

Col hoists himself up on the warden car's landing skid.

He waves for silence.

"Everyone! Just so you know, this is Frey. She might look like one of them, but she's on our side. She saved my life!"

All those eyes turn to me, and for a moment it's like stepping into blinding sun. I'm certain they can see all my secrets, everything I've ever thought or felt.

Of course, these soldiers have no idea what I really am. They must think I'm some kind of spy surged to look like Rafi. They're all in need of a good story about their side winning, and that's what I mean to them.

Then the strangest thing happens—they start clapping.

I've had a lifetime of applause. People clapping for my father when I stand dutifully next to him onstage. For Rafi when I deliver her speeches in front of crowds of randoms.

But this is for me, Frey.

Suddenly dozens of people know my name. And somehow all that attention isn't a pulse knife shredding me to mist.

I stand there, real and solid.

Seen.

There must have been a part of me that was always hungry for this. Because now I want everyone to know my name, my story. At last I'm not afraid they'll all disappear tomorrow for knowing too much.

Because they're an army, not one unlucky tutor.

Col steps down from the landing skid. He pulls me into a hug.

"Thanks for the introduction," I whisper.

"Didn't want anyone starting trouble." He pulls back, shrugs. "And they need a hero right now."

That word sends a mad giggle through me. Just being able to say my own name is enough.

"Flattery. You're going to be a good leader, Col."

"I have to be." His smile stays firm on his face. "Just talked to the ranking officer here. Three troopships, two scout cars, and six light attack craft."

I stare at him. "That's everything?"

He nods. "Eleven surviving hovercars. Counting you, me, and my little brother, the Victorian army is sixty-seven people."

HIGH COMMAND

"The good news is, we have a glacier," Dr. Leyva says. "My math: It contains enough water to last us three million years."

A grim laugh travels around the table.

The Victorian High Command is meeting in a warm, steamy tent the size of my sister's dressing room. Our table is made from a jump deck borrowed from one of the troopships. It's big enough for the seven of us, but we've got nothing to put on it except an airscreen projector and a coffeemaker.

Col and I have been here at the White Mountain for two days, and we're still trying to figure out how to fight my father with next to no army.

"Food is another matter," Leyva says. "We have six days' worth, if we ration. Which *some* of us would prefer not to do."

He gestures to his own belly, and smiles go around the table.

Everyone here adores Dr. Leyva. He was a top scientist in Victoria, and the host of a science-and-cooking feed that the whole city followed. He wasn't in the military, but in the chaotic hours after the war began, he grabbed his medkit, flagged down a Victorian unit, and came here ready to serve his city.

Col shares an unhappy glance with his little brother. Teo has been anti-volcano from the start.

"One of the neutral cities will help," Col says. "Six days is long enough to figure out something."

"Also long enough for the dust to take hold in our city," Dr. Leyva says. "Our fellow citizens can already see it in the air. That means they're starting to watch what they say, what they read, even what they think. A change is coming over our citizens."

"What can we do to stop it?" Col asks.

Leyva shrugs. "Show me a room and I can clear the dust from it—for an hour or so. But once it's in the air, it replicates itself. It comes back, like mold."

"We can't defend every breath of air in Victoria," Zura says. "We're a guerrilla force—we have to *attack*. Disrupt Shreve's power grid. Hit their factories. Make the war so painful that it's not worth occupying us."

Zura is at this meeting as the commander of the House Guard. Because all the other Guard officers are dead, captured, or missing. She's been in a grim mood since her promotion.

But she's wrong about my father.

"Shreve doesn't use much power," Dr. Leyva says. "Their buildings don't hover. And their factories are deep underground— even a plasma gun can't get through five hundred meters of dirt."

"We'll hit their transport, then," Zura says.

"Their trade's already embargoed, and their citizens can't travel without permits." Dr. Leyva leans back, smiling to himself. "It's almost as if Shreve was expecting to fight this kind of war."

"Is there *anything* we can do to hurt them?" Zura asks.

More suggestions come, and I glance at Col. He gives me an encouraging nod. But it's hard, speaking up in front of people who know my real name. Part of me always has to pretend that I'm giving a speech for Rafi.

Finally there's a lull in the conversation.

"Sabotage won't work," I say. "No amount of pain will make my father walk away from a conquest."

The table is silent for a moment. Hearing the words *my father* from my lips still makes them uneasy. In all of Victoria's ragtag army, only the people in this room know what I really am.

"What about the citizens of Shreve?" Major Sarcos asks me. "Don't they have a breaking point?"

"Of course," I say. "But if they're broken, how do they stand up against my father?"

Sarcos doesn't answer the question. He's the highest-ranking officer to make it here to the White Mountain. But he seems too cautious and uncertain to command an army.

"We can't hurt him by force alone," I say.

"Exactly," comes a voice from the end of the table, and my spine contracts a little.

It's Artura Vigil, the head of the Palafoxes' psych warfare team. She's the one who recommended taking me as a hostage, who analyzed me and Rafi from afar, who scanned me while I slept.

She's like a grown-up version of Srin.

"We have to cut his support off at the root," she says. "Prove to his people that he's a monster."

"They know that already!" Teo cries. "He killed my mother, our grandmother. Everyone thinks he raised his own daughter to be a kidnapper—and they don't care!"

"They care about Rafia," I say.

The table goes quiet. I have their attention again.

But then Vigil starts talking. "That means they'll care about you too, Frey. So we tell your story. Show the scans of your body. Let you explain what it was like, watching your sister—"

"We've been over this," Col interrupts. "Reputational damage doesn't win wars."

Vigil just stares at him, uncomprehending.

"We can only make this revelation once," I say. "And what if it doesn't work? What if the whole world hears my tragic story, and the next day my father's still in charge?"

No one has an answer to that.

This was all much simpler when all I wanted was to hurt

him. To make him see me for once. To know that I existed beyond his schemes.

But hurting my father isn't enough anymore. We have a city to save.

I have to destroy him.

"Well, you all know what I think," Zura says.

Col nods, to show he's not ignoring her, but he doesn't reply.

Zura wants to kill my father.

The problem is, he hasn't appeared in public since the start of the war. His house, already a fortress, is now protected by the elite of the Shreve military.

We could raze it to the ground, I suppose. Get close enough to hit it with a hundred plasma guns at once.

But my sister lives there too.

If only there was a way to separate them.

"Rafi's the key to this," I say. "She can change things."

Teo sighs. "But she's not in charge."

"Not yet." This idea has been growing clearer in my brain since we arrived at the White Mountain. "But she's always been more popular than my father. If Shreve had a choice, they'd pick *her*. That's different than asking them to surrender to Victoria."

Dr. Leyva laughs darkly. "Alas, Shreve isn't holding an election anytime soon."

"Not an election." It takes me a few seconds to say the rest. "A coup."

A scout car takes off outside, heading off to do some

recon. The sides of the tent flutter, and for a moment it's too loud to talk.

But it gives my words time to sink in—I'm suggesting a revolt against my own father. An end to his rule forever. The others look confused, but for me it's like a storm is clearing in my head.

This is the only way to really win. To be safe at last.

To fix my sister.

When the sound of the takeoff fades, I go on.

"Rafi hates my father as much as any of you. Since he shot a missile at me, even more."

"You said that in the limo," Teo says. "But does that mean she wants to replace him?"

I hear the promise Rafi made the night before I left.

When I'm in charge, I'll tell the whole city about you.

Back then, I thought she was talking about him dying of old age. But Rafi's virtues have never included patience.

"Even before this war began," I say, "she was making plans to take power."

"Wanting to overthrow him is one thing," Zura says. "But making it happen is another."

I remember the day of the assassination attempt. When Rafi wanted to keep her scar, and Dr. Orteg went quiet. Because if she played up her injury too much, her popularity might exceed our father's in a way that was . . . dangerous.

"Trust me," I say. "This is what he's always feared."

Zura shakes her head. "He has the best army in the world. Why should he be afraid of a sixteen-year-old girl?"

"He's afraid of everything," I tell them. "That's why he made me."

None of them knows how to answer that. But for me this is all becoming clearer, down to the right quote from the warrior Sun Tzu.

" 'When the enemy tries to rest, make them toil. When they want to eat, starve them. When they're settled, make them move,' " I recite. "We'll bleed his army in battle, and make sure the embargo keeps Shreve hungry. And when they're really starting to hurt, Rafi will promise to make it all stop. Our father's army will never surrender to Victoria, but they might give control to *her*."

Everyone looks at me, not quite believing that my sister can pull this off.

It's Artura Vigil who speaks up. "But Rafia hasn't appeared in public since the day the war started. There's no chance of getting her away from your father. She can't declare a coup against him from inside his own house!"

That's when I see it—

"She doesn't have to declare the revolt herself." I give them all my best Rafi smile. "That's what I was born to do."

PART III

COUP D'ETAT

It is twice the pleasure to deceive the deceiver.

—Jean de La Fontaine

SABOTAGE

Three weeks later, a power station splays out below us, a million tiny reflectors mirroring the night sky.

Zura and I are crawling back to the rest of our team, carrying a stolen solar panel. It's bigger, more rugged than the ones in Teo, the size and weight of a combat boot. Like everything in Shreve, it's designed to resist an attack. When I grabbed the panel, it rolled into its ceramic shell, hardy enough to survive a bomb blast.

Luckily, bombing this power station isn't our plan.

Col and Dr. Leyva are waiting for us in the dark, invisible in their own sneak suits.

"This looks easy enough," Leyva says, taking the solar panel from me.

He pulls a cutting tool from his kit and starts to work,

dismantling the panel. He connects it to his handscreen, which comes alight with schematics and code.

"I was right—these things pass system updates to each other, like rumors." Leyva smiles as he taps away.

"How long will this take?" Col asks. He's staring at the city.

Shreve sits on the horizon, its dark skyline dotted with hover-craft on patrol. Only twenty kilometers away, I can make out my father's tower at the city's edge. It rises high above the forest, a corona of guardian hovercraft glinting in the moonlight overhead.

The sight of it makes me twitchy, like a snake in the corner of my vision.

"A piece of Trojan code is like a good ragout," Dr. Leyva says. "You can't rush it."

Col lowers his field glasses and sighs. "This is why no one ever actually *makes* your recipes, Doctor. They're too complicated."

"Indeed," Leyva says. "They only watched for my good looks and charm."

Zura peels away the face of her sneak suit to glare at him. She wants this mission done quickly. Farther up the hill, two more Specials await, invisible in their sneak suits.

With the Victorian army so depleted, Col's soldiers have accepted him fighting alongside them. But this mission has taken us closer to my father's city than we've dared go before, and everyone is nervous.

Last night on our way here, our hovercar was hit with a spray of fléchettes from a hidden ground unit. It sounded like thunder and hail. No one was hurt, but it was a reminder that war can become deadly with no warning at all.

I move next to Col. "Is this the first time you've seen Shreve?"

He lowers the field glasses, still staring at the city. "Yeah. It's not as evil-looking as I expected. But you can't see spy dust, I guess."

"You can at sunset. It turns the horizon brown and red. Like in the history feeds—the death skies after the last Rusty wars."

A shiver goes through Col. "I wonder if the sunsets in Victoria have changed yet."

"Not yet," I say. "We still have time."

He turns to me. "Is it weird, being this close to home?"

It takes a moment to answer. I was the one who asked for our team to take this mission, a chance to be near Shreve again.

No, not the city—Rafi.

I miss her more every day. And now that I'm close, it only hurts to think how near she is.

My sister still hasn't appeared in public. She should be out visiting the troops, or giving speeches in conquered Victoria. But she hasn't been seen, not even to deny that it was her stealing that warden car in Paz.

That means she's not cooperating with my father. There must be open warfare between the two of them inside that tower.

Col's still waiting for an answer.

"I don't miss Shreve," I tell him. "I hardly ever went out into the city. And it's not like I had any friends."

He takes my hand, looking sorry for me. He had a real home, of course, even if it's blown to pieces now. And he still has a whole city that he loves and that loves him back.

He may have lost his mother, but I was born an orphan.

"I just want my sister," I say.

Once Rafi's safe, my father's city can burn to the ground for all I care.

We've been hitting Shreve hard these last weeks. When they collect metal from the conquered ruins, we attack their freighters. When they try to occupy Victoria, we knock their hovercraft down with plasma guns. This leaves the citizens free to fight the spy dust, clearing it house by house with nanos devised by scientists in neutral cities.

None of this will topple my father, of course. But all of it weakens him for the day when his own daughter declares herself the new leader of Shreve.

My last speech in Rafi's voice.

Leyva utters a soft cry of triumph. "Got it!"

He unplugs his screen from the solar panel, reaches for his tool kit again.

"How long to put it back together?" Col asks. "Or is that also a ragout?"

"More like a boiled egg—anything longer than three minutes is the work of a fool." Dr. Leyva's tools move swiftly as he speaks, their metal whispers blending with the night wind.

Now that we're about to leave, the seconds seem to drag. I just want to be out of here. Away from the sight of that baleful tower.

"Got it." Dr. Leyva sets the solar panel down in the grass. It crawls away, back toward the rest of the colony. "They'll all be infected by sunrise."

Col watches with grim satisfaction.

"Sir," Zaru says. "If you please."

"She means come *on*." I take his arm and pull him up the hill. Our hovercar is parked on the other side. Its damaged camo skin won't hide it once the sun comes up.

We meet the other two Specials on the hilltop. They're carrying plasma guns and have those wary, serious expressions that Victorian soldiers wear whenever Col is on a mission with them.

"Too bad we can't stay and watch," Dr. Leyva says as we descend toward the car. "All those solar panels crawling into Shreve and causing havoc!"

I laugh. "This is war, Doctor. Go for stealth, not spectacle."

"War *is* spectacle."

This hovercar is larger than the one we lost to the jump mines. It carries six, with heavier armor and firepower, larger batteries—only the best for the heir of Victoria. Its underside is peppered with scars from the fléchettes last night. But nothing got through.

I settle in the backseat between Col and Dr. Leyva. The three Specials sit in front.

The doors seal around us, vibrations building as the lifting fans spin up.

Something sounds funny to me.

I glance at Col, who's putting on his seat straps. He pauses, frowning, like he hears it too.

As we lift into the air, the car tips sideways. Zura starts swearing, flipping switches.

Dr. Leyva's weight slides into me, squashing us both against Col. The car is sliding down the hill now, our landing skids scraping against grass and rock.

We're crashing.

GYROSCOPE

The skids catch, and we start to roll.

Suddenly I'm hanging upside down, my straps cutting into my shoulders. Col slides up the wall toward the ceiling—he wasn't strapped in. He hits with a *thump*, arms up just in time to protect his head.

I grab onto him. The car is still rolling, and seconds later we're right-side up, then upside down again. The world wheels around me, and Col and I cling to each other.

My stomach lurches. My hair is in my eyes. A loose water bottle bounces around the cabin, along with Dr. Leyva's tool kit.

We crash down onto our skids again and start sliding, and Col's full weight tumbles down on me. We're wrapped around each other like two terrified littlies.

The car is still sliding down the hillside. The lifting fans are shrieking, Zura yelling as she tries to shut them down.

The car's skids catch on hard rock again, and we roll over once more. This time Col and I are ready, and he stays in my arms.

The fans spin down at last. As their whine fades, the car settles on a patch of level ground.

The only problem is, we're upside down . . .

And twenty kilometers from my father's house.

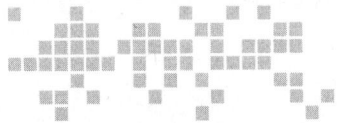

"It was the gyroscope," Zura says.

She and Dr. Leyva are kneeling on the belly of the upended hovercar, staring down into its guts.

The rest of us are on the ground, standing in the gouges left by the sliding car. Col has a medwipe shoved into his bloody nose. My left eye is darkening where his elbow hit, and I have the twitchy-making feeling that I will never leave my father's city behind.

Everyone else is okay. Even the hovercar is mostly undamaged—except for its delicate, crucial sense of balance.

"I missed it last night," Dr. Leyva says. "One of those fléchettes, lodged in the gyro case."

"But we flew level on the way here," Col says.

Leyva nods. "It wasn't a direct hit. But every klick we traveled, the flechette was in there vibrating, nudging the gyro out of whack."

"This is my fault," Zura says. "I knew the controls felt wrong."

"It's just bad luck," Col says, but she doesn't answer. She's still angry with herself for lifting off before the Palafox heir was safely strapped into his seat.

Leyva drops from the hovercar's belly onto the grass. "It's just lucky we're carrying a spare gyroscope. This is the only car in the fleet that has one."

I smile at Col. "It's nice to be the heir."

"We need an ally with a factory," he mutters.

This is our army's real problem—after long weeks in the wild, our ships need maintenance. Our hole in the wall can print clothing and equipment, but not serious military hardware.

This is why the rebels don't use hovercars. The wild is unkind to complicated machines.

"I can switch the new one in," Zura says. "But it'll take a few hours."

"You mean, we'll still be here after dawn," Dr. Leyva says.

Zura nods. "We can't let the sabotage go ahead, or they'll come looking for the people who planted that code. You'll have to save your recipe for another day, Doctor."

Leyva sighs, then picks up his tool kit and handscreen.

"It was too good to be true. Come on, Frey."

Dr. Leyva and I climb back to the other side of the hill, then creep down to the edge of the solar colony.

The sky is already changing color, the stars in the east fading into an inky blue. In the distance, Shreve is lighting up. The factory belt teems with drones and self-driving trucks.

I bring us to a halt thirty meters from the nearest panels.

"Wait here. I'll be back with one in a minute."

"It's too late," he says.

I stare at him. "What is?"

"It would take hours for new code to spread through the whole colony. Once the sun comes up, my sabotage program is going to activate. Shreve will notice something's wrong, no matter what we do."

I stare at him. "Why didn't you tell Zura that?"

"I didn't want her rushing the repair job, like she rushed our takeoff. I've already been in one hovercar crash today." He takes my shoulder. "And you and I will be more useful here. We have a weapon, when Shreve comes looking for who hijacked their power station."

He gestures out at the countless panels, their reflectors rippling into position as dawn spills across the sky.

I shake my head. "You're going to fight off half the Shreve army with a bunch of solar panels?"

"No, with the most powerful object in the solar system. Might I borrow your plasma gun?"

I sigh and hand the weapon over. "Are you being cryptic for dramatic effect, Doctor?"

"You're clever enough to figure it out." He pulls the hydrogen battery off the rifle's plasma chamber.

I stand there, watching him work.

I should warn Zura what's happening, but we're too close to the city to risk a ping. I could climb back, but I don't want to leave Leyva alone. And maybe he's right—a rushed repair job can only make things worse.

There's nothing to do but wait, and try to figure out what Dr. Leyva is up to.

As the sun rises, the colony of solar panels begins to stir.

Instead of jockeying for light, they're flowing away toward the outskirts of Shreve. Leyva's plan was for them to attack the city's infrastructure—clogging drains, getting in the way of loading drones, covering up the markings in the road that guide cargo trucks.

There was also something about starting fires. That must be what he has in mind now. I'm pretty sure the most powerful object in the solar system is the sun. But I'm not sure why he needs to take my weapon apart.

While Dr. Leyva works, I pace back and forth. My father's tower is too close for me to relax. It's all I can do not to stare at it.

I imagine him inside, plotting his next moves against us. Is he still angry that I've turned against him?

Or, now that I've served my purpose, does he even care?

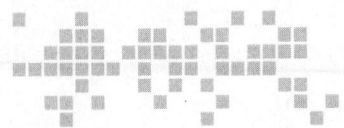

A couple of hours after dawn, someone in Shreve notices the solar colony's strange behavior. A hovercar peels off from the formation over the city and heads toward us.

"Are we ready?" I ask.

"Maybe." Dr. Leyva hands me his improvised contraption. It looks like a demented littlie's science project—the laser torch from his tool kit mated with what's left of my plasma gun. "Have you figured it out yet?"

I look down at the horde of solar panels. They're set to high reflectivity, glittering like mirrors in the sun.

Hundreds of thousands of them.

"Archimedes," I say.

"Ah." The doctor looks impressed with me.

"It's a legend, about an ancient inventor. He burned ships with mirrors, like a pre-Rusty laser. My military tutor taught me that one when I was ten."

When I told Rafi, we spent the day incinerating ants.

I raise my altered plasma gun. "So this is a target indicator?"

"Exactly," Leyva says. "The sabotage code contains a swarming function. Light something up with that, and all the panels will focus on it. But don't fire till you have to. Not sure how many shots you'll get before it all burns out."

I sigh, checking the seals on my sneak suit.

In the sky, the scout ship has come to a halt directly above the colony of panels. It lingers there, drifting back and forth like a survey drone.

The crew probably thinks this is a malfunction, not an attack. Maybe they'll send out a team in a groundcar to investigate. That might buy Zura another hour for her repairs.

The scout car rises up, and for a moment I think it's headed home to Shreve. But then it starts a slow loop around the edges of the solar colony.

Searching.

Motionless in our suits, Leyva and I are invisible. But on the other side of the hill, the hovercar is belly up, its camo skin damaged by flechettes and the crash.

I see the exact moment when the scout spots our car. It drops a little in the sky, taking a closer look. Then the scream of its lifting fans changes in pitch.

It wheels into a tight turn—

—and a ring of plasma streaks up from behind the hill. Two lifting fans vaporized, the scout car spins earthward, out of control.

It crashes against our side of the hill, and begins to roll downward in a gyre of flame.

Headed straight toward us.

SOLAR POWER

Dr. Leyva's staring, transfixed.

"Run!" I grab his arm and pull him out of the scout car's path.

It's hurtling faster as it comes, flinging off hot metal parts. Its remaining lifting fans are still spinning, sending it careening from side to side, a crooked flaming wheel.

Dr. Leyva stumbles, and his tool kit spills.

"Leave it!" I shout.

"Well, obviously." He rises to his feet. "Hold on, Frey. It's going to miss us."

I turn in time to see the wreck thunder past, leaving a dark trail of burned grass behind.

Dr. Leyva looks ecstatic.

"The transcendent spectacle of objects in calamitous motion," he murmurs. "War is such beautiful collisions."

"That *was* pretty bubbly," I say.

The scout car rolls onward until it loses momentum on the flatter ground. It spirals to a stop like a spent coin.

Leyva looks up. "But nothing compared to what comes next."

Half a dozen hovercars are approaching us from Shreve. These aren't scouts—they're armored attack craft, heavier than anything in our fleet.

I let out a whistle. "A bunch of *mirrors* are going to take those down?"

"We'll see." He smiles. "Aim it as you would a gun."

I take another look at the contraption. The laser torch has been fitted with a new lens. I recognize the double-trigger mechanism from the plasma gun, from which the battery and other, more mysterious parts have been borrowed.

When I pull the priming trigger, a familiar whine fills the air. "How many shots?"

Leyva shrugs. "One or two—or maybe zero? Just keep pulling the trigger till it breaks."

I give him a tired look, aim the device at the center of the approaching squadron, and fire.

The laser torch lights up in my hands, hot and buzzing.

A bright spot appears on one of the distant hovercars, a ruby circle of light. My target is moving, and at first it's hard to keep the laser steady.

But as I hold my aim, the car grows brighter and brighter. Thousands of tiny lights join mine, then tens of thousands more, until my target is glowing like the sun.

It doesn't burst into flame—duralloy armor doesn't burn. But its six engines are already spinning a thousand times a second. It doesn't take much for one of them to overheat.

A plume of smoke erupts, then a second, coiling around the hovercar. It banks in the sky, spinning downward like a leaf.

"Wow," I breathe. "This thing really works."

"Solar power," Dr. Leyva says reverently.

I shift the laser to another car in the squadron, and seconds later its engines are smoking too.

The horde of mirrors seems to take on a life of its own. As each car falls, the collective focus shifts to the next brightest in the sky. One by one, the squadron is turned into tumbling motes of smoke and flame.

I release the trigger. Dr. Leyva's contraption is hot in my hands, and a whiff of burned plastic hits my nose. The lens looks darkened in the center.

"Nice work, Doctor. But I think your gun is fried."

"We should probably get back to the ship, then."

We turn and run.

At the top of the hill, Leyva comes to a panting halt. I turn and look back at Shreve.

More hovercraft have formed into attack squadrons. But they aren't hurtling toward us. They've come to a halt at the city's edge, hovering motionless.

"They're afraid," Leyva says, breathless.

Of course. They've seen the panels take down six of their

own, and Shreve is surrounded by solar stations. The crews must think they're all infected.

Until they can figure out what's going on, they're trapped inside the city limits.

I look down the far side of the hill.

Our hovercar is still upside down, but its fans are spinning. Col and the two Specials are waiting a safe distance away. Zura must be at the controls, taking all the risk herself.

Are her repairs really finished? Or is it simply that we have no choice?

The car rises slowly into the air, the engines screaming. It climbs until it's almost level with us, wobbling uncertainly.

"And now the tricky part," Leyva murmurs.

In one motion, two of the four lifting fans roll over in their frames. The car flips to right-side up, then back to upside down, then over again. For a moment it looks like it's going to careen away, end over end—

But it steadies in the air, all four fans pointing downward at last.

I let out an exhausted sigh. "She did it."

"Frey," Leyva says softly. "Your father's house."

I turn back to face the city.

The squadrons that threatened to come at us have pulled back from the edge of the solar colony. Instead of retaking their stations over the city, most of the Shreve fleet is now in a tight ring around my father's tower.

They're guarding him, leaving the rest of the city open to attack.

"Of course," I say. "They think this is just a diversion."

"Not completely incorrect," Dr. Leyva says. "In the long run, we're coming for him. Now we know how he'll react."

I could have told him that. No diversion is big enough for my father to leave himself vulnerable.

Nothing will come easy.

"We should go." Leyva gestures at a last scout car lingering at the city's outskirts.

It's drifting slowly over the infected solar colony, testing the waters, ready to retreat if the mirrors turn on it.

I raise Leyva's contraption. But when I pull the priming trigger, the gun sputters in my hands. The battery is dripping, the last of its hydrogen bound with oxygen in the air, turned to water.

"Bring that along," Leyva says. "If the enemy think it's my usual standard of work, we shall hardly strike terror in their hearts."

"Your secret is safe with me."

We race down the hill.

Zura is landing, and Col is waving for us to hurry.

FLIGHT

As we speed away from Shreve, Dr. Leyva isn't entirely truthful with the others.

". . . and when we couldn't reverse the sabotage code, Frey and I decided to cobble together a weapon."

"Two *hours* without a word from you," Zura grumbles from the pilot seat. "We thought you'd been captured."

Dr. Leyva shrugs. "But think of the results—all it cost us was a plasma gun. Shreve lost six hovercars!"

Col listens, gazing with admiration at the makeshift weapon in my hands. I'll have to tell him later that Leyva's plan was not quite as improvised as he's admitting.

But it got the job done. We're headed back to base. My father's army is bloodied and tentative. And, for the first time, we've brought the fight to the city of Shreve itself.

"Well, you scared them." Col turns to the airscreen in front of him. "There's no pursuit yet."

"Most of the fleet went straight to my father's tower," I say. "He's more concerned with his own safety than catching us."

"They're also guarding Rafia," Dr. Leyva says. "He may have an inkling of our plans for her."

I stare out the window at the forest flashing past. That's still the problem—how do I declare a war against my father with Rafi in his house?

We have to steal her away somehow. Or cut them both off from the feeds so my father can't reveal that I'm an impostor. But as long as she's in his tower, neither option seems likely.

The airscreen lights up.

"Three blips," Col says. "Not from the city—they're right in front of us!"

Zura turns from her controls. "Probably Shreve units coming back from night patrol. They'll be low on juice. Won't be able to chase us for long."

"Right," Col says. "Head for the water, then."

Zura banks us into a sharp turn—southeast, toward the gulf, a long detour on the way back to the White Mountain.

The Shreve hovercars stay on our tail. They aren't fast enough to catch us, but we can't seem to shake them either.

An hour passes. Two. By the time we reach the waters of the gulf, it's almost noon. The high sun sets the ocean sparkling around us.

As I squint in the light, I wonder what it was like for the crews of those doomed hovercars back in Shreve. All those stings of sunlight swarming them, like death from a million bees.

Dr. Leyva's brilliance has a cruel streak.

But maybe I shouldn't judge. I killed someone with a pulse knife when I was fifteen.

We fly farther into the gulf, until there's no land within a hundred klicks. A dangerous place for hovercars with low batteries to follow us.

But the blips on the radar stay in pursuit, like they've got all the juice in the world. Shreve must have hidden recharging bases out in the wild, just like we do.

I lean against Col, trying to get some sleep while I can. But the twitchiness I've felt since seeing the skyline of home lingers in my bones. I can feel those hovercars pursuing us, like fragments of my father's will.

Only the warmth of Col's body keeps me from jumping out of my skin.

"This isn't working," Zura finally says. "If we go any farther out of our way, we won't make it home without stopping to charge."

Col swears. "But we can't lead them back to the White Mountain."

I lean forward in my seat, my muscles coiled tight.

"Then let's fight them."

Zura looks back at me. "It's three to one."

"I didn't say fight *fair*."

"What do you mean?" Col asks.

I look around the cabin. It's full of mission gear—plasma guns, spare sneak suits, body armor, hoverboards, my pulse knife.

A plan starts to form.

"Just get us to an island," I say. "One with mountains, and plenty of cover."

Col's eyes light up. "I know just the place."

AMBUSH

"Five, four, three . . ."

Col and I push ourselves out the hovercar door.

We fall for long, dizzy-making seconds, the board shuddering under our feet in the wind of the drop.

A war cry—more like a scream—leaps from my mouth. My arms are out wide in the warm air, like a tightrope walker's. Col's hands are tight around my waist.

For a moment it feels like we'll fly apart—me, Col, and the board all scattered on the waves below. But the magnetics in our crash bracelets keep us together. And finally the lifting fans spin up, the hoverboard bringing us to a knee-bending halt in midair.

"Whoa," he says in my ear. "This is *not* your safest plan."

I don't answer—while my father is in power, I'll never be safe. We lean sideways and peel away, giving the Specials some room.

They're just overhead, already falling from the car on two hoverboards. Not bothering with midair halts, they execute elegant turns and zoom off toward the island a few kilometers away.

"Show-offs," I say. "Come on."

We lean together, Col's arms still tight around my waist. The board slides down the tropical air currents. The shallow sea below is bright azure, rippled with sunshine and dark stripes of coral beneath the waves.

We're in the Cubans, a string of islands two hundred klicks south of the mainland. The patch of land we've chosen is just a tidal plain with a craggy peak rising at either end.

Col and I head toward the island's highest point. Buffeted by a stiff ocean wind, the board jerks and hitches beneath us. But it's good to stretch my muscles, to feel him pressed against me in the unsettled air.

I try to notice every detail, to hang on to this moment of us alone together over the bright sea—endless, boundless, brief.

We arrive at the summit, step from the board onto a pile of rubble. The peak is crowned with the crumbling remains of an old fort, its view commanding the entire island.

"Looks like someone's had this idea before," Col says, unstrapping the plasma gun from his shoulder.

"Always take the high ground." My sneak suit shifts, taking on the colors of the ancient concrete and its rusted metal skeleton.

I check my plasma gun.

Zura's voice comes in my ear.

Last transmission before they're close enough to hear us—

Everybody in position?

Col taps his ear. "We're ready."

The two Specials answer that they're almost set. I see their board landing a few klicks away, on the island's other peak. A moment later, they've disappeared into the rocks.

Zura's voice comes again.

Don't wait for me to start this.

When you get a shot, take it.

"Will do." Col takes cover beside me. "Be careful, everyone."

Below us, our hovercar is landing on the tidal plain, midway between the two peaks. Its solar panels slowly unfurl, their dark mirrors catching the sun. Exactly like a car that's run out of juice in the worst possible spot.

Our pursuers should pass right between us and the Specials on the other peak.

There's nothing to do now but wait.

Waiting is nervous-making.

"Four plasma guns," I murmur. "And they've got three hovercars. We've only got one shot to spare."

Col raises his field glasses. "Your math is solid."

I look at him. "Shouldn't you be lecturing me on the plant life?"

Col does not disappoint. "Before the seas rose, this whole archipelago was one long island. Mountains, rain forests, swamps—a biological superpower. A paradise."

"Huh." There are more old bunkers strewn below us, their metal skeletons rusting in the sun. "Looks more like a military base than a resort."

Col shrugs. "There was a conflict about economic systems."

"That's Rusties for you," I say.

The birds, at least, are making good use of the bunkers. Feathers and droppings litter the ground. Every cranny is stuffed with the spirals of old nests.

I feel this privacy again, tinged with the hum of an approaching battle.

It makes me want to touch him.

"I miss this, Col. The two of us, alone in the wild."

"Me too. Sorry about my war getting in the way."

I smile, but it's not really a joke. The war that connects us, divides us.

"You've got an army to command, Col. A whole world to convince that Victoria shouldn't be forgotten. That's a lot."

He lowers his field glasses. But he's still looking out over the ocean, not at me.

"Sometimes it's like we're fighting two different wars," he says.

I shrug. "You're trying to save your city. I'm just trying to save my sister. That must seem small to you."

He finally turns to me.

"Frey. Your whole life, you had to hide—private suites, secret compartments, hidden hallways, small spaces. But that doesn't mean *you're* small."

I wrap my arms around myself, wanting to disappear under this open sky. "What am I, then?"

"Angry, unyielding, fierce." He narrows his eyes, like he's looking for the truth of me. "Strange and dangerous."

"Like a pulse knife?"

"I guess. And loyal too. Maybe the best word is *steadfast*."

I look away. "That's a tour guide word."

"Yeah." He shrugs. "How about I make it yours?"

"Okay. Sure."

He drops his hands and bows, like he's asking me to dance. "I swear to you, Frey, I'll never call anyone else steadfast."

As I laugh at this, something crumbles inside me. Something that had turned to stone so gradually, I hadn't even realized.

"That's the nicest promise anyone's ever made me."

A smile breaks on his face.

"I can do better, once we . . ." He turns to the ocean, reaching for his weapon. "Hear that?"

I squint out across the water, switching to heat vision. In the distance, I can make out three bright constellations of lifting fans.

"It's them."

We sink into the rocks. Seal our sneak suits. Hit the priming triggers on our plasma guns.

The pulse of battle builds now. My tension, coiled inside me all day, is strung taut and shimmering.

Col's promise echoes in my ears, and I am steadfast. Ready to fight.

The three hovercars come skimming low across the waves. An iridescent spray plumes from their lifting fans.

They're slowing down. Spreading out, like big cats hunting. Cautious, now that we've stopped running.

Soon they're close enough that I can see their black-and-gray livery, the battle scars on their hulls. One hovers at a crooked angle, its left rear engine flame-blackened and silent.

My finger itches to squeeze the firing trigger.

But the formation glides to a halt, just out of range. I swear softly under my breath, wanting the fight to begin.

One of the three cars rises a little into the air. And something odd happens.

The belly hatch opens, and a long piece of metal is lowered down. At first it looks like an antenna or a signal jammer.

But tied to it is a white flag.

WHITE FLAG

"It's a lie," I say.

Col lowers his aim. "Why would they surrender?"

"They wouldn't. And if they wanted to parley, they'd use radio, not a flag."

I squint through the scope on my gun. The white flag is smudged and threadbare. Like someone's T-shirt pressed into a higher purpose.

It hangs limp in the still air.

"This has to be a trick," I say.

"It's three to one. They don't need to trick us." He reaches for the field glasses. "Or maybe they suspect an ambush?"

I look at our hovercar on the floodplain, its solar panels splayed out, defenseless. The two peaks looming over it with crisscrossing fields of fire.

I shrug. "As ambushes go, it's not what I'd call subtle."

"I'm going to ask Zura." Col reaches for his ear.

I grab his hand. "If we ping her, they'll know we're here. We might as well wave our own white flag!"

"Then what do we do?"

"Wait for them to get closer." I turn back to my rifle, peer through the scope. "Then shoot them."

Col lets out a sigh. In the end, of course, all these decisions are on him. He always feels the weight of keeping his soldiers safe.

But this is where I'm an expert. A false flag of surrender is exactly something my father would do.

A ping comes in my ear—Zura's voice.

Shreve craft. Please state your purpose.

I nod. She's broadcasting on a wide spectrum, so we can hear too.

There's radio silence for a long moment.

Shreve craft, do you read?

Still nothing.

Do you read?

"Maybe their radio's out," Col says.

"All *three* of them?" I shake my head. "This isn't even a particularly good trick. It makes no sense."

"But what if . . ."

Col falls silent—the hovercar with the white flag is easing into motion.

It glides slowly toward the island, headed straight for the tidal plain. Its course will carry it right between us and the Specials on the other peak.

"Well, that makes this easy," I say. "Those pilots are brave, I'll give them that."

"Frey. We can't just . . . *murder* them."

"Col, this is my father—that might be the point! If they trick us, we're dead or captured. If we shoot them, we'll doubt ourselves." I look straight into his eyes. "You can't win. There's *never* a clean victory. Get used to that!"

I turn away. Aim my weapon. The thwarted ecstasy of combat has soured into anger.

"Frey. Look at me."

I don't answer, my eye glued to my scope.

The white flag is fluttering now in the wind of the car's passage. It's not just smudges—someone's deliberately streaked the T-shirt with black.

They're trying to make it *look* improvised.

"That first day of the war," he says, "you didn't let me shoot those soldiers."

My scope lights up—the target is within range now. But I hesitate.

The other two cars are staying back. If I take down this one, they'll open fire on us.

"Col, step on the board and get away from here. I'll handle this." When the two remaining Shreve cars come after me, the Specials on the other peak will have a clean shot.

And Col will be safe.

"This is what your father would do," he says.

"One hit on Zura's car and we're stuck here, Col! What if he knows you were on this mission, and this is all a plan to capture you?"

"Frey, he's not all-knowing."

"If you're a fool, he doesn't have to be. So just—"

My voice chokes off.

The breeze has stiffened, the white flag stretching out to its full length.

It's a T-shirt, all right, but the black marks on it aren't smudges. They're symbols I've seen before—in the ruins.

And words in English . . .

I lower my rifle. "Give me the field glasses."

Col hands them over, and I raise them to my face, thumbing at the focus button.

She's not coming to save us.

I drop the field glasses and tap my ear.

"Everyone, hold your fire."

A sigh rushes out of Col as Zura's voice comes back to me.

State your reasons.

"These aren't Shreve hovercars. They're rebels."

REBELS

We stay hidden on the high ground, watching the black-and-gray hovercar land on the floodplain a hundred meters from our own.

The belly hatch opens, and half a dozen crew spill out.

I was right—instead of uniforms or sneak suits, they're wearing handmade clothes. Fleece jackets, hand-knitted sweaters, shoes made from animal skin. There's no way Shreve soldiers would go to all this trouble just to trick us.

I hand the field glasses back to Col. "You finally got your wish. Looks like we're joining the rebels."

"Or they're joining us," he says.

We ping the two Specials to keep their position, then take the hoverboard down.

Zura and Dr. Leyva are waiting on the wet sand. Most of the

rebels look like young runaways fighting to save the earth—wiry muscles, unsurged faces, threadbare clothes.

One of them looks familiar. From home? From Victoria?

Then it hits me—the last time I saw them, instead of hand-made forest camo they were wearing a feathered blue ball gown.

"Yandre?" Col asks as we step from the board.

"Chico! It's you!"

They embrace, and a torrent of Spanish follows. But when Yandre sees my face, their words break off.

"What the—"

I sigh—life will be easier once the whole world knows. But for now I have to give my little speech again.

"I'm Rafia's twin sister, born twenty-six minutes later. Hidden from birth. Raised as a body double. A decoy."

The rebels all stare at me, dumbfounded.

"And now a 'Fox," Yandre says with a smile, and gives Col a playful punch. "Aren't you the charmer?"

A woman dressed in stitched-together skins comes closer to me, inspecting my face. She's older than the other rebels, with the green armband of a unit boss.

The rebels don't have ranks. Each group elects their own boss, more like pirates than a real army.

"You were the hostage in Victoria, right?" she asks. "You got the 'Foxes to drop their guard—and then switched *sides*?"

I hold her gaze. "That's about right."

"Huh." She turns to Col. "And you're fine with that . . . because she's your *girlfriend* now?"

He looks a little unsteady for a moment. No one in his own forces would dare ask such a question.

But he answers in a firm voice. "Frey saved my life. She's fought beside us—and against her father."

The woman shrugs, turns to me.

"You're sixteen, right? Not a bad age to work out family issues." She turns back to Col. "Well, you 'Foxes might be stuck up, but I've never known you to be stupid. Guess I'll take your word she's on our side."

She waves a hand, and the other two hovercars head in.

"I'm Boss Charles, and we're Carson's Raiders. You 'Foxes got any food?"

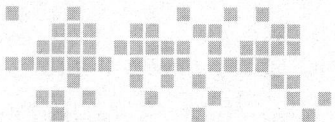

We eat lunch with the Raiders on the beach, in the cool of the ocean breeze and the shade of unfurled solar panels.

There's not much hunting on the island, but Col manages to take down a few birds with his bow while the rebels watch and heckle. We roast those on an open fire and empty all our survival rations to feed our new allies.

Dr. Leyva and Zura are busy gathering information from the Raiders. The rebels have stepped up operations against my father, coming from as far away as Patagon to fight him.

Col sits beside his old friend Yandre, as happy as I've seen him since the war started.

"I should have known it was you, Chico." Yandre's gesture takes in the mountains, the beach, the sky. "Who else is fussy enough to run for four hours, just to find the perfect tropical island for an ambush?"

In our laughter, all the day's anxieties—being so close to my father's house, fighting the Shreve army, almost firing on a white flag—unravel in my chest.

The Palafoxes' bash seems like a thousand years ago, but seeing Yandre again brings back the wonder of that night.

"Since when are you a rebel?" Col asks.

"A confession," Yandre says. "Remember all those stories about my brother? His greenie friends? The playful acts of sabotage?"

Col blinks. "Wait. That was really *you*?"

"I've been a rebel since I was Teo's age." Yandre turns to me. "And just for the record, Frey, I only shoot at people who invade my city. I voted against attacking your convoy."

"Um, thanks?" I say, then shake my head. "It doesn't matter. I was a different person, traveling under a different name."

"Well put."

"But why were you chasing us in Shreve hovercars?" Col asks. "And why the radio silence? We almost shot you!"

Yandre chews slowly, basking in our attention for a moment before sharing the tale.

"Three days ago, we were on patrol in the mountains. We're a light unit—hoverboards and sniper rifles—so we don't usually mess with armored cars. But we stumbled on these three heavy Shreve cars recharging, and it was too good to pass up."

Boss Charles leans into the conversation. "We got the jump on the crews, but the commander managed to run some kind of anti-capture program. The autopilots, radios, codebooks—all of it was smoking when we got inside the cars. Took us a day to get them flying again."

"Okay," I say. "So you didn't have radios. But why were you coming after *us*?"

Yandre looks up at the Shreve cars looming over us.

"We rebels don't fight in tin cans. We can't keep these flying for long—we don't have the parts. But you 'Foxes have a fleet of your own. Now that you're fighting for the planet, we figured you should have them."

"It was Yandre's idea," Boss Charles says. "I voted against it but got out-talked."

Yandre spreads their hands. "My insubordination is matched only by my charm."

"At least we got lunch," the boss grumbles.

I look up at the three machines. They're heavy attack craft, with about as much firepower as the rest of Col's fleet put together.

But they're also hard to maintain. And thanks to that quick-thinking Shreve officer, they're missing most of their software.

"Not sure we can use them either," I say.

"Maybe chop them up for parts?" Col suggests.

I shake my head. "Anything my father builds is incompatible with the rest of the world. So you have to buy your parts from him."

"Told you, 'Dre," Boss Charles says. "Waste of a day. I'm going swimming."

She stands up and walks toward the water, dropping her clothing on the sand along the way.

Half the other rebels spring to their feet and follow her. Soon the beach is covered with handmade clothes, the water full of splashing, naked bodies.

Yandre sighs. "At least I got to see you, Chico."

"It's good to see you too," Col says. "But I'm sure there's something we can do with these ships. Deploy the weapons on the ground, or trade them for something we *can* use."

"Or take a page from my father's book," I say. "Attack Shreve with them, force them to fire on their own ships."

Yandre's eyes light up at that. "Maybe during the peace conference, when he's away."

Col and I both stare at them.

Yandre sees our expressions, and smiles.

"Ah. You mean you haven't heard?"

WAR COUNCIL

A few days later, the rebel delegation lands inside the White Mountain. They seem impressed.

We've got hot showers now—melted glacier water piped along the steaming crater walls—and enough solar panels to recharge a hovercar in just a few hours.

Instead of a tent, we hold the War Council in a real building. It's made from trees and smells like sap and fresh-cut wood. The table is the same recycled jump deck, but someone has burned the Palafox seal into the center.

I'm pretty sure the rebels only care about the showers.

They've sent three bosses—Boss Charles and two others she's fought beside—and Yandre. For us it's me, Col, and Teo at the table, along with Zura, Major Sarcos, Artura Vigil, and Dr. Leyva.

A tight group for keeping secrets.

The first thing Col asks is "How certain are you that this peace conference is real?"

"Our spies in the city governments all say the same thing," Boss Charles says. "Shreve wants to make a deal. But in secret, so they don't look like the pressure's getting to them. The conference location is completely off the grid. A small island in the Pacific. No feeds allowed."

"What's Shreve offering to get the embargo lifted?" Col asks.

"That's also secret."

"Of course," I say. "My father doesn't go into negotiations without a few surprises ready. He'll propose something unexpected, just tempting enough to divide the other cities."

The rebels are watching me closely, still a little perplexed by sitting at parley with their enemy's daughter. Even Yandre gives me a double take every now and then.

I'm starting to wonder if people will always look at me this way, once my secret's out. Maybe pretending to be Rafi was the normal part of my life, and it's all gawking and whispering from here on.

"It doesn't matter what he's offering," Zura says. "If we time our attack right, he'll be out of power before the conference even starts."

Everyone's eyes turn to me again, taking my measure as an impostor.

I'm ready to convince them. I've dressed like Rafi today, in the exact suit she wore for my father's birthday last year. (Or as close as our hole in the wall could come to it, at least.) Yandre did my hair and makeup earlier, and I'm sitting with Rafi's balletic posture. Prim and upright, shoulders back.

Imperious.

"It's time to bring freedom back to Shreve," I say in her voice. "My father's rule must end."

Charles gives a grumbly chuckle, like she always does when I imitate my sister.

Boss X leans forward, his strange eyes slicing through me. He's the most extreme of the rebels, radically surged into a cross between a wolf and a man. He gave up his "human name" when he joined them, and his voice has been surged to a low growl.

"So you're going to conquer him with oratory?"

"Every revolution starts with the right words," I say.

Boss X looks unconvinced. "He's going to make his own speech—threaten them to stay in line, remind them who's in charge. We should cut him off from the feeds."

"We don't have to," I say. "If he speaks up from some island in the middle of the ocean, he'll have to admit he snuck away to bargain for peace."

"And we can't attack the conference," Teo says. "We have allies there."

Boss X shrugs. "Your allies, not ours."

"We don't want to start a larger war," Col says. "We want to end this one."

"But the people in Shreve have breathed dust for ten years,"

Boss Charles says. "They've got no weapons. How do they overthrow an army?"

"They don't have to," I explain. "My father doesn't go anywhere without his favorite officers, his most loyal units. Whatever's left in the city will be easy to sway to our side."

"Even if the revolt isn't total," Col says, "our forces will be there to tip the balance."

He waves a hand, and the airscreen projector sputters to life. A scale model of my home city appears on the table. The stolid skyline, the new defenses and the suborbital pads. The ragtag Victorian fleet appears in the surrounding farm belt.

I stand and point a ringed finger at my father's tower on the outskirts.

"This is our objective—the seat of his power."

Dr. Leyva stands beside me. "From there, we take control of the city feeds to broadcast Frey's speech. We'll also corrupt the dust with a virus. For the first time in a decade, the people of Shreve can say whatever they want about their dear leader. Freedom, all at once!"

The third boss starts to shake his head. He's the oldest of them, with an unsurged face and static tattoos. He has an accent I've never heard before. And a strange name—Andrew Simpson Smith.

According to Yandre, he once fought alongside Tally Youngblood herself.

"I have seen that tower," he says. "Many drones protect it."

"You're right," I say. "It's the best defended spot in the whole city. We'll have to take it by stealth, not force."

A low growl comes from Boss X. "So you're sneaking in? I was promised a stand-up fight."

"A fight is what you'll get." I fix his yellow, lupine eyes with my best Rafi stare. "We'll launch a full-on assault on the city. And once the sky is full of damaged Shreve hovercraft in retreat, my team will slip in alongside them."

With a wave of my hand, the cityscape is replaced with an image of one of our captured hovercars. Zura has skinned it to match the Shreve Home Guard. She's also added some bogus battle scars and smoke bombs on two of the engines.

"This is our Trojan horse—a damaged Shreve car fleeing from the front line. We'll crash-land near the tower, fight our way through any household guards, and grab my sister. Then we take control of the feeds, and I declare a new era for the city."

Yandre speaks up. "What if Rafia's with your father?"

I draw a slow breath, trying not to show any emotion.

"She won't be."

Yandre looks sympathetic, but says, "You can't know that, Frey."

"It won't matter," Col cuts in. "We'll have his tower, his dust, and our own Rafia, ready to make the speech that the people of Shreve have always wanted her to make. All he'll have is a reluctant daughter."

The three rebel bosses look at me.

"Reluctant?" Charles asks.

"My sister despises him." There's certainty in my voice again. "Even if he puts her on the feeds to show that I'm not real, I'll be the more convincing Rafia."

They look like they believe me, but then Artura Vigil speaks up.

"It seems like a gamble, putting everything we've got into one battle." She looks at Major Sarcos. "Isn't that the riskiest thing a guerrilla army can do?"

Sarcos looks uncomfortable. He's never liked the idea of shifting from sabotage to all-out battle.

Vigil turns to me. "And isn't this exactly the sort of dangerous venture your father would *want* us to try, Rafia?"

I give her a cold glare. "My name is Frey."

"So you keep telling us. And yet your plan seems designed to deliver us straight to your father."

Col sits up straighter. "What are you saying, Artura?"

"She tells us there's a real Rafia back in Shreve. But we've only seen that girl for a few moments on a balcony, waving and smiling. That other girl has given no interviews, no speeches on the feeds—as if she's trying to hide something." Artura's eyes sweep the room. "While here in front of us sits a much more convincing Rafia, telling us to send our army into danger. What if this whole story about twins is a lie?"

The world turns inside out for a moment. What if I'm the real Rafi, and the girl back in Shreve is the impostor?

I grip the edge of the table, reminding myself that I'm real.

Col places a hand on mine. "This is absurd. There's no way anyone could've planned all this from the beginning."

"She is no doubt improvising," Vigil says. "But Rafia's already admitted coming to Victoria to make us lower our guard. Why shouldn't she play the same trick twice, if we're foolish enough to fall for it?"

They're all looking at me, but I don't know what to say. I've spent my whole life convincing people that I *am* Rafi. How am I supposed to do the opposite?

Maybe dressing up like my sister today was a bad idea.

"Her name is Frey," Col says softly, and the world settles a little around me. "And we know she's on our side. She could've captured me on the way here!"

"Me too," Teo points out.

Vigil only smiles, her cool expression reminding me a little of Srin.

"Even with you two captured, there'd still be an army, Col."

"No, there wouldn't," I argue. "I could've told my father where this base is. He'd be here already!"

Vigil's smile doesn't fade. "Isn't it easier if we come to him? And better for his reputation he wins this war defending his own city instead of hunting down strays?"

"Frey is exactly who she says she is!" Col shouts. "I'm certain of it. That's the last we'll hear of this ridiculous *theory*."

Vigil bows her head, and the table falls silent.

But that glimmer of distrust stays on all their faces. It's an unlikely story that Vigil is telling, but no stranger than the truth of me.

I was born a lie. Why should any of them believe me now?

I want to speak for myself, to keep the argument going in spite of Col's orders. But the words don't come, because part of me is never really certain who I am.

It's Boss Charles who breaks the silence, letting out a huge laugh.

"What a mess!" She claps me on the shoulder. "Maybe you're Rafia, maybe you're Frey. Maybe your little coup works, maybe it fails. But my Raiders are in either way. It'll be the most chaos we've seen since Tally Youngblood disappeared!"

"She's not coming to save us," Boss Andrew says reverently. "Which is why we have to take chances. My people will join as well."

It's hardly a ringing endorsement, but at least they aren't running away.

We all turn to Boss X.

For a long moment, he doesn't look human at all. The corners of his mouth droop and his ears go back against his head. I don't know what the expression means, but it charges the air in the room.

"My pack will join on one condition," he says. "I'm coming along in your captured hovercar."

"Um, okay." Col gives him a frown. "But I thought you wanted a stand-up fight, not sneaking around."

"There'll be plenty of fighting." A ripple goes across Boss X's fur as he turns to me. "And a little sneaking is worth a visit to your father's house."

"For what purpose?" Col asks.

"It's personal," Boss X says. He leans back and doesn't say another word.

"Rebels," Zura mutters softly.

I give Col the slightest shrug. Boss X's personal business doesn't matter to me. Nor do I care if the rebels are more interested in causing chaos than in trusting me.

All that matters is that we have a plan to save my sister.

GOOD-BYE

As our hoverboards rise above the lip of the crater, the freezing wind sets my blood humming. It's almost sunset, a week after our meeting with the rebels.

At this altitude, the sky is upside down—a layer of red-tinged cloud spreads out beneath our mountaintop, with only cold blue overhead.

It's just me and the brothers Palafox. A last dinner before we leave Teo behind in safety. By this time tomorrow, Col and I will be headed into battle.

"Thank you both," I say. "For trusting me."

Col turns from the sunset. "You're not still worried about Artura, are you? Nobody believes her stupid theory."

I sigh into the cold wind. "She believes it. And I bet she's still whispering in your officers' ears."

"Then she's brain-missing," Teo says. "Srin says that's the

problem with psych warfare. You drive yourself mad along with the enemy."

Col smiles. "Frey and I know all about that. When we met, we were so busy lying to each other, we almost forgot who we were."

"Almost," I say, taking his hand.

A cloud of steam swirls up from the depths of the caldera, setting us wobbling on our boards. We descend to the solid rock of the crater's edge, where the warm volcanic air alternates with the mountain wind.

Teo pulls a few self-heating meals from his pack. He places them in a neat, ceremonious row. This could be our last dinner together here at the White Mountain. It could be Col's and my last dinner ever.

"I've got PadThai, SpagBol, and SwedeBalls," Teo says. "Three timeless classics of camping cuisine."

Col sighs. "Anything without rabbit."

"Same," I say. In the last month, I've seen plenty of volcano rabbits, and eaten most of them.

Teo passes out the meals, and we pull the heating tabs. I cup mine in my hands, grateful for the warmth as it boils the prefab noodles into something edible.

If we win tomorrow, I'll never have to eat camping food again.

And if we lose, it'll be my fault.

Artura Vigil was right about one thing—throwing the whole Victorian army into one battle is a dangerous plan. And now that she's doubted me in front of everyone, they won't ever forget that it was *my* plan.

Their enemy's daughter.

I look up from my food. "You think your soldiers still trust me?"

Teo shrugs. "You heard the rebels—they don't care whose side you're on. They just want to shake things up."

"And my officers will obey orders," Col says.

"Great," I say. "Nothing like comrades-in-arms who have to be *ordered* to trust me."

"Zura trusts you," he says. "That counts for something."

It does, because Zura is coming with me in the stolen hovercar. No other Victorian officer is willing to go on a crash-landing commando mission.

Col himself will stay with the main fleet.

"What if Artura's right about the rest?" I ask. "That it's a terrible plan to begin with?"

"It's the perfect plan," Col says, blowing on his food. "A coup will end the war quickly. And it means freedom not only for Victoria, but for Shreve too."

"But we're risking your whole army, Col."

"Better than risking the soul of my city."

I shake my head, not sure what he means.

"It'll take years to win a guerrilla war," Teo explains. "Long enough for the dust to choke everyone. No one daring to say what they think, or to keep a diary, in case some Shreve warden arrests them for having the wrong opinion."

"Everyone in Victoria has their own feed," Col says, "and tells their own story. That's the soul of our city."

"I grew up breathing spy dust," I say. "And I have a soul."

"Sure," Col says quickly. "I just meant, freedom's easy to lose and hard to get back."

I look away. From the moment I learned to talk, I've had to watch my words, my gestures, the way I stand and walk. I know the value of freedom more intimately than anyone. But I don't have time for philosophical discussions.

Not until my sister is safe.

"You're right," I say. "If we can end this tomorrow, it's worth the risk."

"Which is why you should take *me*," Teo grumbles.

Col just stares into his food. They've had this argument a dozen times in the last week.

"We have to leave someone in charge here, Teo," I say.

"In charge of *what?*" he cries. "You're taking everyone else with you!"

Col turns to his brother, and for a moment I think he's going to be angry.

But his words come softly. "Frey's plan will work, but something might happen to me in the fight. If I have bad luck, we need a Palafox to pull Victoria back together."

I wonder if that's really true. Certainly everyone in this army thinks so, or they wouldn't follow Col's orders just because of his last name. And maybe that's what matters—people believe that the first families bind their cities together, and that belief makes the magic work. At least, I hope so.

Because when Rafi declares war on our father tomorrow, it has to tear Shreve to pieces.

RAIDING PARTY

We take the captured hovercar down a riverbed. Beneath the treetops, out of radar coverage.

Yandre, Boss X, and I are up top, spotting for Zura as she pilots us through tight spots. We crouch behind the rail gun turrets, ducking branches, X's fur rippling in the wind.

There are ten of us in the raiding party—three more of Zura's Specials down below, along with Dr. Leyva and his two best techs. Their job is to take over Shreve's feeds and spy dust, once we have control of my father's tower.

Col's back with the main force, in the largest Victorian ship.

"Why so glum?" Yandre calls to me above the engine noise.

I shrug. "I've never been on a mission without Col before."

"Chica, how sweet."

Boss X is staring at me. "So what are you, exactly?"

I give him a confused look.

"He means, are you a 'Fox or a rebel?" Yandre says. "I've been wondering that myself."

"A Palafox?" I stare at them both. "Are you asking if Col and I got *married*?"

Yandre lets out a long laugh. "Frey, we know you like Col, but that's different from being a 'Fox. That army back there, they *need* a first family. It makes them feel complete, having someone in charge."

I remember how Aribella made me feel that first day. Like she deserved to command a whole city.

But I shake my head. "I'm not in Col's army. I'm not even a Victorian."

"*I'm* a Victorian," Yandre says. "It's my city too. But I'm not a 'Fox. You get it?"

"Sure—you're a rebel. That's bigger than any city."

"Exactly. I'm against anyone who messes with my planet." Yandre waves their hand at the sky, the river, the forest. "*This* is what we rebels are fighting for. So what about you?"

Both of them are watching me now, but I don't know how to answer.

Last night, Col was talking about saving our two cities. But cities don't mean anything to me. My whole life has been spent as a prisoner of my father's schemes, or running from him. Those are the only two realities I understand.

Before I can answer, the hovercar eases to a halt. The banks of the river are tightening, the trees bowing in to scrape our armor.

For the next few minutes, we talk Zura through the squeeze, meter by painstaking meter, pushing aside branches as we go. It's slow going, but we're too close to Shreve to rise above the treetops.

Finally the river widens, and the car can fly freely again.

It's Boss X who gets back to the conversation.

"Ask yourself a simple question," he says. "Who do you fight for? Col Palafox?"

I find myself shaking my head.

Boss X lets out a grumbly laugh. "Don't feel bad if it's true. When I first joined up, it was for a boy. Took me a while to see anything bigger."

"No. I'm fighting *beside* Col—not *for* him." I shrug. "We're allies. And I've never even thought about the whole planet."

Yandre shrugs. "Not everyone's a rebel."

"The truth is, I'm fighting for Rafia," I say. "I was only supposed to be an extension of her, but she saw me as a real person. That's why I exist."

I look away at the lifting fans, wreathed in spray from the river. The sunlight turns to arcs of color in that mist.

"And I'm also fighting *against* my father. There's something wrong with him, worse than his strip mines and his spy dust. Even if we all lived back in the old days, before humans had the power to wreck the planet, I'd still fight him."

Boss X makes a sound between a growl and a laugh. "Nothing

wrong with making it personal. What matters, Frey, is that you fight beside us—up here."

It takes me a moment to understand. The 'Foxes are all down inside the car. The three of us are up in the cold wind, getting whacked by tree branches.

Maybe that makes me an honorary rebel.

"I'm glad you trust me," I say.

"I like a girl who carries a knife," X says. "Blades make it personal. Muscle and metal, point and edge."

"It's higher-tech than it looks," I admit.

His yellow eyes narrow. "Too bad. A knife should be simple."

For a moment, I consider asking him what his personal business is in my father's house. But then the hovercar glides to a halt again.

The riverbanks aren't the issue this time. We're within sight of the valley where Col plans to lure the Shreve army into battle tonight.

This is our hiding spot.

Soon Zura's voice crackles in our ears.

Setting down in thirty seconds. Hold on to something.

And if you rebels don't object to hurting trees, we could use a little camouflage.

BATTLE

We spend the afternoon hidden there, moving our solar panels out of the shifting shadows, getting back to full charge before night comes.

The rest of the Victorian army, along with our rebel allies, will come in high and hard when the sun goes down. We want the added cover of darkness, and for the citizens of Shreve to be home from work and watching the feeds when I declare my coup d'etat.

The waiting gives me time to miss Col.

When his officers didn't let him join the tower raid, it was fine with me. I'd rather have just Rafi to worry about keeping safe tonight.

But I'd somehow forgotten—since my father attacked House Palafox, Col and I haven't been apart for longer than a few hours. It seems like years since then, a lifetime of running and fighting.

If this war ends tonight, what do he and I have left?

"We need to do your face," Yandre says as the sun goes down.

We both smile at the absurdity of this. But Rafi would never go on the feeds looking windblown and disheveled, especially not to declare herself the new leader of Shreve.

Adorning my hands are three rings made of recycled iron, my father's chosen symbol of wealth. My sneak suit has a stored image of Rafi's favorite dress from the waist up.

My hair will have to wait until after the battle. But we do my makeup atop the stolen hovercar in the dimming light, Yandre working with skilled hands to make me look my part.

The imperious first daughter of Shreve.

The battle starts on schedule.

The hoverboards come in first—rebels attacking cargo trucks and greenhouses on the outskirts of Shreve. Like any one of a dozen nuisance raids they've mounted these last weeks.

But this time when my father's light, nimble hovercars respond, the rebels don't scatter and retreat. They open up with Victorian plasma guns, sending a dozen burning wrecks to the ground.

A low growl comes from Boss X as we watch the fight. His fur is twitching, his hands flexing with a wolfish need to join.

"Soon," I say.

Slowly, like a giant waking up, the Shreve military responds.

Two squadrons of heavy attack craft rise over the city. Their massive searchlights wink on, and a blue-tinged daylight spills across the valley.

But instead of venturing out to take on the rebels, they open fire from a distance, safe from the plasma guns. A barrage of steel flechettes glitters across the valley, like sleet in the searchlights.

I wince, seeing distant figures falling from their boards.

"At least we know he's not home," Boss X murmurs, gazing at the edge of the city.

I raise my field glasses. No extra squadrons have moved to protect my father's tower.

Victorian hovercars come forward, and the rebels shelter under their armor. The Shreve response looks sluggish to me— as if they're pinging my father for guidance—but soon they take the bait.

The heavy craft move out to engage the Victorian fleet.

"Get ready," Zura says.

We clear the branches from the topside, stow our gear below, strap in for a crash landing. Beside me, Boss X looks uneasy, staring at his seat restraints like they're strangling him.

We wait, blind to the battle raging overhead—

Until a coded ping comes from our high command.

"Hold on," Zura says as the lifting fans spin up.

We fly low and hard toward my father's tower, our car tipped at a crooked, wounded angle. The metal deck shudders under my feet as our belly armor cracks against treetops. We slew randomly from side to side.

"Do we have to fly *this* badly?" Dr. Leyva asks Zura.

"Afraid so," she says, her hands tight on the flight stick. "The smoke pots malfunctioned. We don't look like we're on fire."

Boss X gives me a sidelong look. He points at his belt, studded with a selection of grenades and a spare pair of crash bracelets. "Topside?"

I'm already unstrapping myself from the seat.

I take the offered crash bracelets and slam them on my wrists. A smoke grenade goes into my pocket.

"Frey," Zura says. "Sit down."

I ignore her. Boss X is already climbing the ladder to the top-side hatch.

"I'm *ordering* you to sit down and strap in," she says.

"I'm not in your army."

Dr. Leyva speaks up. "If you get yourself killed, Frey, this has all been pointless."

"Same if we get shot down! We have to look like the real thing, or my father's house defenses will—"

Boss X opens the hatch above us, and a screaming wind whips my words away. I grab a rung of the ladder and pull myself up into the booming, floodlit night.

I am steadfast.

CRASH LANDING

The wind is a cold gale across the topside.

I twist my crash bracelets on, and their magnetics pull me down. They drag like lead weights on my wrists, clanking against the metal hull as I pull myself toward the right rear engine.

Boss X is making his way forward, his eyes squinting against the wind, his fur pushed flat.

Around us, the night sky flashes and burns—explosions, searchlights, damaged hovercars. A stray fléchette glances off the armor to my right, leaving a dent the size of a fist.

The deck tips and shudders beneath me, Zura flying like a drunk woman.

We skim a stand of tall trees, and our lifting fans hack their tops into wood chips and eye-stinging pine scent.

When I can see again, Shreve sits in the distance. My father's tower is alight, its usual complement of drones swirling around its summit. Most are armed, but some will have sensors, radar, scanners.

This battle damage has to look real.

I haul myself the last few meters. The engine roar grows louder, the hull vibrating, the fan sucking the air down into its blades like a hurricane.

Trying to pull me in . . .

I'm close enough. I pull the smoke grenade out and realize there's nothing to attach it with.

Except my crash bracelets.

I pull one off, twist it to the highest setting. It clings to the vibrating engine casing, and the metal grenade clings to it in turn, immovable when I try to pry them loose.

I pull the pin and crawl back a few meters, counting under my breath.

The grenade flashes, its smoke pouring down into the lifting fan, then outward behind us in a spreading trail.

I turn to Boss X. The front right engine is already spilling smoke, and he's hauled himself to the rear of the car.

He rises into a crouch, unsteady in the wind.

"Ready to jump?" he calls.

"Jump?"

I stare wide-eyed at my father's tower, looming ever closer.

Zura is slowing us, readying to take the car skidding into the dirt. There isn't time to get back inside and strap in.

All we have is our crash bracelets—in fact, I've only got one.

Boss X is wearing both his. The belt is gone from his waist, wrapped around the grenade, I guess.

Then I remember the first time Naya let me take my pulse knife out of the training area.

I showed off for Rafi, making the knife fly around our bedroom. She asked if it was strong enough to pick me up.

Clinging with all the strength in my young hands, I let its magnetic lifters pull me to the ceiling of our bedroom while my sister laughed and threw pillows.

A pulse knife can carry me.

Of course, I probably weighed less then.

I crawl to the rear of the hovercar, find a spot next to Boss X, and look down at the trees whipping past below.

We're still flying very fast.

I pull my hood up over my head and face, switch the suit to light armor mode. It turns black, the nanos stiffening to hardened scales.

Smoke wreathes around us, and sounds of battle shake the air. At the edge of my father's estate, the treetops shooting past below turn to a blur of grass. The lifting fans switch over to silent magnetics.

"On three," X growls, his lips pulled back from his teeth in a beatific smile. "One, two . . ."

We jump straight up, caught in the wind, the car zooming away ahead.

Below us, my father's perfectly manicured gardens are a riot of color in the floodlights. For a moment I'm in free fall, both hands wrapped around my buzzing knife . . .

Then my left wrist snaps taut, the bracelet trying to slow me down. The knife roars to life, and it feels like my shoulders are being yanked from their sockets. My iron-ringed fingers twist painfully in the magnetic fields.

I fall, hit a row of hedges slantways, scraping across the tops of leaves and branches. The stiffened sneak suit is tougher than bare skin, but it still feels like being dragged across thorns and brambles.

The hedges bring me to a gradual, thrashing halt. It takes a painful moment to pull myself from the ruined plants.

Fifty meters farther on, Boss X is standing up, gingerly rubbing his wrists.

He's watching our Shreve hovercar.

It crashes just as planned.

The smoking right-side fans tip down into the gardens, sending up a spray of flowers and dirt. The car tries to slew sideways, but Zura holds it steady. The drag slows it until the fans snap off and career away across the gardens, still smoking.

The car goes into a spin, out of control now. But its magnetics keep it a few meters above the ground, a swirl of smoke and sparks.

Finally it rear-ends into the base of the tower, tearing out a gaping chunk of the cargo bay wall.

As the hatches pop open and Specials spill out, Boss X and I are already running toward the gap.

HOME INVASION

This late, the loading bay is empty of workers. The cargo trucks and lifting drones sit silent, red in the running lights of our crashed hovercar.

The entries to the rest of the house are secured. But Rafi and I have played hide-and-seek a hundred times here—I know what's behind every door.

"This way!" My pulse knife roars to life, flies at the largest roller door. With a shriek of tearing metal, a jagged hole opens up.

We leap through, run across the carpeted lobby floor, and into the largest room in my father's house. The ballroom, full of bare tables and an empty stage.

This is where I saved my sister's life a year ago. When not in use, it's where the house security drones go to recharge.

We catch them sleeping, not expecting attackers pouring from a fallen Shreve ship. The drones try to sputter to life, their weapons crash-charging like the hum of bees. But the Specials' barrage guns open fire, cutting them to pieces.

Boss X extends his pulse lance—like my knife, but two meters long—and chops the supports out from under the balcony. It crashes down onto a dozen waking drones.

I pull the barrage gun from my belt and let my own fire spill wild, hitting the tables, the lights, the ornate ceiling. Some simple, angry part of me thrills to be laying waste to my childhood home.

In seconds, the wreckage of fifty drones litters the ballroom floor. Another twenty or so will be on station throughout the house. Sirens are ringing now.

I start for the stairs, but then I see him—Boss X, up on the stage.

Yandre takes my shoulder. "Five seconds."

X slashes at the stage with his pulse lance. Sparks and sawdust fly, then he kneels and pulls free a jagged triangle of wood. He brings it to his lips.

"The man X joined the rebels for," Yandre says. "He died here."

My mind can't grasp this.

"It wasn't an authorized mission," Yandre says. "And he wasn't trying to kill your sister."

I manage to nod. "My father was meant to give that speech."

I don't tell them the rest. That I made the kill that day—and that it was the best day of my life.

Boss X leaps down from the stage, the token piece of wood clutched in his hand.

We charge up the emergency stairway, up toward the control room, toward my sister. Dr. Leyva and his techs take the lead now, spraying anti-dust nanos and scanning for traps.

Boss X is behind us, sweeping his pulse lance across the landing below. It sends rubble crashing down on anyone who might be following. But it means there's no way back now.

I glance at Yandre.

They shrug. "It's a wolf thing. No retreats."

But it's more than that. This is as personal to Boss X as it is to me.

I bring the party to a halt on the stairwell, ten floors up. Just outside the control room and the medical center, and below my old bedroom.

"There'll be drones on this floor," I say. "Or soldiers."

The Specials push me out of the way, set blast caps on the stairway door.

The roar of the explosion echoes down the stairs.

We charge out the gaping hole. Metal shards of the door are everywhere—

But the med center is empty.

Nothing but shiny furniture and equipment, and that giant picture window showing the battle outside in all its glory. Missiles crisscrossing the night, rings of plasma aflame, hovercars veering, burning, falling. Rebel antiaircraft spider-webs stretch across the sky.

For a moment I can't breathe.

All this destruction—for Victoria, for the planet, for the rule of law and normalcy.

But also for me.

I helped plan this battle, nudging flickering soldiers and machine-like toys across an airscreen table. Quoting Sun Tzu and Niccolò Machiavelli. Pouring out every second of training that my father subjected me to.

His creature.

He made me, and I made this spectacle before us.

"Magnificent," Dr. Leyva says softly. "But we're losing."

It's true. The army of Shreve has left the city almost defense-less, surging out across the farm belt against the rebels and Victorians. So many hovercars, drones, jump troops . . .

Then I realize—the score of ships guarding this tower have joined the fray, tipping the balance. Once we invaded my father's home, it left them with no reason to stay here.

So they headed straight at Col.

"No," I murmur.

"Focus," Zura says. "Where's the control room?"

I point.

"Why is no one here?" Boss X says. His pulse lance buzzes in his hand.

One of the techs raises an instrument. "There's some kind of magnetic field building. Frey, is this room equipped with—"

Her voice cuts off, and she crumples to one knee. Blood spurts from her throat and down her chest, setting off camo reactions in her suit.

I flinch from a metal flash in the corner of my eye. Something shiny darts past, and a lock of my hair falls, cut clean off.

Boss X cries out in pain. A shiny bone pin juts from his shoulder.

Suddenly the air is full of metal—scissors, suturing needles, pins, every medical instrument in flight.

I shut my eyes, knowing this room from endless training injuries, and grab a cushion from the surge table, wrap it around my head.

Some deadly code in the walls is running pinpoint lifter magnets, sending every small piece of metal swirling through the air, thrusting at anything with body heat.

A Special falls, something shiny protruding from his eye. I hear the buzz of Boss X's pulse lance as he fends off flitting projectiles. Objects *thunk* into my cushion, stab at my hardened sneak suit, slice my hands.

Sooner or later, one of them will find a vein.

But then the barrage tapers off.

I peer out.

Yandre stands in the center of the room, their face bleeding, their jacket in ribbons of leather. They hold a crash bracelet high in the air, surrounded by a lacerating hurricane of metal.

Of course. The bracelet's magnet is much stronger than any pinpoint lifter, and has drawn all that flying metal toward itself. But the vortex around Yandre's hand is closing, spinning quicker as it tightens, like water in a drain.

Once it consumes the bracelet—and Yandre's hand—the metal storm will break free again.

I hurl my knife at the picture window. The reinforced glass resists for a moment, then webs, cracks, shatters. Glittering shards spill out into the night, letting in the roar of wind and battle thunder.

Yandre takes slow, steady steps to the window, then drops the bracelet out.

The storm of metal follows, spinning into the dark.

I look around—one tech and two Specials dead. Boss X's fur streaked with blood. Yandre's arm streaming. Zura emerges unscathed from beneath a massage table.

The cold, ten-story wind sets everything rustling around us.

Dr. Leyva goes to work, looking for medspray and bandages. When he turns to me, I wave him off. My hardened sneak suit saved me from the worst.

And the battle is still raging outside.

"The control room's through that door," I say to the surviving tech. "I'll be back in five minutes."

"Frey . . ." Zura warns me.

I shake my head, taking a pair of grenades from Boss X's belt. He only nods.

I make for the stairs. The eleventh floor, where I used to sleep.

Zura doesn't try to stop me.

The stairwell is dark, sirens echoing from all directions. But there's movement below me. In night vision, I can see the two security drones drifting up on silent lifters.

There's no point in stealth anymore.

My barrage gun fills the stairwell with sparks and smoke, leaving them in jittering pieces. I set a grenade on a slow timer and send it bouncing down.

The door to the eleventh floor is secured, but the barrage gun shreds it off its hinges.

I dive through the doorway, aiming and firing at a lone figure in the hall. But my gun sputters, its status light blinking red.

I'm out of ammo.

"Frey," comes a familiar voice. "It's good to see you."

I squint through the soft glow of emergency lights. She stands there, lean and poised and strong.

Unarmed. Unworried by the likes of me.

My trainer, Naya.

NAYA

I drop the empty barrage gun, raise my pulse knife.

"Out of my way. I don't want to hurt you."

"You've never hurt me, Frey."

"Trust me, it wasn't for lack of trying."

Naya wears a familiar expression. That perfect focus, probing for weaknesses, judging me. For a moment, I'm a defenseless seven-year-old again.

"Your stance has gotten sloppy," she says.

I glance down at my feet.

She's right. My weight's too far back.

"I'm out of practice. Not a lot of fistfights in real wars, turns out."

"We can remedy that." She raises her hands, and I remember how beautiful I used to think she was—that blend of elegance, strength, and menace.

Now all I can see is the sadness in her eyes.

"I'm not going to fight you fair, Naya. You'll win."

"Then at least I've taught you something."

"Get out of my way."

"No, Frey. I serve the heir, not you."

I can see past her to Rafi's door. My old bedroom.

A weight lifts from me. "She's here?"

"Yes, Frey. She misses you."

My pulse knife is set humming with a squeeze.

Gently, careful not to crush it.

Firmly, so it doesn't fly away.

"Don't make me hurt you."

Naya shakes her head. "There's no other way."

There are many other ways—the world has taught me that in the last month. But in this house, there is only one.

I throw my knife.

It roars into her. Broken fingers, broken ribs. Sprains and dislocations. Burning muscles, battered pride. All that pain, traded for slivers of praise.

Nothing is left of her but the smell of rust.

I knock on my bedroom door.

"Rafi. It's me."

An endless moment of silence, then softly, "Frey?"

My eyes sting, something rising in my throat. My first answer isn't even a word.

I grip my last grenade. "Stand back. I'm about to blow this—"

The door slides open.

Rafia stands there, her face alight.

She's in the dress she wore for our sixteenth birthday—a gradient of feathers shifting like sunrise from orange to red, rubies tracing her waist. Her eyes are set off by a new necklace of slim gray metal.

For a beautiful moment, I'm certain that the Palafox psych team was wrong. This is Rafi—my confident big sister, every strand of hair in place, every accessory curated.

Until her arms wrap around me, and I feel the shudders in her grip, the panic in her heartbeat.

Her door wasn't even locked. She's too beaten to run.

She pulls away, spins once around. "I dressed up in your favorite, little sister. When the sirens started, I *knew* you'd come."

I can hardly breathe. "You're beautiful."

"And you're . . . *real*." Her words come in a whisper. "He said you were dead. Half of me, gone."

The need in her gaze makes me ashamed. I didn't miss her with that intensity. The world was too busy hitting me. I had a war to fight, a boy to learn.

While she was stuck in this room.

I can see it behind her, the walls set to the same colors she picked when we were ten. The photos of us together, erased from the house servers, but taped to our wall. The velvet dog whose tiny artificial brain learned to tell us apart, even when our father couldn't.

The room looks to me smaller now. Not even half a life.

Rafi reaches out, runs a finger across the scar above my eye—our scar.

"Nice makeup," she says. "Who did it?"

"A friend."

"You have friends now," she murmurs, ecstatic and jealous and sad.

After this long apart, it's strange to see my face in hers. Like some pretty-era software showing what the surgeons will make of me. More elegant, more refined.

More fragile.

She looks at her fingertip—it's slick from touching my face. It's on my hands as well, and in my hair.

"Naya," I say.

"Oh, poor Frey. When the sirens started, I told her to run away. I'm sorry she didn't."

I take my sister's hand.

"It's not our fault. Come on."

We take the stairs down to the med center.

The commandos stare at our identical faces—that baffled expression I'm so used to, redoubled. As if no one ever really believed there were two of me.

Rafi greets them like visitors in our home. A haughty nod and a measuring glance for each. And through her gaze I realize how motley a company we are. The rebels in their skins, Yandre's arm in bandages, all of them are injured in some way.

Dr. Leyva finds his voice first.

"We've corrupted the spy dust, citywide. And the feeds are under our control." He looks out the broken window. "But there isn't much time to turn this fight around."

Against the dark sky, the battle seems muted now. Streaks of light and smoke, but no more burning rings—the Palafoxes' plasma guns must be expended.

"This speech better be good," Boss X says.

"A speech?" Rafi clasps her hands. "Lucky I dressed up."

"No, big sister. This one's mine."

She draws herself taller, imperious again. "And what exactly are you going to say?"

"That you're declaring a coup against him. That we've shut down the dust, so the army and citizens can side with you. That you'll be the leader now, and everything will change."

"You can handle all that?"

For a moment, I'm her little sister again. But I hold her gaze.

"I'm ready for this."

She smiles. "Here's what I think, Frey. If we really want to hit him hard, we should address our city together."

No one speaks.

It slowly ticks into place in my brain—this is all our plans combined. Tearing everything away from him at once. His power, his city, his home, his secrets.

"You're right," I say.

Boss X lets out a rumbling laugh.

SPEECH

We stand side by side.

The camera hovers in the middle of the room, framing me and Rafi in the broken picture window. With the battle blazing behind us, it will be obvious we're talking live from our father's tower.

Bitter cold wind flutters the jagged safety glass, and more Shreve soldiers are storming the stairs now. Others are flying up the tower walls on hoverboards. Shots ring out as our commandos fight them off.

None of it ruffles my sister in the least.

I'd almost forgotten that persuasion was her job, not mine.

When the hovercam winks on, Rafi greets the people of Shreve. She tells them that she is in control of the tower. Then she fulfills her promise from the night before I left, and tells them our secret.

"As you can see," my big sister says, "I am not alone. I have never been alone."

My mouth goes dry. Somehow I can feel the curious gaze of two million people shifting between us, comparing us. One in a damaged sneak suit, her hair wild, covered with a slick of blood. The other, perfect as always.

A knife with two edges.

"I want you all to meet my twin, Frey. Though in fact many of you have met her already, and all of you have cheered for her. She took my place in crowds, in receiving lines, whenever there was danger. She was my first protector." Rafi's voice turns cold. "Because your leader raised one of his daughters to take a bullet."

It's strange, this revelation unfolding here. There are no shocked faces in the crowd. No audience metrics in an eye-screen. Just my sister laying bare the truth of me before a hovering cam.

"Since we were seven years old, Frey has been trained to kill. Every brutal day, she was harmed by her teachers, and there was nothing I could do to help her." Rafi's voice breaks, both genuine and exquisitely artful. "And every time I left our bubble, I had to wipe her from my mind, to pretend to everyone that she didn't exist. Our father made me an accomplice in Frey's pain—in her erasure—every hour, every moment."

Her voice falters again, showing them what Col taught me to see—how hiding me twisted her inside. But she never loses her train of thought, never misses a beat. This speech is so perfect that I wonder if Rafi has been writing it all her life. Practicing it under her breath. Dreaming it in the bed next to mine.

Waiting for this moment.

It was worth risking everything to give her this chance.

"Frey fooled you all, because she is magnificent. But she didn't deserve this. This is not normal."

She looks at me, and I realize it's my turn.

Rafi's already made the speech I practiced. There's no more to say about my broken bones, or hidden passageways, or Sensei Noriko. All I have left to say is what matters to me now.

"When this war began, our father threw me away. I was nothing to him but a way to steal some metal, conquer a city, and murder a family in their own home."

My voice wavers. Not artfully, like Rafi's, but with a shudder in my chest.

"When he sent that missile to destroy House Palafox, he thought I would die with them. A sacrifice to make him look daring and strong. The only reason I'm alive is that one of our father's intended victims was helping me escape. I owe Col Palafox my life."

I wonder if Col is watching. By now the whole world must have tuned in, except for people with a battle to fight. But I hope he's seeing this somehow.

"Col and his army are here to free you. Stop fighting him, and start fighting your real enemy. We call on you, the citizens and army of Shreve, to join us. To reject our father. To make Shreve a normal city again."

It's strange. I expected to utter these words in Rafi's voice. But at long last, I'm using my own.

And suddenly I know how to end this.

"I'm free of my father's lies now, a freedom that you all deserve. It won't be easy, or steady, but it will be *yours*. Because the only sure path to freedom is to seize it for your—"

The lights go out. The hovercam falls to the floor.

Dr. Leyva appears at the door to the control room. "They cut the power! That's all we can do here!"

I turn to face the window.

In the night sky, the booms and streaks of flame are fading, the struggle ending in a whimper. Without the chaos of battle, how can Shreve soldiers declare themselves for Rafia?

There's no Victorian army left to tip the balance. Just a galaxy of lights wheeling in the air, away from the fight, toward us. The army of Shreve is headed home to retake our father's tower.

We were too late.

"Did they hear us?" I ask.

Dr. Leyva nods, staring at a handscreen. "It was on all the feeds. The whole city is talking, reacting. But they can't digest this right away. And we're out of time."

"Poor Frey," Rafi says softly. "Did you think one speech would change everything?"

"I just thought . . ." But I'm not sure of the rest.

"It *was* a good speech," she says. "We're perfect together."

Boss X claps my shoulder. "It was a start, but we need to get out of here."

It takes me a moment to realize that they're all looking at me, waiting for whatever's next.

My head is spinning. The next step was supposed to be victory. But we were too slow in taking the tower, Col's army too weak.

All there is to do is run. But there's shooting all around us.

"We have to get out through the trophy room," I say. "It's one place they can't blow up. Two floors down."

"We *can't* go down!" Zura calls from the broken stairway door. Gunfire lights up the stairwell behind her.

"Yes, we can." I squeeze my knife and let it fall.

It hits the floor screaming, billowing dust. When it leaps back into my hand a moment later, a jagged hole has opened, full of fire-suppression foam and sparking wires.

"Me first," Boss X rumbles.

His pulse lance buzzing, he leaps through. I follow, grabbing onto the edge to swing out of his way.

He's fighting drones, his lance slicing elegant arcs through the air. As I land, my knife takes one out—then sputters to the ground.

Its battery light goes red.

I'm unarmed, but Zura has dropped through, her barrage guns adding to the din. Moments later, the ninth floor is secure.

One more floor to go.

"Cut here," I tell Boss X.

He attacks the floor with his pulse lance. By the time the others are all down behind us, we're ready to descend again.

This room is quiet and dark. As I thought, Father's security wouldn't dare start a firefight here. Nothing is more precious to him than his trophies.

They're mostly portraits. Paintings of his former allies, his enemies, all the people who no longer appear in the Shreve propaganda feeds. Erased people, existing only in this abyss of memory.

Our father never forgets his victories.

There are normal hunting trophies too—the stuffed heads of stags and boars and lions. A hundred kills at least, and a rack of hunting rifles and hoverboards.

"Are these boards charged?" Zura asks.

"Always, in case of a fire. But the guns aren't loaded."

"Good enough." She pulls a hoverboard off the wall.

While the others climb down from the floor above, I orient myself. This room is our father's guilty pleasure, with no windows to let in prying eyes. But the outer wall should be right here, behind this portrait of—

Me.

Frey.

Definitely not Rafi. Not with that mussed hair, the workout clothes, the knife in my hand. A sheen of sweat, and that look of battle ecstasy in my eyes. Wilder than I ever pictured myself.

Our father already has a portrait of me in his trophy room.

But he only thought I was dead for a few days. How long does it take to paint someone?

Was this ready before I left for Victoria?

Then I see her, hanging right across from me—Aribella Palafox.

The painting captures her confidence, her certainty. Every stroke of the brush reminds me how formidable she was.

But she's gone, and I'm still here.

A voice rumbles in my ear. "One day, your father's picture will hang here too."

I look up at Boss X. His fur is blood-matted, one eye clouded by injury. But his expression is very human, very sad.

I wonder if the assassin—his lost love—is among these faces. But that's not for me to ask.

I'm not ready to tell X what I did.

His lance buzzes to life in his hand, and he raises it up, a look of wolfish glee on his face. For a moment I think he knows somehow, and he's going to burn me down.

But all he says is "Time to go. Which wall do I cut?"

COLLAR

I take the portrait of me off the wall, out of Boss X's way.

I don't want it sliced to pieces. I want my father to see my face every day, knowing that I'm still out there. Alive, fighting, looking for more ways to hurt him.

That girl in the painting looks so fierce, so strong. I want her to be the truth of me.

My sister joins me to stare at it.

"*You*, Frey? How sweet. That means he thought about you."

I look around the room, all those lost faces.

"Yeah, but I'm hanging here with his enemies."

"Silly Frey. Dad loves his enemies more than his friends." She waves a hand at the paintings. "For one thing, he knows what to *do* with enemies. You mount them on a wall with the other stuffed heads."

Her voice is trembling. I look into her eyes, and see a kind of panic there.

"I always hated this room." She wraps her arms around herself. "It's like being in his head, the only thing worse than being in his family. You lucked out on that, you know—not being a real daughter. I wish I could give you back those twenty-six minutes."

"I know."

I was only a throwaway, a tool. But she had to be his daughter all those years. I hated not being seen, but being seen was worse. I was never in a room alone with him.

What if all that time, she was protecting me too?

"Do you suppose there's a painting of me?" she asks. "In storage somewhere? Ready to hang?"

"It doesn't matter, Rafi. We're leaving." I take her hands. "It's going to be okay."

"It's not."

"It's different out there, Rafi. There's a whole world where he can't touch you. You never have to see him again!"

Her voice goes soft. "But I can't come."

"What do you mean?"

Rafi's fingers go to her throat, touching the new necklace. "If I leave the house, this goes off."

I stare at it. "He put a tracker on you?"

"No. A bomb."

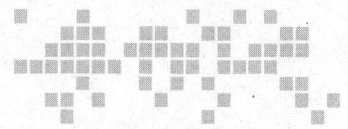

The wall is almost open.

Boss X has carved away the insulation and wiring, but the outer wall of the tower is solid duralloy. Too strong for a pulse lance.

Zura is setting explosive charges.

Shreve forces have occupied most of the building. But the spy dust is corrupted. They don't know where we are, or that we're about to blast our way out of the tower. The floor above us is full of proximity grenades, and Yandre holds our last plasma gun in their good arm, for any hovercars in our path.

But my sister is wearing a bomb around her neck.

"Anything?" I ask Dr. Leyva.

He's staring at his handscreen. "I've pulled all the code from the necklace. It's nothing too head-scratching."

I nod. "He wouldn't bother with anything complicated. Rafi's not great at tech stuff."

She looks at me slantwise. "*Rafi* is standing right here."

"The problem is," Leyva says, "I don't have time to run a hardware schematic."

"What does that mean?" I ask.

Rafi groans. "It means that the bomb around my neck is being defused by *the host of a cooking feed!*"

"A *science* of cooking feed." Leyva stares at his screen. "I've been hacking Shreve code for a month now. It's mostly been easy. But when I see code this simple, I worry there's a trap—a trigger hidden in the hardware."

He looks up at her.

"This is you, after all—*la princessa Rafia*. You're more important than a bunch of solar panels."

Rafi swallows. "So I'm stuck here."

He holds out the screen. "My hack is ready to go. Just push that button. But—"

"But my head might blow up. What are the odds?"

Leyva lowers the screen. "You'd know better than I."

I shake my head, my anger building. "If you don't know, Doctor, how are *we* supposed to?"

Leyva spreads his hands. "It's not about the bomb—it's about your father. If he'd wanted to, he could've made this code too strong to break in a few minutes. But he made it easy."

"Which means?"

"Maybe it's a trick, to kill Rafi if she tries to escape. Or maybe he wanted it simple, so there wasn't any danger of a bogus line of code killing her."

"And you can't tell which?"

"If we had two more hours." Leyva looks back at Zura.

She's almost done setting the charges. Our surviving tech has the hoverboards ready to go. Yandre has the plasma gun shouldered.

"What do you think, little sister?" Rafi fingers the necklace. "Would he rather kill me than let me go?"

Everything I know about our father goes rushing through me. It's acid in my veins.

"He hates to lose, Rafi." My voice starts to shake. "If you get away from him, it's like losing Seanan again. He can't let that happen."

"He wouldn't kill me," she says.

I step closer to her.

"The whole time I was at House Palafox, I thought the same. But he tried to, because nothing matters to him except *winning*. I'm sorry, Rafi. I swear to you I'll come back and save—"

Rafi takes the handscreen from Leyva, pushes the button.

The necklace pops open.

I stare—relieved, astonished, a sliver of me shattered.

"Sorry, little sister." She gives me a gentle smile. "It sucks, I know. But it's not like he'd ever throw *me* away."

CLICK

We stand on our hoverboards, ready to fly.

The charges are set. Yandre has already pulled the priming trigger on their plasma gun. The whine of its battery fills the trophy room like a boiling tea kettle.

Above us, the proximity grenades are going off one by one. The enemy clearing that floor. But they're taking their time—

They think we're trapped here.

We're only waiting for an opening outside.

"We should have a clear path in five, four, three . . ." Dr. Leyva begins, then shakes his head. "No, wait. Heavy attack ship in the way."

I groan. "Stop *doing* that!"

Leyva shrugs, staring at his handscreen. "You think this is easy?"

He's watching the newly free and rampant feeds of the citizens of Shreve. Two million people, all broadcasting whatever they want for the first time since our father took over.

Most of them are covering the battle, of course. Thousands are standing on their roofs, pointing cams at the tower, where signs of combat still flash in the windows.

They all want to know if they're really free yet.

They aren't, because we failed.

But at least I've saved my sister.

She's waiting on her board with the rest of us, wearing a sneak suit stripped from a dead Special. The camo is set to midnight black, but on Rafi it looks like a fashion choice.

Her feathered dress is neatly folded in the corner. The open bomb collar sits on top, a good-bye note from a runaway.

Boss X shifts nervously on his motionless board. "You're sure blowing out that wall won't kill us?"

"The charges are ninety-eight percent directional," Zura says. "You can trust Victorian tech."

"Ninety-eight." Boss X spits on the floor.

"Let's go, Doctor," Zura says. "We're just giving them more time to surround us."

Leyva shakes his head. "Actually, they're moving away from the tower and back toward the city. There are demonstrations popping up—fireworks, crowds, like All Saints' Day in Victoria. The military's more worried about its own citizens than us!"

"*Told* you it was a good speech," Rafi says.

I share a smile with her, but I'm worried about what happens to all those protestors next week, when the spy dust is back in the air again.

Does one night of freedom really change anything?

"There's still the matter of soldiers coming for us." Zura glances up at the hole in the ceiling.

Searchlights are crawling the floor up there.

"Another heavy unit's peeling away," Leyva says, staring at his screen. "Heading back out to the battlefield. Something's happening out there!"

I stand straighter on my hoverboard, hopeful for a moment.

Maybe the Victorians held some units in reserve. Maybe they're still fighting, and there's time for the rebellion in Shreve to take hold . . .

But then Dr. Leyva's face crumples.

"No," he says softly.

"What *now*?" Zura yells.

Leyva looks straight at me. "I'm sorry, Frey. It's just coming on the feeds. Why the battle ended sooner than we thought—his car was shot down."

I shake my head. "What do you mean?"

He hands the screen to me. "That heavy unit just went out to take custody of him."

I stare at the image on the feeds.

Col Palafox.

He's dirty, bloody. His eyes glazed, his wrists tied with smart plastic. Surrounded by two Shreve soldiers.

My father's prisoner.

"Please, no." My voice breaks.

Rafi puts a hand softly on my shoulder. "Poor Frey. You looked so sweet in that red jacket."

I look up at the others, pleading for a plan, some way to rescue Col. Yandre turns away, swearing under their breath.

Only Zura meets my eyes, her expression one of utter hatred. She must be wondering if Artura Vigil was right.

"It's not your fault," Rafi whispers in my ear.

But it is. This was all my plan.

A *whomp* comes from the floor above us, a smoke canister exploding. The billowing edge of a thick cloud pushes through the hole in the ceiling.

"Doctor," Zura says. "We have to go *now*."

Leyva doesn't take the screen from me, just nods his assent. Everyone steps back onto their boards.

Zura hits the charges. The wall blows outward in a furious roar, shards of duralloy tearing through the hovercars and drones outside. The force of the blast sends me staggering backward.

And all I can think is: Col is being brought here to this tower, a captive. Because he listened to me, followed my plan. Threw his army away for my sister.

The hoverboards rise up, their lifting fans at maximum speed. The wind ripples the paintings around us, stirs the dust and smoke in the room.

My team shoots off into the night, Yandre sending a blazing spheromak of plasma bolting out ahead of them, shredding still more hovercars in their path.

All in camo black, they disappear against the dark sky.

They won't notice I'm missing until it's too late to turn around.

I step from my hoverboard. Strip my sneak suit off, my gloves, and earpiece.

Shivering in the cold wind coming through the jagged hole, I cross to the dress that Rafi wore for our sixteenth birthday. They never made a copy for me. The party was only for half a dozen friends—no need for a body double.

But Rafi never forgot that I liked this dress. She wore it for me tonight.

I slip it over my head. The smart fibers beneath the feathers stretch; our bodies have parted ways over the last month, just a little. But once it slides down and around my hips, the dress feels like it was made for me.

I hide Dr. Leyva's handscreen behind the painting of Aribella Palafox. Then I close the bomb collar around my neck.

Click.

When Col is brought here, I'll be waiting. Ready to free him, to fight for him. To take him back to his brother and whatever's left of the Victorian army.

It will be okay.

The Shreve commandos come crashing down into the trophy room a minute later. Twenty of them in full armor, with stun guns and a dozen screaming battle drones.

They find me fixing my hair.

"You're late," I say in my best Rafi voice. "Our visitors have already gone."

FATHER

"Your father will see you now," Dona Oliver says.

I give her a bored sigh as I stand up and smooth my dress. He's kept me waiting for two hours outside his office.

How petty. Just because I helped my sister make a little speech. What was I going to do—let her pretend to be *me*?

Dona watches as I walk past, but there's no suspicion in her eyes. Only fear of what he'll do to me.

I'm more worried about Dona than anyone else. The last time Rafi and I switched places, she was the one who caught us.

But it's one thing, telling twins apart when they're standing side by side, another when there's only one in front of you. And quite *another* to believe that anyone would snap a bomb collar around her own neck.

I can still hear that *click*.

The office door closes behind me.

For the first time in my life, I'm alone with my father.

From behind his desk, he looks up at me. His eyes travel across what I'm wearing.

I spent all morning in Rafi's closet, remembering all the times I've watched her get dressed. Trying not to get lost in the maze of materials, cuts, and biases, the rules of formal, casual, cocktail, creative. Trying to imagine that it all really belongs to me.

Only the *best* clothes for the first daughter of Shreve.

With Rafi's voice in my head, I stayed conservative—a buttoned white shirt and dark skirt, modest shoes. Like someone applying for a job.

My father looks like he hasn't slept. He flew straight back from the peace conference, of course. He must have spent the night trying to put his city back in order.

He gestures to a pair of chairs by the window.

We sit together, the city of Shreve spread out below us. The scars of battle blacken the farm belt, and the debris of protests fills the streets.

But nothing shows more damage than this tower, a gaping chunk blown out of my father's edifice. From my bedroom window, I saw people on the rooftops gazing up at it.

We've made him look weak, at least.

"Have you seen what they're saying about us?" he asks.

It takes me a moment to answer. The city feeds must still be churning after the revelations in our speech last night. Rafi would have read them all by now; choosing the right clothes would've taken her only seconds.

At the edge of her mocking voice, I ask him, "You haven't got the feeds under control yet?"

"In time. For now, let them talk, so we'll know who to deal with once the dust is back in the air."

I smile at his logic, my stomach churning. How many people has my call for rebellion put at risk?

My father leans forward in the chair, closer to me than he's ever been before.

"Do you finally understand?" He waves a hand at the city. "With nothing but a few rebels and Palafox diehards, Frey did all this. And she forced you to make that . . . *speech*."

His whole frame shudders with anger.

But not at me. At my little sister.

For a moment, I'm too head-spun to speak. A hundred excuses were ready on my tongue. How I had no choice. How it was better with me, Rafi, in front of the camera, to take control if Frey went too far. How I knew the battle was already won.

But my father has already made the excuses for me.

"We made your sister too well, too dangerous," he says. "Do you see now why I tried to kill her at the start of this?"

He's pleading for my approval.

After Col's diagnosis of Rafi's psyche, I almost forgot how formidable she can be. But this was always her job—making people feel she was on their side, no matter what crimes my father committed.

Maybe she's worked the same magic with him.

"Frey isn't my sister anymore," I say softly. "She killed Naya right in front of me. It was grisly, Daddy."

"Of course it was. I'm so sorry, Rafia." But he doesn't look sorry. He looks pleased, maybe a little surprised that I'm agreeing with him so easily.

Rafi would have made him work harder.

I run a fingertip along my necklace.

"Don't you think it's time we took this off?"

His smile fades, his eyes narrowing a little. He reaches over to take my hand, and a shiver travels down my spine.

It's the first time he's ever touched me.

"But without my little gift, she would've taken you away. It protects you from her."

He thinks I should be grateful for this collar.

Rafi's maxim rings in my head—*This is not normal.*

I give him a shrug. "I suppose. But maybe she'll stop bothering us, now that you've destroyed the Palafoxes."

"She won't. Not while we have him in our house." He makes a gesture.

The door to his private office opens, and two people step through. One is a soldier—not a house guard in a crisp gray uniform, but one of the commandos from last night, still in full body armor.

The other is Col Palafox.

COL

I turn, pulling from my father's touch, and give Col a bored look as my heart breaks.

"So *this* is the boy who's riled up my little sister?"

He's dirty, though they've wiped most of the blood from his face. His Victorian uniform has been replaced with a jumpsuit made by a hole in the wall. It doesn't fit right, like they scanned him with his hands bound.

Still I want to wrap my arms around him, to breathe him in.

My father chuckles. "Frey had nothing to compare him to. Our fault, perhaps, for not widening her education."

Col stares back at me.

For a brain-missing moment, I expect him to see through my disguise. As if he'll somehow just *know* who I really am.

But he looks horrified by me. Like I'm some uncanny plastic

replica of myself. I promised him that Rafia was on our side, and yet here she is, plotting with her father.

I stare into Col's eyes, imploring him to read my thoughts.

It's going to be okay.

But it isn't—he's wearing a bomb collar too. Not a necklace, like mine. A thick dark ring, like a dog collar.

"I was going to keep him hostage," my father says. "To make the Victorians behave. But what's the point now? Their army's gone."

"So we let him go?" I ask lightly. "A gesture of goodwill?"

My father lets out a roaring laugh. "I've missed your sense of humor, Rafia."

I nod, taking the compliment, as always. "Then what do we do with him?"

My father shrugs. "We show those protestors how we deal with our enemies."

I stare, not understanding.

"And think what it will do to Frey," my father says. "Watching him executed will finally break her spirit."

Executed.

For an awful moment, the room darkens around me. I see a portrait of Col hanging down in the trophy room, across from his mother's. My heart rails in the cage of my chest.

My father narrows his eyes.

"What is it, Rafia?"

I draw a slow breath, my mind racing for an answer.

"An execution, Daddy?" My voice is quivering. "On the *feeds*? What will the other cities think?"

He gives a tired sigh. "It's too late to worry about our reputation. Your sister's speech has seen to that."

"But what if there's a way to fix it? To make them accept your control of Victoria?"

He stares at me, his eyes bored and heavy lidded. Like he's made and discarded a hundred plans to rehabilitate himself.

"Like what, darling?"

I don't know what to say. I don't know how to save someone with words. All I understand is improvised weapons, finding weaknesses, and fighting with all my heart.

All I know is war.

I stand up and turn toward Col, my eyes pleading. He stares back at me, uncertain why I'm trying so hard to save him.

We connect, a slant of air kindling between us—

And I see the answer.

"What if Col Palafox wasn't your prisoner, or your enemy at all? What if he was your son?"

I turn back to my father, twisting my lips into Rafi's cruelest smile.

"What if instead of killing Col, you give him to *me*?"

There's a moment of silence. Thoughts scuttle across my father's face, too quick to interpret.

It feels like the tower is tipping around us, broken by last night's blast. Broken by all my mistakes.

At last my father murmurs, "An alliance of blood."

"No more Victorian citizens resisting. No legitimate claim to Victoria for Teo Palafox. The perfect excuse for the other cities to buy our metal again."

A low roll of laughter comes from my father. But he's shaking his head.

"No one would believe it, unless we put the wedding on the feeds. Are you going to hold a knife to his throat?"

I turn to Col and reach out, stroke his arm. He shudders at my touch.

It's going to be okay.

"I'll persuade him, Father. You know how persistent I can be when it comes to getting what I want. How steadfast."

A realization flashes across Col's face—then he drops back into character, turning away from me, defiant.

I lean closer to my father, like I'm whispering a joke.

"The two of us married. Think what *that* will do to poor Frey."

That's when he laughs the hardest, rising grandly from his chair to gather me into a hug. My first hug from my father ever. I've never felt this before—the heat of his body, the mass of him, the *greed*.

And that's when the rest of the plan comes clear . . .

The same night I escape this tower, my father will die at my hands.

ABOUT THE AUTHOR

Scott Westerfeld is the author of the Uglies series, the Leviathan trilogy, the Midnighters trilogy, the New York trilogy, the Zeroes series, as well as the Spill Zone graphic novels, the novel *Afterworlds*, and the first book in the Horizon series. He has also written books for adults. Born in Texas, he and his wife now split their time between Sydney, Australia and New York City. You can find him online at scottwesterfeld.com

EVERY NOTE
PLAYED

a novel

Lisa Genova

SCOUT PRESS
New York   London   Toronto   Sydney   New Delhi

Scout Press
An Imprint of Simon & Schuster, Inc.
1230 Avenue of the Americas
New York, NY 10020

This book is a work of fiction. Any references to historical events, real people, or real places are used fictitiously. Other names, characters, places, and events are products of the author's imagination, and any resemblance to actual events or places or persons, living or dead, is entirely coincidental.

Copyright © 2018 by Lisa Genova

All rights reserved, including the right to reproduce this book or portions thereof in any form whatsoever. For information address Scout Press Subsidiary Rights Department, 1230 Avenue of the Americas, New York, NY 10020.

First Scout Press hardcover edition March 2018

SCOUT PRESS and colophon are registered trademarks of Simon & Schuster, Inc.

For information about special discounts for bulk purchases, please contact Simon & Schuster Special Sales at 1-866-506-1949 or business@simonandschuster.com.

The Simon & Schuster Speakers Bureau can bring authors to your live event. For more information or to book an event contact the Simon & Schuster Speakers Bureau at 1-866-248-3049 or visit our website at www.simonspeakers.com.

Interior design by Davina Mock-Maniscalco

Manufactured in the United States of America

10   9   8   7   6   5   4   3   2   1

Library of Congress Cataloging-in-Publication Data is available.

ISBN 978-1-4767-1780-7
ISBN 978-1-4767-1782-1 (ebook)

RO451313785

For my parents

In loving memory of
Richard Glatzer
Kevin Gosnell
Chris Connors
Chris Engstrom

Why do you stay in prison when the door is so wide open?

—Rumi

EVERY NOTE
PLAYED

PROLOGUE

Richard is playing the second movement of Schumann's Fantasie in C Major, op. 17, the final piece of his solo recital at the Adrienne Arsht Center in Miami. The concert hall is sold-out, yet the energy here doesn't feel full. This venue doesn't carry the prestige or intimidating pressure of Lincoln Center or the Royal Albert Hall. Maybe that's it. This recital is no big deal.

Without a conductor or orchestra behind him, all audience eyes are on him. He prefers this. He loves possessing their undivided attention, the adrenaline rush of being the star. Playing solo is his version of skydiving.

But this entire night, he's noticed that he's playing on top of the notes, not inside them. His thoughts are drifting elsewhere, to the steak dinner he's going to eat back at the hotel, to the self-conscious examination of his imperfect posture, criticizing the flatness of his performance, aware of himself instead of losing himself.

He's technically flawless. Not many pianists alive today could traverse this demandingly fast and complex section without error. He normally loves playing this piece, especially the bombastic chords of the second movement, its power and grandiosity. Yet, he's not emotionally connected to any of it.

He trusts that most, if not all, of the people in the audience aren't sophisticated enough to hear the difference. Hell, most people have probably never even heard Schumann's Fantasie in C Major, op. 17. It forever breaks his heart that millions listen to Justin Bieber all day long and will live and die without ever hearing Schumann or Liszt or Chopin.

Being married is more than wearing a ring comes to mind. Karina said this to him some years ago. Tonight, he's just wearing the ring. He's mailing it in, and he's not sure why. He'll get through this last piece and have another chance here tomorrow night before flying out to LA. Five more weeks of this tour. It'll be summer by the time he gets home. Good. He loves summer in Boston.

He plays the final phrasing of the third-movement adagio, and the notes are gentle, solemn, hopeful. He's often moved to tears at this point, a permeable conduit for this exquisite expression of tender vulnerability, but tonight he's unaffected. He doesn't feel hopeful.

He plays the final note, and the sound lingers on the stage before dissipating, floating away. A moment of quiet stillness hangs in the hall, and then the bubble is punctured by applause. Richard stands and faces the audience. He hinges at the waist, his fingers grazing the bottom of his tuxedo jacket, bowing. The people rise to their feet. The houselights are up a bit now, and he can see their faces, smiling, enthusiastic, appreciating him, in awe of him. He bows again.

He is loved by everyone.

And no one.

ONE YEAR LATER

CHAPTER ONE

If Karina had grown up fifteen kilometers down the road in either direction north or south, in Gliwice or Bytom instead of Zabrze, her whole life would be different. Even as a child, she never doubted this. Location matters in destiny as much as it does in real estate.

In Gliwice, it was every girl's birthright to take ballet. The ballet teacher there was Miss Gosia, a former celebrated prima ballerina for the Polish National Ballet prior to Russian martial law, and because of this, it was considered a perk to raise daughters in otherwise grim Gliwice, an unrivaled privilege that every young girl would have access to such an accomplished teacher. These girls grew up wearing leotards and buns and tulle-spun hopes of pirouetting their way out of Gliwice someday. Without knowing specifically what has become of the girls who grew up in Gliwice, she's sure that most, if not all, remain firmly anchored where they began and are now school-teachers or miners' wives whose unrequited ballerina dreams have been passed on to their daughters, the next generation of Miss Gosia's students.

If Karina had grown up in Gliwice, she would most certainly not have become a ballerina. She has horrible feet, wide, clumsy flippers with virtually no arch, a sturdy frame cast on a long torso and short legs, a body built more for milking cows than for pas de bourrée. She would never have been Miss Gosia's star pupil. Karina's parents would have put an end to bartering valuable coal and eggs for ballet lessons long before pointe shoes. Had her life started in Gliwice, she'd still be in Gliwice.

The girls down the road in Bytom had no ballet lessons. The children in Bytom had the Catholic Church. The boys were groomed for the priesthood, the girls the convent. Karina might have become a nun had she grown up in Bytom. Her parents would've been so proud. Maybe her life would be content and honorable had she chosen God.

But her life was never really a choice. She grew up in Zabrze, and in Zabrze lived Mr. Borowitz, the town's piano teacher. He didn't have a prestigious pedigree like Miss Gosia's or a professional studio. Lessons were taught in his living room, which reeked of cat piss, yellowing books, and cigarettes. But Mr. Borowitz was a fine teacher. He was dedicated, stern but encouraging, and most important, he taught every one of his pupils to play Chopin.

In Poland, Chopin is as revered as Pope John Paul II and God. Poland's Holy Trinity.

Karina wasn't born with the lithe body of a ballerina, but she was graced with the strong arms and long fingers of a pianist. She still remembers her first lesson with Mr. Borowitz. She was five. The glossy keys, the immediacy of pleasing sound, the story of the notes told by her fingers. She took to it instantly. Unlike most children, she never had to be ordered to practice. Quite the opposite, she had to be told to stop. *Stop playing, and do your homework. Stop playing, and set the dinner table. Stop playing, it's time for bed.* She couldn't resist playing. She still can't.

Ultimately, piano became her ticket out of oppressive Poland, to Curtis and America and everything after. *Everything* after. That single decision—to learn piano—set everything that was to follow in motion, the ball in her life's Rube Goldberg machine. She wouldn't be here, right now, attending Hannah Chu's graduation party, had she never played piano.

She parks her Honda behind a Mercedes, the last in a conga line of cars along the side of the road at least three blocks from Hannah's house, assuming this is the closest she'll get. She checks the clock on the dash. She's a half hour late. Good. She'll make a brief appearance, offer her congratulations, and leave.

Her heels click against the street as she walks, a human metronome, and her thoughts continue in pace with this rhythm. Without piano, she would never have met Richard. What would her life be like had she never met him? How many hours has she spent indulging in this fantasy?

If added up, the hours would accumulate into days and weeks, possibly more. More time wasted. What could've been. What will never be.

Maybe she would've been satisfied had she never left her home country to pursue piano. She'd still be living with her parents, sleeping in her childhood bedroom. Or she'd be married to a boring man from Zabrze, a coal miner who earns a hard but respectable living, and she'd be a homemaker, raising their five children. Both wretched scenarios appeal to her now for a commonality she hates to acknowledge: a lack of loneliness.

Or what if she had attended Eastman instead of Curtis? She almost did. That single, arbitrary choice. She would never have met Richard. She would never have taken a step back, assuming with the arrogant and immortal optimism of a twenty-five-year-old that she'd have another chance, that the Wheel of Fortune's spin would once again tick to a stop with its almighty arrow pointing directly at her. She'd waited years for another turn. Sometimes life gives you only one.

But then, if she'd never met Richard, their daughter, Grace, wouldn't be here. Karina imagines an alternative reality in which her only daughter was never conceived and catches herself enjoying the variation almost to the point of wishing for it. She scolds herself, ashamed for allowing such a horrible thought. She loves Grace more than anything else. But the truth is, having Grace was another critical, fork-in-the-road, Gliwice-versus-Bytom-versus-Zabrze moment. *Left* brought Grace and tied Karina to Richard, the rope tight around her neck like a

LISA GENOVA

leash or a noose, depending on the day, for the next seventeen years. *Right* was the path not chosen. Who knows where that might've led?

Regret shadows her every step, a dog at her heels, as she now follows the winding stone path into the Chu family's backyard. Hannah was accepted to Notre Dame, her first choice. Another piano student off to college. Hannah won't continue with piano there. Like most of Karina's students, Hannah took lessons because she wanted to add "plays piano" to her college application. The parents have the same motive, often exponentially more intense and unapologetic. So Hannah went through the motions, and their weekly half hour together was a soulless chore for both student and teacher.

A rare few of Karina's students authentically like playing, and a couple even have talent and potential, but none of them love it enough to pursue it. You have to love it. She can't blame them. These kids are all overscheduled, stressed-out, and too focused on getting into "the best" college to allow the nourishment passion needs to grow. A flower doesn't blossom from a seed without the persistent love of sun and water.

But Hannah isn't just one of Karina's piano students. Hannah was Grace's closest friend from the age of six through middle school. Playdates, sleepovers, Girl Scouts, soccer, trips to the mall and the movies—for most of Grace's childhood, Hannah was like a younger sister. When Grace moved up to the high school and Hannah remained in middle school, the girls migrated naturally into older and younger social circles. There was never a falling-out.

Instead, the friends endured a passive drifting on calm currents to separate but neighboring islands. They visited from time to time.

Hannah's graduation milestone shouldn't mean much to Karina, but it feels monumental, as if she's sustaining a bigger loss than another matriculated piano student. It trips the switch of memories from this time last year, and it's the end of Grace's childhood all over again. Karina leaves her card for Hannah on the gift table and sighs.

Even though Hannah's at the far end of the expansive backyard, Karina spots her straightaway, standing on the edge of the diving board, laughing, a line of wet girls and boys behind her, mostly boys in the pool, cheering her name, goading her to do something. Karina waits to see what it will be. Hannah launches into the air and cannonballs into the water, splashing the parents gathered near the pool. The parents complain, wiping water from their arms and faces, but they're smiling. It's a hot day, and the momentary spray probably felt refreshing. Karina notices Hannah's mom, Pam, among them.

Now that Hannah is moving to Indiana, Karina assumes she won't see Pam at all anymore. They stopped their Thursday-night wine dates some time ago, not long after Grace started high school. Over the past couple of years, their friendship dwindled to the handful of unfulfilling moments before or after Hannah's weekly piano lesson. Tasked with shuttling her three kids to and from a dizzying schedule of extracurricular activities all over town, Pam was often too rushed to even come inside and

LISA GENOVA

waited for Hannah in her running car. Karina waved to her from the front door every Tuesday at 5:30 as Pam pulled away.

Karina almost didn't come today. She feels self-conscious about showing up alone. Naturally introverted, she'd been extremely private about her marriage and even more shut-in about her divorce. Assuming Richard didn't air their dirty laundry either, and that's a safe bet, no one knows the details. So the gossip mill scripted the drama it wasn't supplied. Someone has to be right, and someone has to be wrong. Based on the hushed stares, vanished chitchat, and pulled plastic smiles, Karina knows how she's been cast.

The women in particular sympathize with him. Of course they do. They paint him as a sainted celebrity. He deserves to be with someone more elegant, someone who appreciates how extraordinary he is, someone more his equal. They assume she's jealous of his accomplishments, resentful of his acclaim, bitter about his fame. She's nothing but a rinky-dink suburban piano teacher instructing disinterested sixteen-year-olds on how to play Chopin. She clearly doesn't have the self-esteem to be the wife of such a great man.

They don't know. They don't know a damn thing.

Grace just finished her freshman year at the University of Chicago. Karina had anticipated that Grace would be home for the summer by now and would be at Hannah's party, but Grace decided to stay on campus through the summer, interning on a project with her math professor. Something about statistics. Karina's proud of her daughter for being selected for the internship and thinks it's a great opportunity, and yet, there's that pang in Karina's stomach, the familiar letdown. Grace could've chosen to come home, to spend the summer with her mother, but she didn't. Karina knows it's ridiculous to feel slighted, forsaken even, but her emotions sit on the throne of her intellect. This is how she's built, and like any castle, her foundational stones aren't easily rearranged.

Her divorce became absolute in September of Grace's senior year, and exactly one year later, Grace moved a thousand miles away. First Richard left. Then Grace. Karina wonders when she'll get used to the silence in her home, the emptiness, the memories that hang in each room as real as the artwork on the walls. She misses her daughter's voice chatting on the phone; her giggling girl-friends; her shoes in every room; her hair elastics, towels, and clothes on the floor; the lights left on. She misses her daughter.

She does not miss Richard. When he moved out, his absence felt more like a new presence than a subtraction. The sweet calm that took up residence after he left filled more space than his human form and colossal ego ever did. She did not miss him then or now.

But going to these kinds of family events alone, without a husband, tilts her off-balance as if she were one cheek atop a two-legged stool. So in that sense, she misses him. For the stability. She's forty-five and divorced. Single. In Poland, she'd be considered a disgrace. But she's been in America now for over half her life. Her situation is

LISA GENOVA

common in this secular culture and imposes no shame. Yet, she feels ashamed. You can take the girl out of Poland, but you can't take Poland out of the girl.

Not recognizing any of the other parents, she takes a deep breath and begins the long, awkward walk alone over to Pam. Karina spent an absurdly long time getting ready for this party. Which dress, which shoes, which earrings? She blew out her hair. She even got a manicure yesterday. For what? It's not as if she's trying to impress Hannah or Pam or any of the parents. And it's not as if there will be any single men here, not that she's looking for a man anyway.

She knows why. She'll be damned if anyone here looks at her and thinks, *Poor Karina. Her life's a mess, and she looks it, too.* The other reason is Richard. Pam and Scott Chu are his friends, too. Richard was probably invited. She could've asked Pam if Richard was on the guest list—not that it mattered, just to be forewarned—but she chickened out.

So there it is, the stomach-turning possibility that he might be here, and the even more putrid thought that he might show up with the latest skinny little twentysomething tart hanging on his arm and every self-important word. Karina rubs her lips together, making sure her lipstick hasn't clumped.

Her eyes poke around the yard. He's not standing with Pam and the cluster of parents by the pool house. Karina scans the pool, the grilling island, the lawn. She doesn't see him.

She arrives at the pool house and inserts herself into

the circle of Pam and Scott and other parents. Their voices instantly drop, their eyes conspiring. Time pauses.

"Hey, what's going on?" Karina asks.

The circle looks to Pam.

"Um . . ." Pam hesitates. "We were just talking about Richard."

"Oh?" Karina waits, her heart bracing for something humiliating. No one says a word. "What about him?"

"He canceled his tour."

"Oh." This isn't earth-shattering news. He's canceled gigs and touring dates before. Once, he couldn't stand the conductor and refused to set foot onstage with him. Another time, Richard had to be replaced last minute because he got drunk at an airport bar and missed his flight. She wonders what reason he has this time. But Pam and Scott and the others stare at her with grave expressions, as if she should have something more compassionate to say on the subject.

Her stomach floods with emotion, her inner streets crowding fast as a fervent protest stands upon its soapbox in her center, outraged that she has to deal with this, that Pam especially can't be more sensitive to her. Richard's canceled tour isn't her concern. She divorced him. His life isn't her problem anymore.

"You really don't know?" asks Pam.

They all wait for her answer, lips shut, bodies still, an audience engrossed in watching a play.

"What? What, is he dying or something?"

A nervous half-laugh escapes her, and the sound finds no harmony. She searches the circle of parents for connection, even if the comment was slightly inappropriate, for someone to forgive her a bit of dark humor. But everyone either looks horrified or away. Everyone but Pam. Her eyes betray a reluctant nod.

"Karina, he has ALS."

CHAPTER TWO

Richard lies in bed awake, satisfied by a full night's sleep, his eyes alert and unblinking, staring vaguely at a curled slice of peeling paint on the vaulted ceiling directly above him. He can feel it coming, an invisible presence creeping, like ions charged and buzzing in the air before an approaching electrical storm, and all he can do is lie still and wait for it to pass through him.

He's in his own bedroom when he should be waking up in the Mandarin Oriental in New York City. He was supposed to play a solo recital at David Geffen Hall at Lincoln Center last night. He loves Lincoln Center. The almost-three-thousand-seat venue had been sold-out for months. If he were at the Mandarin, he'd be about ready to order breakfast. Possibly for two.

But he's not at the Mandarin in New York, and he's not in the company of a lovely woman. He's alone in his bed in his condo on Commonwealth Avenue in Boston. And even though he's hungry, he waits.

Trevor, his agent, sent out a press release canceling his tour, claiming tendinitis. Richard can't understand the point of publicizing this misleading information. They bite the bullet now or they bite the bullet later. Either way, the barrel of the gun stays firmly pointed at Richard's head. True, he first assumed he was dealing with tendinitis, a frustratingly inconvenient but common injury that would heal with rest and physical therapy. He'd been so frustrated with taking even a few weeks away from the piano, worried about what it would do to his playing. That was seven months and a lifetime ago. What he wouldn't give to have tendinitis.

It's possible his agent is still in denial. Richard is scheduled to play with the Chicago Symphony Orchestra in the fall. Trevor hasn't canceled this gig yet, just in case Richard is somehow better by then. Richard gets it. Even now, six months after his diagnosis, he still can't fully wrap his mind around what he has, what's going to happen. Many times in any given day, when he's reading or drinking a cup of coffee, he's symptom-free. He'll feel totally normal, and he'll either forget that the past several months have happened, or a confident rebellion rises.

The neurologist was wrong. It's a virus. A pinched nerve. Lyme disease. Tendinitis. A temporary problem, and now it's resolved. Nothing's wrong.

And then his right hand won't keep time when playing

Rachmaninoff's Prelude in G-sharp Minor, chasing and not catching the tempo. Or he'll drop his half-full cup of coffee because it's too heavy. Or he doesn't have the strength to manage the fingernail clipper. He looks down at the grotesquely long fingernails of his left hand, the neatly trimmed nails of his right.

This is not a temporary problem.

He will not be playing in Chicago in the fall.

He's naked, has always slept in the nude. All those years next to Karina in her high-necked flannel pajamas and kneesocks. He tries to picture her naked but can only imagine the other women. This would normally arouse him, and he'd welcome the pleasant distraction of masturbation right now, but the dreadful anticipation of what's coming has him anxious, and his dick lies limp and still like the rest of him.

His body heat has created a cozy cocoon beneath the covers, a stark contrast to the uninviting temperature of his bedroom. He braces for the shocking sharpness of cold air against his skin as he whips the sheet and comforter off his body. He wants to see it when it comes.

His eyes scrutinize the length of his arms, each knuckle of each finger, especially the index and middle fingers of his right hand. He evaluates his chest and stomach for irregularities amid the rise and fall of his breathing. He drops his gaze to his legs, his toes; his senses heightened and ready, a hunter scanning for a flash of white fur.

He waits, his body a pot of water on the stove, the setting dialed to high. It's only a matter of time. A watched pot will eventually boil. Of course, he hopes it won't come.

But also, perversely, he lies there welcoming it, its familiarity dancing through his body.

The first bubble breaks the surface, a pop in his left calf. It vibrates there for a few seconds, the opening act, then jumps to his right quadriceps, just above the knee. Then the pad at the base of his right thumb flickers. Over and over and over.

He can't bear to witness this one in particular, this spasm in his dominant thumb, yet he cannot look away. He silently pleads with it, this microscopic enemy within. By sheer coincidence, for he knows he possesses no power over its intentions, it leaves his hand, tunneling in the space between his skin and fascia like a mouse burrowing within the walls of a house, and invades his right biceps next. Then his bottom lip. These rapid, fluttering seizures ripple from one part of his body to another in rapid succession, a roiling boil.

Sometimes, the twitching lingers in one place. Yesterday, it got stuck in a quarter-size segment of his right triceps, contracting in intermittent, repetitive pulses for several hours. It set up shop there, obsessed there, fell in love and couldn't move on, and he panicked that it would never stop.

Yet he knows with absolute certainty that it will stop. At some point, the twitching in every single muscle group—in his arms, his legs, his mouth, his diaphragm— will stop forever, and so he should embrace the twitching. Be grateful for it. The twitching means his muscles are still there, still capable of responding.

For now.

His motor neurons are being poisoned by a cocktail of toxins, the recipe unknown to his doctor and every scientist on the planet, and his entire motor neuron system is in a death spiral. His neurons are dying, and the muscles they feed are literally starving for input. Every twitch is a muscle stammering, gasping, begging to be saved.

They can't be saved.

But they aren't dead yet. Like the fuel light in his car that alerts him when he's low on gas, these fasciculations are an early-warning system. As he lies naked and cold on his bed, he starts doing math. Assuming he has about two gallons left in the tank when his fuel light is triggered and that his BMW conservatively does twenty-two miles per gallon in the city, he could go forty-four more miles before running out of gas. He imagines this scenario. The last drop of gas used. The engine gears ground to a halt. Seized. The car stopped. Dead.

The right side of his bottom lip twitches. Without understanding the biology, he wonders how much muscle fuel remains in his body and wishes the twitching could be enumerated.

How many miles does he have left?

CHAPTER THREE

As Karina walks a little over five blocks to Commonwealth Avenue, she's barely aware of her surroundings—sparrows nibbling on crumbs of a dropped muffin beneath a park bench; a fierce dragon tattoo covering the bare chest of a skateboarder; the aggressive whir of the board's wheels as he whizzes by her; a young Asian couple strolling hip to hip, hand in hand; a breeze perfumed with cigarette smoke; a baby wailing in a stroller; a dog barking; the alternating choreography of cars and pedestrians at every intersection. Instead, her attention is held inward.

Her heart races faster than required for her walking pace, making her anxious. Or maybe, likely, she was anxious first, and her heart rate responded. She speeds up in an effort to synchronize her external action with her inner physiology, which only makes her feel as if she were rushing, late. She checks her watch, which is utterly unnecessary. She can't be early or late when he doesn't know she's coming.

She's worked up a sweat. Stopped at the next corner, waiting for a WALK signal, she pulls a tissue from her purse, reaches under her shirt, and blots her armpits. She digs around for another tissue but can't find one. She wipes her forehead and nose with her hands.

She arrives at Richard's address and stops at the base of the stairs, looking up to the fourth-floor windows. Behind her, the spires of Trinity Church and the sheer vertical glass of the John Hancock building rise above the rooftops of the brownstones on the other side of Comm Ave. He has a lovely view.

This street in the Back Bay is especially posh, housing Boston's Brahmins, cousins to their neighbors on Beacon Hill. Richard lives on the same block as many of Boston's elegant and elite—the president of BioGO, a Massachusetts General Hospital surgeon, the fourth-generation owner of a two-hundred-year-old art gallery on Newbury Street. Richard makes decent money, exceptional for a pianist, but this address is way out of his league, probably his version of a midlife crisis, his shiny red Porsche. He must be mortgaged to the hilt.

She hasn't seen him since Grace's high school graduation, over a year ago now. And she's never been here. Well, she's driven by twice before, both times at night, both times ostensibly to avoid traffic, purposefully rerouting from her preferred course home from downtown Boston, slowing to a crawl just long enough to avoid instigating honks from behind her, barely long enough to capture a quick blur of high ceilings and a nonspecific golden glow of a home inhabited.

She resents that Richard got to be the one to move out, to start over, fresh in a new place. Memories of him haunt her in every room of their once-shared home, the rare good as unsettling as the common bad. She replaced their mattress and their dinnerware. She removed their framed wedding picture from the living-room wall and hung a pretty mirror there instead. It doesn't matter. She's exactly where he left her, still living in their house, his energetic impression left behind like a red-wine stain on a white blouse. Even washed a thousand times, that brown spot is never coming out.

She could move, especially now that Grace has gone off to college. But where would she go? And do what? Her stubbornness, that impenetrable bedrock of her personality, refuses to give these questions actual consideration beyond calling them nonsense. So she stays put, frozen in the three-bedroom colonial museum of her devastated marriage.

Grace already had her license when Karina and Richard separated, so she was able to drive herself over to her father's "house." His bachelor pad. Karina walks up the stairs to the front door of his brownstone, and her mouth goes sour. At the top step, her stomach matches the taste in her mouth, and the word *sicken* grabs the microphone of her inner monologue. She feels sick. But she's not sick, she reminds herself. Richard is.

The sour in her stomach turns, fermenting. Why is she here? To say or do what? Offer pity, sympathy, help? To see how bad off he is with her own eyes, the same reason drivers rubberneck when passing the site of an accident—to get a good look at the wreckage before moving along?

What will he look like? She has no reference point other than Stephen Hawking. A hand puppet with no hand in the body, paralyzed, emaciated, unable to breathe without a machine, his limbs, torso, and head positioned in a wheelchair like a little girl's floppy, cotton-limbed rag doll, his voice computer generated. Is that what Richard will look like?

He might not even be home. Maybe he's in a hospital. She should've called first. Calling somehow seemed scarier than drumming up the nerve to show up at his front door unannounced. Part of her believes that she caused his illness, even though she knows that such thinking is narcissistically absurd. How many times has she wished him dead? Now he's dying, and she's a despicable, hellbound, horrible woman for ever wishing such a thing, and worse, for having derived sick pleasure from it.

She stands before the doorbell, torn between following through and turning around, passionate counterpoints creating a quagmire of indecision, pushing and pulling her from within. If she were the gambling kind, she'd put her money on leaving. She breaks through her inertia and rings the bell, surprising herself.

"Hello?" asks Richard's voice over the intercom speaker.

Karina's heart beats in her tight, acidic throat. "It's Karina."

She tucks her hair behind her ears and pulls at her bra strap, which is sticking uncomfortably to her sweaty body. She waits for him to buzz her in, but nothing happens. Opaque white curtains cover the windows in the door, making it impossible to see if anyone is coming. Then she hears footsteps. The door opens.

Richard says nothing. She waits for him to look stunned that she's here, but that doesn't happen. Instead his face is motionless but for his eyes, which hint at a smile, not exactly happy to see her, but satisfied, right about something, and her heart in her throat already knows that this visit was a disastrous idea. He continues to say nothing and she says nothing, and this nonverbal game of chicken probably takes up two seconds, but it stretches out in agonizing slow motion beyond the boundaries of space and time.

"I should've called."

"Come on in."

As she follows him up the three flights, she studies his footing, assured and steady and normal. His left hand slides along the banister, and although it never loses contact, the banister doesn't appear to be assisting him. It's not a handicapped railing. From behind, he looks perfectly healthy.

It was a rumor.

She is a fool.

Inside his condo, he leads her to the kitchen, dark wood and black counters and stainless steel, modern and masculine. He offers her a seat on a stool at the island, overlooking the living room—his Steinway grand, a brown leather couch, the Oriental carpet from their den, a laptop computer on a desk by the window, a bookcase—sparse and tidy and singularly focused. Very Richard.

An army of at least two dozen bottles of wine stands at attention on the kitchen counter, an uncorked neck and a puddle of red at the bottom of a goblet in front of him. He loves wine, likes to fancy himself a connoisseur, but typically indulges in a special selection only after a performance or in celebration of an achievement or a holiday or at least with dinner. It's not even noon on a Wednesday.

"These were from the cellar. This 2000 Château Mouton Rothschild is exquisite." He pulls a glass from a cabinet. "Join me?"

"No, thanks."

"This"—he waves his hand back and forth in the air between them—"unexpected visit or whatever it is needs alcohol, don't you think?"

"Should you be drinking so much?"

He laughs. "I'm not tackling all of these today. Tomorrow and tomorrow and tomorrow."

He grabs a beautiful black bottle with a golden sheep embossed on it, already open, and pours her a generous glass, ignoring her answer. She sips, then smiles out of obligation, unimpressed.

He laughs again. "You still have the discriminating palette of a farm animal."

It's true. She can't discern the difference between an

expensive bottle of Mouton and a jug of Gallo, nor does she care, and both traits have always driven Richard mad. And true to patronizing form, he's essentially just called her a stupid pig. Karina clenches her teeth, biting back the comment that will leave her mouth if she opens it and the urge to throw $100 worth of his precious wine in his face.

He swirls, smells, sips, closes his eyes, waits, swallows, and licks his lips. He opens his eyes and mouth and looks at her as if he's just had an orgasm or seen God.

"How can you not appreciate this? The timing is perfect. Taste it again. Smell the cherries?"

She tries another sip. It's okay. She doesn't smell cherries. "I can't remember the last time we shared a bottle of wine."

"Four years ago, November. I was just home from Japan, wrecked from the flights. You made *golabki*, and we drank a bottle of Châteaux Margaux."

She stares at him, surprised and intrigued. She has no memory of this evening, so readily and fondly retrieved by Richard, and wonders if it simply wasn't significant enough to her to hold on to or if the memory faded, crowded out by too many other experiences that didn't jibe. Funny how the story of their lives can be an entirely different genre depending on the narrator.

They lock eyes. His look a bit older than she remembers. Or not older. Sadder. And his face looks more defined. Although he's always been thin, he's definitely lost weight. And he's grown a beard.

"I see you've stopped shaving."

"Trying something new. You like it?"

♪

"No."

He grins and takes another sip of wine. He taps the rim of his glass with his finger and says nothing, and she can't figure out whether he's deciding which of her buttons to push or showing restraint. Restraint would be new.

"So you canceled your tour."

"How did you hear?"

"The *Globe* said it was tendinitis."

"So is that why you're here, to check on my tendinitis?"

He's baiting her, asking her to spell it out, to say the three letters, and her apprehensive heart beats too fast again. She brings the goblet to her lips, avoiding his question and her answer, swallowing a mouthful of wine along with her real reason for being here.

"I used to think you sometimes canceled for the attention."

"Karina, I'm abandoning several thousand people over the next three weeks who were all planning on spending an entire evening paying attention to me. Canceling is the opposite of calling attention."

Again, they lock eyes, and the energy exchanged is somewhere between an intimate connection and a showdown.

"Of course, it did get your attention." He smiles.

He sticks his nose into his goblet and inhales, then drains the remaining gulp. He looks over the bottles on the counter and pulls a soldier from the back row. He fits the hood of the opener over the top of the neck and begins to twist, but he keeps losing his grip before making any progress. He lifts the opener off the bottle and examines

LISA GENOVA

the top, rubbing it with his finger. He wipes his hand on his pants, as if it had been wet.

"These hard-wax-capsule corks are a bitch to open."

He repositions the opener and tries and tries, but his fingers keep slipping and have no command over the twisting mechanism. Without thinking much of it, she's about to offer to do it for him when he stops and hurls the bottle opener across the room. Karina ducks reflexively, even though she was never in danger from the object's trajectory.

"There it is," he accuses her. "That's what you came to see, yes?"

"I don't know. I didn't know."

"You happy now?"

"No."

"That's why you came here. To see me humiliated like this."

"No."

"I can't play anymore, not well enough, and I won't be able to ever again. That's why my tour was canceled, Karina. Is that what you wanted to hear?"

"No."

She stares into his eyes, and standing squarely in the windows of his rage is pure terror.

"Then why are you here?"

"I thought it was the right thing to do."

"Look at you, suddenly a model Catholic, concerned about right and wrong. With all due respect, my dear, you wouldn't know right from wrong if it fucked you up the ass."

She shakes her head, sickened by him, disgusted with herself for not knowing better. She stands. "I didn't come here to be abused by you."

"Oh, there you go, carting out that word. No one's abusing you. Stop using that word. You've brainwashed Grace. This is why she won't talk to me."

"Don't blame me for that. If she's not talking to you, maybe it's because you're a prick."

"Or maybe it's because her mother is a vindictive bitch."

Karina takes the bottle he couldn't open by the neck and smashes it against the edge of the counter. She drops the broken bottleneck and steps away from the expanding puddle of wine on the floor.

"That one smells like cherries," she says, her voice shaking.

"Leave. Right now."

"I'm sorry I ever came here."

She slams the door behind her and runs down the three flights as if she were being chased. She had such good intentions. How did that go so wrong?

How did it all go so wrong?

Rage and grief assault her from all sides, and her legs suddenly feel loosened and drained, powerless to continue. She sits on the top step of the front stoop, facing the beautiful view—the joggers on Comm Ave., the pigeons in the park, the spires of Trinity Church, and the blue glass of the Hancock—not caring who sees or hears her, and sobs.

CHAPTER FOUR

Richard sits down at his piano for the first time in three weeks, since August 17, the day his right index finger gave up the fight, the last of his right-handed fingers to fall deaf to his wishes. He'd been testing it daily. On August 16, he could tap his right index finger ever so slightly. He clung to this accomplishment, pathetically celebrating this movement that required massive mental and physical effort and that looked more like a feeble tremor than a tap. He placed his entire life's hope on that finger, which eight months ago could dance across the keys of the most complex, athletic pieces without missing a beat, striking each note with just the right amount of force.

FORTISSIMO!

Diminuendo.

His index finger, every finger of his right hand, a finely calibrated instrument. If he made a single mistake while rehearsing, if one of his fingers lacked confidence, strength, or memory and stumbled, he'd stop instantly and start the piece over from the beginning. There was never room for error. No excuse for his fingers.

Eight months ago, his right hand held five of the finest fingers in the world. Today, his entire right arm and hand are paralyzed. Dead to him, as if they already belong to a corpse.

He picks up his lifeless hand with his left and places it on the keys, setting his right thumb onto middle C, pinkie on G. He feels the cool sleekness of the keys, and the touch is sensual, seductive. The keys want to be caressed, the relationship ready and available to him, but he can't respond, and this is suddenly the cruelest moment of his life.

He stares in horror at his dead hand on the beautiful keys. It's not simply that his hand is motionless that makes it appear dead. There's no curl to his fingers. His entire hand is too straight, too flat, devoid of tone, personality, possibility. It's atrophied, flaccid, impotent. It appears fake, like a Halloween costume, a Hollywood prop, a wax prosthetic. It can't belong to him.

The air in the room thickens, too solid to breathe, and he can't seem to remember how to inhale. A wave of panic slips through him. He places his left fingers on the keys, arm extended, wrist up, fingers curled, loving the keys they touch, and he inhales sharply. He heaves air through his lungs as if running for his life while his desperate eyes search the keys and his two hands for what to do. What the hell can he do?

He begins to play Brahms I, actual notes with only his left hand, the right-hand notes with his mind's ear. He played this fifty-minute concerto with the Boston Symphony Orchestra at Tanglewood last summer. Eighty-seven pages memorized and played as near to perfection as anyone ever has. Some nights the music is well played and applauded, and other nights, the music is transcendent. He lives for those transcendent nights.

That evening on the lawn, the entire orchestra was more than simply a cover band for Brahms. They were an open conduit, breathing life into the music, and he felt that ecstatic, energetic connection between his soul, the souls of the other musicians, the souls of the audience on the lawn, and the soul of the notes. He's never been able to adequately describe the equation or the experience of this alchemy. Using language to convey the magic of Brahms would be like using a wooden classroom ruler to measure the speed of light.

While playing solely with his left hand, he closes his eyes to lose sight of his immovable corpse hand, and this cut-and-paste, mind-body performance is satisfying to him for a bit. But then he's rocking his torso back and forth, an unshakable habit criticized by many of his teachers as being either distracting or indulgent, and accidently knocks his right hand off its position on the keys. His entire dead arm dangles from his shoulder like a dropped anchor, heavy and painful, likely dislocated again.

He uses it. The pain in Brahms I, the gravitas, the

longing, the loss, the battle in the stormy first movement, like walking into war. The haunting solo played by his left hand. The lonely memory of the melody playing in his mind. The agony in his shoulder. The loss of his right hand.

He dares to wonder what part of himself he'll lose next. His gut and his mind agree.

Your other hand.

He wails aloud and strikes the keys harder with his left hand while he still can. He loses the sound of the melody in his memory and can now hear only what is real, vibrations produced by hammers and felt and strings and vocal cords, and the absence of the right-handed notes feels like a death, a loss of true love, the bitter end of a relationship, a divorce.

It feels just like his divorce. He lifts his left hand high above the keys and hesitates, stopping the piece just before the crescendo of the first movement, his heart pounding in his shoulder and in the sudden silence, the unfinished song, his interrupted life. He curls his left hand into a fist and pounds the keys as hard as he can as if in a street fight as he weeps, betrayed and heartbroken all over again.

CHAPTER FIVE

It's Family Weekend at the University of Chicago. Grace insisted that it wasn't necessary for Karina to come. Karina already knew what the campus looked like, Grace argued. They'd bought sweatshirts and T-shirts and bumper stickers and coffee mugs from the campus store last year. Karina sees Grace's dorm room and roommate and gets caught up every Sunday when Grace FaceTimes her. Karina thought Grace seemed a little too invested in her opposition to the visit, as if protecting her privacy or independence or some big secret. But Karina could not be dissuaded. The airfare was reasonable, and she was missing her daughter.

They're at Common Grounds, a homey hipster campus coffee shop, and the big secret is sitting next to Grace, one hand on his triple-shot latte, the other on Grace's thigh. Matt has overly styled brown hair, a shadow of a beard, and blue eyes that become amused whenever he talks. He's clearly crazy about Grace. And although she's trying to play it cool in front of her mother, Grace is crazy about him, too.

"So Grace says you're an amazing pianist," says Matt.

Karina holds her pumpkin-spice latte midway between her lips and the table, suddenly unsure of which way she was going with it. She's caught surprised, moved that Grace would describe her this way. Brag even. Richard is the amazing pianist, not her. Or maybe Matt simply has them confused. Or he's kissing up to his girlfriend's mother.

She sets her cup on the table. "No, that's her father. I'm just a piano teacher."

"She's amazing," says Grace, assertively correcting her mother. "But she gave up her career to stay home with me. This is why I'm never getting pregnant. I'm not wasting my education on raising some kid."

"Some bratty kid," says Matt, smiling.

Grace playfully shoves his arm, squeezing his biceps before letting go. Karina sips her latte and licks the foam from her lips as she watches them. They're definitely having sex.

Karina and Grace are close, but they don't discuss such things, a trait seemingly passed down from Karina's mother, like her green eyes and proclivity for waking before dawn no matter how exhausted she was. Karina had exactly one conversation with her mother about sex. She was twelve and forgets the wording of what she asked, but she remembers her mother's response as she washed dishes at the sink, her back to Karina: "Sex is how babies are made. It's a sacred act between husbands and wives. Now go bring the towels in off the line." End of story, forever.

Karina got little more from the nuns and her friends. She remembers feeling horrified and embarrassed when Zofia told her that Natalia was giving boys blow jobs under the bleachers in the gymnasium, mostly because Karina wasn't quite sure what a blow job was and didn't have the courage to ask. Whatever it was, she knew for sure that Natalia was going to hell for it.

When Karina was sixteen, her boisterous and beautiful friend, Martyna, was sent away to live with an aunt. She returned nine months later, her disposition subdued, her eyes averting others, pointing to her shoes. Everyone in town gossiped about her. Martyna was damaged goods. No one would ever marry her now. Such a shame.

Karina had imagined the baby Martyna left behind, a daughter or son she would never know, and the spinster's life ahead of her. Right then, she'd made a promise to herself. She would not end up ruined like Martyna or imprisoned like her mother, chained to the kitchen, cooking and cleaning day and night for decades, raising five children. Karina would not lose control of her life.

When Grace was a freshman in high school, they had "the talk." Karina was determined to make it more informative than the "wisdom" her mother had imparted to her and consciously didn't include any Catholic shame or misogynistic mythology. *No sex before marriage, no birth control—those aren't God's rules, honey. Those rules were made*

♪

by men. They were in the car, on their way to one of Grace's soccer games, more side by side than face-to-face, but a big improvement over Karina's mother's back side. Karina's speech included information about condoms and the pill, STDs and pregnancy, intimacy and love.

Sex isn't a sin. But you have to protect yourself. Birth control is the woman's responsibility. She winces now as the words play in her mind, just as she did when she said them aloud to Grace in the car, reliving the guilt. Using birth control isn't a sin. She did what she had to do.

Thou shalt not lie.

Lying is a sin.

If Grace remembered one thing from that conversation, Karina always hoped it was the admonition *Whatever you do, don't get pregnant.* She's sure she repeated it several times, and although she could only glance at the side of Grace's face while driving, Karina could sense Grace's embarrassment and eye rolling.

She looks at Grace straight on now, and her face is self-assured and radiant. She's in control of her life. Karina's glad to see the message was received, but she didn't mean *ever.* Did she somehow communicate that as well?

"Well, I am pretty awesome. So it was all worth it, right, Mom?"

"Yes, honey."

"Do you teach at a school?" asks Matt.

"No, at home. In my living room."

"Oh."

"Really, she's at least as good as my dad, but he gets all the glory."

"Have you talked with your father?" asks Karina.

"Not recently. Why?"

Karina hasn't heard anything about Richard since that horrible day in July when she went to see him. Although he couldn't open the wine bottle, she's still not convinced he really has ALS. He probably has something like carpal tunnel or tendinitis, injuries common to every pianist at some point, pesky but ultimately benign. If Richard really has ALS, he'd tell his only daughter, wouldn't he?

"I think he's supposed to play here in Chicago next month."

"I don't know anything about it." Grace shrugs her right shoulder. "Why are you still keeping track of where he's going to be? You need to get your own life, Mom."

Karina feels her cheeks flush. Grace's quick comment is too sharp, an insulting slap, and it feels cruel, especially in front of Matt, someone who doesn't know Karina's complicated history. But she believes Grace's insensitivity was unintentional and swallows the urge to defend herself. She and Grace have had many heart-to-hearts about this over the past year. Now that Grace is in college, Karina could move. She could live in New York or New Orleans or Paris. She could give up teaching and play again. She could reinvent her life. Or at least track down the one she abandoned. She could do anything. Or at least something.

"Where's *your* musical talent?" Matt asks Grace.

"I'm, like, the best karaoke singer ever."

"The best worst. You sure you weren't adopted?"

"I look just like her."

"Or maybe you were dropped on your head?"

"That would explain my taste in men."

This time Matt shoves Grace's arm, and Grace giggles. *Men*, not *boys*. When did her little girl become a young woman?

It occurs to her that Grace is the same age Karina was when she met Richard. They were in Sherman Leiper's Technique class together. She knew nothing about Richard except that he seemed awkward and intensely driven. She could feel him staring at her in class, too shy to talk, for almost an entire semester. Then one day, he did.

They were at a keg party at one of the dorms. Emboldened by beer, he introduced himself. One beer turned into many, catalyzing their attraction, but not until she heard him play piano did she fall for him. They were alone in a practice room, and he played Schumann's Fantasie in C Major, op. 17. He was so connected to the piece that he seemed to become unconscious of her presence. His playing was powerful yet gentle, assured, masterful. And the composition is so utterly romantic, still one of her favorites. By the time he played the final note, she was in love.

They had sex morning and night, more often than she brushed her teeth. She spent her days memorizing Bach and Mozart and her nights memorizing the shape of him, the first and last notes of every day played on each other's body. They were passionate, insatiable for piano and each other. Nothing else existed. She'd never been happier.

She knows this is her history, the early chapters in the biography of her life, yet she feels utterly disconnected from it. She remembers that first year with Richard, yet these memories, these snapshots of body parts tangled up in bedsheets, feel as if they must belong to someone else, a character in a book she read long ago.

The thought of Richard even kissing her now is revolting, that she ever desired him crazy, that they were married surreal. Yet it all happened.

She watches Grace listening to Matt, smiling, flirting, enamored, and wonders what their narrative will be. She hopes her daughter fares better in love and marriage than she did. *Don't repeat the mistakes I made.*

Could Karina have seen the red flags through the thick haze of lust at twenty? Was there any way to predict all that would unfold? Possibly. Richard was always a bit of a narcissist, a fragile egomaniac, a selfish prick. She naïvely thought these were the character traits of any talented, ambitious man. The price of admission. She respected his dedication to piano and admired his confidence. Looking back, she can see that his dedication was desperation, his confidence was arrogance, that he was always a house of cards.

Still, in the beginning, their relationship was intoxicating and held the promise of a great love story. In the end, it was dog shit. *Till death do us part.* That's a man-made rule, too. An unreasonable one, she thinks. Everything begins and ends. Every day and night, every concerto, every relationship, every life. Everything ends eventually. She wishes she and Richard had ended better.

The playlist in the coffee shop, which had been a steady stream of pop songs—Ed Sheeran and Rihanna and Taylor Swift—switches abruptly to Thelonious Monk.

"Mom, listen. You used to play something like this when I was little. Remember?"

Karina stares at Grace with her mouth open, shocked. Grace had to have been three or four. "Yes. I can't believe you do."

"What kind of music do you play now?" asks Matt.

"Classical. Mostly Chopin, Mozart, Bach."

"Oh, nice."

"How come you don't play this?" asks Grace.

A million reasons.

"I don't know."

Grace looks up and away, at nothing in particular, and listens. The song is "'Round Midnight," a late-night loungy ballad that makes Karina feel as if she should have her hands around a gin and tonic instead of a pumpkin-spice latte. She imagines the keys under her fingers as she plays along with her mind's ear, the motor plan unfolded like an old family recipe, still legible after so many years. She feels the notes vibrating in her heart, and she's swept up in an intense longing, approaching something close to sorrow. Regret. She listens to Monk playing jazz, and her heart fills with regret.

A smile enlivens Grace's face, and her eyes brighten. "I love it, don't you?"

Karina's cheeks flush pink again. She nods.

"I do."

CHAPTER SIX

In the languid, not-quite-conscious moments before Richard opens his eyes, newly familiar black notes dance across crisp white sheets of paper behind his lids. He hears the sound of the notes as his mind sees them, ascending arpeggios that call him like a siren to his bench. He opens his eyes. A ribbon of bright white light slices through the midline of the drawn heavy drapes of his bedroom. Another day.

He instructs the fingers of his left hand to play scales on the fitted white sheet, his morning ritual. His daily exam. He studies this symphony of simple movement, the sequential, rapid lift and drop of each finger like a sewing-machine needle, the machinery of tendons, knuckles, veins, and muscle, no less miraculous and essential to him than his beating heart.

Satisfied, he gets up, pees, and walks into the kitchen to prepare breakfast, resisting the impatient pull of his Steinway for the moment. Sitting naked at the kitchen-island counter, he sips hot coffee through a straw while vaguely studying his feet. He commands his toes to wiggle. They comply. Bending his neck and curling his upper torso down, he stretches his lips to meet a powdered doughnut in his hand. His left shoulder has started to lock, limiting the vertical mobility of his arm. He tries not to dwell on the advancing paralysis that this new symptom likely predicts. Maybe the disease will stop there, in his left shoulder. He could live with that.

As he alternates between doughnut and coffee, he allows his thoughts to peer down the rabbit hole and imagines the impact if this disease doesn't stop there. He pans around the room, his field of view narrowed like a series of close-up shots in a horror movie—the cabinet knobs (most already out of reach), the coffeemaker, the sink, the refrigerator-door handle, the light switches, his phone, his computer. His piano. He'll have two paralyzed arms. No hands. He won't be able to feed himself, scratch his head, wipe his ass. He stares at his piano as he sucks up the last drops of coffee. Maybe the disease will stop in his shoulder.

Finished with coffee and doughnut, he wants to lick clean the dusty white sugar covering his fingertips but instead wipes it onto the bare skin of his thigh. He'll continue brewing coffee throughout the day, but only for the invigorating aroma it diffuses throughout his home. More than a cup gives him the shakes.

Done with breakfast, he showers, bending over to shampoo his hair, in and out before the bathroom mirror fogs. He examines his furry face at the vanity. It's been almost two weeks since he last shaved. He can still adequately manage the job with his left hand, but he hasn't felt like bothering. Maybe he'll shave today.

Although he's right-handed, a life at the piano has made him essentially ambidextrous. He feels so lucky. He smiles. But his smile in the mirror is dressed in a beard he doesn't want, and he thinks of all the people in the world with two healthy, functional hands and clean-shaven faces who don't have ALS, and his mind mocks him for feeling fortunate. His smile is a betrayal of his grim reality, a Pollyanna fool's mission. *What do you have to smile about?* Shamed, he stops. His closed-lipped face is somber, serious, covered in black hair, a bit menacing, a much more appropriate portrayal of a forty-five-year-old man with a fatal neuromuscular disease. He decides to keep the beard.

He stands before his closet, demoralized by so many sleeves and buttons, and considers not dressing at all. But then he remembers what he's ready to play, and inspired, he goes in the completely opposite sartorial direction. He pulls out his best tuxedo.

Socks and trousers are challenging but doable. Lace-up shoes are history. He slides his feet into patent-leather loafers. Now the top half. His eyes fill with sinking dread as he hopelessly puzzles over the pleated shirt, the waistcoat, the cuff links, the bow tie. To hell with all that. He threads his tuxedo-jacket sleeve over his lifeless right arm and buttons a single button over his bare-chested body with relative ease. There. Ready to perform.

Being mathematically minded, he'd assumed that playing the piano with one hand would be at most only half as satisfying as with two, but he was 100 percent wrong. For the past three days, he's been rapt and obsessed with Maurice Ravel's Piano Concerto for the Left Hand. It's about a fifteen-minute piece played alone, eighteen with a whole orchestra, a single movement originally composed for Austrian pianist Paul Wittgenstein, who lost his right arm in World War I.

Richard sits tall at his bench, places his right hand on his lap, and turns the sheet music over, hiding the notes. He'll play it this time from memory. He positions his left hand on the keys and waits. He imagines an audience of several hundred in his living room, the conductor and orchestra in his kitchen.

The concerto begins immersed in darkness, a foreboding storm in the bass and tenor registers, the solemn contrabassoon, the thundering drums. Richard's solo begins about a minute and a half in. His hand climbs the scales, lifting everyone out of the sinister storm, evoking visions of shimmering sunlight. His left fingers have full command over all eighty-eight keys, traversing from hell to heaven, the piece richly embodied with one hand.

His concentration is fiercely devoted to every note, yet he isn't thinking. He's been practicing Ravel for nine hours a day, and now the music is pulsing inside him, the memory of every sharp and rest and staccato encoded in the muscles of his hand as well as his mind. He can't tell if his eyes are directing his fingers or following them, witnessing. He's reached that magical part of the curve where he's no longer playing the music. The music is playing him.

He hears the whimsical cat-and-mouse game, the call-and-answer conversation between the music he's creating and his mind's rendition of the strings and horns. The song now ascends into hopeful possibility, each note and imagined marching drumbeat reaching toward triumphant ecstasy. Closer and faster without rushing, a crescendo that vibrates and steadily rises in his body like the expectation of certain orgasm, he plays along with the imagined massive orchestra, louder, closer, higher, finally ending all at once, like the dramatic climax of an epic film, in heroic victory.

And with that last resonating note, the victory is his. He looks to the darkened living room, the shades still drawn, adrenaline dancing through his heart as he receives the applause, the audience rising in a standing ovation. He turns to the kitchen to acknowledge the orchestra and thank the conductor. He stands and bows to the couch.

In the stark silence of his apartment, the experience of Ravel's concerto exciting his soul, he imagines taking this performance to a real venue with a real orchestra. He could do this. He could tour this piece as a guest with symphonies the world over. Of course he could. His career isn't over. His agent is going to love this.

He sits back at his bench, readying to play it again. He positions his left hand on the keys, but instead of hearing the orchestra begin in his mind's ear, he hears only the oppressive silence of his empty apartment and a voice in his head, an arrogant naysayer stealing his confidence, talking him out of this pathetic plan.

Richard lifts his left arm straight out in front of him. It begins to tremor just below shoulder height. He tries to will it higher, recruiting every muscle fiber he can conjure to the job, but his arm won't budge any farther. Exhausted, he lowers his hand back onto the piano keys.

Instead of beginning his solo, in opposition to the overbearing silence and the voice in his head, he plays a single note, D, with his pinkie. He holds the key and the foot pedal down, listening to the singular sound, bold and three-dimensional at first, then drifting, dispersing, fragile, decaying. He inhales. The smell of coffee lingers. He listens. The note is gone.

Every note played is a life and death.

Maybe the disease will stay in his shoulder. The voice in his head knows better and insists on another peek down the rabbit hole. No hands.

Richard leaves the piano. He retreats to his bedroom, undresses, and crawls back into bed. He does not call his agent. He lies on his back, staring at the ceiling, wishing he could stop time, hiding from his future, knowing without any doubt or hope that someday soon he won't simply be peeking down that rabbit hole.

He's going to live and die in there.

CHAPTER SEVEN

Alone in a cheerless examining room, Richard waits for Kathy DeVillo. It's the beginning of October, and this is the fourth time he's waited in a similarly impersonal room for her, the first instance almost a year ago. Kathy is the nurse-practitioner overseeing his medical care at the ALS clinic. *Care* is the term they use here, and Richard doesn't openly object, but care is not what's provided every three months when he comes for his appointment. The staff all mean well. He has no doubt of this. Kathy is nice and clearly cares about her job and him. But as an ALS care coordinator, her pockets contain little more than tongue depressors.

These clinic visits primarily amount to data collection, a chronicling of worsening symptoms indicative of disease progression. Every three months, the losses are noticeable, significant, and Kathy and others record these losses in various charts. Each clinic day is a Q&A series aimed at measuring what has gone from bad to worse. Kathy will offer some practical strategies for coping, some sympathetic nodding, and a preview of coming attractions: *You think this is bad, wait till you see what's next!* His neurologist might adjust the dosage of Rilutek. He might not.

It takes at least three hours to do all the measuring, and by the end of every clinic day, Richard's morale is battered and defeated. He swears he won't come back. What's the point? Given that he has only a limited number of hours left as an animated being on this planet, to squander any of them sitting still in this room with Kathy, or waiting for Kathy as the case may be, feels like an egregious injustice or at least utterly irresponsible. Yet, he comes. He does as he's told, which surprises him, as passive obedience isn't at all consistent with his character.

If he had to put his soon-to-be-paralyzed left finger on it, he'd admit that he dutifully comes to each clinic appointment because he still has hope. Maybe there will be a breakthrough, a new clinical trial drug, something to slow it down, a cure. It could happen. What were the odds that a boy raised to devote his time equally between football, tractors, and Bud Light in rural "Live Free or Die" New Hampshire would grow up to be a world-renowned concert pianist? Probably the same as some scientist discovering the cure for ALS. It could happen. So he waits for Kathy.

She finally enters the room, pink faced and out of breath, as if she'd just jogged over from another wing of the hospital. She's wearing tortoiseshell glasses, a black knit sweater unbuttoned over an untucked white blouse, pants that are too short for her, and flat shoes fit for running the halls of the hospital, her look more librarian than nurse. She washes her hands while saying hello, then settles into the chair opposite Richard and reads his record of decline from three months ago, his new baseline, the treacherous edge from which he'll now cliff dive.

She looks up at him and raises her eyebrows. "Where's Maxine?"

"No longer together."

"Oh, I'm so sorry."

"That's okay."

With the exception of Maxine, Richard's relationships with women had about the same shelf life as a carton of milk. Most met him after a performance, at a VIP cocktail party or charity fund-raiser, starstruck and fascinated. They fell hard and fast, looking past his wedding band when he was married. In the beginning, they also tolerated his moodiness and the time he committed to the piano instead of them. They saw his passion for the music of Brahms, Chopin, and Liszt, the love and devotion he was capable of, and assumed the skills were transferable. To everyone's disappointment, he's never been able to love a woman the way he loves the piano. Not even Karina.

So, invariably, the women became frustrated, lonely, and dissatisfied with their lot as second fiddle. Third, if

♪

they realized they were in line behind his wife. At first they tried even harder. It never worked. He doesn't know why. Maybe human beings are capable of only so much passion. The pie has only so many pieces. For Richard, all but a sliver is devoted to piano. He loves women, appreciates them as much as any man, but ultimately they find themselves achingly hungry with him. And he refuses to feed them. His artistry for playing piano seduces them. His lack of artistry as a man is why they leave.

Steeped in denial, he started seeing Maxine two months after he was diagnosed. She didn't notice that he couldn't lift his right arm above his elbow or that he always positioned himself to her right so he could hold her hand with his left. He might've slurred his words a touch in the evening when his energy waned, but they'd just shared two bottles of wine. Then one morning she caught him weeping, his hands in his lap at the piano, and he confessed everything.

Instead of running for the hills, she rolled up her sleeves. An acupuncturist, she was convinced she could save him. But no amount of needling, cupping, or burning moxa could prevent his right arm from steadily filling with concrete. She kept at it, but they both knew the effort had become insincere.

Decency laced with guilt prevented her escape. The situation wasn't healthy for either of them. Sex became quick and unimaginative. She became afraid of his body. He became indifferent to hers. He focused on her imperfections. She wore too much eye makeup. She had bad breath. She wasn't beautiful enough, interesting enough, challenging enough. Her list of complaints was just as lengthy.

For four months, they argued and sulked and danced silently around the real reason the relationship had to end. It took him that long to accumulate the courage he needed to break up with her. She didn't protest. They hugged for a long time, then she walked out the door. It was the most unselfish act of his life.

"Anyone looking after you?"

"No. I'm doing okay on my own."

"You're going to need help. Your parents, a relative, friends. You can hire private nurses, home health aides, but that will get expensive. Can you call on someone?"

"Uh-huh."

His mother died of cervical cancer when she was forty-five. Richard is forty-five. Apparently, a rough age in his lineage. He hasn't spoken to his father in years. His two brothers live in New Hampshire. They work full-time, and their wives are raising young kids. They aren't options. Grace is in school, and that's where she belongs. He still hasn't told her. He doesn't know how. He draws Karina's name next but immediately returns that card to the deck. There's no way.

"How's your living situation? Did you find a new place?"

"No. I'm still good where I am."

"Richard, you're on the fourth floor of a walk-up. Really, you have to get into a new place ASAP, before you need a wheelchair. You're going to need elevators, ramps. Okay?"

He keeps his gaze steady, refusing any sign of agreement. He can still walk. How could he be in a wheelchair ASAP? He knows this is where the disease goes, yet he can't bring himself to fully imagine it. He looks into Kathy's big brown eyes. She can. Easy-peasy.

"So tell me what's going on."

"It's starting in my left arm. I can't raise my hand above my shoulder, and my fingers are a bit weaker. I can't lift anything heavy. I'm dropping things. Walking is still mostly okay."

"Mostly."

"Yeah."

"Okay. What about eating, drinking, talking?"

"Mostly okay."

"Okay, we'll check out these mostly's, see what's happening. Let's start with your left hand. Spread your fingers and don't let me bunch them back together."

He spreads his fingers like a starfish. She scrunches them together with one second's minimal effort.

"Hold your hand straight out in front of you and don't let me push it down. Resist me."

She applies a bit of pressure, and his arm collapses to his side. The last time he was here, he still had the use of both arms and could raise both hands when asked. But his right arm crumbled with the mere suggestion of force on Kathy's part, and he remembers the terror that rushed through him like a cold blue current, chilling his heart, realizing that he possessed almost no strength in that arm and that he was about to lose the use of it entirely and forever. He remembers thinking, *At least I still have my left*

LISA GENOVA

56

arm. He glances now at his left hand, defeated and shamed by his side, and he knows what this profoundly simple exercise will look like in three months' time.

"Make an A-OK sign with your thumb and index finger and lock them into a ring. Don't let me pull them apart."

She pulls them apart.

He wants to punch this nice lady in the face with his feeble hand.

"Show me a big smile, so big it's fake. Like Hillary."

He does.

"Now pucker. Like Trump."

He does.

"Open your mouth and don't let me shut it."

He opens his mouth, and with the heel of her hand under his chin, she steadily closes his bottom jaw.

"Stick your tongue out and don't let me move it."

She pushes down and right and left on his tongue with a Popsicle stick, shifting it in each direction.

"Lick your lips all the way around."

Her eyes track his tongue in a circle.

"Fill your cheeks with air and don't let me pop them."

She does.

"Are you having any trouble blowing your nose?"

"No."

"Any trouble with saliva?"

"Like, am I drooling?"

"Yeah."

"No."

"How about coughing? Any trouble clearing your throat?"

♪

"Not really."

"Let me see. Cough from deep down. Give me a big throat clear."

He tries to take a deep breath but hits a wall sooner than expected, and so his cough comes out shallow and sputtering. He's embarrassed. He was going for the cough of a lion, but instead he's a kitten hacking up a hair ball.

"Take a big breath and expel a note for as long as you can. Ready? Go."

He chooses middle C and runs out of air at about fifteen seconds. Is that normal? Kathy doesn't say.

She goes to the sink and fills a plastic cup with water.

"Here. Take a few sips and then chug the rest."

He does while she appears to study something about his Adam's apple.

"Is taking your meds giving you any trouble?"

"No."

"Good. Taking pills is the highest level of swallowing. So that's great. Water's the fastest liquid and will give you the most trouble. You drink coffee?"

"Yeah."

"How do you take it?"

"Black."

"Okay, you need to switch now to cream. Thicken all of your liquids. Make them slower. Thin liquids can lead to aspiration. How's your weight?" She looks through the pages of his various charts.

"I've lost a few pounds."

Eating has become a joyless, necessary chore. Anything that requires a knife and fork is out. Gone are medium-rare filets mignons at Grill 23. Opening jars and the packaging to his favorite cheese and the twist tie on a new loaf of bread requires a collaboration between his left hand and his knees and his teeth and a patient persistence he often doesn't possess. Unable to lift his hand to even shoulder height at the end of the day, he has to lower his mouth to meet his fork or spoon. It's painstaking and sloppy, and he looks ridiculous, and because he can't get over worrying about what he looks like, he refuses to eat in public. Dining used to be a social and savored experience. Now he mostly orders takeout and eats alone.

And he's started choking. The muscles that coordinate the safe movement of food from the back of his mouth down the esophagus to his stomach must be weakening because sometimes food gets lodged halfway down the tube or, worse, sucked down the wrong pipe. And as they just witnessed, he now has the coughing capacity of a kitty cat, so a small bite of cracker has been a life-threatening endeavor more than once. Almost killed by a cracker. He doesn't share this with Kathy.

"Okay, yup, you've lost seven pounds in three months. We need to stabilize your weight. You need to eat more. High-fat, high-density foods and liquids."

"Okay."

"Cream in your coffee, butter on your bread, pies à la mode."

"Everything my cardiologist recommends."

"We're not going to worry about heart disease."

Right. A heart attack would be a blessing.

"Can you lift your right leg for me and don't let me push it down?"

He resists her for many sustained seconds through increasing pressure before he finally fails. They do the same exercise on the left until he fails.

"Good. You experiencing any foot drop, any falls?"

"No."

He's lying, and his heart beats faster as he waits to see if she catches him. He clipped his right toe on a step going up his front stoop last week, and he fell hard, bashing the right side of his chin and trampling his paralyzed forearm underneath his body. He's wearing a long-sleeve shirt, hiding the massive bruises covering his right arm, and his beard is apparently thick and dark enough to mask the scabbed gash on his chin.

She taps his knees, checking his reflexes. She performs various strength tests on his feet. He gets a passing grade.

"Any cramping?"

"No."

"Your legs are looking good for now. But your arm is going, so you won't be using a cane or a walker once your legs weaken. The power wheelchairs take three to six months to get, so we'll have PT put in an order for you now."

Again, he stares at her with a flat gaze. She can go ahead and order the chair, but he won't endorse this decision with a blink or a nod.

"I'm worried about your dysphagia and the weight loss. Have you thought at all about whether you want to get a feeding tube?"

Only in that he doesn't want to think about it. "No."

"Okay, Dr. Prince will talk you through what's involved and schedule you for the procedure if you decide to go ahead."

He was scheduled to play in Chicago, Baltimore, Oslo, Copenhagen. He's supposed to schedule piano concerts, not feeding-tube surgery. His head swims.

"Your breathing still seems strong. Dr. Kim's going to see you next to check you out more thoroughly there."

Dr. Kim is the pulmonologist.

"Have you banked your voice yet?"

"No."

"Is this something you want to do?"

"I'm not sure."

"It might be a good idea to look into that now. When the time comes, you can always use the synthetic, computer-generated voice, but it's really nice to have the option of still using your own. The guy who does the banking is at Children's Hospital. I'll make sure you have his contact information before you leave today. If you want to do it, I wouldn't put it off much longer."

Kathy flips through his charts, pencils in some additional notes that Richard can't decipher, then looks up at him and smiles, satisfied.

"That's all for me. Do you have any questions? Anything you need that I can help you with?"

Let's see. What does he need? He needs to bank his voice because he'll soon be unable to speak, and the alternatives are to sound like Stephen Hawking or be totally mute. He might need a feeding tube. He's going to need a wheelchair ASAP. He needs a new apartment with an elevator and ramps. He needs someone to look after him.

It's too much to take in. Too many losses and needs at once. He tries to focus on what is most immediate. The loss of his left hand. He'll have no hands. He'll no longer be able to feed himself, dress himself, wash himself. He'll empty his bank accounts and hire help. He won't be able to type on the computer. He'll use his big toes.

He's going to lose Ravel's Piano Concerto for the Left Hand. He'll never play the piano again.

This is the loss he's imagined in microscopic detail from the first hints of this disease, the one that guts him through his center and keeps him from sleeping and makes him want to swallow a bottle of pills and end his life now. Because without the piano, how can he live?

Yet, this isn't the loss that has him suddenly stunned and panic-stricken, unable to swallow his own pooling saliva. He's thinking about Maxine again, and he's revisiting their good-bye hug. He can still feel her body in this remembered embrace, her breasts pressed against his chest, her wet cheek on his shoulder, her breath on his neck. He can feel the apology, the tragic love story in the memory of that hug. He let go first. Maxine quickly followed his lead, slipped out of his arms, and left his life. He wishes now that he'd hung on a little longer.

He's about to lose his left arm. Three months ago, he hugged Maxine for the last time. Could that be the last embrace of his entire life?

He swallows hard, but he chokes on his spit, and the coughing quickly turns to crying. Kathy offers him a tissue. Humiliated, he takes it. But then again, he decides he doesn't care. What hasn't she already seen in this room? He sputters, coughs, cries, and drools through three more tissues, then collects himself just enough to find his voice.

"I need a hug."

Kathy sets the tissue box aside without hesitating and stands in front of him. Richard rises to meet her, and she wraps him in a firm embrace. He's dousing her sweater with his tears and runny snot, and Kathy doesn't flinch. He hugs her with his left arm, pressing her into him, and she responds, hugging him back, and their contact creates a human connection that feels as vital to him as the air he can still breathe.

He can't name the element at first. The connection isn't about hope. It doesn't contain sympathy. It's not made of love.

It's care.

Richard exhales and doesn't let go. Kathy stays with him.

This is care.

CHAPTER EIGHT

While her neighborhood still sleeps, Karina is standing on the sidewalk in front of her house, waiting for Elise. The cold air crowds her, penetrating her clothing, and she wishes Elise would materialize so Karina can get her blood moving. She hugs herself as she watches her exhales, white puffs that lift and disperse into the sky as if returning to the clouds. Realizing that she's standing beneath one of the towering oak trees lining her street, she shifts her position a few feet to the middle of the road. She tilts her face toward the sky, searching for warmth from the sun, but it hasn't risen yet. The door finally opens, and Elise emerges.

"Sorry. I couldn't find my gloves."

They fall in step and walk wordlessly through their

tidy neighborhood of landscaped yards and two-car garages, still-darkened windows adorned with school-made ghosts and witches, front porches hosting impressively carved jack-o'-lanterns, pots of green and purple kale, and golden hardy mums. Without stopping, Karina plucks a Tootsie Roll wrapper from the street and pockets it. Karina and Elise won't break into conversation until they reach the reservoir. Anxious to get there, Karina walks a touch faster. Without questioning, Elise keeps up.

They've been walking together one morning a week for three years. Although only recently neighbors, Karina and Elise met at a faculty dinner at the New England Conservatory of Music twenty years ago. Richard had just accepted a highly coveted teaching position in the piano department. They'd moved from New York City because of this prestigious job offer, from the jazz scene at Smalls and 55 Bar, the network of rising musicians Karina jammed with and loved, the steady gigs she played on weekends, and a promising footing in the career she dreamed of.

She didn't realize this at the time, how one-sided the move would be when she agreed to it. She's often wondered how much Richard understood before they packed up and left. Not being from this country, she simply assumed Boston would have a significant jazz culture. Surely, she would find other hip clubs, other talented artists, other opportunities for expression and hire. Boston loves the classical concerts of the Boston Symphony Orchestra and the Pops at Symphony Hall and the Esplanade. Bostonians are fanatically loyal to the rock and pop music of hometown bands such as Aerosmith, the Drop-kick Murphys, and New Kids on the Block.

Jazz in New York, New Orleans, Berlin, Paris, and even Chicago is considered a renegade and revered art. There is no jazz scene in Boston. The musicians who play at the handful of jazz clubs in town are one-night guests. They come and they go. They don't live and breathe here. Even before she'd unpacked their dinner plates, she realized this devastating truth and hated herself for being so naïve, so easily duped, as if she'd been promised sushi at a Mexican restaurant and never even asked to see the menu.

Elise was Karina's beacon of hope at that first faculty dinner. A bassist and professor of contemporary improvisation, Elise talked about ragtime and Wynton Marsalis and African jazz. She'd recorded an album with her students the previous year, a campus production, not exactly Blue Note, but still exciting. Karina couldn't wait to connect with her again, to ask her about playing somewhere, anywhere, maybe auditing one of her classes, possibly even teaching, but Elise was missing from the next faculty dinner. She'd been diagnosed with an aggressive form of breast cancer and had taken a leave of absence to undergo treatment.

Then Karina became unexpectedly pregnant with Grace, and Richard left New England Conservatory for what became an endless year of touring, so there were no more faculty dinners. Over time, Karina forgot about Elise. She retreated into the intensity, responsibility, and loneliness of full-time motherhood, resigning herself to living in Richard's immense shadow, darker, lonelier, and far more inescapable than the pre-dawn sky of a grim November morning.

While she never planned on being a mother, she loved Grace fiercely from the moment she was born and couldn't imagine choosing the kind of life Richard was living—gone for weeks at a time, devoting his days and weeks and years so singularly to his career. Even when he was home, he'd practice for eight to ten hours a day. He was there but not there.

She couldn't bear the thought of being separated from Grace, of missing any milestone. She wanted to witness her daughter discovering the world—the magic of seeing her first rainbow, the feel of a dog's fur and tongue, the silky sweet taste of vanilla ice cream. Karina wanted to be the person Grace saw when she awoke from her naps, who hugged her when she cried, who kissed her a hundred times a day. She couldn't abandon this enormous, precious love, this gift. She loved Grace more than piano.

And if she chose Grace over piano because she loved her daughter more, then Richard must not have loved Grace at all. This is the script she wrote and read to herself for years. He must be some kind of selfish monster to not love his own daughter, and she hated him for it. She built this case against him, black-and-white and indefensible. But now, looking back, she admits to herself that her conclusion was too extreme and not necessarily true. Love isn't measured by the number of hours a person logs. For the first time, she wonders if his affairs started before or after she began hating him.

At some point, she can't locate exactly when, she abandoned any possibility of a career in jazz piano. The goal became too implausible, childish, foolish. She thinks about it now as she walks, the vague dream of that intended life she never lived, and it feels like a comet she'd once seen long ago blazing across the night sky, witnessed for the briefest breathtaking moment and then gone for another hundred years.

While Karina was raising Grace and resenting Richard, Elise beat breast cancer, joined the faculty at Berklee College of Music, divorced her husband, and started dating her radiologist. They married and four years ago moved from Boston to the suburbs, directly across the street from Karina. Kindred spirits reunited. Karina still marvels at this serendipity, and her Catholic mind can't help but wonder if God led Elise here for a reason.

As they walk past Oak Hill Cemetery, the date returns to Karina's consciousness. Today is November 1, All Saints' Day, a national holiday in Poland. As a child, she would spend the entire day at the cemetery with her family. Everyone did this. Having lived in the United States her entire adult life, this tradition now seems a bit morbid and creepy, even in comparison to Halloween, but she always liked it. She remembers the white votive candles placed on the raised gravestones, dots of light sprinkled around her as far as she could see like stars spread across the universe.

She remembers her family gathered, her parents, aunts, uncles, and cousins telling stories of those who'd passed away. She savored the stability she felt listening to

LISA GENOVA

those stories, in being connected to that history, a single bead strung on an infinitely long, uniquely beautiful necklace. She loved hearing how her grandparents on both sides met, courted, married, had children. She remembers studying their names etched on the gravestones, imagining the lives she barely and never knew, and that double-edged feeling of importance and insignificance, of fate and random chance this still generates, that every moment of those four lives had to unfold exactly as it did or she wouldn't be here.

They reach the dirt path along the reservoir and begin the three-mile loop. Here they'll begin chatting, as if they're finally out of earshot of their neighbors, their words safe among the trees, the Canada geese in the water, an occasional jogger, dog and dog walker.

"How was school this week?" This is always Karina's first question, inviting the conversation that both inspires and tortures her, like a recovering addict asking for a sip of wine.

"Good. I'm loving that new student I told you about, Claire. She's got such a great ear, and she's so totally open to listening and failing. You've got to come hear her play. There's a class show in two weeks."

"Okay."

"And we're planning the student trip to New Orleans. You should come this year."

"Maybe."

Karina won't go to either. Elise invites her to all kinds of shows and classes and guest lectures and every year to the New Orleans trip, and Karina declines it all. Her excuse used to be Grace. She couldn't go because Richard was out of town, and she was needed at home. Now that she's divorced and her excuse is at the University of Chicago, she has to come up with some other reason. She'll be too tired the evening of the class show. And maybe she'll plan a visit to see Grace the same week Elise and her students are in New Orleans. The thought of being immersed in the jazz scene in New Orleans, that magical hodgepodge of Delta-blues guitar riffs, brassy ragtime horns, and sultry French Gypsy music is too painful for Karina to stomach. Every girl loves a wedding unless the groom is the lost love of her life.

"And maybe one of these days, you'll come play with us, please."

"Someday."

Elise plays bass in a contemporary improvisation band called the Dish Pans with faculty from Berklee, New England Conservatory, and Longy, mostly in bohemian restaurants and hipster bars that have a rotating roster of live music. *Someday* is always Karina's reply, and she'd like to believe that it's true. While she plays and teaches piano almost every day, she's restricted herself to the classical music of Chopin, Beethoven, Schumann, Mozart. The dots are already on the page, and she plays them with the obsequious reverence of a Catholic priest reading from the Bible or an actor quoting Shakespeare.

Jazz improvisation is a speech without a script. It's twelve notes and doing anything she pleases. There are no rules, no boundaries. Verbs don't have to follow nouns. There is no gravity. Up can be down.

LISA GENOVA

70

And it's collaborative. She hasn't played jazz with anyone since before Grace was born. It shatters her heart every time she realizes how many years it's been. She could remedy this by taking Elise up on her offer. What if someday was today? Her breath goes shallow, and the wind off the reservoir chills the sweat on her forehead. She's too out of practice. It's been too long. A runner laid up for years with an Achilles injury can't simply show up at the Olympic trials. Karina imagines playing with such practiced and accomplished musicians, and the fear of her certain and overwhelming inadequacy locks her life's greatest wish in a box.

"So I need to come clean," says Elise. "I visited Richard."

Karina stops walking, every muscle's action suspended, stuck in stunned betrayal.

Elise pauses several steps ahead and turns around. "Roz from the Conservatory called. It was nice of her to remember me. She organized a bunch of the staff who knew him from his teaching days, and we all went over. I felt like it was the decent thing to do."

Begrudgingly satisfied with this explanation and fueled by curiosity, Karina starts up again. The two women walk side by side.

"So how is he?" Karina asks, a reluctant toe edging into muddy water.

"His arms are completely paralyzed. That was upsetting to actually see."

The previously dormant pit in Karina's stomach, planted months ago, sprouts roots. *This is really happening.*

Aside from not being able to open the bottle of wine, he'd looked and acted perfectly normal when she last saw him in July. She'd been holding on to the possibility that his diagnosis was a rumor or a mistake. She still hates him, but palpably less than she did last year, and hasn't wished him dead since before the divorce. She wouldn't wish ALS on anyone, not even Richard. She kept waiting to see a correction in the newspaper, his tour back on, that the reports of his imminent death had been greatly exaggerated.

"I'd planned on giving him the stink eye for you, but his arms were just hanging off his body like dead branches, and there was his piano in the room with all of us trying to pretend it wasn't there. None of us mentioned it. It was too sad."

Richard without the piano. A fish without water. A planet without a sun.

"How did he seem about it?"

"His spirits were good. He was happy to see us all. But you could tell he was trying really hard to be positive, like he was performing."

They continue walking in silence, and soon the silence fills with sound—the muffled steps of their sneakers on the dirt path, softened by a bed of brown pine needles and then the crunching of dry, brown-paper-bag oak leaves; Elise sniffling; the huffing of their exhales.

"Does Grace know?" asks Elise.

"Not unless someone else told her. I would know if she knew. No, honestly, I wasn't even a hundred percent sure he had it until this very conversation."

Grace. She's in the middle of midterms. It would be

cruel to break this news to her right now. She might get distracted and fail her exams. And why hasn't Richard told her? Of course he hasn't told her.

"Maybe I should go see him again," says Karina.

"That's your Catholic guilt talking."

"No."

"Remember what happened last time."

"I know."

"Seeing him is not good for you."

Richard always seemed invincible to Karina, as if he could conquer anything, and he did. He was an unstoppable force that awed and intimidated her and, at times when she was most vulnerable, trampled her. Now he's the vulnerable one, and she can't help but wonder what it would feel like to sit at the other end of the table.

"Yeah, but—"

"What are you hoping for? Tuesdays with Morrie?"

"I don't know."

"He's still Richard, honey."

"Believe me, I know who he is."

"Just don't get hurt."

"I won't," Karina says, her voice utterly void of conviction.

CHAPTER NINE

Karina is carrying a foil-covered plate of pierogi in one hand, a $50 bottle of red wine in the other, and several months of unrelenting guilt down Commonwealth Avenue. It's a gunmetal-gray November morning, raining hard, and she has no hands for an umbrella and four more blocks. She picks up her pace, almost running, and the wind whips the hood off her head. *Damn it*. She has no available hand to pull it back on.

The weather hits her like an assault, and since she's the only pedestrian in sight, the attack feels personal. Raindrops pummel the aluminum foil like machine-gun fire. The bitter-cold wind stings her face raw. Rain soaks through her socks, pants, and hair, chilling her skin like a punishment. She blames Richard. She wouldn't be subjected to this misery if he hadn't provoked her. Of course, she reacted. Just as she always did. It's as if she were programmed to respond to him, an unthinking and immediate ouch to his pinch.

It was already raining when she left the safety of her house, and she knew she wouldn't likely find a parking space within four blocks. She could've waited another day. Tomorrow's weather forecast is cold but clear. But she made the pierogi last night, and she needs to make at least this one thing between Richard and her right, clean up her side of the street, deliver her penance, and be done. Carpe diem. Weather be damned.

Focused on the numbers on the door and the promise of shelter, she barely registers the FOR SALE sign planted in the minuscule square patch of front lawn as she races past it. Out of breath and shoulders hugging her ears at the top of the stairs, she presses the doorbell and waits. Her hands, wet and lacking circulation and painfully cold, are aching to let go of her peace offerings and find comfort inside her coat pockets. Without a greeting or question as to who's there, she's buzzed inside.

When she reaches Richard's unit, the door is ajar. She knocks as she edges the door open a bit more to be heard. "Hello?"

"Come on in!" a man's voice, not Richard's, hollers from somewhere inside. "We'll be done in a minute!"

Karina enters, steps out of her shoes at the door, and returns to the kitchen, the scene of the crime. The lights are on. The room smells of coffee. The kitchen island and counters are wiped clean and are bare but for three glasses filled to the top with what looks to be vanilla milk shake, a tall straw standing erect in each. There's no noise, no sign of anyone. She sets the wine and pierogi down on the counter, removes her raincoat, and drapes it over one of the barstools. She waits, not knowing whether to sit or stand, growing increasingly uneasy. Maybe she should find a piece of paper and pen, write a note, and leave.

Her attention wanders to the living room and screeches to a sudden stop, stunned. A wheelchair. A wheelchair unlike any other she's ever seen. The tipped headrest and seat resemble a dentist's chair. The two strapped footrests remind her of the stirrups on a gynecologist's exam table. There are six wheels and shock absorbers and a joystick affixed to one of the arms. This is not a chair for a broken leg. It looks futuristic and barbaric. Cold rainwater drains from her hairline, trickling down her neck. She shivers.

The chair is positioned next to Richard's piano. She looks again, and the piano is as unfamiliar and formidable as the wheelchair. An inner chill more penetrating than the rain on her skin drips down her spine. The key cover is shut. The music rack is bare. The bench is pushed in. She approaches Richard's Steinway as if she were trespassing on sacred ground, her mind still disbelieving the incongruity of the sight before her. She hesitates, gathering courage, then slides her index finger along its lid, clearing a thick layer of fine dust, revealing a snail trail of the piano's glossy black finish.

"Hi."

She spins around, heart pounding, as if she were a criminal caught in an illicit act. Richard is standing behind a bald man with black-rimmed glasses.

"I'm Bill." He wields an energetic wide smile, extending his hand to hers. "Richard's home health aide."

"Karina." She shakes his hand.

"Okay, well, that's it for me. Gotta run," Bill says. "Melanie will be here for lunch, Rob or Kevin for dinner and bed. You've got three shakes in the kitchen. You all good?"

Richard nods. Bill checks something on Richard's iPhone, worn on his chest and attached to a lanyard hung around his neck like a conference badge.

"Okay, my friend. Call us if you need us. See you in the morning."

Richard stares at Karina as Bill leaves and says nothing. His hair is wet, combed, and parted too severely and neatly to the side. He looks like a young boy on school-picture day. He's clean shaven, his face gaunt. His black sweater and jeans hang on him, long and baggy, as if they belonged to a big brother or were borrowed from Bill. Unsettled by the wheelchair, the abandoned piano, Richard's emaciated appearance and prolonged silence, Karina forgets why she's here and begins to wonder if he can speak at all.

He notices her apology on the counter.

"Pierogi," she says. "I'm sure the wine is below your standards, but it's the thought that counts."

"Thank you."

He walks into the kitchen, and that's when she notices.

♪

His arms don't swing. They sag from his shoulders, still, lifeless. And both hands look wrong, inhuman. The fingers of his right hand are stick straight, flattened. The other hand is fixed in a grotesquely curled claw. He positions himself in front of one of the milk shakes, lowers his head to the straw, and sips.

His arms are completely paralyzed. He watches her absorb this information. She smiles, trying to mask her real reaction, a trench coat wrapped around her naked horror.

"Want to have a seat?" He returns to the living room. "I don't recommend that one." He nods at the wheel-chair.

The melody in his voice is gone. Every syllable is the same note, softer in volume, and slow, as if each monotone word is being dredged through molasses.

"You can still walk," she says, confused.

"Ah. That's my future. You have to order the chair before you need it or I guess you end up getting it six months after you die. I told Bill they might as well deliver my coffin, too."

He laughs, but the sound of his amusement quickly turns into something else, a runaway choking wheeze, sounding nasty and villainous, gripping him tighter and tighter around the throat as if it aims to kill him. She sits a few feet in front of him, watching, a silent bystander, holding her own breath and strangely paralyzed, not knowing what to do. His final wheeze ejaculates a gob of spittle that lands on the face of his iPhone. She pretends not to notice as it oozes down the screen.

She looks away, over her shoulder, back at the piano and the wheelchair. Richard's past and future. She thinks of all the time he used to fill learning, practicing, memorizing, perfecting—nine to ten hours and more a day. She looks back at Richard, at his useless hands. What on earth does he do all day now?

"Once you need that, how will you ever leave your apartment?" He's on the fourth floor of a 150-year-old brownstone. No elevators. No ramps.

"I won't."

He'll be trapped inside this apartment, locked inside his body, a Russian nesting doll. She suddenly remembers the FOR SALE sign out front.

"So you're moving."

"Trying. I can't afford a new place until this one sells. Even to rent. Keeping me alive is already an expensive project. Might not be worth the investment. Don't expect any more alimony checks."

"No. Of course."

She goes silent. The checking-account balance, her meager piano-lesson income, the monthly bills. She begins doing math, mostly subtraction, equations that scare her and can't be entirely solved right now in her head.

"How's Grace?"

"Richard, she doesn't know. She doesn't know any of this. I didn't realize you would change so much so fast. You have to tell her what's going on."

"I know. I was going to. Many times. I just kept putting it off. Then my voice. I sound like a robot. I don't want to call and scare her."

♪

"Write her an email." Karina's stomach cringes, and her eyes widen, embarrassed. His hands. He can't type.

"I have speech-recognition software and toes. I can still email. But she doesn't return my emails about school and the weather. I couldn't stand it if I wrote her about this and she didn't reply."

Given what Grace knows and doesn't know, it's not surprising she took sides. Loyal to her mother, Grace hasn't spoken to her father in over a year. Karina can't help but enjoy the victory in this allegiance and has done nothing to encourage an end to his daughter's cold war. Karina looks down at the floor, at her damp socks.

"I didn't want to drop this bomb on her while she was at school. I thought it could wait—"

"For the coffin to get here?" Karina asks, transforming her shame to blame, an alchemy she's long mastered.

"Until she was home for Thanksgiving. To tell her in person. And I know this is dumb, but I think I thought if I didn't tell people I had ALS, maybe I really didn't have it."

Four months ago, she couldn't tell if he had ALS by looking at him. But now, it's unmistakable. How could he be in such crazy denial? Her heart tightens as she imagines Grace absorbing the news, this view of her father for the first time, this threat to everyone's well-being.

"She's not coming home for Thanksgiving. She's got a boyfriend. Matt. His parents live in Chicago. She's staying out there for the long weekend. We won't see her until Christmas."

Just over a month away. Only a few weeks. Richard looks past Karina to the wheelchair behind her. His eyes well up, and he blinks repeatedly, working hard to keep his tears contained.

"Can you tell her for me?"

She considers his request and him, sitting opposite her, so vulnerable, a fragile bird with no wings. He's lost his arms. He's losing his voice. He's going to lose his legs. His life. She should pity him, this flightless, dying bird. But she doesn't. He's not a bird. He's Richard. She feels her posture harden, a familiar numbness.

"No."

Her reply is cruel, but she can find no other, and the thickening silence between them is pressing on her walled-off heart, begging her to reconsider. She crosses her arms, steeling her resolve. She feels his eyes on her as she stands.

"I have to go."

"Okay. Before you do?"

She looks at him, trying not to see him.

"Would you scratch the top of my head? Please?"

She takes a breath, crosses the impossible distance between them, sits on the couch next to him, and scratches his head.

"Oh my God, thank you. A little harder. All over, please."

She uses both hands. Her nails are unmanicured, but they're hard and strong, and she rakes them all over his head, messing up his neatly combed schoolboy hairstyle. After a good scrubbing, she stops and checks on him. His eyes are closed, and a deeply satisfied closed-lipped smile is stretched across his thin face. It's been a long time since she's touched him, since she gave him any kind of pleasure. Without her permission, a sweet memory massages an un-hardened piece of her heart.

"I have to go now. You okay?" She stands.

Richard opens his eyes. They're glossy. He blinks, and a couple of tears escape, spilling down his face. He can't wipe them.

"I'm okay."

She hesitates but then grabs her raincoat, slips into her wet shoes, and leaves without another word. As she's descending the stairs, she thinks of the many times she's left Richard—walking away in the middle of innumerable arguments; storming out in the middle of dinner, deserting him in a restaurant, leaving him to take a cab home alone; the last time she was here, marching out of his apartment after breaking his bottle of wine; leaving the courthouse on the day the judge declared their marriage irretrievably broken, the dissolution no-fault, the divorce absolute. As she walks out the front door, fixing her hood onto her head, shoving her hands into the cozy safety of her coat pockets, she remembers walking down the courthouse steps, scared that it was she who was irretrievably broken, knowing there was plenty of fault to this failure, and daring to admit that she might be as much to blame for it all as he was.

CHAPTER TEN

Richard closes his eyes against the muted morning light, wishing he could fall back to sleep, knowing he can't. He used to sleep through the night without waking, oblivious to the stirrings of his wife or whoever might be next to him, deaf to car alarms and police sirens and phone alerts. He used to sleep for six to seven hours straight every night, lifting gently out of slumber into consciousness each morning with no memory of dreams or thoughts beyond shutting off the bedside light. He turns his head to see the time. He just spent eleven hours in bed, and he's exhausted. He doesn't sleep well anymore.

With two lifeless arms, he's essentially stuck on his back all night. He can rock himself to one side, but it's risky. The last time he did this was a few weeks ago. His right arm became trapped at a painful angle under his torso, cutting off the circulation, and he had a hell of a time freeing it.

And he can't risk beaching himself on his stomach. Because his abdominal muscles have weakened, he's not able to draw in enough air when lying flat either prone or supine. Propped up on three pillows, he sleeps with his torso angled upright so that gravity can assist him with breathing. When three pillows and gravity aren't enough, the solution won't be four pillows.

His pulmonologist says Richard will need a BiPAP machine likely within the next month. It's already been ordered for him. He'll have to wear a mask strapped over his nose and mouth, and pressurized air will be forced in and out of his lungs all night long. His pulmonologist says it's no big deal. The BiPAP is noninvasive. Chronic snorers with sleep apnea use a similar machine all the time. But to Richard, the BiPAP is a very big deal. And everything he needs feels invasive.

The introduction of each new medicine, adaptive device, specialist, and piece of equipment comes with a corresponding loss of function and independence. The new medications for drooling and depression, the new voice-to-text phone app, the ankle foot orthotic he's supposed to wear to keep his right foot from dropping, the feeding tube he'll soon need, the power wheelchair waiting for him in the living room, the BiPAP already ordered. Each one is his signature on the dotted line of a contract agreeing to the next phase of ALS. He's standing in a lake of dense quicksand, and every offer of assistance is a block of concrete placed atop his head, sinking him irrevocably deeper.

And although Richard can't bear to talk about it, he's keenly aware of the last concrete block in the queue. When his diaphragm and abdominal muscles quit their jobs entirely and he can't produce any respiratory pressure on his own, the final offering from his multidisciplinary medical team will be mechanical ventilation through a tracheostomy tube. Twenty-four/seven life support. Up to his eyeballs in quicksand, he'll be asked to blink once if he wants to live.

It's ten after seven, and Bill won't be here until nine. Richard has almost two hours to fill. Not long ago, it wouldn't be unusual for him to spend an entire day alone with his Steinway, perfecting the sonatas and preludes of Schubert or Debussy or Liszt. He'd begin in the morning, the sun streaming in through the bay windows, a spotlight for his private stage, and he'd be stunned to look up, seemingly only minutes later, to see his reflection in the darkened windowpanes. An entire day, here and gone in a snap. He was never lonely when he was alone with his piano. Without the piano, two hours is seven thousand two hundred seconds. An anxious eternity.

Torn between competing desires, aching to sleep and aching to move off his back, he spends several minutes doing neither. He turns his head to the side, pressing his nose into the pillowcase, and inhales the smell of freshly laundered sheets. He breathes steadily there, and the experience is heavenly, as sensually enveloping as walking into a bread bakery, but more specific, more personal. He can't remember the brands of detergent and fabric softener his mother used, but Trevor, who instead of managing Richard's career is now managing Richard's bills, services, and the delivery of groceries and household supplies, must be purchasing the exact combination Richard's mother bought. He inhales as deeply as he can, and just as the smell of onions sautéing on a stove puts him in his grandmother's kitchen, he's transported to his childhood bedroom.

He's Ricky, seven years old and waking in his twin bed on a Saturday morning. He'll have bacon and pancakes drenched in maple syrup for breakfast before his piano lesson with Mrs. Postma. He'll play Chopin and Bach. His feet don't yet reach the pedals. Mrs. Postma loves teaching him. She sometimes gives him a pack of Life Savers at the end of his lesson as a reward for being such a good student. He likes the five-flavor rolls best. Cherry is his favorite. A feeling of safety and innocence washes over him as delicious as creamy hot soup, but it passes through him too quickly and without pausing. He's Richard, back in his adult body, in his adult bed, and he wants to cry for that little boy, for what he's destined to face as a man, for all that he'll lose.

Eleven hours of locked-up pain in his hips and spine intensifies, annihilating any hope of sleep, so he shimmies himself out of bed. He walks through his darkened bedroom. He can't draw back the drapes. He can't pull up the shades. He flips the bathroom light switch on with his mouth.

Naked, he straddles the toilet and empties his bladder

into the bowl, aiming with his hips. His stream is accurate at first but then, as usual, goes astray. Before he's done, he's sprayed urine onto the back of the lid, splattered it across the seat, and dribbled some onto the floor. He hears his mother's voice in his head. In a household inhabited by a husband and three boys, she was regularly scolding one of them about the god-awful filthy state of their toilet. He assesses the mess he's made, powerless to wipe any of it up. *Sorry, Mom.*

He looks down at his distended stomach. He's not fat. Despite a steady diet of milk shakes, he's alarmingly underweight. His abdominal muscles have started loosening their grip, letting go. He stands sideways in front of his bathroom mirror and examines his profile. He's got the tummy of a toddler, the beer gut of an old man.

He's also five days constipated. His neurologist recently put him on glycopyrrolate, an anticholinergic that decreases the secretion of saliva in his mouth and throat, so there's less drool, less pooling in the back of his mouth. Before going on this medication, he had several unrelenting coughing fits that carried on for so long that Bill and whatever aide or therapist was in the room believed that Richard might drown right then and there in a puddle of his own spit. Thankfully, the drug works, but it comes with a trade-off. Less spit but full of shit.

His overall lack of mobility and the mostly liquid, rather fiberless diet he's on can also cause constipation, but since this is a new issue, he's blaming the glycopyrrolate. He's also on Rilutek. It's said to prolong survival by 10 percent. Richard did the math. The average duration of

this disease is twenty-seven to forty-three months, so he stands to gain about three months of life on Rilutek. A single bonus season. According to his most optimistic calculations, he won't see his fiftieth birthday.

Not necessarily, people say. *Look at Stephen Hawking,* they say. Sure, the disease will paralyze every muscle he owns but for those in his intestines and his beating heart, but he could live on artificial ventilation for thirty more years! This is the hope people want him to adopt, the inspirational speech aimed to fuel his will to live and persevere. Although Richard hasn't reached a definitive decision on a tracheostomy yet, if he had to choose today, he would rather die than rely on invasive ventilation. Stephen Hawking is a theoretical physicist and a genius. He can live in the realm of his mind. Richard can't. He looks down at his dangling hands. His world, his fascination, his reason, was the piano. If he were a brilliant theoretical physicist with ALS, he might hope for thirty more years. As a pianist with ALS, he's not buying any new calendars.

Hungry, he walks into the kitchen out of habit. He faces the refrigerator and tries to penetrate it with his eyes as if he had X-ray vision, imagining the food inside that he can't eat unless Bill or Melanie or Kevin opens the door and prepares it for him. His stomach growls. Two more hours until breakfast. For some reason, he pictures the bottle of balsamic salad dressing in the door and thinks about its expiration date, wondering if it will outlast him. He imagines Trevor, tasked with sorting through Richard's belongings after his death, fixing himself a salad,

LISA GENOVA

pouring the balsamic dressing over a bowl of mixed greens.

Richard leaves the refrigerator and now stands in front of his bookcase, reading the spines of his books. He can't pull one from the shelf and flip through it. Photo albums from his various tours and concerts are stacked on the shelf below the books containing pictures he can't see of himself playing at some of his favorite venues—the Sydney Opera House, Roy Thomson Hall in Toronto, the Oslo Opera House, Merkin Hall, Carnegie Hall, Tanglewood, and of course Boston Symphony Hall. The cover of the photo album on top is blanketed with dust. He can't wipe it off. Programs from several hundred shows line the bottom shelf. There will never be another program to add to the line, never another picture to slide into the next clear plastic sleeve of his dusty photo album. This realization isn't a new loss, but he never gets used to it. He'll never play again.

His chest tightens, and his heart and lungs feel sluggish as if filling with wet sand. Despite the glycopyrrolate, tears well at the back of his eyes. He coughs several times and steps away from the bookcase.

He continues walking through his apartment, a tourist in his own home, a visitor at a museum where he's allowed to look but not touch. He wanders over to his desk and visits the two framed photographs of Grace. Baby Grace with no hair and one bottom tooth. Grace in her cap and gown, her long chestnut hair worn down, one of the few times he can remember it not in a ponytail. He wonders if she's wearing it up or down these days.

He imagines the space between the two photographs.

He missed so much of her childhood. His heart twinges with regret, wishing he could go back. He thinks of the framed moments he'll likely never see—her college graduation, her wedding day, her children. He sits at his desk and leans in to get a closer look, hoping to see something in the tilt of her head, the light reflecting in her eyes, to absorb something new and lasting about her while he still can. The hunger within his distended stomach widens, aching for more than breakfast.

And that single, lonely frame on his desk hurts his heart. There should've been more. When he and Karina were first married, he dreamed of a traditional family with great excitement—three or four children, a house in the suburbs, the regular hours of an instructor at New England Conservatory, and Karina teaching or playing somewhere. He hoped for a son especially, a boy who played piano or violin or any instrument, a young man Richard could inspire, mentor, and celebrate. He promised himself as a young man that he'd be a better father to his children than his father was to him.

He studies Grace's face in the photograph, and his heart is pummeled by regret, anger, blame, and shame. He didn't live the life he intended, and there's no way to do it over. Maybe he's no better than his father after all. He blinks back tears and clenches his teeth, swallowing over and over, stuffing these ancient and new emotions down, absorbing them into his body.

Richard's father was the quarterback captain of his high school football team, division champions class of 1958, married to the prettiest cheerleader on the squad, and Pop Warner coach to two of his three boys. Walt Evans felt no pride or joy in his awkward skinny son who loved classical piano. He still doesn't. Real men love Tom Brady, not Wolfgang Mozart. Although Richard hasn't been back home in years, he'd bet that his brothers' football trophies are still standing gleaming tall on the fireplace mantel in the living room, proudly on public display. His father is probably still bragging about Mikey's one-handed touchdown catch that won the Thanksgiving Day game against Hanover High. Richard's many piano competition awards were kept in his bedroom, hidden, private. If they haven't been thrown away or donated to the YMCA, they're now most likely in an unmarked cardboard box in the attic.

Growing up, Richard felt his father's disinterest in him as disdain, disgust, dishonor. He's not sure Grace's experience of her father is much better. She had two highly trained pianists for parents, and no matter how he and Karina sold it, zero interest in the piano. She loved sports. Soccer and volleyball. Oh, the irony. For the first time in his life, Richard empathized with the disappointment his father felt in him. But he swore he wouldn't pick up the thread in the pattern his father had woven, that he wouldn't in turn reject his daughter. She could love anything she wanted, even if it involved nets and balls instead of strings and keys.

He understood this, yet her nonmusical interests created real distance between them. They literally had no common ground—she was on a field or a court, and he was in a practice room or on a stage. The demands on his time, both rehearsing and performing, kept him from being home much, and when he was, he had trouble relating to her. He's always loved her, but they were never close.

Then he and Karina split. Karina lobbied hard for Grace's allegiance, disclosing all of Richard's many sins. He hated Karina for doing that, accused her of stealing his only daughter's love, and threatened to reveal his side of the story. But in truth Karina didn't need a smear campaign to secure Grace's love and loyalty. Karina already had it. And pointing out the rotting heap of trash on Karina's side of the street wouldn't have served to clean up his.

Hidden behind the photo from Grace's graduation is a picture of Richard and Karina on their wedding day. He almost didn't bother taking it with him when he moved out, and he almost tossed it in the trash when he needed a frame for Grace's graduation picture. He and Karina are holding hands and smiling in the photo, young and in love, assuming everything will work out for them. Oblivious. He thinks of how far they strayed from the life he wanted in that photograph, of what she stole from him, of the second chance at happiness that he'll now never have, and a wild anger snakes through him, coiling in the dark emptiness of his stomach. If he could use his hands, he'd remove that hidden wedding photo from the frame and rip it to shreds.

He needs something to do, something to distract him from the bottomless sorrow and anger inside his gut, from the tortured thoughts circling like vultures in his head.

LISA GENOVA

He can't use the computer until Bill affixes Richard's Head Mouse, a reflective-dot sticker stuck to the tip of his nose. Well, he could go "old school" and peck at the keys with a pen held by his teeth or with his big toe as he did before getting the Head Mouse, but he doesn't feel like it.

He considers watching TV. The remote is taped to the hardwood floor where he can press the on-button with his big toe. Once the TV and cable are on, he can press the voice-command button with his toe and say, "Channel Five." He could watch CNN or PBS or a movie, but it's too passive.

He wants to run, scream, cry, punch something, break something, kill something. Instead, he sits on the couch, powerless, laboring to breathe, staring vaguely at his pathetic reflection in the glassy black TV screen. He tries to imagine the life he might've lived if he hadn't met Karina, if he had forty more years, if he didn't have to sit here alone for two hours with no hands, if he didn't have ALS. His breathing eventually settles as he stares and waits. He thinks of nothing coherent for a long time.

He's playing Debussy's *Préludes* in the TV screen as he falls asleep.

CHAPTER ELEVEN

Richard is awakened by the sound of a key at the door. He looks to his left wrist for the time, an obstinate and futile habit. He hasn't worn a watch in six months, since the fingers of his right hand lost the strength and dexterity to work the latch on the band. His eyes find the time on the cable box as the door opens: 9:00 on the dot. Ever punctual.

"Mornin'!"

Bill bursts into Richard's condo, whistling an upbeat song Richard doesn't recognize, jingling a metal ring of keys like a tambourine. The kitchen and living room lights flick on, and Richard squints against this assault on his senses. Bill puts something in the refrigerator, places an earth-friendly grocery bag on the counter, removes his hat, and hangs his coat on the back of one of the bar chairs. He's all movement and high energy, a diametrical contrast to the silent inertia he entered. He walks past Richard and lifts the window shades.

"Let there be light!" he says in a dramatic stage voice as he does every morning. "Where you at with the BM?"

"Nothing yet."

Bill smiles and heads toward the kitchen. Richard can't imagine how this answer can be a cause for joy, even considering Bill's often-inappropriate sense of humor. Richard assumes he must've misunderstood and is about to correct him when Bill pulls a small white bottle from the bag on the counter.

"This'll fix you."

Knowing that breakfast with a side of laxative is not the first item on his morning menu, Richard stands and waits for his Rilutek. Bill pops the pill into Richard's mouth, tips a glass of water gently at Richard's lips, and studies Richard's eyes as he swallows, watching for signs of distress. Richard gets the pill down without any fuss and then follows Bill into the master bathroom.

He doesn't flinch about being naked in front of Bill. Any modesty Richard had was pulverized to fine dust after their first week together. Bill's seen it all. He cared for his partner who was diagnosed with HIV in 1989 through full-blown AIDS, Kaposi's sarcoma, and the pneumonia that killed him in 1991. The experience catalyzed a change in career from travel agent specializing in excursions to exotic destinations on private islands to home health aide specializing in excursions to exotic diseases in ordinary living rooms.

On the books, he's officially Richard's morning home health aide, but Richard has come to think of him as equal parts brother, doctor, therapist, and friend. Richard wishes every day that he didn't have ALS and therefore no reason to have ever crossed paths with Bill, but since Richard does have ALS, he thanks God every morning for this strange, beautiful man. God bless Bill.

Bill turns on the shower, rolls up a sleeve, and checks the temperature several times with his hand before he's satisfied.

"There you go. Hop in."

Richard steps up and over the wall of the tub, less than two feet high, an elevation he's actually measured and is acutely concerned with. Clearing it already takes concentration and conscious effort. At some point in the coming months, his legs won't possess the strength to raise his feet over the wall. Maybe by then he'll be in a new condo with a walk-in shower, one he can shuffle his feet into while he can still walk, wide enough to accommodate a shower chair that can roll right into the stall when walking becomes a memory. If not, Bill will have to sponge bathe him. So many wonderful changes to look forward to.

Richard stands with his back to the showerhead, grateful for the heat and pressure and touch of the water spraying his skin, one of the few moments of each day when he still enjoys being in a physical body. He pees. No mess to clean up in here. Just outside the open shower curtain, Bill is rubbing a dollop of shampoo between his latex-gloved palms.

"Let's have that gorgeous head of yours."

Bill is bald and openly jealous of Richard's head of thick, wavy black hair. Richard is openly jealous of Bill's healthy motor neurons and strong muscles. Slightly taller than Bill, Richard bends over, offering the crown of his head as if he were being knighted. Bill works the shampoo into Richard's hair, and Richard smiles with his eyes closed, diving deep into this newly discovered carnal indulgence. Head scrubbing for Richard is a hedonistic experience approaching nirvana, almost as sensually pleasing as a blow job. If Bill were an attractive woman, Richard's pretty sure he could climax off an intense head scrub. He channels every unresolved, agonizing itch he's suffered through since yesterday's shower into the sublime satisfaction of Bill's nails combing the base of Richard's skull, raking the top of his head, scratching circles above his temples.

The scrubbing stops, and Richard peeks his eyes open. Water is spraying past the open curtain, and suds are dripping down Bill's forearm. Bill adjusts the curtain and continues. He massages Richard's scalp well past the point of clean hair. Again, God bless Bill.

He finishes, and Richard rinses. Bill squirts bath gel onto a sponge, and Richard moves out of the shower's spray to be washed, front side first, then back. Rubbing the sudsy sponge along every inch of Richard's body, Bill sings "They Say It's Wonderful" from *Annie Get Your Gun*.

The whistling and the singing drive Richard nuts. Bill is a Broadway buff and a karaoke fanatic. Every morning he belts out a medley of songs from every era of Broadway, from *Porgy and Bess* to *Oklahoma!* to *The Lion King* to *Hamilton*. Richard sits proudly on the other end of the musical spectrum. He loves classical piano, the notes alone evoking powerful emotion, each wordless composition translating a privately interpreted journey. Listening to Schumann is like looking at a Picasso, like breathing in God. Listening to Bill serenade him with Broadway tunes is a fork dipped in vinegar, stabbing him in the eye.

But Richard hasn't shared his distaste for Broadway with Bill. He figures it's not wise to risk offending the man who washes his penis. So he quietly endures every maddening medley. He's thought about asking Bill to play music from Richard's iTunes playlists. They could enjoy getting bathed and dressed to Bach's *Goldberg Variations*, Schumann's fantasies, Chopin's preludes. As there are no lyrics, this would shut Bill up.

But Richard can't bear it. He can't bear to listen to the masterpieces of these great composers, the music playing in the practiced circuits of his mind, never again to be executed by his fingers. The exquisite agony in hearing the music he loves but can never play is far more painful than Bill's rendition of "Everything's Coming Up Roses." So Richard tolerates Bill's singing. In a million ways, living with ALS is a practice in the art of Zen.

Bill shuts off the water and dries Richard with a towel. The two men move over to the sink. Bill wipes shaving cream onto Richard's face, finger painting his cheeks, chin, neck, and upper lip. Bill stops singing once he has the razor in hand. Richard watches Bill's brown eyes devote themselves to every contour of Richard's face. Bill is breathing deeply and audibly through his nose, and as if it has its own gravitational pull, Richard finds himself inhaling and exhaling in sync. When Bill is finished, he wipes Richard's face clean with a hot, wet facecloth.

"You look tired," says Richard.

"Queeraoke last night. I was up late."

"With anyone special?"

Bill hesitates. "No."

"Anyone unspecial?"

"I'll let you know when Ryan Gosling realizes I'm the one for him." Bill works some styling gel through Richard's hair and combs it. "You lucky bastard. Look at this head of hair."

"Yeah, I'm the lucky guy in the room."

Richard hears the monotone sound of his own voice, still unfamiliar to him, every last syllable of one word bleeding into the first syllable of the next, every word a single note played over and over. D-D-D-D-D-D. Every sentence is the same song. It's the ALS anthem, lullaby, number one hit.

"You're not getting any pity parties from me, Handsome. Open."

Bill brushes Richard's teeth with an electric toothbrush and wipes the white froth off his lips with the now cold, wet facecloth when finished. The last step of their morning bathroom ritual is the arm massage. Bill begins with Richard's right arm. He rubs moisture cream onto Richard's shoulder, biceps, elbow, forearm, and hand, Bill's strong fingers sliding along Richard's skin, pressing into

♪

abandoned muscles. As with the shampoo, it feels like heaven to be touched.

His right arm and hand are flaccid and passively accept everything Bill does. He wiggles and pulls on each finger. He holds Richard's arm, the elbow in one hand and the wrist in the other, and gingerly rotates the arm at the shoulder, circling forward, then backward, moving this frozen joint. He lifts Richard's arm above his head, dragging his fingers down Richard's skin, squeezing from wrist to armpit, trying to drain some of the edema that plagues Richard in this hand. His limp fingers look like tight sausages due to the fluid that seeps from his leaky veins, pooling in his hands.

Richard watches this exercise somewhat detached, as if his fingers and arm belong to someone else. Yet he feels everything Bill does in vivid detail. Each touch reminds Richard that his arms aren't completely severed from his body. Even though the efferent pathways are forever out of order, his arms are still connected to his nervous system, the afferent signals of pain, pressure, temperature, and touch completely intact. Somehow, this is comforting.

Bill moves over to Richard's left arm. Although both arms are completely paralyzed, they look and act nothing alike. While his right arm is hypotonic, a limp noodle of skin and bones, his left arm is rigid, his fingers locked in a deformed claw. The spasticity in Richard's left arm resists Bill's touch as if in rebellious disobedience. Bill has to work hard to rotate the arm, to uncurl each stiff finger. Richard tries to will his misbehaving fingers to relax. He has no influence over them.

Done in the bathroom, they walk to Richard's bed-room dresser. Bill knows where everything is. He chooses underwear, socks, jeans, and a gray crewneck, each with Richard's approval. Bill then dresses Richard like a parent dresses a small child, like a girl dresses a favorite doll, like a home health aide dresses a grown man with ALS.

Bill pulls a pair of old loafers from the closet, and Richard worms his feet into them. Lastly, Bill loops the lanyard holding Richard's iPhone over Richard's neck as if it were an Olympic medal, clips the Bluetooth connec-tor to his shirt collar, and presses the Head Mouse target sticker to the tip of his nose. There. Richard checks him-self in the mirror. As always, Bill did a fine job. Richard is dressed and ready to go out, as if he has somewhere to go, as if he'll ever be expected anywhere other than the hospital ever again. Except for the ghoulish hang of his arms, his protruding belly, the extreme thinness of his face, and the absurd sticker on his nose, he still recog-nizes himself in the mirror. He wonders if at some point he won't.

They make their way to the kitchen. Bill opens the re-frigerator door, that impenetrable vault, with an easy, un-remarkable tug and begins pulling ingredients for this morning's smoothies. Richard's favorite recipe is peanut butter, banana, yogurt, and whole milk, with dashes of pro-tein powder, flaxseed, citalopram, and glycopyrrolate. To-day's special will include the addition of a laxative. Yum.

Richard looks out the living-room window. He knows from Bill's winter coat, hat, and gloves that it's cold out-side, but the day appears sunny, inviting. He looks at his

♪

desk, the bookcase, the TV, the piano, exactly as they were earlier this morning, yesterday, the day before that, the month before that.

"I think I'd like to go for a walk when you leave."

Bill removes the lid from the blender and gives Richard a long, serious look. Richard hasn't gone out alone, unattended, since his left hand went dead.

"I'd feel better if you waited for Melanie."

Melanie comes at 1:30, three hours after Bill leaves. Richard hates that he needs Bill's permission to leave his own home, but there's no other way. If Bill shuts the door behind him when he leaves, Richard is trapped inside his condo, his living tomb.

"I'll be fine. Just leave my door open."

"What about the front door?"

"I have my neighbors' phone numbers. Someone will let me back in."

"Who's home?"

"Beverly Haffmans should be around."

Bill approaches Richard and leans his mouth over the phone resting on Richard's chest. "Launch voice control," Bill says slowly and clearly. "Call Beverly Haffmans."

The phone rings on speaker.

"Hello?"

"Hi, Beverly, this is Bill Swain, your neighbor Richard Evans's home health aide."

"Oh, hi there. Is everything okay?"

"Yup, everything is fine here. He's going to go for a walk this morning. Are you going to be home to let him back in the building?"

"Oh, yes. I'll be here. I can do that."

"Okay, great. Thank you, Beverly. Bye now."

Bill returns to the blender and peels a banana. "I still don't like it. If I didn't have my next client right after you, I'd go with you. You sure you can't wait until Melanie?"

"I'm sick of being in here. I can still walk. I'll be fine."

"You're wearing your brace."

"Okay."

Bill makes four smoothies without singing, a sure sign that he's uncomfortable with this plan. Worried that conversation might lead Bill into verbalizing his concerns, and that might in turn convince him to change his mind, Richard keeps quiet. Bill plops a straw into each drink and then leaves the kitchen.

Richard steps up to the counter, bends his head to the straw of the first glass, and sucks the smoothie steadily down. He was so hungry. And while these drinks are thick and filling, they're far from satisfying. What he wouldn't give to chew on a steak. Or even a piece of toast.

Bill returns with the foot brace and a winter coat, hat, and mittens and squats down in front of Richard. Familiar with this drill, Richard lifts his right foot without direction. While holding Richard's leg to stabilize him, Bill removes the shoe, fits the ankle foot orthotic over Richard's sock, and returns the shoe to his foot. Bill then threads Richard into his coat, pulls the iPhone out so it lies on top of the zipper, clips the Bluetooth connector to the coat collar, fits his hat on his head, and works his lifeless hands into the mittens.

"I'm putting a key to your building in your right coat

♪

pocket in case Beverly doesn't answer. You'll ask someone to open the door for you, okay?"

Richard nods, knowing this won't be necessary.

"Okay, my friend." Bill dons his own coat. "You're all set. I'm still not a fan of this idea. You sure I can't set you up with something on Netflix?"

"No. I want to get out of here. I know you have to get going. Let me just drink one more."

He finishes a second smoothie while Bill slips on his hat and gloves.

"Okay, let's do it."

Bill opens the door, and they leave without shutting it behind them. Richard takes each step down the stairs consciously and carefully, wanting to prove to Bill, who is walking backward in front of him and most certainly assessing the competence of every step, that he's perfectly capable of walking alone. They pass through the grand foyer, Bill opens the front door, and they walk outside.

The air is face-pinking cold, but it's clean and breezy and instantly feels far more vital than the confined air Richard has been stewing in for too long inside. He takes a deep breath and sighs out the exhale. He takes in the passing traffic, the people walking on the sidewalk and in the park, a baby stroller, a bicyclist, a dog, a squirrel. He smiles. He's among the living again.

Bill pats him on the back. "You'll be okay. See you in the morning, Ricardo."

"Thank you, William."

Before he sets off on his own, Richard watches Bill hurry down the street, an angel on his way to the next bathroom, bedroom, and kitchen, to someone with MS or cancer or Alzheimer's, washing hair and teeth and genitals, massaging and dressing and feeding, singing show tunes to all as he does, and, for some, giving them the freedom to do as much as they can while they still can.

God bless Bill.

CHAPTER TWELVE

Three blocks from home, Richard walks through the gate of the Public Garden and is already exhausted. When he's simply standing still or walking from his bedroom to the living room, his legs feel sturdy beneath him, still capable and responsive, normal. At home, he can convince himself that ALS might only ever affect him from the waist up. Maybe he'll return that hideous $27,000 wheelchair that wasn't covered by insurance. But in his fourteen-hundred-square-foot, one-bedroom condo, he's not asking much of his quads and hamstrings and calves.

Three blocks from the front step where Bill left him, he's completely sapped. His legs have become sandbags, his bones filled with rocks, impossibly heavy, and he lacks the energy to move them. Even standing still is shaky. He needs to sit down. Around the bend past the statue of George Washington on his horse, Richard spots the nearest bench and tries to estimate how many steps away he is. He guesses about thirty and seriously wonders if he can make it.

This is not normal. It's not normal for a three-block walk to wear out a forty-five-year-old man, potentially defeating him thirty steps shy of his destination. There's no denying it. ALS has crawled its way into the motor neurons that feed the muscles of his legs, and walking three blocks is the pathetic molehill large enough to unmask its sinister invasion. He imagines his body's resistance to this attack, the molecular war in the fight against ALS at every neuromuscular junction, an invisible army, outnumbered and outgunned, deployed to fight this insidious enemy for as long as it can. The army holds its ground in Richard's legs when he is home, but when it has to divert half its soldiers to the mission of walking to the Public Garden, the resistance becomes compromised, ALS advances, and the enemy is poised to take control. His army calls back the troops. Every soldier is needed in the trenches. No more walking!

But he presses on, every step a grueling punishment. He hears Bill's, Kathy DeVillo's, and his neurologist's voices scolding him in his mind. It's dangerous for him to keep walking when he's tired like this. His coordination gets sloppy. He's especially worried about the possibility of dragging one of his tired feet, stubbing a toe on the uneven pavement, tumbling him to the ground. With no arms or hands to break his fall, every wipeout is a potential head trauma, broken bone, and trip to the emergency room.

Twenty feet from his goal, he's fast running out of gas and faith. Still heavy, his legs now also feel flimsy, a teetering tower of wooden blocks that threaten to collapse beneath him with every step. His blood races through the vessels of his body, rushing through the chambers of his heart, begging him to hurry up and get to the bench before he falls. He looks around. He counts five other people close enough to hear him if he yells, but they might as well be in Timbuktu because he'll never ask any of these strangers for help.

And he'll never ask his father or brothers in New Hampshire or his daughter in Chicago. And he can't ask Trevor in New York or his medical team at Mass General or even Bill, who is somewhere with his next client. He is alone in the Public Garden. He's alone in his home. He's alone in his ALS. And he's suddenly, overwhelmingly terrified.

He can barely breathe, but it's fear that's strangling him, not ALS. Each inhale seems to stoke a building terror, as if his blood now carries panic instead of oxygen. The fear grips his entire body like a vise, a cage around his lungs, more paralyzing than his disease, and he can't move. Sipping sharp tastes of air, he has to keep going if he's going to make it to the bench. He finds a pep talk, a mission statement. *Keep going.* He takes small steps, small breaths. His eyes are married to the bench, and when he's close enough, he leans forward, forcing his legs to *keep going*. It's the bench or bust. *Keep. Going. Keep. Going.*

Two more wobbled steps, and he crash-lands face-first into the bench. His right cheek, shoulder, and hip already throb. He'll have bruises by morning, which Bill will demand explanations for. He rights himself and sits victorious but feels nothing like a winner. The panicked fear flushes out of his system, leaving him rattled, wrung out, warned. He looks back along the path he traveled and beyond the garden gate. A little more than three blocks and a long way home. Too many steps to estimate. Too many steps, period.

Worst-case scenario, he'll spend the next two hours on this bench. Melanie will call him at 1:30 and retrieve him. But he hopes for better than the worst-case scenario. Always has. He'll rest awhile and hopefully recharge his leg muscles and courage enough to make the journey home on his own.

The garden is tranquil this time of year. He spots a couple of ducks in the pond, but the swans and swan boats are gone for the season. The tourists are gone, too. The people walking by him are Bostonians: a young Asian man, likely a student, bent over at the waist, hauling a backpack thicker than he is; a woman in sneakers and a massive black winter coat carrying a large black umbrella, her eyes focused on the ground—Richard looks up at the clear blue sky, perplexed—a corporate woman carrying her dry cleaning with two fingers, the winter wind blowing the clear plastic sheath covering her hanging clothes behind her like a sail, her purse bouncing off her hip on the downbeat of every left step, her heels beating the ground in a half-time tempo, late for something; a short Italian guy, his stomach leading way out in front of him, gabbing on his phone in a thick Boston accent, his walk a swagger in expensive-looking leather shoes.

Most of the people who pass Richard are traveling alone, stone-faced, white cords dangling from their ears as if they're robots powered by the devices they hold. No one looks at him. It's not that they see him and look away. They never notice him in the first place. He's part of the background, as uninteresting as the bench he's sitting on.

A sparrow leaps onto the wooden seat a brazen few inches from him and tilts its head from side to side. They make eye contact, and then the sparrow hops to the ground. It pecks at something there and flies away.

Everything living is in motion, going somewhere, talking, walking, pecking, flying, doing. Life is not a static organism. Every day, he's a little more shut down, shut in, turned off. A little less in motion. A little less alive. He's becoming a two-dimensional still-life painting, slipping inexorably into the alternate dimension of the sick and dying.

A woman passes him. Something about her reminds him of Karina twenty years ago. Her long hair and that purple scarf. He met Karina in Sherman Leiper's Technique class. Although he noticed her on the very first day, it took him most of the semester to talk to her. Fresh out of public high school in New Hampshire, he had no experience with girls yet. When he was a teenager, his father regularly discredited Richard's masculinity in obvious digs and under-his-breath derogatory comments. In a home and town where jocks ruled, a boy who loved tickling the ivories was seen as unmanly and decidedly uncool. Already cast aside by his father and brothers and boys in his grade, he couldn't risk adding more rejection from Jenny or Stacey or any of the other cute girls he had crushes on. Instead, he channeled his private feelings of longing and unrequited love into his playing. He devoted his attention to piano instead of girls, and he insulated his young heart from the pain of being judged weird or wrong or not good enough by pretending not to care what anyone thought of him.

At Curtis, music ruled, not athletics. Every girl there was attracted to music, and even better, to musicians. Like a seed waiting for healthy soil and sunshine, Richard's confidence around girls blossomed at Curtis.

That first day of Technique class, Karina was wearing a lavender scarf wrapped around her long brown hair. He remembers her big green eyes and pale skin, her plump bottom lip distracting him from the lecture as he imagined how soft it would feel to kiss it. Then she spoke, called upon by Sherman Leiper. He can't remember the question, but he can still remember the sound of her answer in that Polish accent, her perfectly charming broken English. He sat there captivated, fascinated, turned on, jealous that she wasn't speaking to him. Her voice was a melody of exotic sounds and intonation, a song he wanted to learn.

He loved the melody of her voice, but it was her fearlessness that he eventually fell in love with. At eighteen, she'd left her country, her family, her first language, everything she knew. Although his story was less dramatic, he felt a kinship in this. They had a common independence, a sense of no return, that music would be their savior, that everything was riding on this education. Curtis was Richard's path to freedom and fulfillment, and he found Karina on that same path with him, matching him stride for stride, holding his hand, smiling next to him. Their mutual passion for playing the music of Chopin and Schumann bled into a passion for each other. Their relationship at Curtis was heady and intense, their days and nights consumed in classes, lessons, practice, and sex.

Richard sighs as the bitter memories rise up from the shadowed corners of his mind, dialing into vivid focus. He's surprised they held back from intruding for as long as they did. It's hard for him to visit those old, happy memories of Karina without every horrible memory demanding equal viewing. *In good times and in bad.* The good and the bad—insoluble elements, prime numbers, oil and water. His good and bad memories of Karina don't blend, balance, neutralize, or cancel each other out, and he's stuck holding both, perfectly intact.

Videos from his memory bank play—their first coffee date in the student lounge, the first time they had sex, the last time they had sex, watching her play piano, which was always feeling her play piano, her green eyes loving him when he got his first big break, playing with the Cleveland Orchestra, her green eyes hating him at the dinner table after they moved to Boston, the morning Grace was born, Karina's surgery, the day everything he believed unraveled—and too many emotions run through him. He's happy, in love, betrayed, heartbroken, overcome with lust, disgust, rage, regret. The release he needs is laughter or

LISA GENOVA

crying or screaming or possibly all three, which would be fine if he were home and not on a bench in the Public Garden. The people walking by will think he's nuts. He feels a little nuts.

He needs to get Karina off his mind. He'll walk back home now. Walking will consume all of his mental energy and focus.

He's standing next to the statue of George Washington when the laxative kicks in. A massive cramp seizes his large intestine, followed by urgent pressure, a five-day-late freight train barreling into the station, right now. The pain and fear of losing control keep him pinned in place, unable to move. But he must. He's three blocks from home.

A few steps onward and the cold air against the sweat on his forehead makes him feel clammy, sick, as if he might pass out. He's not going to make it. He has to. He reinstates his pep talk. *Keep going.* Five days of stagnant waste are now in motion, insisting on evacuation, and the struggle to walk combined with the struggle to hold it all in brings tears to his eyes. *Keep going. Keep. Going.*

Through sheer will and some kind of a miracle, he reaches his front step. The urge to shit is now screaming full tilt, a peristalsis of feces and water churning inside him, pressing downward. He won't be able to hold it in much longer.

Dipping his chin to his chest, he summons all of his strength and pours it into his voice.

"Launch voice control. Call Beverly Haffmans."

The phone rings and rings and rings and rings.

"Hi, you've reached Beverly Haffmans. Please leave a message after the beep."

"Beverly, it's Richard Evans, your neighbor. I'm at the front door. Are you there? Open the door if you get this message. Please. I need to get in. . . . End call."

Shit. Where did she go? He presses her doorbell with his chin. No one answers. Unable to think of what else to do, he tries calling her again. The phone rings once and goes straight to voice mail.

"End call."

He literally held his shit together with the promise to his body that he would relieve himself when he got home. He can't pull down his pants, but he imagined soiling himself in the privacy of his own bathroom. Now that he's on the stoop, he has no reserve left. His bowels have run out of patience and composure, and he swears he can feel the pressure in his eyeballs.

He has nowhere to go. Public restrooms aren't an option. He has no hands. He could call 911, the lesser of two humiliating options. Wait. He remembers his other neighbor.

"Launch voice control. Call Peter Dickson."

The phone rings twice.

"This is Peter."

"Hi, Peter, this is Richard Evans, your neighbor. Are you home?"

"No, I'm in New York. What can I do you for?"

"Nothing, never mind, thanks."

"Everything okay?"

"Yup. I gotta go. End call."

He remembers the key in his pocket. In his fucking pocket, and he can't reach it. He turns to the street to look for help. A young woman is jogging on the sidewalk, approaching his stoop.

"Excuse me!" he yells from the top step, unable to walk down fast enough to meet her, unable to wave his arms.

She notices him. Thank God. She removes an earbud and slows down.

"Can you help me get my key out of my pocket and open my front door for me?"

Her face closes off, scared. "Sorry," she says quickly, and jogs away without looking back.

"Wait! Please!"

She practically sprints down the street. He can only imagine what he looks and sounds like—a sweaty, bashed forehead; his arms hanging; his torso bent over; his voice monotone and creepy. He'd run, too.

No one else is on his side of the street, and his voice is too weak to reach the dog walker he sees in the park. He looks down at his phone. It's 12:20, over an hour until Melanie arrives. He won't make it. Maybe they can send someone else, someone now. Yes!

He activates the voice control on his phone. A wave of pain and pressure rolls through him, doubling him over at the waist. He knows this is his last chance. He can barely speak.

"Call Caring Health."

It rings three times.

"Hello?"

"This is Richard Evans. Can you send someone out right now? I can't wait for Melanie. It's an emergency."

"Richard? This is Karina."

What? How? His voice, his slurring, sloppy, barely audible monotone voice. Caring Health. Karina.

"Sorry, I . . . I—"

"I'm in the city. I'll be there in five minutes."

CHAPTER THIRTEEN

"Please just leave me. Melanie will be here at one thirty."

"Shut up."

In the pause that follows, the last kicks and screams of their mutual dread settle into surrender. They're in Richard's bathroom. She could leave him here. But for some reason that she doesn't yet understand, she's not going to, and so it's not worth discussing.

She unclips a device labeled BlueAnt from his coat collar, lifts his phone up and over his head, and places both on the vanity counter. She then unzips his winter coat, unsealing the stench that had been trapped beneath the insulating layers of down and weather-resistant outer shell. She covers her nose and mouth with her hand, an utterly ineffective shield against the noxious odor that is quickly saturating the air in the room.

She flashes to a summer afternoon when Grace was two. Armed with nothing but the innocent intention of retrieving a beach chair from the car, she popped the trunk and was assaulted by the putrid, violent stink of a forgotten diaper filled with poop, baked in eighty-degree weather for several days. The smell emanating from Richard right now is similar but far worse. She removes her useless hand from her face and gags.

About to take a deep breath as she would before attempting anything potentially painful or scary—striking the first key of Bach's *Goldberg Variations* in a recital a million years ago; pushing in concert with the labor contractions that delivered Grace; picking up the phone today, knowing it was Richard calling—she thinks better of it. Taking a deep breath now would mean consuming more of this aerosolized cesspool. Instead, she lifts the top of her sweater and hangs it over her nose, creating a mask, and breathes short, timid breaths through the woven fibers.

She looks up and finds herself accidently eye to eye with Richard. His thin, clean-shaven cheeks are wet with untouched tears, and his eyes, ever formidable in her experience, submit to her gaze, humiliated, apologizing, holding an expression so stunningly uncharacteristic of him that she can't look away. He closes his eyes and keeps them shut, likely unable to bear being seen like this, and she's grateful for the curtain between them, that he's not able to see the tears welling in her eyes.

While music, especially live music, can easily over-

LISA GENOVA

come her—the swell of the notes, an overwhelming awe of the artistry before her, the sorrow in the story of the song—she never cries for the crying. Raised under Russian oppression, she'd seen more than a lifetime's worth of weeping before she could tie her own shoes. At a young age, she learned to pretend that nothing bothered her, to dam up any tears of pity or compassion with great, impenetrable walls. She watched dry-eyed as scrawny toddlers wailed in the bread line where she stood dutifully for over two hours every day after school; as Mr. Nowak, who lived across the street, was hauled off to prison in front of his hysterical wife and six crying children for stealing a pig's head from a neighboring farm; as her mother wept while Karina packed her suitcase, leaving for a six-month job as a nanny in Switzerland, knowing that six months was a lie and that the nanny job was simply the plausible excuse necessary to obtain a passport, a way station on the way to school in America, and that she might never see her daughter again.

So it unnerves her that Richard's tears have somehow found a wormhole. She clears her throat, attempting to shake it off, reorienting her focus toward the task at hand. She unbuttons and unzips his jeans, grabs the waistband of his pants and boxers at both hips, and, in one hard yank, pulls them down to his knees.

It took her longer than five minutes to get to Richard's front stoop. She was only about a mile away when he called, but parking took several additional minutes. Some of the wet, runny shit that had dripped down his legs has already dried, his coarse black hairs poking through like weeds in droughty earth. A substantial heap is in his underwear, and the rest is stuck like cake frosting to his ass and balls. More than she bargained for.

"Okay, can you balance on one foot?"

"I'm too tired. I don't want to fall."

"Hold on to my shoulders."

"I can't."

"Oh, right. Here, lean against the wall behind you."

She holds him firmly by his bare waist, and he shuffles back a few steps until he's flush to the wall. She squats down in front of him.

"Lift." She taps his left shin with the palm of her hand.

His shoes already off, she tugs the pants and boxers down and off one leg. In doing so, she slides his leg through the soiled clothing, and now his entire leg is smeared with shit. A substantial hunk of it falls out of his boxers and onto the bathroom floor. The white wall behind him has been painted brown by his rear end. Good God.

"Switch."

He lifts his right foot, and she drags the pants and boxers down, threads them over his socked foot and off. She looks at her hands and wishes she hadn't—Richard's shit on her right thumb, across her knuckles, beneath her freshly painted nails, pressed into her neatly trimmed cuticles. Her sweater mask has fallen off her nose, but she doesn't want to touch her sweater with her contaminated hands, so she leaves it. The stench, the mess, her hands. She wretches twice.

"I'm sorry," he says.

She can't pause now to clean herself up or she won't be able to finish. She has to keep going.

"Lift."

She peels the left sock off, then the right. She stands and grabs the bottom of his crewneck and tries to pull it up and over his head, but his arms won't cooperate, and he's stuck, a puzzle she can't solve.

"You have to go one arm at a time," says Richard.

She wrestles his left arm through the hole, then the right, then his head. He's now totally naked, smeared with shit and tears and shame.

She runs the shower. Richard steps in. She grabs the sponge on the tub's edge and saturates it with liquid soap.

"I'm good like this. Melanie can do the rest."

"Shut up."

As she begins to wash him, to touch his shoulders and chest and stomach, she has the split-second recognition that, although much bonier than she remembers, this is Richard's naked body before her, a body she has loved, kissed, hugged, held, spooned, sucked, fucked, avoided, despised, resented, cursed, hated. A comprehensive menu of memories and feelings related to this body, inappropriate to this bizarre situation, scrolls across her consciousness. She refuses it, ignoring his body's history, and focuses instead on the impersonal job in front of her. The sponge, the bum, the soap, the leg, the water, the penis, more soap, the balls, the sponge, the other leg.

Finally, the water circling the drain is clear. She leaves him there, goes to the kitchen, finds a trash bag, and returns to the bathroom. She locates a clean segment of his pants and, fashioning her hand like a pair of tweezers, transfers his trousers into the trash bag. She does the same to the socks, boxers, and shirt, then knots the top of the bag to seal off the smell. Even though she's sure she didn't touch any poop, her hands feel contaminated again. She washes them thoroughly in the sink under the hottest water she can stand and then washes them again.

She returns to the shower and shuts off the water. Richard steps out of the tub, and she dries him with a clean towel. They then walk wordlessly to his bedroom. Without input or direction, Karina finds his clothes and dresses him.

There. It's done. They look at each other now.

"Holy shit," says Karina.

Richard laughs. She didn't mean to be funny, but she's too adrenaline buzzed to remain straight-faced and joins him. They laugh deep, hard, sighing cackles, and the release feels good. It's been a long time since she's been on the same side of joy with Richard.

"I'll wait until Melanie gets here," she says, realizing that it's now almost 1:30.

"Okay."

She follows Richard into the living room and sits next to him on the couch. He turns the TV on by stepping on a remote control taped to the floor. He surfs a few channels, finds nothing of interest, and shuts the TV off. They sit side by side in silence, waiting for Melanie, and the lack of anything to say or do stretches on well past uncomfortable, feeling somehow more awkward than the shit show they just endured in the bathroom.

"So what were you doing in Boston?"

"I had a doctor's appointment."

"Oh." He doesn't ask what for or if she's okay. She doesn't blame him. Pandora's box is better left locked shut.

"I was just leaving the parking garage when you called."

She was at her annual gyn physical, not due to be in that office again for another year. What are the odds that she'd be barely over a mile away and available when he called? She looks around the room—the piano, the wheelchair, the desk and chair, the TV and coffee table. She looks at him.

"How long does Melanie stay with you?"

"About an hour."

"Does anyone else come here to help you?"

"Someone comes in the morning, usually Bill, for an hour and a half. Then another person comes at night to help me with dinner and get ready for bed."

"So about four hours a day?"

"Yeah, about that."

She thinks about the twelve or so waking hours in each day when he's alone with no help and all the trouble he could get into. What if he falls? What if he's hungry? What if he chokes? What if he shits his pants on the front step and is locked out of the building?

"You need a lot more help that that."

"I know. I don't work anymore. I can't afford it."

She thinks about the stairs and that wheelchair. This situation is untenable.

"You're selling this place."

"My realtor says I have it priced too high, but I don't want to come down or I'll lose money on it. Suppose it doesn't matter. I have a huge mortgage. It won't free up enough cash."

She doesn't point out that leaving here might be more about living somewhere without stairs than the potential for liquidity. She knows his father and his brothers. His father won't help, and his brothers can't. It's too bad his mother isn't still alive. She would be here for him. His agent is in New York City.

"Is there a girlfriend?"

"No."

"You can't go on like this."

Isn't that exactly what she said to him when she finally asked for a divorce, but with an *I* instead of a *you*? She pinches her mouth shut, trying to withhold what she's about to say next, thinking that maybe if she makes it past this moment, if Melanie walks through the door and takes over the conversation, then she won't say what she's about to say.

She looks at Richard, and he nods, and she can't tell if he's agreeing with what she said or what she's thinking, believing suddenly that he can read her mind. This is nuts. She can't do this. She can't say what she's about to say. She'd have to be a masochist, an idiot, insane. Elise will call her crazy for sure. She can't undo all that has happened by saying what she feels compelled to say.

Just as she's sliding down a slick hill to panic, a sense of calm settles over her instead, leveling her tilted inner landscape, and she realizes that it doesn't matter whether she says it now or not. She sighs. She looks at Richard and his lifeless arms and the wheelchair and his piano, and it's already true and done, as if this moment, this whole day, her entire life, were fated, and she agreed to say what's next before she was even born.

"You need to come back home."

"I know."

CHAPTER FOURTEEN

There aren't any Hallmark cards illustrated with doe-eyed characters or inspirational quotes that celebrate the life moment when a man moves back in with his ex-wife. For eight days now, Richard has been living at 450 Walnut Street, the house he lived in with Karina and Grace for thirteen years, the house he left when he and Karina separated a little over three years ago, the house conveyed to Karina free and clear in the divorce settlement. More specifically, he's been living in the old den, now his new bedroom, on the first floor.

Practically speaking, the move was a summer breeze. Aside from his clothes and toiletries, he needed only to move his computer, his TV, his Vitamix, and his wheelchair. He left everything else behind for his real estate agent to use in staging his condo. She says the piano in particular shows well, helps potential buyers to imagine a cultured life there, especially once they learn whom it belonged to and that it comes with the unit if they want it. She was ecstatic to see the wheelchair go. In her thirty-two years in the real estate business, she says that nothing ruined the feng shui of a home more than a power wheelchair.

He even left his king bed, as his occupational therapist convinced him that now was the perfect opportunity to order the hospital bed he needs. Weakening abdominal muscles plus no arms equals one hell of a time getting up from a flat mattress. He hated agreeing to it, but he has to admit that he sleeps much better in the twin hospital bed with the back raised to about sixty degrees than he did propped up on two or three pillows on his horizontal Posturepedic, and getting up without assistance is infinitely easier.

Emotionally speaking, the move was a Category 5 hurricane. Getting out of this house, away from Karina and the unsettled turmoil between them, and starting over in his own place in Boston had felt like a glorious victory, as if he'd won some grand prize or been released from prison or been allowed to graduate despite failing a required class for years. He remembers those first few mornings alone, the delicious moment upon wakening when he realized that she wasn't next to him or anywhere under the same roof, and he felt relieved, revitalized, ten years younger. And now, here he is, back under the same roof, demoralized, pathetic, emasculated, dying.

His new bed sits where his piano used to be. Where

♪

his passion, his love, his life, used to be. Now, in all likelihood, unless Karina panics and calls 911, this is where his death will be. He tries to ignore his deathbed, but there's no avoiding it. Even when he's not sleeping or sitting on it, when he's at his desk or watching TV from the easy chair, he feels it near him, waiting for him.

He is grateful to be living on ground level, to no longer have to negotiate three flights of stairs or a locked front door if he wants to go for a walk. He can open and close the garage door though voice activation of an app on his phone, and Karina keeps the door from the garage to the foyer propped open. So he can come and go without the need for keys or contingency plans.

But there's a rub. In Boston, he could go anywhere anonymous, unseen. Here, he knows all the neighbors. Despite their well-meaning smiles and hugs and conversation, he wishes he could step outside and be alone, unnoticed. He doesn't want to be seen like this.

His wheelchair is currently stored in the back corner of the garage, blessedly out of everyday sight. When he needs it, a construction project will be necessary. Karina assumes that it'll fit through the doorway, but she hasn't checked. He's spent countless hours alone in his living room sitting opposite that chair, as if they were staring each other down, and he's memorized the size and shape of his enemy. A quick eyeball of the entryway and he's already surmised that the geometry doesn't work. Twelve steps lead up to the front door. They'll either need to widen the doorway from the garage to the foyer or build a ramp over the front steps. The ramp will likely be cheaper. That or a bottle of pills.

He's at his computer, writing the seventh letter to his father that he won't send. He hasn't sent the other six. All are saved, but none are sent. Saved for what? When? Later. Later, which used to mean some nebulous, indeterminate time in his infinite future, has taken on a sense of immediacy since his diagnosis. Diagnosed a year ago with a disease that comes with an average life expectancy of three years, later is right fucking now. Yet, time for him is strangely both compressed and spun out. A day can seem to drag on for a week by midday, then pass by in a skinny minute during that same evening.

Is he saving these letters for his deathbed? His funeral? Will his father even come? The father he wants would be heartbroken to read that his youngest son has ALS. He'd drop everything to be by his son's side, supporting him with whatever he needs, his biggest champion to the end. The father he has might not even reply, which is probably why Richard can't bring himself to hit SEND. Maybe he'll print the letters, roll them, stuff them in glass bottles, and toss them into Boston Harbor for some other father to find. Maybe he'll delete them.

He's using a Head Mouse to type. A camera clipped to the top of his laptop screen detects the shiny target stuck to the tip of his nose, and the cursor moves wherever he points his face. When this technology was first introduced, the directions suggested sticking the mouse target to the user's forehead, hence the name. But most people wear the sticker on the bridge of their glasses or, like Richard, on their noses.

The door to his old den/new bedroom is intentionally

left open, a lack of privacy traded for the ability to come and go without needing to call for Karina to come and open the door. Like letting the dog out. He's an animal in a cage. A pig in a pen. An ex-husband in the old den.

Despite being able to come and go, he restricts the majority of his time to this room, mostly for fear of stepping on any number of unresolved eggshells and land mines hiding beneath the floorboards of this home. And in the private company of his desk, TV, and hospital bed, he can sometimes forget that he's living under the same roof, under the care of his ex-wife. While he feels some relief in knowing that Karina is around should he need help, he's also loath to ask her for it.

He's hungry. He'll wait two hours for the next home health aide to come and make him a smoothie. He's cold and could use another layer. Think warm thoughts. He has to move his bowels and will need to be wiped. It doesn't matter that Karina already dealt with far worse on that fateful, humiliating day at his condo. He'll hold it in.

He lost Melanie and Kevin and the other home health aide regulars in the move due to geography. They serve only clients who live in the city of Boston. But Bill worked his magic and stayed on even though Richard now lives nine miles outside Bill's official territory. God bless Bill.

Through the open door, he can hear Karina's piano student playing in the next room. The student is dreadful. Richard leaves his unfinished letter to his father and peeks through the open door. A girl, a teenager. She has terrible posture, neck and shoulders slumped forward and down. Karina should correct that. It takes him a minute to figure out that it's Chopin's Nocturne no. 2 in E-flat Major that she's slaughtering. Her playing is uninspired and sloppy with many fits and starts, and Richard agonizes through every hesitation, the unfinished phrases hanging in the air, and he keeps impatiently begging her under his breath to strike the proper next note. To top it all off, she keeps forgetting the flats. This girl clearly didn't practice last week on her own. If he were her teacher, he'd send her home without finishing the lesson.

He returns to his desk but grows tired of using the Head Mouse. He switches to pecking the keys with a pen held in his mouth, but that's even more painstaking, and he soon gives up altogether. Instead, he sucks a sip of the milk shake left over from lunch. He doesn't care for this one. It's bland and too chalky, probably Ensure. His new early-afternoon aide, Kensia, left it on the desk for him. He takes another sip. It's definitely from a can and definitely not one of the freshly made elixirs from heaven that Bill concocts for him. But he's hungry and needs the calories, and Karina is busy, and Bill won't be here until the morning, so Richard sucks it up.

This is his new mantra, for Kensia's tasteless milk shakes and most everything else about this disease. He can't play piano ever again but has to listen to some shit student butchering a masterpiece in the next room. Suck it up. He can't live safely alone so he has to move back into his old house with his estranged ex-wife. Suck it up. An itch at the tip of his nose is intensifying every second that he doesn't address it, but if he scratches it by rubbing his nose against the edge of his desk or the wall or his bed comforter, he risks wiping off his Head Mouse sticker and not being able to use the computer again without pen pecking until the next aide comes. Suck it up.

He returns to his chair and stares out the window, listening vaguely to the piano lesson through the open door. As his thoughts often do if given too much unstructured time, they wander into the unsolvable realm of whys. Why did he get ALS? Why him? He runs up and down the familiar streets of these frequently traveled neural circuits in his mind, knocking on doors and ringing bells, not in a self-pitying way, but more in a scientific-discovery kind of questioning. It's always an answerless quest.

Ten percent of ALS cases are purely genetic. One of his parents would've had to have had ALS for his ALS to be this hereditary kind. His father is alive and well, as far as Richard knows, and will probably live to be a hundred. His mother died of cervical cancer when she was forty-five, so he supposes that she could've had the mutation and would've developed ALS had she lived longer. But he dismissed this possibility seconds after he first considered it shortly after his diagnosis. First, it's just too freakishly unlikely and cruel that she would've been dealt cervical cancer *and* ALS. Second, and more convincing, his mother's parents, Gramma and Papa, died in their eighties. Both from strokes, if he remembers correctly. No ALS. So his ALS didn't come from his mother.

Five to 10 percent of ALS cases are familial, caused by a collaboration of genetic mutations. Conspiring DNA. Without genetic screening, the quick and dirty test to identify ALS as familial is the diagnosis of ALS in two

LISA GENOVA

other blood relatives. There is no ALS on either side of Richard's family tree. He's the only bad apple, rotting on a withering branch. So he doesn't have familial ALS. This is the single satisfying part of his why line of ALS questioning because it means that Grace is safe from this hideous monster. Or at least as safe as anyone else.

His form of ALS is called sporadic, caused by something other than or in addition to the DNA he inherited. He must've exposed himself to something or done something to cause this. But what? Why did this happen to him? He's not a vet and has never been a smoker. Both, for reasons no one understands, increase a person's odds of developing ALS. Did he have some degree of lead poisoning, mercury toxicity, or exposure to radiation that led to this? Did he have undiagnosed Lyme disease? Could Lyme trigger ALS? There is no scientifically based evidence to support any of these speculations.

Was he too sedentary? Maybe too many hours sitting at a piano bench causes ALS. He pictures the warning labels printed on all future Steinways: NEUROLOGIST'S WARNING: PLAYING MAY CAUSE ALS. Obviously not.

He grew up in the seventies and eighties, when processed foods were all the rage. Maybe his ALS was caused by consuming too many chemical preservatives or additives or saccharin. Maybe it was a dietary deficiency, a lack of some necessary vitamin at a critical age. He ate and drank almost nothing but bologna, Doritos, and Tang in 1977. Is that why he has ALS? Did he drink too many cups of Kool-Aid? Did he eat too many Steak-Umms, Twinkies, and bowls of Lucky Charms?

Maybe ALS is triggered by a sexually transmitted disease, a virus yet to be identified. Are virgins safe from ALS?

Who gets ALS? From what he's witnessed at the clinic, the answer is anyone. He's seen a twenty-five-year-old medical student, a sixty-five-year-old retired Navy SEAL, a social worker, an artist, an architect, a triathlete, an entrepreneur, men and women, black, Jewish, Japanese, Latino. This disease is as politically correct as they get. It has no bigotries, allergies, or fetishes. ALS is an equal opportunity killer.

Why did a forty-five-year-old concert pianist get ALS? Why not? He hears his mother's voice: *Don't answer a question with another question.* But this is the only answer he can find.

Only when the playing from the next room stops does he realize that his jaw has been clenched. God, how can Karina stand it? The music begins again, but this time, it's Karina playing, showing her student what the piece is supposed to sound like, what's possible given those same notes. Her playing is beautiful, a soft blanket calming his agitated nerves. He gets up and walks to the slightly open door to hear her better.

Why did Karina stop playing piano? Teaching kids half-hour lessons after school doesn't count. Why did she give up on her career as a pianist? He pretends as he often does when he first flirts with this particular why that he doesn't already know. Unlike the ALS whys, this why has at least one verifiable answer, one that he's never admitted aloud.

As students, she was inarguably more talented and technically proficient than he was and might've stayed the better player and had his career and more, but she abandoned classical piano for improvisational jazz. It was heartbreaking for him, disgusting even, to watch such God-given talent go misdirected, unappreciated, wasted. Granted, he's more than a little biased, but to him, Mozart and Bach and Chopin are gods, and their sonatas, fantasies, études, and concertos are timeless masterpieces, every note divine brilliance. Playing them on a world stage requires education, talent, passion, technical precision, and endless hours of disciplined practice. Few people on the planet can do this. Karina was one of them. He finds jazz sloppy, incomprehensible, unlistenable, played by mostly untrained amateurs in dive bars, and he never understood how it moved Karina's soul.

His admittedly snobbish preference for classical music aside, her singular pursuit of jazz was a doomed decision, and he told her so, many times, which probably only glued her faster to it. If a stable, well-paying, and respectable career in classical piano is a fringe endeavor, then a sustainable life playing jazz is akin to landing a job on the moon. The only shot in hell a jazz pianist has of making it is to play with the very best, to develop and nurture and elevate her playing with the other elite musicians called to do this rarest of things. Karina needed to be where these musicians were—in New Orleans, New York City, Paris, or Berlin.

After Curtis, he and Karina lived in New York. She found a regular gig playing with a phenomenal saxophonist and drummer at the Village Vanguard, which paid squat but made her so happy. She was at the beginning of something real and possible, and they both felt it. Who knows what might've happened for her had they stayed?

Instead, he relocated them to Boston, accepting a coveted teaching offer at New England Conservatory, a faculty position he sold to her as necessary for his career, a job that, as it turned out, wasn't so necessary, as he readily left it barely two years later for a life of touring. He knew that moving to Boston put the brakes on Karina's momentum and was potentially cheating her out of her life's dream, but he never admitted this to her. And he knew this not just in retrospect, but while they were on the train from Penn Station to Boston's Back Bay. And he said nothing. Looking back, this was possibly the most selfish thing he'd ever done.

Until eight days ago.

But that wasn't her only chance. When he began touring, playing with a different symphony orchestra in a different city every week, every month, for years on end, he was willing to move and told her so. His home could've been based out of any city, out of New York or New Orleans just as easily as Boston if she wanted. Karina chose 450 Walnut Street in a suburb nine miles outside Boston. He'll never understand why she did this to herself. Maybe fearless Karina had become afraid. Maybe that's when he began falling out of love with her.

Karina switches to Mozart's "Rondo alla Turca." He listens to her play, remembering how remarkable she is and the choices they made and didn't make and where it all got them—Richard in the den with ALS and Karina in the living room teaching a moron—and Mozart's light-hearted notes suddenly turn dark and sinister. An anger rises inside him, not a logical notion or a fleeting feeling, but a deeply stored thick black poison.

Why is she teaching pitiful high school students when she should be a world-class, revered musician? What does she earn—maybe $50, $100 an hour? Does she do four half-hour lessons a day? How is she going to live on this?

Grace's college tuition is already in the bank, thank God, but what little savings he has beyond this is dwindling fast. He hates himself for not having long-term disability or life insurance. But he didn't work for a company that offered benefits. He was the company, and he was relatively young and healthy and had forever in front of him to earn more than enough money to suit his lifestyle. The worst he could imagine was a career-ending injury to his hands. But in that highly unlikely case, he'd then teach, go on a lecturing tour, take a faculty position at some school. There would always be options. He never considered the possibility of needing insurance. He assumed nothing bad would ever befall him. Certainly nothing catastrophic. Now look at them. Living catastrophes.

After all the lies and betrayals, he's still devastated that she gave up such a rare, God-given talent for classical piano to chase jazz and then never even catch it. His mind sends fruitless signals to clench his hands into fists. His anger mixes with impotence.

It's not all his fault.

She blames him for everything.

She lied about everything.

She would say that he betrayed her first.

Cold and wishing for a fleece for the past couple of hours, he's now running hot. Sweat is soaking his undershirt beneath his paralyzed armpits. He feels shaken, disturbed, as if he needs to sit down or leave the house, but instead he stays pinned to the open door.

Karina's playing stops, and now it's the student's turn with "Rondo alla Turca." Nothing about it is sweet or lighthearted. He's reminded of Grace reading aloud when she was five or six, stammering through each syllable of *Frog and Toad*, despairing several times a page, losing any hope of comprehension as every ounce of focus was drilled into the effort of microscopically sounding out the letters. A joyless experience. Except he loves Grace. He hates this student.

He shouldn't do that. He shouldn't hate this poor student. But a poisonous black hate lives inside him, and his hatred needs a subject. The easy choice would be ALS, but ALS doesn't have a face or a voice or a heartbeat. It's hard to hate something that isn't human.

He hates Karina. Her excuses. Her lies.

He hates himself. His selfishness. His infidelities.

Why does a forty-five-year-old concert pianist have ALS? Maybe it has something to do with karma. Maybe his ALS is retribution for something he did equally horrendous in magnitude. Or maybe it's because of what she did. Maybe his ALS is punishment for their mutual sins.

Or, strangely, maybe ALS is their chance to make amends. If they admit where they'd been wrong and apologize for all the hurt they caused each other and are for-given, if they settle their bad karmic debt in this other way, maybe he'd be cured. Or, if not cured, maybe healed in some way. For both of them. He realizes that this kind of mystical wondering is akin to wishing on a star, praying to God, or believing in the prophecies of a Magic 8 Ball.

But why not try?

He pulls the door shut with his foot. He can't tolerate one more second of listening to this wretched piano les-son. And he'd rather go on hating Karina and himself than answer that why.

CHAPTER FIFTEEN

From his reclining chair in the den, Richard can hear Karina singing "Baby, It's Cold Outside." She's been in the kitchen all day preparing for Wigilia, a traditional twelve-dish Polish supper served on Christmas Eve, her favorite day of the year. She's been singing and cooking since early morning, determined to enjoy this day even if no one else at 450 Walnut Street will join her. Or maybe she's hoping that her dogged cheerfulness might hitch a ride with the velvety smells of cooked onions, garlic, ginger, and yeasty dough permeating the house and infect her daughter and ex-husband.

As far as Richard knows, Grace has always helped her mother cook for Wigilia. They wear matching red aprons. Grace specializes in baking the *makowiec*, a sumptuous poppy-seed rolled cake. They're an adorable team, singing and chatting while preparing this special feast from scratch.

Not this year.

Grace has been holed up in her room since walking through the front door two days ago. Her muttered excuses for reclusion have so far included exhaustion, headache, and reading. Every now and then, Richard hears the water running in the pipes overhead, so he knows she's in the bathroom above the den. She came downstairs a couple of hours ago for a wordless visit to the kitchen, probably to grab some food to go, and scurried back to her cave. It's now 6:00 p.m., and she's still up there.

He and Karina agonized over how much to tell Grace before she came home for Christmas break. Karina didn't want to risk distracting her from her studies and cause her to bomb her finals, but Richard didn't want her to come home to his ALS with absolutely no warning. There was no good choice here. They compromised. Since Karina's voice doesn't sound like Siri on a bender, she called Grace and gave her a hint of what she'd be coming home to.

Just wanted to let you know, your dad is living here back at the house. . . . No, we're not getting back together. He needed some help, so he's staying here for a while. . . . I'm not crazy. . . . It's fine. We'll talk about it when you get home.

He keeps replaying the shock on Grace's face at the first sight of him. It was more than the simple discomfort of seeing her divorced, estranged father living back at the house. That would've been mind spinning enough. It was his ALS—his slumped, hanging, lifeless arms; his slurry,

♪

monotone voice; his emaciated frame. He's had a year to get used to this creeping metamorphosis. He adjusts to each incremental loss, each distortion along the way, and so when he looks in the mirror or hears the sound of his voice, he usually notices only the most recent change. He registers the difference from ninety-nine to one hundred and adapts to it. He doesn't have to start from zero with every new symptom, every pound or consonant lost. He mostly still sees and hears himself. Every week, a new normal.

But Grace hadn't seen him since before he was diagnosed. He watched her absorb the entire transformation, from zero to one hundred, in less than a second, and the stunned impact on her face made him breathless, horrified to be the source of it. She averted her eyes and forced a soft hello. Stiff and mute, she endured their carefully planned introduction to ALS 101. Then, without a word, she withdrew to her room.

Karina announces that supper is ready. Richard emerges from his room, and Grace materializes, hovering at the edge of the dining room like a nervous rabbit about to dart. Karina calls her into the kitchen. Alone in the dining room, Richard sits at the head of the table, where he sat for holidays and dinner parties for thirteen years, but instead of feeling familiar, it feels strange, unsettling, wrong. The dining room is exactly as he remembers— same oak table and ivory slip-covered chairs, same crystal chandelier, same silver and china, same mint-and-copper-colored abstract oil painting on the wall. Everything is the same.

But he couldn't be more different. He's an ex-husband, an ALS patient, a former concert pianist. In this chair, he's an interloper, an uninvited guest, a walk-on assuming a starring role. As is Polish tradition, Karina has included an additional place setting for an unexpected visitor, someone who might be lost in the night and needing a meal. Richard stands and changes seats. There. Far more suitable.

Karina and Grace shuttle in and out of the dining room, making several trips, transporting plates and platters and bowls and serving spoons while Richard sits and watches like a powerless king. The table fills up with colors and smells and memories. *Barszcz*—a tangy bright red beetroot soup. *Uszka*—little ear-shaped pastas filled with sautéed wild mushrooms. Pierogi, braised sauerkraut, herring in sour cream. Twelve dishes in all. A splendid feast before him.

Returning from her last trip to the kitchen, Karina pauses, noting without objection that Richard has changed seats, then places a vanilla ice-cream milk shake smack in the middle of his plate. She sits, recites a quick prayer, blessing them for the upcoming year, then breaks off a piece of bread from a loaf instead of using a traditional wafer and passes the loaf to Grace. Grace does not pass the loaf to Richard. Karina and Grace begin eating this decadent meal, and Richard sips his shake.

Although he's still capable of eating certain soft foods such as mashed potatoes and macaroni and cheese, and he could certainly handle the soup and pasta on the table tonight, he can't stand being fed. He's tried it, gone along with the song and dance a few times with various home health aides. He wore the bib and opened wide. It made him feel helpless, emasculated, infantile. He quickly put a stop to it, trading beloved flavors and textures and favorite foods that require forks and spoons for the rather limited menu of drinkable soups, smoothies, and shakes. He's losing control of his muscles, his independence, his life. While he still can, he's going to feed himself.

So he sips his vanilla shake while watching Grace and Karina eat Wigilia supper in front of him, annoyed that Karina didn't think to offer him the beetroot soup in a glass with a straw. He's too stubborn, too stupidly offended, to ask. Instead, he keys into the sights and sounds of them eating—the clinking of the silverware against the china, Karina slurping the soup off her spoon, steaming bowls being passed, Grace chewing with her mouth open. The entire sensory experience—every festive, forbidden molecule of it—disgusts him. Even Bing Crosby singing "White Christmas" is a personal affront.

No one is talking. Naturally chatty, Grace hasn't offered a single word. Silence has always been the cloak she wears to conceal her anger or fear. She's shoveling one forkful after another into her mouth, clearing her plate as if she were in a race, gunning for first prize. She's done before Bing Crosby finishes his song. She pushes back her chair, stacks her soup bowl onto her plate, and stands, on her way to the kitchen.

"Hold on there," says Karina. "You're not excused from the table."

"Why not? I'm done."

"You didn't have any *piernik* or *makowiec*."

"I don't want any *piernik* or *makowiec*."

Grace loves *piernik* and *makowiec*. So does Richard.

"Fine, then sit and keep us company. Wigilia isn't over."

Grace relents and sits but doesn't add any dessert to her plate. Richard catches her stealing fast, microscopic glances at him, as if looking directly at him for more than a moment might be dangerous. It's one thing to read about ALS on the Internet, as he assumes she's been doing up in her room over the past two days, it's quite another to sit across the table from it, a plate of *piernik* and a couple of flickering candles away, to witness it live and in the flesh, residing in her father.

"How were your finals?" Karina asks.

"Terrible."

"Oh no, why?"

"I didn't study because I was too busy reading about ALS."

Richard and Karina turn to each other, stunned.

"But how—"

"You tell me Dad is back living with you, and you won't tell me why? I texted Hannah Chu and told her how freaky this was, and she told me."

"I'm sorry, honey—"

"So Hannah Chu and God knows who else already knew that my father had ALS, and I didn't. Glad I'm part of this family or whatever you want to call this."

"We didn't want to tell you before finals for that very reason."

"This didn't happen overnight. Why didn't you tell me sooner?"

"I didn't know myself until recently," says Karina.

She's known since July if not before. Always deflecting blame, always right, always innocent. Richard wants to pounce on this lie, argue the facts and for once expose Karina in front of Grace, but his voice is too slow to produce to jump in, and he lets it be.

"What about you?" asks Grace, addressing her father for the first time. "Why didn't you tell me about this?"

He was diagnosed just before Christmas last year. He didn't want to ruin Grace's holiday with his grim news. Then full denial set in. He couldn't have even whispered, alone in his condo with no one to hear him, that he had ALS, never mind speak the three letters aloud to his only child. He continued to tour, pretending everything was fine, and didn't reveal his diagnosis to Trevor for three more months. Shortly after, his right hand weakened further—threatening his playing, his reputation, his life—and the jig was up. Still, he didn't announce his disease to the world. Trevor hid it behind the guise of tendinitis for a while. So at first, keeping the news from Grace wasn't personal.

Then it was. He was afraid of giving her yet one more reason to push him away, that she might reject him so completely that they'd never have a chance to recover. Before ALS, he had no idea how to make things right between them, if it was even possible. Admittedly, he was lazy and figured they had time. And now he has ALS, and they don't have twenty years of therapy or living to sort it all out, and he still has no idea how to make things right. He's not off to a good start.

"I tried to, many times. It's hard. You had finals and then the second semester of your first year of college. I didn't want to ruin this exciting time in your life."

"Don't worry, you won't."

Born loyal to her mother, Grace has always blamed Richard for Karina's unhappiness and the divorce. As she sits across from him, arms crossed, eyes glaring, Richard sees an additional edge to Grace's anger, one that has probably been there for years, but that he'd never noticed until just now. Betrayal.

Every time Richard cheated on Karina, he was also cheating on Grace. He repeats this theory in his mind, chewing on it like a fresh stick of gum. It's one thing to have missed Grace's Saturday soccer game or Sunday dinner or an awards night at school because he had a concert in Miami. It's another to have missed those things because he chose to linger in Miami with a woman whose name he can no longer remember. Grace spent much of her childhood without a father at home, and some of those days and nights were because of his various infidelities. So in that sense, he cheated on Grace, too.

He looks at his daughter, who has always so closely resembled her mother with her wide-set green eyes and espresso-brown hair, and sees resentment in those green eyes, defiance in her strong jaw, her mouth a weapon. He sees himself in his daughter's face, and his heart aches. Neither of them got the father they wanted.

"So what happens next?" Grace asks.

Barring any special weekend trips or time off, Grace won't be home again until the end of March, if she doesn't go to Daytona Beach or Key West or wherever college kids go these days for spring break. Three more months. Any number of depressing changes could transpire in that time, changes that could necessitate a feeding tube, a BiPAP, a wheelchair, eye-gaze communication, a trach tube and invasive ventilation. Hopefully, he won't be dead.

"I don't know."

Both the ultimate certainty and immediate uncertainty of Richard's future, imaginable and unimaginable, hang in the air over Wigilia supper. No one says a word, and no one eats. The last track of the Bing Crosby Christmas album ends. The room is silent. Richard examines the uneaten meal on the table, the comfort food Grace has refused, refusing to be comforted, the twelve dishes Karina cooked from scratch by herself, recipes handed down from her parents and grandparents. He focuses on the untouched *makowiec*—a sweet poppy-seed cake, his favorite—and decides to take a risk.

"Karina, would you please feed me a bite or two of the *makowiec*?"

She doesn't react at all at first, her blank face not seeming to comprehend his request. He's never asked her to feed him. Apprehension fills her eyes as she registers his question.

"I don't know. Is that allowed?"

"Just a couple small bites. I'll wash them down with milk shake. It's not Wigilia without *makowiec*."

That won her. Karina's a sucker for tradition. Still unsure, she cuts a thin slice of the cake and sets it onto Richard's plate. She then sits in the empty chair next to Richard

LISA GENOVA

and faces him. She pinches off a small piece of cake between her thumb and finger, barely the size of a corn ker-
nel, and holds it up.

"I'm not a bird. A real bite, please."

Still uncertain, she takes an unused fork from the unexpected guest's place setting and cuts a modest helping of
cake. She makes eye contact with Richard and gingerly
sends the piece of *makowiec* into his open mouth.

Richard closes his lips and lets the cake sit on his
tongue. If his taste buds could weep with joy, they would.
His mouth is watering, so maybe they are. The moist cake,
the sour cream and butter, the sweet honey, a hint of
lemon, the bumpy poppy seeds. He chews. He chews! He
can't remember the last time he chewed. It might've been
a bagel. Whatever food it was, it wasn't memorable. This
cake is divine, every taste and texture swirling through his
mouth a scrumptious celebration.

Once he's mashed this small bite of heaven into a liquid paste that could be sucked through a straw like a
smoothie, he begins consciously swallowing. No problem.
He sticks his tongue out like a child to prove that it's gone.

He raises his eyebrows and tips his head toward the
plate. Karina loads up another forkful. Richard opens his
mouth, and she feeds him. They stay connected through
eye contact as he chews, Karina vigilantly searching for
any issues, Richard wordlessly letting her know that he's
all right.

He clears that bite and asks for another. As he chews,
he looks into Karina's unwavering green eyes, and the
cruel awkwardness and pity he dreaded in being fed by her

in particular isn't there. Instead, a gentle intimacy, a quiet tenderness passes between them that he never expected. After the next bite, she wipes his bottom lip with a napkin, and he feels appreciative instead of ashamed. She smiles. He wishes he hadn't sworn off being fed so many months ago and is imagining all the delicious chewable meals and lovely moments he's unnecessarily forgone when he begins to choke.

Maybe he got a little cocky. Maybe he was distracted by the unexpected connection with Karina. He inadvertently moved the bolus of cake to the back of his mouth before it was entirely pureed, triggering the swallowing reflex before he was ready. He doesn't know if he panicked first and caused the problem, or if a piece of cake went down the wrong pipe and caused him to panic, but he's got a hunk of gooey *makowiec* paste stuck in his windpipe, and he can't breathe.

Worse, because his abdominal muscles and diaphragm are weak, he can't produce the simple cough a normal person could to blast the gob of food out of there. His eyes bulge wide-open, unblinking, and Karina stares back, terrified but unmoving, paralyzed. He's straining every muscle and vein in his neck, trying desperately to cough, to breathe, to yell for help, silently choking.

"Mom!" Grace screams, waking her mother into action.

Karina starts pounding on his back with the heel of her hand as if he were bongo drum. It's not working. He envisions the half-chewed lump of cake as a wet concrete stopper in his trachea. He looks across the table at Grace, who appears fuzzy and scared through his watery eyes.

Karina switches tack. She stands behind his chair, wraps her arms around his middle, and starts rapidly pumping her fisted hands into the soft space below his sternum, between the bones of his rib cage. Over and over she thrusts her fists into his abdomen. The *makowiec* won't budge. He tries and tries to help her, but he can't cough with any real force. His head begins to tingle. Grace and the entire room blur. Karina's saying his name, and he knows she's right here, pounding on him harder and harder from behind his chair, but she sounds far away.

Maybe this is how it ends. Maybe this is what happens next.

CHAPTER SIXTEEN

Karina uncaps the plastic MIC-KEY button that lies flush against Richard's skin two or so inches above his belly button, attaches a small length of tubing, and begins pressing on a fifty-milliliter syringe plunger, delivering a total of 500 cc of Liquid Gold over the next half hour directly into his stomach, his fifth and final "meal" of the day. They watch a rerun of *Friends* on TV while they wait for the syringe to empty.

The past three weeks have been all about tubes. After his nearly fatal choking episode on Christmas Eve, Karina took him to the ALS clinic. His neurologist, pulmonologist, radiologist, speech-language pathologist, and gastroenterologist listened to what had been going on and assessed his breathing and swallowing. Two major things were discovered. Two monumental decisions, both involving tubes, were made. The mother of all decisions, involving the mother of all tubes, still awaits a verdict.

First, he had a swallowing study. He drank barium dissolved in a thin liquid and sputtered as he swallowed. He next consumed barium mixed in applesauce and had to swallow several times to clear the feeling of mush stuck to the side of his throat. He then suffered a violent coughing fit trying to eat the tiniest bite of a barium-sprinkled cookie. A radiologist and the speech-language pathologist studied the X-ray video and determined that his ability to reliably and safely swallow had become significantly compromised in the past three months. No kidding.

The muscles of his tongue and palate have further atrophied, making them weak and lazy. Most dangerous, his epiglottis is slow to close off his larynx while swallowing, which means that food can be aspirated into his trachea and lungs. This is what likely happened with the *makowiec* on Christmas Eve. While liquid milk shakes won't lodge in his windpipe like poppy-seed cake, they can drain down the wrong pipe and drip into his lungs, causing aspiration pneumonia. Anything that goes into his mouth now could easily kill him.

Not yet ready to surrender to dying, he surrendered to a feeding tube. He had the surgery the day after Grace returned to school. The twenty-minute procedure was straightforward and routine for his surgeon. Dr. Fletcher fed an endoscope through Richard's mouth, down his esophagus, and into his stomach. He then threaded a thin plastic tube through the scope and out a small hole incised in Richard's abdominal wall.

Karina waits a good ten minutes after the first 250 cc for his stomach to settle before delivering the rest. When given too rapidly, he gets too full too fast, nauseous, and vomits. Liquid Gold has a foul, acidic, nutty flavor on the way up that makes him cringe just thinking about it. That stuff was never meant to be tasted. Thankfully, Karina takes her time.

When *Friends* is over and the final food syringe is emptied, Karina dissolves his evening meds in water and delivers that through the syringe as well. The water feels cool and refreshing and weirdly quenches his thirst without ever touching his lips. She then flushes the tubing two more times with water, recaps the MIC-KEY button, and lowers Richard's lifted shirt. There. Done with dinner or his nightcap or his feeding or whatever this is called. His stomach is now filled with five hundred calories in a half liter of liquid. He can't say that he's hungry, but he's hardly sated. Although the service was impeccable, he'd give the meal itself a one-star Yelp rating.

He remembers when he first started touring, he ordered steak from room service every night. By maybe the eighth or ninth night, he couldn't stomach even the thought of one more steak. He'd had his fill. He ordered pizza and didn't touch another steak for months. The only item on the room-service menu now is Liquid Gold, every meal for twenty-three days straight and counting. What he wouldn't give now for a medium-rare dry-aged New York strip.

He tries not to think about food. For one, it's torture to imagine what he can never again have. Second, like Pavlov's dog anticipating the steak his master is about to plop in its dish after the bell is rung, remembering food makes Richard's mouth water. While the PEG tube eliminates the potential threats of eating and drinking, he still has to contend with his own saliva, which, like any liquid, can go down the wrong pipe when swallowed.

Even with the help of the glycopyrrolate, his drool, which has for some reason become the consistency of Elmer's glue, is constantly accumulating, either spilling over his bottom lip and hanging from his chin in shimmering, stringy ribbons or gurgling at the back of his mouth. Thinking about steak turned the faucet on. He's gurgling.

Karina flips on his new suctioning machine, pokes the wand into his mouth, and slides it around in there, vacuuming between his teeth and gums and under his tongue, slurping up his excessive spit, drying out his flooding mouth. He feels like he's at the dentist every time she does this.

The second big discovery at his clinic appointment was the treacherous state of his breathing. His forced vital capacity, the amount of air he's able to forcibly exhale, was down to 42 percent. Over the past three months, he'd started to notice that he was regularly out of breath when walking from room to room, that he had to pause every four or five words when talking because he was out of air, and that he was speaking only on the exhales.

"Are you waking up throughout the night?" asked his doctor.

"Yes."

"Are you starting the day already fatigued?"

"Yes."

"And do you have a headache when you wake up?"

He did, almost every morning for weeks.

"You're hypoventilated during the night. You're not getting in enough oxygen, and you're retaining too much carbon dioxide. I want you on a BiPAP."

He had no idea that his insomnia and morning headaches were due to a continual lack of air throughout the night. So now he sleeps with a mask attached to a machine by a long tube. It's ten o'clock, and the only thing left on his exciting daily itinerary is getting hooked up to the BiPAP.

Karina fills the humidifier and plugs it in. Richard watches her weary but focused eyes as she works. She applies Vaseline with her pinkie to the many raw sores on his face. The moist air and prolonged contact of the mask against his skin every night have caused it to break down, creating a painful rash. He tried switching to nasal pillows instead of a full-face mask, but he couldn't keep his mouth closed while sleeping and found wearing the chinstrap to keep it shut too aggravating. So he wears the full mask and endures the sores. Karina wipes her hands on a towel, turns the BiPAP on, then secures the mask over his nose and mouth.

The relief is instantaneous. Initiated by his own inhale, air is forced in. His lungs fully inflate, and his rib cage expands. When he exhales, the machine inverts the pressure, and air is forced out as if his lungs were a pair of bellows and the machine were pressing the handles together. Every night, in this moment when Karina seals the mask onto his face, he realizes exactly how labored and shallow his breathing has been all day, as if he's been wearing a tight corset around his lungs since morning and Karina finally released it. With the mask on his face, he breathes an abundant flow of sweet oxygen in and carbon dioxide out, and a deep tension lifts out of his body like steam rising off a hot cake. He won't suffocate in the night.

His pulmonologist says that his forced vital capacity appears to be declining at about 3 percent per month. The BiPAP is only capable of producing pressure that supports breathing. It doesn't breathe for him. It breathes with him. At some point, the BiPAP will no longer sustain him. The only options then will be death or a tracheostomy tube coupled with mechanical ventilation and 24-7 care. Like the medium-rare dry-aged New York strip, he tries not to think about it.

While the introduction of the BiPAP has meant a better night's sleep for Richard, it has meant the opposite for Karina. She adjusts the mask, making sure it's entirely sealed, knowing without question that, like all things, the seal is temporary. When he yawns, when he scrunches up his nose because it itches, when he turns his head to the right, the mask can come loose. If it does, the machine will then sound an alarm, and Karina will have to get up to re-adjust the mask. Several times a night. She sleeps on the couch in the living room now to shorten her commute.

He's like a newborn, and Karina is the sleep-deprived new mother, a walking zombie. But with newborns, there is light at the end of the tunnel. The baby starts eating solid food or gains weight or turns one—some developmental milestone is achieved and miraculously the baby sleeps through the blessed night. There is no light at the end of this tunnel, no developmental milestone that will graduate Richard from needing assistance all hours of the night. Unless they consider his death a milestone. Maybe Karina does.

He watches her face, her pretty green eyes. She's inspecting the perimeter of his mask, but because the mask is over the midline of his face, it looks as if she were studying him. Her eyes appear dull, disconnected from the source of any internal spark. Her long hair is gathered into a low ponytail, but a section from the front has fallen loose, draping over her right eyebrow. He wants to reach out and tuck it behind her ear.

She looks him in the eye and sighs. He wants to tell her that he's sorry that she's so tired. He's sorry that he has this and had nowhere else to go. He's sorry he's become such a burden to her. And then suddenly, strangely, for the first time, he wants to tell her that he's sorry for all of it.

And he's sorry without the usual accessories, the excuses that absolve him or an equivalent list of her crimes weighing down the other side of the scale, blaming her, making them even. There is only his apology. He's sorry he was so careless with her, their family, their life. He's sorry that he cheated on her, that he didn't know what to do with his loneliness, that he felt unappreciated, unseen, unloved by her and didn't know how to talk to her about it. He was lonelier in bed with Karina than anywhere else

LISA GENOVA

on the planet. He never told her. He remembers those green eyes looking straight at him, simmering with resentment, punishing him, looking straight through him, indifferent, shunning him. He was too afraid to ask her what was wrong, too afraid to hear her answer. They never talked about any of it. They were complicit in their mutual silence.

Her exhausted eyes, likely praying that the mask stays put for at least a couple of hours, connect with his. He wants to tell her now that he's sorry, before she leaves the room, before this revelation and urge to confess evaporate, before he goes to sleep and, as if it were a dream in the nighttime, he awakens in the morning with only the vaguest sense of having known something. He holds his apology like a helium balloon, the slipknotted string fast loosening from his wrist, soon to be a dot in the stratosphere. He has to say it now or possibly never.

"I'm sorry."

But his voice, already thin and weak like the rest of him, can't be heard through the mask, over the vacuum-cleaner-like whir of the BiPAP.

"Good night," she says.

Karina turns off the TV and the light, leaving the door open a crack as she disappears from his room without ever hearing him, not knowing.

CHAPTER SEVENTEEN

Finished with his morning shift, Bill walks into the sunlit but chilly living room, leaving the door to the den wide-open. Cuddled under a blanket on the couch and draining the last still-hot sip of her second cup of coffee, Karina is distracted by this, bothered even, as if she'd witnessed someone leave a bed unmade or the cap off a tube of toothpaste, nagging her like an aggressive itch she can't yet scratch. She doesn't keep the den door wide-open. She can't shut it entirely as she would prefer, as Richard would be trapped inside, but there needs to be some physical, visible barrier between them. She keeps the den door positioned open only a crack, creating at least a semblance of separation and privacy. She feels safer that way. Not wanting to reveal this probably diagnosable compulsion to Bill, she'll close the den door to an inch shy of shut after he goes. Then she'll finally take a shower.

Karina anticipates their daily good-bye as Bill checks a text on his phone. Done, he looks up at her, but instead of offering his usual cheery hug and a kiss on the cheek, he stands there with his arms crossed, studying Karina as if she were a math problem he can't quite figure out or a piece of art that sort of offends him but he's not sure why.

"Okay, girlfriend, my one-thirty just canceled. Kensia will be here with Richard then. You're meeting me for coffee."

"I can put on a pot here if you want some coffee."

"No. You're getting out of this house, and we need to chat."

"About what?"

"About you," he says, assertive and concerned.

"Me?" She's suddenly self-conscious about her bed-head and sweatpants, that she's not wearing a bra under her T-shirt or any makeup, and that she doesn't smell so good. "I'm fine."

"You are so not fine. Ryan Gosling in *The Notebook* is fine. You're Mickey Rourke in *The Wrestler*."

Mortified, she wants to pull the blanket she's wrapped in up and over her head.

"I'm just tellin' it like I see it."

"I haven't showered yet," she confesses, as if this weren't obvious. "And I've already had two cups of coffee and can't have any more caffeine or I won't sleep at all tonight."

"You can order decaf."

"Honestly, I'm okay, Bill."

"Decaf coffee at one thirty, or we're going for martinis after I get off work tonight at six thirty. And don't throw any more excuses at me 'cause I have a really big bat, and I'll just keep hitting 'em back at ya."

"I'm good."

"You're bad."

"I can't leave at six thirty. Kevin's only here until six."

Bill squints at her through his black-rimmed glasses as if he were contemplating his next move in a game of chess. "You're driving me nuts." He checks his phone again. "Okay, my next visit lives nearby, so let's do this now. Come."

He marches into the kitchen, a man on a mission, and not knowing what else to do, Karina follows him. They sit opposite each other at the square breakfast table. He looks into her eyes and says nothing, taking her in, and she feels so utterly exposed and yet safely held in his gaze that she finds herself working hard not to cry.

"Okay, honey, tell me what is going on. I need to know more about this situation."

"What do you mean?"

"I mean about the two of you. Not for nothing, but the tension in this house is killing me."

Karina sits back in her chair, blinking, stunned. She thought she'd been nothing but perfectly civil, polite, and dutiful around Richard, especially in front of Bill, whom she adores and admires and wants to impress. She can feel the razor-sharp point of every edge between Richard and her, but she assumed their animosity was traveling on a

LISA GENOVA

private, restricted highway. She didn't think Bill or anyone else visiting or tending to Richard could possibly pick up on it.

"Really?"

"You both do anything to avoid making eye contact with each other. Seriously, if you're in the same room, your eyes dart around so much I practically have to sit down I'm so dizzy."

"Well, you know we're divorced," she says in a hushed voice, not wanting Richard to hear her through the wide-open den door, wondering what details he's already shared with Bill.

"Are you ever going to talk about your whole history?"

"To you?"

"To Richard."

She pauses. She didn't see that coming. She picks at a flake of skin on her chapped bottom lip with her thumb, smelling her coffee breath on her hand as she does. The skin peels too far without letting go, and a quick pinch stops her from continuing. She licks her lip, tasting blood.

Bill waits, watching her.

"Part of the reason we're divorced is because we don't know how to talk to each other."

"Look, I don't walk in your shoes, but I see what I see, and I've been through a lot. I've lost people close to me, and in the end, it's all about peace of mind and closure. You've gotta get to forgiveness."

She has taken Richard in. She pulls down his underpants so he can pee, she wipes his urine off the toilet seat and the floor when he's done, she suctions mucus out of his mouth all day, she reseals that damn mask onto his face all night, she pushes liquid food and water through a syringe into his stomach, she makes sure the den door is cracked open instead of shut so he can come and go. And a thousand other things. Now she's supposed to forgive him, too? She wants to do the right thing, and she wants to please Bill, but she's maxed out. Totally tapped.

"I can't do any more than what I'm already doing for Richard." She crosses her arms over her chest.

"Sweetheart, forgiving Richard is for you. Not for him."

She softens her stance, surprised to be considering this perspective. *Forgiving Richard would be for me. Could that really be true?* She tries it on, but instead of feeling true like *the sky is blue*, it feels more like *the sky is infinite space extending through more than one hundred billion galaxies.* It could be true, but she can't comprehend it.

"I don't know if you've fully grasped this, but he's probably not going to live to be ninety."

"I know."

"I wouldn't wait too long then. You might just miss your chance."

Bill looks her straight in the eye, making sure his words landed, and her heart beats faster as if it's been warned or dared or threatened. She nods but has no idea yet what she's agreeing to.

"I gotta run. But also, honey, please. You gotta take care of yourself. I've seen too many caregivers burn out. You gotta get out of this house and have time that's just for you."

"I walk with Elise every week."

"That's not enough. What about meeting someone?"

"Like a man?"

"Yes, a man. Or a woman if you're into it. Whichever. A date."

"No." She shakes her head for emphasis, dismissing the suggestion.

"Look at you. You're beautiful. Or, you would be after a long shower and some makeup and maybe a trip to the mall."

"The last thing I need is another man to take care of, thank you."

"I'm not telling you to marry him, for God's sake. I'm talking someone to wine and dine you. And getting laid wouldn't hurt either, girl. I'm just sayin'. You know I love you."

"Thanks. I just . . . I'm good."

"Okay." Bill stands, not believing her, but satisfied enough for now, needing to go. "But find something outside of this that's just for you. ALS is going to take Richard down. Don't let it take you, too."

He kisses the top of her head and leaves the kitchen. She stays in her seat, listening to the squeaky sound of his rubber-soled footsteps on the hardwood floor of the living room and then the front foyer, the rising chord progression of his coat zipper, the questioning intonation of the front door as it creaks open, and the satisfying thump of it closing all the way shut.

CHAPTER EIGHTEEN

Karina and Elise walk together every week, regardless of the weather. Neither snow nor rain nor heat nor gloom of early dawn keeps them from completing their three-mile loop. It's an admirable policy in theory, but questionable on mornings such as this when the temperature, with the windchill, is below zero. They leave the paved roads of their neighborhood for the dirt path that encircles the reservoir, walking much faster than they normally do. The sharp, frigid air stings Karina's cheeks and seems to penetrate her brain through her exposed eyeballs, every blink a temporary shield, a noticeable moment of relief. She wishes she'd remembered her sunglasses. The normally soft pine-needle-strewn dirt path has no give, feeling petrified beneath her feet, the earth frozen solid. Frequent bursts of wind slice her body and steal her breath. It's too cold to be out here. It's almost too cold to talk.

"She definitely needs more help," says Grace, walking fast behind Elise's heels as if pursuing her.

Grace arrived home yesterday for a long weekend. Before bed, Karina invited Grace to join her and Elise in the morning but didn't pin any hopes and dreams on Grace's actually coming. A night owl who hates the cold and hasn't seen 6:00 a.m. since elementary school, Grace didn't verbalize any interest, and Karina took her nonanswer to mean *Thanks, but no thanks*. So Karina was more than a little surprised, and happy, to see her daughter dressed and waiting at the front door when Karina was ready to leave.

It's been a month since Grace was last home. It feels like a year. In December, Karina came and went without too much thought regarding Richard's safety. He could always reach her on her cell. But his voice has significantly weakened since Christmas, and the voice-activation app on his phone can't reliably comprehend his muted, slurred speech. His whole life has changed in one month. He needs Karina's help regularly, throughout the day and night, and so her whole life has changed, too. She worries about leaving him alone, but she's not giving up her weekly walk. He'll be fine.

"What about his father and brothers?" asks Elise.

"They're not going to take him in," says Karina.

"How do you know if you don't ask?"

"Believe me, I know."

"They can at least give you some money for more help."

"I can do it."

Richard has thirty hours a week of home health aides, not covered by insurance. The rest is on Karina.

"But why do you want to?"

"Yeah, Mom, what are you trying to prove?"

Karina's not sure. Maybe having Richard in the house gives her something useful to do, something that fills the many hours every day when she's not teaching children to play piano. When Grace moved to Chicago, an enormous, lonely void moved into Karina's home and heart. No amount of therapy, chocolate, wine, sleep, or Netflix could evict it. Richard in the den with ALS has elbowed out some of the void, which is admittedly strange, as his presence had never before been the cure for her loneliness. Are these really her only two options—live with Richard or live with the void?

She must be a saint. Or a martyr. Or screwed up.

"It's not forever."

"That's what Jane Wilde thought."

"Who?" asks Grace.

"Stephen Hawking's first wife," says Elise. "They were in their twenties when he was diagnosed, and she married him anyway, thinking he had only a couple of years left. He's in his seventies now."

"So Dad could live that long?"

"If for some reason the disease stops progressing," says Karina, not believing this is possible in Richard's case, given the decline he's experienced in the past month. "Or if he gets a trach and goes on a ventilator."

"You can't do this indefinitely, Karina."

LISA GENOVA

"I know. If he goes on a ventilator, he needs to move to a facility."

She's not a nurse. And she's not his wife.

"He'd probably qualify for some kind of assisted living now," says Elise.

"I'm okay for now."

"I don't get it," says Grace. "You couldn't stand living with him. You said the day he moved out was the happiest day of your life."

Karina bristles. She shouldn't have said such a thing within ear's distance of Grace. Karina's hoping she didn't lack all judgment and say this directly to Grace. She might've. She doesn't ask.

"Let me look after him for a few hours here and there. How about Tuesday and Wednesday evenings?" asks Elise.

"No. I couldn't ask you to do that."

"You're not asking. I am."

"No, really, I'm okay."

"I could at least come over and keep you company."

Reluctantly, Karina acquiesces. "Okay."

Elise puts an arm around Karina and hugs her as they walk.

"I'm worried about leaving you alone with Dad."

"I'm not alone. Elise is coming over Tuesday and Wednesday evenings. Don't worry, honey. I have plenty of help."

"You don't. And this is only going to get harder. You realize this, right?"

Karina does, but she doesn't answer Grace or acknowledge her with a nod. Karina keeps walking, her frozen eyeballs focused on the ground. One step at a time.

"Maybe I should stay home and take this semester off."

"No, you're not doing that," says Karina.

"What if I figured out a way to do the next semester at BU or Northeastern?"

"No. We're not discussing this. Your father would never want you to do that for him."

"I'd be doing it for you, not him."

As much as Karina would love for Grace to stay, to help with Richard and fill the void, she won't risk Grace's future. Karina knows all too well that a life derailed, even for a short time, can't always find its way back to its original track. She never even made it back to the station. No, she won't let Grace pause her studies, her relationship with Matt, her pursuit of happiness for a semester. For one second. Especially not for Richard. She won't let Grace make the same mistake she made. That pattern ends with her.

Restless ghosts of unresolved resentment rise to the surface, as full and fresh and haunting as they were twenty years ago, ten years ago, last week. Karina lets the aching pain run through her, the tragic story of how Richard ruined her life, welcoming it for its familiarity, for the way it makes her feel justified.

"You're not disrupting your life out there."

"You're disrupting yours," says Grace.

"That's different."

"She has a point," says Elise. "You're not exactly moving on if Richard is living in the den. Can you see your mom bringing a date home? This is the living room, and that's my ex-husband in the den."

"Richard isn't keeping me from dating. I'm not interested in dating."

"What are you interested in then?" asks Elise.

Getting warm. Ending this conversation.

"How about coming with me and my students on the New Orleans trip?"

"I can't this year."

"Why?"

Her ex-husband in the den.

"I think you like having Richard around to blame for things. It's like a comfortable habit."

Karina hates to admit it, but there is truth to this. If she blames him, she never has to blame herself.

"You can hire help for a few days, someone to stay the nights," says Elise.

"I can't."

"You won't."

"Fine. I won't."

"Why?"

Karina doesn't answer because she doesn't know. Or maybe she's beginning to but can't yet articulate it. She senses something like a program running in the background, an awareness creeping up the basement stairs of her subconscious.

Maybe this horrible, bizarre living situation is giving her and Richard a chance at resolution, at forgiveness. She considers this possibility, first suggested by Bill last week, as the three walk in silence, Elise and Grace waiting patiently for an answer. Karina would like to forgive Richard for uprooting them to Boston; for missing most of Grace's childhood; for cheating on her, betraying and humiliating her, robbing her of happiness. She's tried many times over the years. After giving it much thought, she believes Bill, that forgiving Richard would be good for her. What's the saying? Not forgiving someone is like drinking poison and expecting the other person to die. But she hasn't been big enough or spiritually evolved enough or brave enough to do it. Richard is sick and dying, and she still can't let him off the hook. Making him wrong allows her to feel right, and feeling right is her drug of choice.

And she'd like to be forgiven. But she can't bring herself to apologize to Richard, to say the words. She's handcuffed by shame and a stubborn, self-righteous logic that supports her side of the story. She had her reasons. Maybe her actions now can be the words she's still too afraid to offer.

"I don't know," says Karina.

"I could come back for that," says Grace. "Go to New Orleans."

"No, you don't need to."

"How many days is it?" asks Grace.

"Four," says Elise. "Thursday to Sunday. First week of March."

"I can do that."

"It's too much," says Karina.

"It's four days, Mom."

"I mean it's too much, taking care of him. I'm up all night."

LISA GENOVA

"I'm young. I stay up all night all the time. I got this. You're going to New Orleans."

Elise smiles, patting Grace on the back. "I love this girl."

They reach the beginning of the trail, where they began. Before stepping off the path and onto the paved road of their neighborhood, Karina looks back for a moment at the frozen reservoir, at the loop they just completed. Like her morning walk, her thoughts and emotions run in circles. Richard is living with her again, and caring for him is more than she can handle, but she can't ask him to leave, and her entire life is a circle. She's trapped, never getting anywhere.

"Okay, I'll go to New Orleans."

Grace and Elise high-five, celebrating their victory, but Karina doesn't join in. The trip is a month a way. As she's recently learned, anything can happen in a month.

They stop in the street in front of their houses to say a brief good-bye. Grace and Elise hug, and Elise wishes her good luck at school. Karina checks the time on her phone. They've been gone for forty-five minutes. She hurries to the front door, anxious to get inside, to sit at the table in her warm kitchen with a cozy hot cup of coffee.

She swings open the door, and her stomach drops. Without thinking, she runs toward the den, toward the piercing sound of the BiPAP alarm.

CHAPTER NINETEEN

Karina barrels into the den, breathless. Richard is propped up in his hospital bed, the mask askew on his face, much like it was at 4:00 a.m. He smiles sheepishly beneath it. She quickly sizes up the situation: he's fine. But instead of feeling relieved, she's pissed, as if he's played the same cruel trick on her for the millionth time, and she stupidly fell for it.

"Is he okay?" asks Grace, running in right behind her mother, her voice high and terrified.

"He's fine."

Grace looks him over, assessing the state of her father herself. His face is alert and calm. He's clearly breathing.

"Jeez. Okay, I'm gonna take a shower," says Grace, only temporarily inconvenienced by the false alarm, her spiked emotional temperature already back to normal.

But Karina's heart is still feverish, adrenaline whipping through her body, searching for danger. The shrill sound of that damn alarm sends shock waves through her nervous system, activating some automatic primal instinct for crisis. She can't seem to override her response to it. But nothing about the BiPAP machine is yet life-and-death. He can still breathe without it. He breathes entirely on his own without it all day long. It only *assists* him at night.

So the sound of the BiPAP alarm shouldn't send her running. The sound of his choking on rivers of goopy spit *is* life-threatening. He could aspirate and develop pneumonia. But oddly, she often ignores the first minute or more of these routine, seismic coughing fits, listening patiently and somewhat annoyed from another room, hoping he'll work it out on his own. He almost never does.

She turns the BiPAP and the humidifier off, silencing the alarm, then pulls the mask up and over his head.

"I-ha-fa-pee."

Of all the undignified ALS-related chores, she hates the morning pee the most. She swears he yawns or turns his head on purpose, breaking the seal on the mask, sounding the alarm so she'll magically materialize before him. He then wants her to unhook him from the machine so he can get up and use the bathroom.

She shouldn't resent him for having to pee in the morning, but she does. It's always about 7:00 a.m. when he makes this request, shocking her out of a dead sleep. She begins almost every day exhausted, hollowed out and nauseated from lack of sleep. Granted she's already up today, but normally, she's out cold at seven. Bill comes at nine.

Why can't he just lie there and wait for Bill? She should be grateful that he doesn't piss the bed.

He swings his legs over the side of the bed and worms his butt to the edge. Using his weakening core, he works to pull himself to standing. She watches him struggle and doesn't offer a hand. She follows him out of the den, through the living room, and into the first-floor bathroom.

He stands in front of the toilet, waiting for her. She pulls his boxers down to his ankles, and he steps out. She picks his shorts up off the floor and rests them on the vanity, keeping them safely dry.

He stands over the bowl, thrusts his bony hips forward, and pees. She crosses her arms and grits her teeth, irritated with him for not sitting. Granted, sitting doesn't guarantee that everything will land neatly in the toilet, but she feels the odds are better. What does he care if he misses? He's not the one who has to clean up the mess.

She closes her eyes, an absurd and unnecessary offer of privacy, listening for him to finish. She can tell by the intermittent sound of trickling, of urine splashing into water and then nothing, that he's peeing all over the floor. Just as she predicted. She's sweating, stifling hot beneath her winter coat and hat, which she still hasn't had time to remove. She wonders when she's going to get her cup of coffee.

When he's done, he presents himself to her. She squats in front of him, holding open each hole of his boxers for him to step into. She pulls them up.

"Can-a-pu-on-my Hea-Mus?"

"Give me a minute. I have to clean up this mess."

He leaves her—his ex-wife; his dutiful, unpaid, unthanked nursemaid—to the job of wiping up his piss. She unzips and removes her coat and hat, sprays disinfecting cleaner all over the toilet seat and floor, and wipes everything dry with a wad of paper towels. There. Clean until the next time he pees.

While washing her hands in the sink longer than necessary, she studies her face in the mirror. Her mouth is turned down at the corners, a resting frown. Her skin and eyes are dull. Her hair is flat and oily. She hasn't bothered washing it in days. She needs a long, hot shower. She needs a good, long nap. She needs breakfast and a cup of coffee. But instead, she has to return to Richard's room to stick a silver Head Mouse dot to the tip of his nose. It will take two seconds. But he gets to go first, and she hates him for it.

Back in the den, he's sitting at the desk in front of his laptop, waiting for her. She peels a dot from the sticker strip and presses it onto the tip of his big nose. He begins typing, selecting letters one at a time by aiming his nose at the keyboard displayed on the screen. As usual, Bill will get him showered and dressed when he arrives at nine. While she's in there, she opens the shades and strips the bed. With an armful of bedding, she's on her way to the laundry room when her eyes unintentionally catch the words *Dear Dad* at the top of his computer screen.

"You're writing to your father?"

"Ya-na-su-po-sta see-tha. Don-rea-dova-my-shoul."

"I'm not. Are you asking him for help?"

"No."

♪

"Why not?"

"Why-do-we nee-hel?"

She stares at the back of his head, incredulous. She's pretty sure her frowning mouth is hanging open. Maybe she misheard him. Did he really just ask, *Why do we need help?*

"Bill-an-tha-otha-aides do-mo-satha hea-vy-lif-ting. You-do-wun meal-a-day but-o-tha-than-that I-mo-sly-stay ou-ta-ya-hair."

She squeezes the sheets in her fists. She wants to pull every strand of hair out of his ungrateful head. Who does he think just wiped up his piss? Who will interrupt every piano lesson this afternoon to suck his mouth dry so the students don't have to listen to him sputter and gag between notes and worry that he's dying in the next room? Who is up all hours of the night adjusting his mask so he can breathe? Who does he think washes his bedding and clothes and takes him to his doctor's appointments? But, otherwise, yeah, he mostly stays out of her hair.

"I'm exhausted."

"Yuh-firs-les-son is-no-un-til afa-noon. Why-don-you go-ba-to bed?"

"Why don't you go to hell?"

She drops the pile of bedding on the floor, marches out of the room, and shuts the door behind her. She doesn't want to see him. He can stay in there until Bill arrives.

Standing in the living room, shaking with fury, she's unable to decide what to do. She's too angry to enjoy breakfast and a cup of coffee, too incensed to take a nap, and Grace is still in the shower. Karina stands there, paralyzed in her rage, and wonders what would happen if she stopped helping him. What would happen if the next time he chokes, she doesn't stop her piano lesson midnote to suction him? At some point, the BiPAP won't simply be used for the quality of Richard's sleep. He'll need it all day and night for adequate ventilation. What happens when they reach that point in one month, in two months, this summer, and his mask comes loose in the night, and she ignores the sound of the BiPAP alarm? What if she awakens the next morning, refreshed from a full night's sleep, to find Richard with his mask askew, asphyxiated in the den?

She stands in the living room, exhausted, unappreciated, unshowered, and hungry, wondering if she'd be charged with murder if he dies on her watch.

CHAPTER TWENTY

The first half of every piano lesson is devoted to technique—scales in four octaves, Schmitt exercises, chords, and arpeggios—training fingers and ears. The second half is focused on playing the piece of music assigned to the student the previous week. Ideally, the student has practiced twenty minutes a day at home.

This student has not.

Now that he's finished the technique part of his lesson, Karina waits for Dylan to begin playing, and every minute of waiting increases the temperature of her exasperation. Dylan is thirteen and has probably grown six inches since last year. He's got long arms and fingers, knobby shoulders and knees, and appears uncomfortable in his own body, as if he hasn't quite moved into all that new space. Pink, inflamed acne covers his otherwise pale face. A whisper of fuzzy brown hair has sprouted above his lip. He's wearing bright golden yellow shorts and a matching sweatshirt. His mother will shuttle him to basketball practice immediately after his piano lesson. Every few seconds, he snorts phlegm from somewhere in his throat up into his brain.

"Would you like a tissue?" asks Karina.

"Huh? No, I'm good."

No, you are not good, she wants to say.

He studies the sheet music in front of him as if reading Greek for the first time. Maybe he has a learning disability or some kind of musical dyslexia or amnesia and she shouldn't judge him. Or maybe, he simply doesn't want to be here. That makes both of them. She was up half the night, and sitting on this bench in silence is draining the last drops of her depleted energy. Her eyelids rest shut for a second or two with each blink. She's desperate for a nap.

Dylan lifts his left hand, but then retreats, placing it back onto his lap. He can't decide where to put his fingers. He won't even sample a note unless he's sure he's got it right. Millennials. They're all afraid to make a mistake. Dylan would rather sit on this bench, paralyzed in fear and indecision, than play the wrong note.

If she just tells him, she can end this infuriating stalemate. But she's not going to. Not today. She provides the answers for this kid every week, and he never learns. She blames his mother. She probably sits next to him while he does his homework and checks his answers, irons his clothes, wakes him up in the morning. The boy is helpless. Well, Karina is done coddling him. She sits and waits and says nothing, letting him sweat it out.

He snorts again as he squints at the music, leaning closer to the sheet of paper, searching for where to put his left hand. She's given him many bass-clef mnemonics. All Cows Eat Grass, for the spaces. Good Boys Deserve Fudge Always, for the lines. Or, Grizzly Bears Don't Fly Airplanes. No matter how it's packaged, he can't retain it and is forever perplexed by the arrangement of black dots on the five lines and four spaces of the bass clef.

She wishes he'd quit. She's tired of teaching students who don't want to play piano. She wishes all of them would quit. Aghast by this reckless thought, by the misfortune she just invited into her life, she crosses her fingers in her lap. How would she keep this roof over her head if that happened? She needs to be more careful about what she thinks.

Dylan snorts again. He shouldn't be here with a chest cold. If Richard catches it, it could easily lead to pneumonia, and with ALS, that could be the end of him. She thinks about telling Dylan that they need to end the lesson early, but he doesn't have his license. They'd have to wait for his mother to pick him up, and his half-hour lesson would be done by the time she returns anyway.

The indecipherable music in front of him is Prelude in C by Johann Sebastian Bach. No sharps. No flats. It's as simple a piece of music as she can imagine that is still lovely to play and hear. The first note is middle C. Granted, the note is written for the left hand, and so it's on the ledger line above the bass staff and not on the ledger line below the treble staff, as he's used to seeing it. But still. It's middle fucking C.

His awkward presence and the even more awkward silence continue to provoke her, itching her hot, weary nerves, making her crazy. She grinds her teeth and breathes impatiently through her nose, suffering in her resistance. She will not tell him what to do. Not one little hint. These kids are handed everything with a pretty little gold bow tied around it. Everyone's a winner. Everyone gets a trophy. Not on this bench. Welcome to real life, Dylan.

He snorts again, and she wants to scream. *Play a note! Blow your nose! Do SOMETHING!* On another day, she might blame herself. If only she were a better teacher, more inspiring and encouraging, he'd know how to play this piece. Today, she's letting him own the blame. They'll both sit here for the remaining ten minutes in silence if they have to.

She gazes vaguely out the living-room window and notices three birds in the distance, possibly doves, sitting on electrical wires, two on the top line, the third on the wire below them. These round, black birds blur into treble-clef notes that she plays in her desperately bored mind. G-G-E. G-G-E. She begins to compose a piece of music prompted by these avian notes, and her foul mood is somewhat lifted by the sweet melody when Richard's coughing intrudes. Not the sound she was hoping for.

She listens for the shape and meaning of it and hopes that, like young Dylan here, Richard will work it out on his own. The cough is wet and gurgling, unrelenting.

Richard's abdominal muscles have weakened considerably in the past month, and he often can't produce a cough effective enough to simply clear his throat. To Dylan, it probably sounds as if someone were drowning in his own spit in the next room, but Karina has grown hardened to these now-familiar noises.

Richard suddenly goes quiet, and it's the silence between the bursts of choking that she never gets used to, that fill her with dread. She can picture him straining, his body shaking and taut with effort as if he were trying to pull the cough up from his toes, the stringy vessels swelling in his neck, frothy spittle dripping over his mouth. She waits, listening, and she's reminded of years ago, lying awake in bed, waiting to hear the sound of the front door creaking open after midnight, the sound of Richard's heavy footsteps in the foyer, the wheels of his carry-on rolling across the hardwood floors. She resented him for being away, and then she immediately hated him for being home. Here he is, back home. And she still hates him.

If the situation were reversed, if she was sick, and Richard was stuck tending to her, everyone would canonize him. No one makes her feel like a saint for doing this. She feels pathetic, foolish, resentful, and stupid, probably how Dylan feels sitting at her piano for thirty minutes once a week.

Richard coughs again, breaking the silence. He hacks and sputters, obviously fighting for air, and the sound of his failing to clear his throat crawls up Karina's spine and screeches in her ear. That's it. She's had enough.

She stands abruptly, leaving Dylan in his endless confusion over Bach's impossible notes, and rages into the den. For the briefest moment, she considers the cough-assist machine. But her heart and mind are saturated in a burning-hot soup of hatred, and she can't take one more minute of any of this. She pulls out one of the two pillows from behind Richard's head and registers the split-second, wide-eyed recognition in his eyes before she covers them and his entire face. His head moves side to side beneath the pillow but not violently so. Paralyzed, his hands lie still by his side, unable to resist. She presses down harder.

It takes only about a minute for his head to go still. She waits a bit longer before lifting the pillow. His eyes are open, his pupils fixed in place, uninhabited.

She hears the sound of middle C.

"Is that right?" Dylan asks.

Karina blinks. The doves have taken flight from the electrical wires outside. She turns her head to see Bach's Prelude in C on the rack and pulls herself fully back into the living room, releasing that sinful, warm chocolate torte of a daydream. She listens as the pleasing tone of middle C fades, and Richard begins coughing in the den.

"Yes, Dylan. That's right. Congratulations."

She checks the time on her watch: 4:00. Lesson's over.

CHAPTER TWENTY-ONE

Grace is sitting at Richard's desk, slumped and sullen, her body swiveled in the seat so she's angled toward the door, the way out, instead of facing him squarely. Aside from Karina and Bill and the other aides and doctors who are used to seeing people with ALS, most people choose not to face him directly. He's gaunt and often drooling, and his arms are lifeless and his voice is messed up. Strangers can tell by the quickest glance, because that's typically all they'll stay for, that something is really wrong with that guy. But he understands that, even if he were healthy, facing him is hard for Grace.

He'd been watching *Game of Thrones* from his easy chair when she knocked on the slightly open door a few minutes ago and asked if she could come in, but she hasn't said a word since. She's clearly been sent in against her will, dutifully obeying her mother's directive. She keeps glancing down at her phone, possibly checking the time, wondering how long will be long enough for her to endure this nonconversation. She's been in here for three minutes going on eternity. Or maybe she's reading texts. He can't tell. She's leaving for the airport in an hour, going back to school. This is good-bye.

"I-wan-you-to-know, how-eh-va-ex-pen-sih thi-gets, yah-tu-i-sha mo-ney-wo-be tussed. Yah-ed-u-ca-sha is-safe."

"Okay. Thank you."

Whatever he didn't give Grace growing up, at least he will have given her this.

"Are there any new drugs coming out soon that might cure it or at least slow it down?" she asks, as if finally remembering something she planned to say.

"I'm-ina-clin-i-ca-tri. May-be-thata-be-a mag-ic-bul-le."

"Oh, good."

She seems satisfied and doesn't inquire any more on the topic. Like most twenty-year-olds, she probably can't imagine death in any real way. So of course something will save him. And there it is, the solution, the clinical trial drug. Problem solved. She can move on to a safer, more palatable topic. Or return to their mutually uncomfortable silence. Either way, no one's dying in this room.

Every morning, Bill dissolves the mystery clinical trial pill in water and pushes it through the syringe into Richard's stomach. He wants to feel some kind of difference when this happens—he can take a deeper breath, his articulation improves, the fasciculations in his tongue subside, he can miraculously wiggle his left thumb. But aside from the quenching cool rush of water filling his belly, he feels nothing.

Maybe he's in the control group. Or maybe, likely, this isn't the cure. But he stays in the trial, not because he's betting on this little white pill. He's not deluded into thinking modern medicine can save him. He's already gone too far down the rabbit hole, and he knows it. It's too late for him to be saved. He's in the trial because he's doing his part, contributing this small step in the long march toward the cure.

He figures every single thing that didn't work before scientists discovered the polio vaccine, for example, was necessary to get them to that cure. How many mistakes did he make in learning to play Chopin's Étude op. 10, no. 3, in learning any masterpiece, before being able to play it flawlessly? On the road leading to any great achievement are a thousand missteps, a thousand more dead ends. Success cannot be born without the life and death of failure.

Someday, scientists will discover a vaccine, a prophylactic, a cure, and people will talk about ALS the way they talk about polio. Parents will tell their children that people used to get something called ALS, and they died from it. It was a horrible disease that paralyzed its victims. Children will vaguely imagine the horror of it for a moment before skipping along to a sunnier topic, fleetingly grateful for a reality that will never include those three letters.

But not yet. Today, there is only one lame excuse for a treatment and no cure, and children like Grace sit in front-row seats, opposite their fathers, witnessing ALS in all its grotesque, unspeakable detail.

Even if, by some miracle, his little white clinical trial pill was the magic bullet, at most it would stop the advancing ALS army from taking over any more territory, arresting the disease where it is. From what he understands, this drug can't rebuild what has already been destroyed. So he wouldn't get any worse, but nothing could be reversed. He'd still have two paralyzed arms and hands, a barely intelligible voice, difficulty breathing, a feeding tube, and a right foot that drops and trips him regularly. As much as the prospect of dying in one year freaks him out, a dozen more years of living like this is even more unappealing. It's downright terrifying if he dwells on it.

He needs a magic pill and a time machine. He'd stop the disease and then go back in time, before ALS stole his hands. And then he'd go back even further, to when Grace was two, when he started touring to play with faraway symphony orchestras; to when Grace was four, when he was traveling to hide from Karina and her discontent; to when Grace was six, and he'd teach her how to tie her shoes and ride a bike, he'd celebrate her 100 percents on spelling tests, he'd read bedtime stories to her and kiss her good-night; to when she was eight, nine, ten. To know his daughter.

But here they are instead, in the den, strangers saying good-bye. They have no time machine and no cure for ALS and no cure for this broken relationship. No supplements can fill all that was lost, no pills can be pushed through his PEG tube to make everything right between them.

She swivels her chair back and forth, back and forth, then stops, her feet planted, as if she's decided something. It must be time for her to go. She folds her arms around her middle as if she were cold or feeling ill or protecting herself and looks directly at him.

"My whole childhood, I felt like you picked piano over me."

It's one thing to house shortcomings and failures within the privacy of his own thoughts; it's another to hear the words aloud, publicly spoken by another, called out by his daughter. He feels a crashing wave of shame, and then, to his surprise, he's washed in relief. He holds his daughter's fierce gaze and feels so proud of her.

"I did."

Her face reads surprised, and her eyes don't know where to look. She wasn't expecting agreement. It's time to take responsibility, to accept blame, to be the grown-up, to be her father, right now or never. She's going back to school. He might not have another chance.

He wants to say more, to let her know that while he chose piano over her, he didn't love piano more. It was just easier for him to love piano than to show his love for her. He was good at piano. What if he wasn't a good father? What if he was like his father? Piano was consuming, demanding his full attention, his passion, his time. He'd have time for Grace later. And later was always later. This is the biggest regret of his life.

He was a terrible father. He didn't play a starring or even supporting role in her upbringing. At best, he was an ancillary, recurring character, and now he's a nonunion extra with no lines. When he's thought about his legacy, it's always been about his body of work, the music he's played and recorded, his piano career. He now sees his real legacy sitting opposite him, his daughter, a beautiful young woman he doesn't know, and he's out of time. He likely won't meet her boyfriend, her husband, her children. He won't see her graduate college or where she'll live or what she'll do. He looks at her pale green eyes, soulful like her mother's, her long hair pulled back into a ponytail, and realizes that he's never known her, and now he never will.

Maybe if he'd had more children as he wanted, he would've been a different father. Maybe he would've made better choices, been more involved. Karina was so capable, so totally committed to mothering Grace, he genuinely felt he wasn't needed at home. Over time, he felt he wasn't wanted there either. So he buried his head and dreams in his career and assumed he'd have more chances, that he and Karina would have more children. There would never be any more children. He clenches his jaw, swallows, and holds his breath, but the tears come anyway.

Grace pulls a tissue from the box on the desk, walks over to her father, and wipes the tears from his face and eyes. She returns to her seat and dabs the corners of her own eyes with the same tissue. He gives her a gentle, grateful smile. He wants to give her so much more.

"I have to go."

"Wi-you-be ba-home-fah spa-ring-brea?"

♪

"I was planning on going to Lake Tahoe with Matt and some friends. But, I dunno, maybe."

"Tha-souns-fuh. You-sha-do-tha."

"I'll probably be here for a weekend in March. I'll definitely be home for the summer."

"O-kay."

"See you then."

"See-you-then."

She stands, walks over to him, and with her hand on his shoulder, kisses him on the forehead.

"Bye, Dad."

As she leaves the room, he wants to reach out and touch her, to wrap his arms around her and hug her tight, to show her with touch what he can't seem to execute in words, but his hands are even more useless than his voice. He's plagued with regret and the inability to articulate the apology he wants to give her because of the sweeping scope of it, because his voice production is so damn slow and there are too many and not enough words, because he's entirely unpracticed with this kind of conversation. As she leaves the room, he thinks about the story of his own father—the one he's carried his entire adult life, heavy and cumbersome and painful—and wonders what story Grace carries about him. When her boyfriend asks, "What's your dad like?," what is her answer? How heavy and cumbersome and painful is her story?

CHAPTER TWENTY-TWO

Richard and Karina are sitting side by side in the small office of Dr. George, an augmentative communications specialist. Dr. George has just spent the past few minutes giving them an overview of who he is and what he does, and he's jazzed about all of it. He's probably in his midthirties, pale and thin, wearing metal-rimmed glasses, and is excessively cheerful bordering on goofy, effervescing with energy as if he's had three too many shots of espresso, but Richard suspects that this is simply how this guy rolls. His sunny demeanor is as unexpected as it is disarming, so unlike that of the many other specialists Richard sees. Not that he can blame the others. Treating ALS isn't exactly a barrel of laughs.

"So tell me what's been going on," says Dr. George.

"Well," says Karina, "it's hard to understand him when—"

"I'm sorry, forgive me for interrupting. I'm going to stop you right there. I want to hear straight from the horse's mouth. Make sense? Richard?" Dr. George nods at Richard, eyebrows lifted, smiling. "Giddyup."

"I'm-los-ih my-voice an-we-wa-na-know wha-ta-do so-I-ca-still co-mu-ni-cay."

"Okay, great. I'm a little heartbroken I'm just meeting you now. I wish you'd come in after you were first diagnosed or even a few months ago."

Richard's neurologist, who referred him to Dr. George, said Richard was told about voice banking when he was first diagnosed and many times thereafter, but Richard has zero recollection of it. He was in shock when he was diagnosed and then in denial for at least a season. Dr. George's information was buried somewhere in a packet of other terrifying information he wanted no part of, such as PEG-tube surgery and invasive ventilation and power wheelchairs. Even after he accepted his diagnosis, he didn't accept that he would someday lose his voice. Some people with ALS don't. Maybe he wouldn't. Banking his voice feels like the equivalent of setting up a baby's nursery or creating a baseball diamond in a cornfield. If he builds a voice bank, he will come to need it.

"I-know-I-ma lil-lay-to the-par-ty."

"That's okay. The party's still going. Even though your voice has lost a lot of its melody and isn't as robust as I'm sure it used to be, it's still you. The way you accent sylla-bles, idiosyncratic phrases you might use or even noises you make—your laugh, for example—are all specific to you. By recording these, we can help keep your communications personal and human."

Richard wonders about the sound of his laugh. Is it the same as it was before ALS? He tries to remember the last time he laughed out loud but comes up blank. His life hasn't been funny in quite a while. As every other sound coming out of his mouth has changed, he suspects that his laugh is different, too. He tries to hear it in his mind's ear but finds only silence. He'll have to try laughing when he gets home.

"Even with the sound of your voice being mostly monotone, you'd be surprised. Even the smallest inflection can convey emotional nuance and personality you just can't get from the computer-synthesized voice options."

Dr. George doesn't have to convince Richard of the value of using his own voice versus a computer-generated one. He understands the breadth of what can be communicated in the smallest subtlety of sound. A single key played on the piano can convey the entire range of human experience. Middle C can be played staccato and fortissimo, a loud and sudden *yell!* It could mean anger, danger, surprise. The same note played pianissimo is a whisper, a tiptoe, a gentle kiss. Middle C held down, along with the foot pedal, can convey a longing, a wondering, a fading life.

The same note played by a novice versus a master is a completely different experience. What does Mozart's Concerto no. 23 in A Major have to say? How does it make a listener feel? It depends entirely on who is playing. So, yes, Richard understands.

"I like to think of voice banking as an acoustical fingerprint. Our voices are part of our unique personalities and identities. As you know, with ALS, everything gets taken away. Voice banking is a way we can preserve a piece of who you are before it's gone."

Before *he's* gone.

"Synthetic speech is flat. That's the voice Stephen Hawking uses that you've probably heard. There's no musicality in it. Musicality is so important for conveying meaning, you know?"

More than Dr. George knows. Richard's voice now is a one-note instrument, a child's annoying party horn. His articulation is indistinct, his once-sharpened consonants filed down to a soft, rounded nub. Even Karina and Bill, familiar and trained in Richard-speak every day, are having a hard time comprehending what he's saying. His production is painstakingly slow, every syllable hard labor, and he runs out of air every three to four words. He often runs out of patience for what he wants to say before he even begins and then doesn't bother.

"You can pick and choose what to record. It can feel like a tiresome process, and it does take time. But I promise it's worth it. Don't record in the afternoon or evening, your voice and energy will be at their lowest quality. That's why your appointment today is at four. I want to hear you when your voice is tired. Record in the morning. Make sense?"

Richard nods.

"And we want to conserve your energy. Things like 'I'm thirsty' can be the synthetic voice generated by the computer. 'Thank you so much' would be better in your voice. You get what I'm saying?"

Richard does, but he can't think of anything to record beyond *Thank you so much*.

"Do-you-ha-va liss?"

"We do! You're so on top of this. Yes, we have a list of ideas to get you started. But there are no rules to this. You can record anything you want. You might also want to record what I call legacy messages. These are longer than a phrase or a sentence and not about the activities of daily living. They can be reflections of who you are or messages you want to leave for the people you love, like your wife."

Dr. George settles his gaze on Karina and smiles big.

"I'm his ex-wife," says Karina, correcting him swiftly, the clear tone and volume of her voice leaving no room for miscommunication.

"Oh. Good for you guys," says Dr. George, still smiling, completely unfazed. "Some people like to record movie quotes, a fun way to inject a little humor into the day. So, like, 'Frankly, my dear, I don't give a damn.' Make it fun."

Yeah, Richard can record movie quotes while he's having his Liquid Gold dinner. ALS is a blast. Although the technology is cool, it sounds time-consuming, and Richard's not sure any of this will be worth it. He has only so much time left.

He often checks the time on his laptop and on the TV cable box many times an hour, a vague and persistent dread harassing him, as if he needs to buy something at a store before it closes soon, or he's increasingly late for an appointment, or he's waiting for someone to arrive, the doorbell to ring any minute. Yet, he knows that he has nothing to purchase, no appointments to keep, and isn't expecting the arrival of anyone at the front door other than Karina, home health aides, and therapists. It doesn't matter. He still checks the time. Over and over and over.

Every minute that goes by is one less minute. But what exactly is he doing with those minutes? If he weren't in Dr. George's office right now, he'd be in the den sipping on a coffee milk shake and bingeing on the next season of *House of Cards*. He's squandering his minutes, but what else is there for him? He can't play piano. He can't teach piano. He can't even bear to listen to the classical music he loves unless it's played by Karina.

He looks forward to the moments in her lessons when she takes over. He'll notice the antecedent extended pause and imagines her student scooting over, Karina positioning herself at the center of the bench. He stops whatever he's doing when this happens and waits. She begins playing, showing her student how the piece is supposed to sound and feel, developing the student's ear.

He'll close his eyes, and he's transported into the music. He's traveling with the notes, feeling whatever Karina feels as she plays, as if he were no longer trapped in his prison cage of a body, flying. Listening to Karina play is transcendent, as free as he's felt since he was diagnosed. He wishes she'd play more, when her students are gone for the day, just for him.

"Aside from voice banking, there are some other communication aids I can offer you. You'll want this." Dr. George produces a round red plastic button from one of his desk drawers, something that a clown might pull out of his prop bag. "It's a simple call button. So, for example, say you're choking and you can't call for help, you can step on this call button, and the receiver end will buzz loudly like a doorbell, and so even if Karina is somewhere else in the house, she'll be alerted. It's kind of like a baby monitor. This is a great option for you because you're still walking. So you can get to the button and step on it. You're lucky you still have your legs."

While Richard knows he's lucky to still have use of his legs, and he's lucky that he can still talk, and he's lucky he can still breathe, these kinds of comments strike him as both ridiculous and insulting. But he tries not to take offense.

His legs will soon be leaving him. For the past week, he's felt a long-distance pause between the decision to take a step and stepping, a loosening of body from mind, of muscle from bone, of intent from action. ALS is extending its evil tendrils south.

Maybe he's just being paranoid. Maybe he's imagining the weakening in his right leg, creating a somatization. Maybe it's psychosomatic. His mother used to tell him, *If you're looking for trouble, you'll find it.* That may be true, but he certainly never went looking for ALS. He knew that Lou Gehrig had it, that Stephen Hawking has it, and was peripherally aware of the Ice Bucket Challenge. That was the extent of his knowledge on the subject, and he wasn't seeking to know more.

Trouble came looking for him. He was diagnosed fourteen months ago, and paralysis from the waist down, one leg at a time, is what comes next, whether he's a paranoid hypochondriac looking for trouble or not. But for now, he agrees with Dr. George. He's lucky to still have his legs.

"An-yah-lu-cky you-still-ha-vyah ki-neys."

Dr. George laughs, a high-pitched, tickled, unguarded giggle. Richard should record it and use that as his banked laugh. He likes Dr. George. He wonders if George might actually be his first name and not his last, if he's choosing to be addressed with a title that's less stuffy and more intimate, like Dr. Phil or like an unrelated friend who goes by Uncle instead of Mr. He's Uncle George.

"You're also going to want a bunch of these low-tech alphabet boards and flip charts. I know they're not as sexy as the eye-gaze and Tobii technology, and you'll get your sexy on eventually, but you'll use these first, and they're actually quicker and easier to use. As his voice goes, or maybe later in the day when his energy is low, you'll want to use these, Karina."

Dr. George hands her a stack of charts. Richard reads the tabs: *In Bed*; *Comfort*; *Transfer and Position*; *Wheelchair*; *Computer*; *Bathroom*. Karina opens to the *In Bed* chart. Richard scans the page.

Raise/Lower Head	Take Arm Out of Cover	Raise/Lower Foot of Bed
Hot/Cold	Take off BiPAP	Adjust Mask
Turn on BiPAP	Mouth Dry/Water	TV and Lights Out
Chap Stick	Pee	Nose/Saline
Nose/Wipe	Scratch My Head	Wipe My Eyes

In bed used to mean something entirely different. Karina turns the page before Richard has the chance to absorb every option. She spends only a second or so on each additional chart before flipping, looking overwhelmed and scared.

"I know it can feel a bit like being on a game show, and this kind of intense listening can feel awkward and frustrating at first, but you'll get good at it. Ask yes-and-no questions or point to what you're asking. Richard, when you can no longer speak, as long as you can nod and shake your head, great. If you can't move your head, you'll blink for yes and do nothing for no."

The same message is printed at the top of every chart: *You have to keep looking at my face and DON'T guess please!* Richard wonders what happens if he can no longer raise his eyebrows or blink. What happens if his face can't offer any clues? He doesn't ask.

"Okay, I know this was a lot. Only a couple more things, then you're good to go. You're going to love this." Dr. George retrieves something from a box under his desk. "It's a head mic and voice amplifier. We're going to turn Richard's volume way up. Super-lightweight and easy-breezy. Here, try it."

Dr. George hooks one end of the microphone over Richard's ear and bends the wire so the tiny mouthpiece sits in front of his left cheek.

"Try saying something."

He feels like a rock star in concert. Madonna comes to mind.

"Sss-tri-ka-pose."

Dr. George stands up and vogues. "Isn't that great? It can amplify a whisper and make what you said audible. It'll save your energy by a lot. Our goal is for you to be fatigued from talking after four hours instead of two."

Richard's fatigued after talking for five minutes.

"Okay, so you have the call button and the voice amplifier, the alphabet and flip charts, and here's the voice recorder for you to use." Dr. George hands the recorder to Karina. "Each file you create is automatically saved in the format we use to build your bank. You don't have to do anything but hit RECORD. It's not voice activated though. You have to turn it on and off by pressing here, so Karina will have to help you."

Karina holds the recorder out in front of her with both hands as if she's been given something fragile or dangerous or sacred. Maybe it's all of those.

"Okay, that's all I have for today. Please contact me with any questions at all, and come back to see me as things change. And I'd say if you're going to bank your voice, do it now."

The change in Dr. George's voice in that last sentence was subtle but unquestionable. The key was slightly lower, the intonation narrowed, and his articulation crisper. The sound of a spoken sentence can add layers of meaning beyond the mere definition of the words strung together. Dr. George's last sentence was a rich concerto, and Richard clearly heard the subtext.

You don't have much time left.

CHAPTER TWENTY-THREE

Dear Dad,

I'm writing to let you know that I've been diagnosed with ALS (Lou Gehrig's disease). Both of my arms are paralyzed, I'm having difficulty breathing and talking and swallowing. I can no longer safely eat food, so I have a feeding tube in my stomach. I can still walk, but this, too, will go. Despite all of these losses, I'm mainly in good spirits. Because I could no longer manage living alone, I've moved back in with Karina, where she and a wonderful team of caregivers help me get through the days and nights. Just wanted you to know.

Your son,

Richard

This is the simplest of the nine letters he's composed, saved, and not sent to his father. He reads it again. Nothing but straightforward information. Just the facts, ma'am. He wrote the first draft of this letter back when he still had use of his left arm, when he still lived alone on Comm Ave. and spent his days and nights obsessively playing Ravel's Piano Concerto for the Left Hand. That was this past summer. He can't decide if August was a lifetime ago or yesterday.

After Bill leaves him showered and dressed and fed, he spends his mornings at the computer. He'll scan the news, but he's conscious not to spend too much time surfing these treacherous global waters. War, terrorism, nasty politics, racial tensions, murders, ignorance, blame—the news either frustrates, angers, or depresses him. He has enough to be frustrated, angry, and depressed about.

He invariably finds himself using this time every day to write and reread the letters he's written to his father. Periodically, he edits his "coming out" letter, updating the list of losses to keep it current, just in case he should decide to send it someday. He added the part about the feeding tube just after Christmas.

He reads the letter again. Pointing the tip of his nose to FILE, he pulls down the menu, then points his nose to PRINT and hovers there just shy of long enough for the computer to register a click before turning his head to the right, his nose aimed at the window, disconnecting the cursor from his mouse target. A game of printing chicken.

He has no idea if his eighty-two-year-old father has an email account, so sending him anything would require actual paper, an envelope, and a stamp. If Richard's ever going to print and mail any of the letters he's written, this would be the one. Unlike the other eight letters he's composed, this disclosure contains no blame or indignant rants. He's almost printed it many times, flirted with the fantasy of his father holding the envelope in his hands before opening it, but Richard's heart gets all twisted as he hovers the cursor over PRINT, and he bails.

Part of him doesn't want his father to know. Keeping his diagnosis from his father fills Richard with an exhilarating sense of winning. He was born into a father-son game he never wanted to play, the rules still cruel and incomprehensible to him, but damn it, he's going to win. He's living with a disease that shaves off another layer of control every single day. Possessing control of whether his father knows or not puts a sword in Richard's hand, a power that's too seductive to resist. He's going to prove, in an ultimate and final test, that he doesn't want or need his father for anything and wouldn't turn to him for help or love even in the most dire circumstances. He won't give his father the satisfaction of knowing he'll soon be rid of the son he never wanted.

But when Richard's bombastic offense tires of wielding its sword and takes a seat, his defense is clearly visible, cowering in the corner. More than anything, he's afraid of his father's indifference. He wonders if his father already knows, if word of mouth has spread north to cow country, and Walt Evans is the one doing the snubbing.

Or his father doesn't know and wouldn't respond if he did. Richard imagines his father opening the envelope, reading the letter through once, crumpling the paper in his fist, and tossing it into the trash. Or he reads it, refolds it, and slides the letter into his coat pocket, where it will be forgotten along with some lint and a gas receipt. In all the fantasies Richard entertains about his father's potential reaction to this letter, Richard's mind won't allow for the possibility of his father picking up the phone or showing up at the door. The father Richard knows would offer no words of shock, horror, empathy, sympathy, or love for his youngest son.

This is why Richard doesn't print the letter.

He knows he'll never send the others. He'll never get what he wants from his father. What does he want? He wants his father to admit that he was wrong for making Richard feel as if he weren't good enough to be in the family. He wants his father to tell him that he's okay exactly as he is. He wants his father to say that he's proud of him. He wants his father to say he's sorry for showing no interest in his piano career, his wife, his daughter. In him. He wants a big fat heartfelt apology.

But Walt Evans is an old dog, and he's not going to change, and he's certainly never going to apologize. And it doesn't matter now. Sorry won't do Richard any good. What's done cannot be undone.

Yet, Richard continues to write to his father. It feels good to get the words out—words Richard felt when he was six but didn't have the vocabulary to articulate, words he wanted to yell when he was sixteen but didn't have the courage, words he wanted to argue when he was twenty-six but didn't have the composure, words he wanted to speak when he was forty-six but literally no longer had the voice. The letters he writes communicate what he could never say, every typed word carrying an ancient scar on its back, every typed sentence fracking a bevy of silenced wounds stored in his deepest, darkest core, releasing a lifetime of outrage and resentment. But it seems no matter how many sentences he writes, the injustices buried within him are never fully mined.

He considers writing another letter, but he lacks the energy. His neck muscles tire faster when sitting up at the desk versus reclined in his chair or propped against the back of his bed. It's becoming conscious work to hold up his ten-pound head. His accuracy declines after typing only a few minutes, the cursor drifting down the screen as his head drops forward. He's probably ready for one of those neck braces, the standard soft white collars people wear when they've been injured in an accident.

He opens the second letter instead. It begins as a résumé, a list of Richard's achievements, appearances, and critical reviews (only the good ones). If he never sends it to his father, maybe Trevor can use it for Richard's obituary.

He graduated with honors from Curtis. He was an associate professor at New England Conservatory. He's played with the Chicago and Boston Symphony Orchestras; the New York, Cleveland, Berlin, and Vienna Philharmonic Orchestras. He's played at Boston Symphony Hall, Carnegie Hall, Lincoln Center, London's Royal Albert Hall, Tanglewood, Aspen, and many more. His playing has been hailed as "inspirational," "spellbinding," and "possessing great virtuosity."

I was a great pianist. Audiences all over the world ap-

plauded me. They gave me standing ovations. They loved me.
Why couldn't you applaud me, Dad? Why couldn't you love me?
Richard has never found a satisfying answer to either of
these questions, but staring at his bio on the computer
screen, he's proven, at least to himself, that he's worthy of a
father's love. *There is something wrong with him, not me.* It
took Richard forty-six years and ALS to get that far, which
feels like progress but is probably just shifting blame, the
pea transferred to another shell under deft sleight of hand,
the truth still hidden from everyone.

Maybe if he'd loved to play something more accessible
to his father, if he'd been into playing Billy Joel or the
Beatles, if he'd wanted to play in a rock 'n' roll band in a
pub instead of classical piano in a recital hall, if he'd also
played football and baseball like Mikey and Tommy, his father would've approved. Walt hated classical music. They
lived in a one-hundred-year-old three-bedroom farm-
house with thin rugs and thinner walls. Whenever Richard
practiced, which was all the time, there was nowhere in the
house that didn't fill with sound. If Richard was playing
Bach, the entire house was listening to Bach.

Walt Evans hated Bach. Ten minutes was about all he
could tolerate before he either stormed out of the house to
do yard work or got in his pickup and drove to Moe's, the
local bar. If for some reason he wasn't allowed to leave the
house, if Richard's mother told them supper would be
ready in a few minutes, and Walt was forced to endure a
few more minutes of Richard's practicing, he'd explode.
"Would you *stop* with all the goddamn noise?!"

Richard opens another letter, and every familiar sentence, every ancient accusation, is a bugle call to his oldest, darkest suffering, summoning an army of resentment and hatred to rise up within him. *You called me a pansy for playing piano instead of football. . . . You called me a fag for loving Mozart. . . . You threatened to hack my piano to pieces with an ax and use the wood for kindling. . . . You never came to my recitals. . . . You never accepted me. . . . You never even knew me. . . . You never loved me, Karina, or Grace.*

Grace. An electric ripple runs through him, decimating the tortured battlefield within, leaving him hollowed out, staring in helpless horror at his computer screen, seeing history repeated. The letters on the screen blur as he imagines a similar letter addressed to him, written by Grace.

You picked piano over me. You never came to my games. And now you have ALS, and you'll never know me. You never loved Mom or me.

Tears roll down his face. *Please don't think that.* He can't stand the thought of this kind of letter, penned by her hand, of this legacy of pain he's leaving her. Maybe what's done can be undone. Maybe that's what apology is for.

After a quick knock on his door Karina enters the room without pausing. It irritates him that she doesn't even allow him to respond, for the possibility that he might not want her to enter. He's still upset, his face wet with tears. He can't wipe them away.

"It's Tommy." She's holding Richard's cell phone, faceup.

"Who?"

"Your brother," a voice says from the phone on speaker. "Hey, Ricky, I'm sorry I'm not calling with better news. But, well . . ." Tommy's voice thins out and disappears. He sighs and clears his throat. "Dad died last night."

Richard stares at Karina. The puddle of agony he was just knee-deep in over Grace's imagined letter evaporates. He waits for what replaces it. He feels nothing.

"Mikey found him early this morning. He was in his chair with the TV on. We think he died in his sleep. Probably a heart attack. . . . You there?"

"Yah."

"I'm so sorry," says Karina.

"Thank you. The wake is Thursday at Knight's Funeral Home and the funeral is Friday at St. Jude's."

"O-kay," says Richard.

"I know. I'm having trouble talking, too. He lived a good life. Almost eighty-three. And dying in your own home in your sleep, no hospitals or long, drawn-out disease, you can't ask for better than that, right?"

Richard and Karina trade a silent conversation about ALS and death with their eyes before Richard realizes that Tommy is waiting for an answer.

"No."

"Hey, I know we haven't seen you in a long time, but you're welcome to stay with Mikey or at Dad's house. I'd have you here, but we literally got kids sleeping in closets and don't have any room."

Richard looks up at Karina. She nods. She'll go with him to New Hampshire.

"Thaks-Tom-my. We'll-be-there."

LISA GENOVA

"You okay, man?"

"Yeah."

"All right. We'll see you Thursday then."

Tommy doesn't know that Richard has ALS. Neither does Mikey. None of them knows. They're about to find out.

Karina hangs up the phone and eyes Richard's impassive-yet-already-tear-strewn face. "I'm sorry. Are you really okay?"

"Fine." He swivels his chair toward the computer and away from her, showing her the back of his head.

He hears her leave the room without a word. He swivels the chair to be sure that she's gone, then returns to his computer. He takes a deep breath, or at least a deep shallow breath. He points his nose at the screen, holding the position of his heavy head steady, focused on the folder labeled *Letters to My Father*. The folder opens. One by one, he selects each of the nine files and drags them to the trash. He studies the screen. The folder remains. The cursor darts and shimmies and his heart pounds hard in his throat as he works to select and then direct the folder to the trash bin.

There.

In an instant, his father and any possibility of apology are dead and gone.

CHAPTER TWENTY-FOUR

They're the last to arrive at Walt's house after the funeral. Karina and Grace hover awkwardly behind Richard in the living room, waiting for him to continue walking or sit down or do something. He just stands there, paralyzed, observing empty space. His upright piano, a fixture in his childhood home as seemingly permanent as its foundation, is gone. There is nothing in its place. Richard stands still, trying to comprehend its incomprehensible absence, feeling as if the only record of his childhood has been expunged. As he imagines his dead father erasing his past and ALS erasing his future, there is too little of him left. Time feels as if it's collapsing in on him, and his bones are suddenly too fragile, his skin too transparent, his presence sliced too thin, and he wonders if he might cease to exist right then and there.

"Whe-did-he geh-ri-do-vit?" he asks of no one in particular, his voice barely audible even with the voice amplifier.

Karina moves to his right side, wraps her arm around his waist, and holds him by the hip, offering him stability.

His brother Tommy wanders in from the kitchen. "What's going on?"

"Where's the piano?" asks Karina.

"I have it. Lucy and Jessie take lessons. I hope that's okay."

Relief washes through Richard. He breathes, and he's back in his body. Lucy and Jessie are his nieces, ages nine and twelve. He nods.

"Yes. Thas-per-feck."

"They're really good. I tell them they get it from their uncle."

Richard smiles with his eyes and looks down at his feet, uncertain how to handle this unexpected compliment.

"You guys hungry? We've got food in the kitchen. Grace?"

"Sure." Grace follows her uncle into the other room.

Richard takes a seat in the rocking chair and looks around the living room as if he were visiting for the first time. It may well be the last time. Much like its former occupant, the house is old and outdated. The floorboards are worn and creaky, the paint on the cracked walls is chipped, the ceiling is mottled with water stains. With the exception of the missing piano and the additions of a

♪

giant-screen TV and an oversized recliner, the living room is furnished exactly as Richard remembers it.

There are still no curtains on the windows. His mother believed in sunshine and having nothing to hide. She often said she wouldn't do anything she wouldn't mind the neighbors seeing. On this four-acre, heavily wooded property, the nearest neighbor would've needed the Hubble telescope to see Sandy Evans smoking cigarettes in her pink curlers and nightgown.

Even though his mother has been gone for twenty-eight years, it's her absence and not his father's that Richard feels most acutely in this room. She was his only ally in the family, the only one who truly saw and accepted him. Without his mother, he couldn't have played piano. She arranged for his lessons, insisted on the money from Walt to pay for them, drove him to every lesson, every recital and competition, and defended his right to practice.

He remembers the time she put herself between Richard's piano and Walt's chain saw. Richard can't remember what set him off. Maybe he'd had a half dozen beers, and the Patriots lost. Richard does remember the thumping of his heart in his ears playing percussion with the distant buzz of his father's chain saw slicing through the branches of a maple tree in the backyard after Walt stood down, determined to destroy something. Richard remembers sitting at the kitchen table while he listened, his mother's hands shaking as she measured out flour and salt for apple-pie dough. He remembers stupidly asking, "Can I play now?"—his mother answering, "Not now, honey." He remembers he was ten.

LISA GENOVA

She was so proud of him for getting into Curtis on scholarship. She died just before he turned nineteen. She never met Karina, never got to see him graduate or play professionally, never got to hold her granddaughter. She never knew that her son would someday have ALS.

He thinks his mother would've approved of Karina. What little his father experienced of her, he was never a fan. Walt didn't trust anyone from out of town, never mind from out of state, never mind from Poland. His world played out within his zip code, his life revolving around his job at the local quarry, the town church, the bank, the school, and Moe's tavern. He didn't like that he didn't know Karina's parents, that he couldn't judge what kind of family she came from. When asked about her religion, she told him she was a lapsed Catholic. The only kind of person Walt, a Protestant and faithful Sunday churchgoer, trusted less than a Catholic was a godless woman. He found no charm in her accent and didn't appreciate her sophisticated vocabulary, which, even spoken in broken English, was far superior to Walt's. He blamed Karina for his son's name preference of Richard over Ricky when she had nothing to do with it. Walt took her to be uppity, a snob, a heathen, probably a communist, a lazy immigrant only interested in Richard as a ticket to a green card.

The grown-ups filter into the room carrying food and drinks and take seats. No one chooses the recliner. That must've been "the chair." Richard's not sure if everyone is staying off it in reverence to Walt or if they all find it too creepy, knowing he died there a few days ago. On Monday,

♪

his father was sitting in that chair watching TV. Today he's in a box in the ground.

Grace says she isn't hungry after all and joins seven of her eight cousins outside, sledding on the hill. They range in age from three to twenty-two, nieces and nephews Richard doesn't know. They were all stone-faced and tearless during the funeral, seemingly more weirded out by their drooling, unfamiliar uncle than their dead grandfather. It's probably easier to bear witness to the graceful exit of an old man than the sloppy, slow-motion, paralytic crawl to death that is ALS in someone who should be in the prime of life. The older kids snuck periodic glances at him as if on a dare, and when caught staring, their eyes fled to somewhere safer, often the coffin.

Brendan, age eight, wiry with a buzz cut, a sharp nose, and curious eyes, doesn't feel like getting wet or cold and is sitting sandwiched between his parents, Mikey and Emily, on the small couch. Tommy and Karina are on the love seat. Tommy's wife, Rachael, is outside, helping her two youngest kids up and down the steep hill. Everyone is eating deli-meat sandwiches and Buffalo chicken wings on paper plates. The men are drinking Budweiser out of cans, and the women are drinking white wine.

Richard watches his brothers eat, massive bites of bread, ham, and cheese churning around in their open mouths like clothes in a circular dryer window while they talk, and he's a kid again at the supper table. Skinny, he ate modest meals, always a single helping, and finished quickly. Never allowed to be excused early, he felt as if he spent hours at the table every night, waiting in lonely silence as his brothers gorged on several platefuls of meat and potatoes. Unlike Richard, they were big boys with big muscles to feed. Athletes who were every day running on a field or bench-pressing at the gym, they were in good physical shape when they were young, but now, they're both overweight. They've got beer guts and full-moon faces and beefy arms and legs that look stiff when they walk, like growing kids stuffed into last winter's snowsuits.

"Want me to get you a plate?" asks Mikey, noticing that Richard isn't eating.

"I-can't-eee-tha."

"You need one of us to hold the sandwich for you?"

"It's not that. He can't swallow the bites without chok-ing," says Karina.

"I-ha-va fee-ding tu."

"There's a tube in his stomach," says Karina to wide-eyed Brendan.

"Can I see it?" asks Brendan.

"Sure," says Richard.

They all sit, watching him, as if waiting in the audi-ence for the curtain to rise and the show to start.

"One-a-you has-to-lif-my shir. I-ca-na do-it."

Richard looks to Brendan and raises his eyebrows twice. Brendan tentatively leaves his seat, walks over to his uncle, and pauses. He looks back at his parents.

"Go-fo-rit."

He gently lifts his uncle's shirt, exposing a quarter-size white plastic disk flush with the upper part of Richard's hairy stomach.

"Ew," says Brendan, releasing the shirt.

"Brendan!" says Emily. "That's not nice."

Brendan quickly retreats to his seat between his parents. Mikey swats him on the head with a rolled funeral missalette. Richard's shirt has fallen back down over his stomach, but everyone in the room is still studying the spot where the tube lives, imagining what they just saw.

"So what goes in that?" asks Mikey.

"It's called Liquid Gold," says Karina. "It's like baby formula."

"Tase-lie chi-cken."

"Really?" asks Tommy.

"No." Richard smiles. "I-am ki-ding."

"What are you doing to fight it?" asks Mikey.

"Wha-do-you-mean?"

"Look at that guy who started the Ice Bucket Challenge, right? And the movie *Gleason*. Did you see it? That defensive back from the New Orleans Saints. He got ALS and started a nonprofit. Their slogan is 'No White Flags.' Guy's an inspiration. A real hero. You can't just take this lying down, Ricky. You gotta fight it."

Former captain of their high school football and baseball teams, cornerback at the University of New Hampshire, Mikey sees every obstacle as an opponent that can be beaten, a game that can be won.

"How-do-you thin-I-shu fight?"

"I dunno. Look at what those guys did."

"You-wa-me-to dum-pa bu-cket a-ice o-vah-my-head?"

Or block a punt? Get a trach and go on life support when he can no longer breathe? Is living at any cost winning? ALS isn't a game of football. This disease doesn't wear a numbered jersey, lose a star player to injury, or suffer a bad season. It is a faceless enemy, an opponent with no Achilles' heel and an undefeated record.

"I dunno. I'd do something though. Start another challenge or make a documentary or something. Something that helps find the cure. The key is fighting and not giving up."

"O-kay."

"It's good you're still walking. Those other guys are in wheelchairs."

"I-will-be in-one-soo."

"Maybe not. You never know. You gotta stay positive. You should go to the gym, lift some weights and strengthen your leg muscles. If this disease starts stealing your muscle mass, you get ahead of it and build more. You beat it."

Richard smiles. He appreciates the thought, but that isn't how muscle atrophy in ALS works. The disease doesn't discriminate between strong and weak muscles, old or new. It takes them all. Exercise won't buy him more time. High tide is coming. The height and grandeur of the sand castle doesn't matter. The sea is eventually going to rush in, sweeping every single grain of sand away.

"Goo-i-de-a."

"I don't know how you do it," says Tommy. "I don't think I could ever go without food."

"Then-you-be gi-vin-up. This-tu-bis how-you fi-ALS."

It ain't sexy. Richard's PEG tube and BiPAP aren't interesting enough fodder for a movie or a global Internet phenomenon. His fight is a quiet, personal, daily struggle to simply breathe and consume enough calories to keep being here.

"It's good to see that you two are back together," says Emily.

"We're not back together," says Karina.

"Yah." Richard smiles. "We-jus li-vin-in sin."

"No," says Karina. "There's no sinning going on what-soever."

"That's too bad," says Mikey.

Emily laughs. "Well, that's really amazing then, what you're doing for him."

Karina says nothing. Richard says nothing and doesn't look in Karina's direction, embarrassed that Emily has so easily articulated what Richard has never said. And although he'd like to, he can't blame ALS for his silence.

"So, Ricky," says Mikey. "We want to talk to you about Dad's will. We already knew about this before he died, but he left the house to me and Tommy."

Of course he did.

"But we talked it over and agreed that we're going to sell the house and split it three ways."

Everyone waits.

Richard repeats what he just heard in his head and asks, "Really?"

"Yeah. He had three sons, not two. That ain't right, and we want to do the right thing."

"Yeah, man," says Tommy. "I hate that I never stood up for you when we were kids. Dad was really hard on you."

"He could be a bullheaded bastard," says Mikey.

Tommy nods. "We're standing up for you now."

It never occurred to Richard that his big, brave, tough jock brothers were scared of their father, too. To show any allegiance with their youngest brother would've risked being forsaken, ostracized, disowned. Like Richard. His brothers weren't as macho as he thought they were. And he doesn't blame them.

"He was also a great father," says Mikey, his voice out of air, jaw clamped, wiping the outside corner of his eyes with his fingers. "Sorry you never got that side of him, Ricky."

"You know, you were better at piano than either of us clowns have ever been at anything," says Tommy. "He should've been proud of you. Jessie Googled you, and we all watched your performance at Lincoln Center."

"Holy shit, man," says Mikey.

"Yeah, you're amazing," says Emily.

"I wish Mom could've seen you play there," says Tommy.

"Tha-means-so much to-me." Tears spill down Richard's face.

He never saw that coming. With the death of the autocratic dictator, their Berlin Wall crumbled, and his brothers were right there, waiting for him on the other side. Karina pulls a tissue from her purse, walks over to Richard, and mops up his wet face.

"Three ways," says Mikey. "That's the fair thing. It wasn't right how Dad treated you. Our son, Alex, is a junior now, hasn't willingly picked up a ball since he was six. He's into musicals. Loves to sing and dance."

♪

"He's really good," says Emily.

"Yeah. And he's a great kid. Can't imagine doing to him what Dad did to you." Mikey sighs. "And I wouldn't be the man I am without him."

Tommy nods. Mikey knocks back his Budweiser. Richard absorbs the acceptance and apology given to him by his brothers, and a space begins clearing inside him, a field stretched to the horizon, a morning sky, a universe of stars. Still overwhelmed and unable to speak, he silently thanks his brothers, one generation healing the wounds inflicted by another.

"I'm sorry to break this up, but we really have to get going," says Karina.

"Can't you stay another night?" asks Emily.

"No, we have to get Grace to the airport. She needs to get back to school."

"Let's do a toast to Dad before you go," says Mikey, cracking open another can. "Can you pour beer into that thing?" He points his finger to the center of Richard.

Karina looks to Richard, and he nods. Every now and then, when he asks her to, she delivers a syringe full of wine through the PEG tube and wets his lips with the smallest taste, one of the few pleasures he still indulges in. It's not the same as drinking wine from a glass. It'll never be the same. But he can still taste a Château Haut-Brion on his tongue. He can still feel its warm infusion in his belly.

Karina attaches the tubing and flushes it with water. She fills a fifty-milliliter syringe with Budweiser and slowly presses on the plunger while everyone watches.

Richard belches. Brendan laughs. It tastes like a teenage memory, horrible and wonderful.

"Okay, save some for the toast," says Mikey. "Karina, you have your wine?"

She picks up her wineglass in her right hand, holding the syringe of Bud attached to Richard's stomach in her left. "Ready."

Tommy and Mikey raise their beer cans. Emily and Karina lift their wineglasses. Brendan raises his Coke.

"To Walt Evans," says Mikey. "May he rest in peace."

Rest in peace, Dad.

CHAPTER TWENTY-FIVE

It's 8:28, four minutes later than last he looked. For the past three days, time has been a fat slug napping on a shady stone. Karina is in New Orleans, joining Elise and her students on their annual pilgrimage to the holy motherland of jazz. Sitting in front of his computer, Richard aims his nose like a conductor's baton, directing the cursor arrow across the letters of the keyboard, typing the names of various jazz artists in iTunes. He plays a few seconds of Herbie Hancock. Then Oscar Peterson. A few seconds of John Coltrane. He can tolerate Miles Davis for just over a minute. The notes wander without any apparent destination, a lost dog in a field, sniffing and tail wagging, scampering here and there, no one calling it home. The compositions are scribbles, run-on sentences without proper grammar and no punctuation, indulgent explorations in incongruous sound.

He clicks on Thelonious Monk, and his mouth cringes as if tasting something noxious, something too sour or bitter or rotten, and he wishes he could spit the sound out. The saxophone and the trumpet sound like an escalating argument, both sides shrill and unreasonable. He hurries the aim of his nose to the PAUSE button. He can't take one more second of this assault, this madness, this noise.

For Richard, music is like language. While he doesn't speak Italian or Chinese, he finds the experience of listening to Italians chatting over cups of espresso to be a melodious pleasure. Chinese, on the other hand, feels like cacophonous machine-gun fire, every word a needle inserted into his spine next to the sound of someone rubbing the surface of a rubber balloon. For Richard, jazz is Chinese.

Or, it's like abstract expressionism. Richard can look at *Number 5* by Jackson Pollock, a supposed masterpiece revered for its artistry and worth millions, and see only unappealing, splattered bullshit, utterly lacking in structure or talent. Jazz is Pollock. Mozart, on the other hand, is Michelangelo, Rembrandt, Picasso, painters who've mastered the art of seeing. To look up at the ceiling of the Sistine Chapel is to be with God.

Bach, Chopin, Schumann, these composers have mastered the art of listening. Richard hears Debussy's "Clair de lune," and every cell in his body has a broken heart and bare feet dancing in the moonlight. Playing Brahms is communing with God.

♪

Richard doesn't feel jazz in his body. It doesn't move through his heart and soul. He doesn't get it. It's always been impossible for him to understand what he can't feel.

While Karina is away, Grace is home, babysitting her father. They've been under the same roof for three days, two lines rarely intersecting, alone together. She mostly stays in her room. She says she has a ton of homework, but to call or come get her or step on the call button if he needs anything. So far, he hasn't needed her for anything other than his last meal of the day and getting hooked up to the BiPAP mask at bedtime. So he hasn't called for her.

While Grace is here, he's been waiting for Bill to arrive at nine in the mornings to pee, saving both Richard and Grace the indignity of a daughter pulling down her father's pants so he can urinate. Two days ago, he asked her if she wanted to watch a movie with him. Any movie. She had statistics, economics, and physics homework and no time for a movie. Yesterday, he asked her if she wanted to go for quick walk. His right leg is too weak and his right foot is too droopy for him to risk going for a walk alone. She said it was too cold outside. Today, he didn't ask her anything.

It's now 8:40 p.m. He keeps looking over to the door, expecting to see her. She pokes her head in the den every couple of hours to check on him. He hasn't seen her since five. *Do you need anything? . . . No.*

But he does need something from her. He needs things to be right between them before . . . He needs things to be right between them before his circumstances force him into finishing that sentence. For now, not finish-

LISA GENOVA

ing that sentence, not squinting his eyes to bring into focus what's blurry and waiting for him on the horizon, or even ignoring what is hovering two feet in front of his face, is his only line of defense against this disease. Denial, blunt and dull and shaped more like a spoon than a knife, is the only weapon he's got.

He's not sure how to go about making things right with Grace but realizes it probably involves being in the same room. Admitting that he chose piano over her has maybe loosened a few bricks in the wall dividing them, but it's still standing strong and tall, an imposing, ancient fortress. Karina comes home tomorrow, and then Grace goes back to school until the summer. She might not be back home again before . . .

It's 8:43, and he's running out of time.

He thinks about asking Grace to help him with the recording device that Dr. George gave him for banking his voice. He's done little so far. He and Karina recorded a few simple phrases: *I have an itch. I have to use the bathroom. Will you wipe my nose? Will you wipe my eyes? I'm cold. I'm hot.* Karina played these back to make sure the device was actually recording, and after hearing what his voice sounded like, he lost all motivation for the project. He wishes he'd gone to Dr. George sooner, while his voice was still robust and full of melody and inflection and personality, while his voice was still his and not this stripped-down, aerated, soulless, robotic monotone. He'd rather listen to free jazz than the sound of his voice. He might as well use the computer-generated speech when the time comes.

♪

It's 8:51. That time is coming.

But the banking project would give him an easy excuse to need Grace for something. He looks to the door, to the red call button on the floor. He doesn't call for her. He's too tired. He hasn't done a damn thing all day, and he's exhausted.

It feels later than it is. His room is dark but for the glow of his laptop screen and a sliver of light from the hall intruding through the slant of the cracked door. He gets up, stands at the edge of his room, and listens for signs of Grace. He hears nothing. Restless, he leaves the den and wanders the living room, studying the furniture and decor like a curious museum patron after hours. Or a creepy prowler. The living room is dim, gently illuminated by lights Grace must've left on in the kitchen. The cold black night is framed in every window. If Karina were home, she would've drawn the shades.

The living room is neat and tidy, everything in its place. It's too tidy. Sterile. Before he moved out, before Grace left for college, the entire house felt like Grace's home. Her backpack and clothes and books and papers were strewn about. Her music and phone conversations could be heard throughout the house no matter what room she was in. Her personality and presence loomed large here. But Grace doesn't live here anymore. Karina does. Other than revealing that the person who lives here plays piano, observing Karina's home gives little sense of who she is.

But this is her home, her life. Not his. He's not supposed to be living here anymore.

LISA GENOVA

He visits her piano, the same Baldwin upright they bought used when they first moved to Boston. His eyes travel from one end of the keyboard to the other. From watching and listening to Karina and her students play these past few months, he knows the action of the keys is slow compared to that of his grand, and he imagines the frustrating stickiness within the pads of his paralyzed fingers. For years, he tried to convince Karina to upgrade to a grand piano, but she always refused.

The top sheet on the shelf is Beethoven's "Für Elise." One of Karina's students was mutilating this composition in a lesson last week. When Richard was eleven, "Für Elise" was his favorite piece to play. He hesitates, then sits down at the bench. As his eyes travel the notes, he hears the music in his mind's ear, and he is eleven again. He's playing for his mother, and when he finishes, she kisses him on the head and tells him it's the most beautiful song she's ever heard.

He reads the notes to this simple, overplayed, yet lovely piece, and without trying, he feels it in his body—in his beating heart, in his unmoving fingers that still fondly remember, in his tapping foot. This is music.

He aches to touch the keys. While he can feel the imagined music playing in his body, the experience of participating in its creation and hearing it live resonates in his soul. He tries to remember the last time he played, the feelings coursing through his body and soul as he lived the notes of Ravel's Piano Concerto for the Left Hand, and he gets only a faded sense of it. He can't grab on to it. The memory is but a passing ghost. Tears flood

EVERY NOTE PLAYED

229

his eyes, and he leaves Karina's piano before he's reduced to sobbing.

He follows the light into the kitchen. A bowl of lemons is centered on the square table. One of the lemons has gone moldy. He wants to pluck it out and throw it in the trash. He thinks about calling Grace down from her bedroom and asking her to remove the bad lemon but, assuming his diminished voice couldn't reach her anyway, decides not to bother.

He walks over to the pizza box on the counter, the lid tilted slightly open. He peeks inside. Three pieces left. He inhales the smells of peppers and onions and dough and with a tortured sadness remembers the sensory pleasure of eating, like a lover he'll never kiss again, a piano he'll never play again. He imagines the chewiness of the toppings and cheese, the crunchy bite of the crust, the hot temperature of the tangy sauce and salty cheese in his mouth, the rapid responsive action of his grand piano, his hands in Maxine's thick black hair, his mouth on hers.

Almost dizzy with desire, he notices that he doesn't imagine Karina's hair or lips. He tries to remember the last time they kissed, the last time he held her, the last time he got hard thinking about her. He can't find it. His memories of touching her, wanting her, loving her, feel like yellowed, unlabeled snapshots in someone else's scrapbook. Too much time has passed.

It's 9:03.

Stepping away from the pizza box, he approaches Grace's coffee mug from this morning, next to the sink. He bends over, leans his face into the mug, and inhales whatever he can draw out of the sticky, bittersweet hoop of desiccated coffee at the bottom. He exhales. Nirvana. And pure hell. Desperate, he extends his tongue into the mug, hoping to lick the dry ring, but his tongue isn't long enough and the mug is too deep. He gives up.

The phone numbers for Caring Health, his neurologist, and Bill's cell are written on a piece of paper and held by a magnet to the refrigerator. Next to this is a photograph of Grace and Karina at Grace's high school graduation. They're both wearing black, both beaming. Grace has her mother's smile.

There are no other photographs. No other smiling children on what used to be his refrigerator. The son he always wanted. A sister for Grace. All those years trying to get Karina pregnant, believing in her doctor's appointments, jerking off into plastic cups, hoping. None of it was real. Maybe this is why he can't remember loving her.

All that time wasted.

It's 9:06.

With nothing more to explore, he's walking back to the den when he's struck with the sudden, out-of-body, slow-motion realization that he's falling. He went to step right, but his leg never responded. Something in the interplay between neurons and muscles broke off. Something didn't fire or listen or land. Something let go, unplugged, and the command to walk fizzled out, the connection severed. In the split second before he hits the floor, he's aware that he cannot break his fall and thinks to turn his head, but not soon enough. His chin and nose take the brunt of the impact.

Warm blood drains down his right nostril. He can taste its metallic saltiness in his mouth. He registers the pain, throbbing and sharp, mostly at the bridge of his nose, between his eyes. Internally, he scans his limbs, trying to discern if anything is broken. He can't seem to find his right leg. A realization sinks in like liquid concrete funneling into his body, transforming him into immovable stone. Nothing is broken, but he's not getting up. His right leg is gone, consumed by ALS. As he lies facedown on the kitchen floor, he knows he'll never walk again.

He tries to yell for Grace, but he can barely get enough air into his lungs in this position to breathe, never mind produce loud sound. He lifts his head and tries again.

"Graaa."

He lowers his head, resting his right cheek on the cold tile floor. A puddle of drool mingled with blood pools beneath his chin. He's not sure he has the strength to lift his head again. He finds the only part of his body still available to him. His left foot. He lifts and drops it over and over, banging his wool-slippered foot against the floor like a foreboding, muffled drumbeat.

Several minutes pass. Tired, he stops tapping his foot. Panic wants him now. It forms a fist in his stomach, its claw reaching for his throat. He won't be able to breathe if panic takes him. Grace. She comes down every night at ten for his last feeding and to hook him up to the BiPAP machine. What time is it? It won't be long now. He has to fight against the panic and keep breathing.

He's lost in the feeble yet steady rhythm of his inhales

LISA GENOVA

and has no sense of how much time has passed when he hears Grace's footsteps.

"Oh my God!"

He opens his eyes, and Grace appears over him like an angel.

"What happened?"

He doesn't expend his limited energy to state the obvious.

"Okay, I'm calling 911."

"No," he whispers. "Please-don."

"Why? I'll call Bill or someone at Caring Health."

She looks over at the refrigerator, at the phone numbers on the door.

"No. Is-late."

"What if you broke something?"

"I-din."

"Your face is all bloody. I think you broke your nose."

"There-goes-my mo-de-ling ca-reer."

"I have to roll you over then."

His head is turned to the left. She places a hand on his left shoulder and hip and pulls on him carefully but with great effort. He assists as much as he can with his left foot, and she finally manages to turn him onto his back. She grabs a dish towel from the counter, runs it under the tap, crouches over him, and wipes his mouth, cheek, and neck. As she scrubs the cloth too roughly against his skin, working to loosen the blood that has dried and crusted on his face, cold water drips down his neck, soaking his back. She's gentler around his nose.

She stands up and studies him now. He studies her,

too, and can't tell if she's worried, disgusted, or scared. Probably all of the above.

"I'm not strong enough to get you into bed."

"Thas o-kay. I-ca slee-here."

She folds her arms over her chest.

"I'll be right back."

He sees the light flick on in the den, and a few moments later, he hears the wheels of the BiPAP cart rolling toward him. She wiggles three pillows under his head, adjusts his arms to match their position on either side of his body, and drapes his bed comforter over him. She leaves again. This time, he hears her footsteps running up the stairs. She returns with her pillow, a blanket, and her blue-and-white gingham comforter.

"I'll sleep next to you. In case something happens."

She plugs in the humidifier and the BiPAP, turns them on, and checks the settings. He doesn't bother to mention that she's forgotten to feed him. He's not hungry. She holds the mask in her hand, and he's afraid of how much it's going to hurt when pressed against the bridge of his nose.

"I'm sorry I didn't hear you right away."

"Don-be-sor-ry. I'm-the-one who-sor-ry."

"For what?"

He's sorry he didn't give enough of his time to her. He's sorry he's running out of it. He's afraid he doesn't have much left. He's sorry he wasn't a better father to her. He's sorry she didn't feel loved by him.

It's now or never.

"Ev-er-y thin. I-love-you-Grace. I'm-so sor-ry."

She closes her eyes, and a gentle close-lipped smile settles on her mouth. She opens her eyes, and tears stream down her beautiful face. She doesn't wipe them.

"I love you, too, Dad."

She fits the BiPAP mask over his face, and he endures the screaming pain between his eyes as air flows in and out of his lungs. For the first time in as long as he can remember, he feels peace when he breathes.

CHAPTER TWENTY-SIX

Karina, Elise, and her students are early, sitting at a cluster of four round tables, three chairs at each huddled in a half-moon facing the stage. They're at Snug Harbor Jazz Bistro on Frenchmen Street, just outside the French Quarter, tucked away in a windowless, candlelit, cozy room behind the dive bar out front, waiting for the show to start. Tonight features up-and-coming jazz pianist Alexander Lynch, accompanied by drums and a bass, a simple trio. With a background in classical piano and then Broadway, Alexander is new to the jazz scene. Elise saw him in New York at Blue Note in October and can't stop raving about him, says he reminds her of Oscar Peterson.

The room hasn't filled in yet. Karina counts fifteen tables plus a balcony above them. Their seats are right up front, inches from the stage, which feels intimidating, threatening even, as if she were sitting too close to an open flame, as if being here could be dangerous.

She pulls at her lavender silk scarf, spreading it across her front like a bib, covering her cleavage as much as possible. After much angst, she decided to wear her best black dress, spaghetti strapped and tight around the bust, flaring and flowy from the waist to the knees, probably too short and too revealing for her age. She bought it over a decade ago. It fit her better then. She fears she looks like ten pounds of potatoes in a five-pound bag. Elise is in jeans and black suede ankle boots, a black velvet blazer over a graphic T-shirt, laughing and chatting with her students, totally at ease, as if she were a regular, as if this were her seat and the club was expecting her. She fits into everything.

The students are also in black and jeans, edgy and casual and cool. They belong here, too. They're all in their early twenties, about where Karina left off before giving up, still believing it's all possible.

Karina slides the bottom olive off the plastic skewer in her martini and chews on it while Elise leans over to the table to their right. As Elise's back is now to her, Karina can't hear the conversation and feels excluded, out of place, conspicuous. She doesn't deserve to be on this field trip. She's not a teacher at Berklee. She's not a student. She's not even a real musician.

She's Elise's sad, pathetic neighbor. She's an old, suburban piano teacher, a has-been, a never-was. Once upon a time, an almost-was.

She wants to be home, in her flannel pajamas, reading a book in her living room. But as soon as she imagines being on her couch, she hears Richard calling her from the den. She drags a long sip from her martini and pulls another olive into her mouth with her teeth. It's an enormous relief to be away from him, to have a break from the distressing sound of his struggling to clear a cough, from having to tend to him all day and night. She blinked her eyes open this morning in her hotel bed and felt almost giddy, realizing that she had just slept through the night undisturbed.

And then Guilt came marching in, stomping with its monster feet and pounding its drum, scaring any nascent feelings of relief and lightness back into their holes. She shouldn't have stuck Grace with him for four days. Grace shouldn't have to clean up her father's piss and be up all hours of the night while Karina is well rested and wearing a poorly fitting black dress, drinking a dirty martini, and listening to jazz with a bunch of kids. What if something goes wrong?

"I can't wait for you to hear this guy," says Elise, leaning back over to Karina. "Abby just called him the Mozart of jazz."

Karina nods. It's been so long since she's been to any kind of live musical performance, years since she's been to Symphony Hall, the Hatch Shell, Jordan Hall. The last time might've been to see Richard at Tanglewood. He played *The Marriage of Figaro* overture. Eight years ago? Can it really be that long?

She wouldn't feel so uneasy if they were at a concert

hall, if she were tucked somewhere safe and civilized in the orchestra or mezzanine section, waiting to hear a recital or concerto. Classical music has always been her home base, her comfort food, her security blanket. At Curtis, she started as a classical pianist, and by third year, her career looked more promising than Richard's. They never acknowledged this aloud, but they both knew it. Her teachers praised her and gave her opportunities normally reserved for seniors or graduates. They did not offer these opportunities to Richard.

He congratulated her whenever this happened, but his words were rigid and cold, spoken through his teeth, and would leave her feeling insulted instead of championed. Whenever she privately or publically surpassed his playing, he'd grow distant and critical of her in other ways. He didn't like her hair. He ridiculed her grammar. He withheld affection, refused sex, and pouted. She craved nothing more than to be loved by him when he felt self-confident and admired in the spotlight. Ironically, the biggest obstacle to his center-stage bravado seemed to be her.

When they were students, their technical skills were similarly matched, but her playing was emotionally connected and far more mature. While Richard could master the technical complexity of any piece, listening to him play often made her picture the notes on the page, the chords, the key, intellectually appreciating his athleticism, hearing the music as dissected elements rather than a whole. Not until after graduation, when they lived in New York, did something click in him, and he

♪

began to play the emotion of a piece and not simply the notes.

She remembers Professor Cohen and the Test. Each student was asked to play a piece but not until Professor Cohen left the classroom. The Test was simple. Could the student make the teacher cry in the hallway?

The first time Karina took the Test, she played Schumann's *Fantasiestücke*, op. 12, no. 1. She played the closing gesture, tender and quiet, and waited, breath held, for Professor Cohen to return. The door opened, and Professor Cohen was smiling with clasped hands and wet eyes. She made him cry several times that semester. Richard never did.

She discovered jazz first semester of her senior year. She breezed into the campus coffeehouse for a quick espresso, on her way to something else, and stayed for two hours, mesmerized by three of her classmates, a trio of piano, drums, and trumpet playing Miles Davis. This music was so different from the sacred, rigid exactness of Mozart or Chopin. It had an exhilarating freedom, a playful exploration outside the structure of the melody. She watched the three improvise, detour, collaborate, creating something original, discovering the music as they played it, following a free association, a harmony, an embellishment, wherever it led them. They generated a momentum, a magical chemistry, a river that flowed through everyone there. Her heart was captivated, dizzy, spellbound.

She doesn't think her relationship with Richard would've lasted beyond graduation if she hadn't discovered jazz. In abandoning classical piano for jazz, she ensured that they would never compete, that the classical spotlight would be his to shine in. But switching from classical piano to jazz wasn't an easy transition. Jazz is complex and in many ways technically more difficult than classical piano. And her decision was at best frowned upon, more often snubbed and mocked. Although neither genres are mainstream music, the world of classical piano is privileged and white, played in grand symphony halls to audiences who sip champagne. The jazz world is historically poor and black, played in hole-in-the-wall nightclubs for patrons drunk on bourbon.

Alexander, the drummer, and the bassist take the stage, and the audience applauds while the musicians ready themselves at their instruments. Alexander is slender, about Karina's age, with a mop of glossy black hair and fingers that extend for miles, poised on the keys like a sprinter in the blocks, ready to explode into action, holding for the gun to fire. Alexander nods, and the three begin.

The melody is a simple repetition, a catchy, easy-breezy tune, but soon breaks into improvised solos. As Alexander plays, Karina closes her eyes, and the notes become a summer-evening stroll down a country road drenched in moonlight, more of a mood than a melody, sultry and slow, in no hurry at all. Softened by vodka, she rides the notes, allowing herself to be carried, and her blood is flowing hotter. She's turned on.

Karina remembers living on East Sixth Street in New York City, hanging around the Village Vanguard, listening to Branford Marsalis, Herbie Hancock, Sonny Rollins, and

Brad Mehldau, learning through listening, watching, asking, performing, and improvising. Learning jazz was a three-dimensional experience of unique expressive discovery, lived and breathed on the fly in spontaneous jam sessions. Learning classical piano had been an academic exercise in practiced techniques, adherence to strict rules, memorizing the notes on the page, practicing alone. She never felt more challenged, more alive, than when she was playing jazz.

The next two pieces are high energy, a call to action and a celebration. Alexander's fingers are a fiddler crab running from a seagull's pursuing shadow; a hummingbird drinking nectar from the keys, trilling arpeggios inhabited by God.

He's traveling low to high on the keyboard, coloring outside the lines, hitting notes that land just shy of displeasing. This is renegade music, exciting, provocative.

"Holy shit, right?" says Elise.

Karina nods. She closes her eyes again during the fourth piece, entranced by Alexander's riffs, the way his chord extensions wander from the head. He's playing outside now, and the song becomes about the journey, not the destination, about getting lost along the way and what he might discover, an embellished grace note, an ascending harmonic progression, a meandering Sunday drive. He varies the phrasing, changing the shape and texture, inserting blue notes and trills that sound like children laughing. He dances across the keys, courting the notes, loving them, and the music is a gentle morning rain playing on a windowpane, delicate, lonely, longing for a lover, a childhood friend, a mother.

The song ends, and the audience applauds. Karina opens her eyes and tears spill down her face. She is enraptured, changed, remembering who she is.

She is a jazz pianist.

With stunning clarity, she suddenly sees the role she's been playing, the costume and mask she chose and has been wearing for twenty years. She's been hiding, an impostor, unable to give herself permission to do this, to play jazz, to be who she is, shackled inside a prison of blame and excuses.

At first it was all Richard's fault for moving them to Boston. Jazz pianists live in New York, not Boston. Then Richard started traveling. He was hardly ever home. They rarely had sex anymore. She needed to refill her birth control pill prescription, but it was February and so cold outside, and she didn't feel like walking to the pharmacy.

She was lazy. She was stupid. She was pregnant.

Her excuse then chasséd over to Grace and motherhood. Now she couldn't be a jazz pianist because her baby needed her. Richard still spent much of the year touring. She was essentially a single mother. She was consumed and devastatingly lonely in the demands of young motherhood. There was often no room for a shower, never mind for getting back to playing jazz. So she tended to Grace full-time, creating a safe nest where Karina could hide. She promised herself it would be a temporary shelter.

Karina remembers her mother, born in an oppressed country, stuck in an economically depressed town by her husband's meager coal-mining wages, trapped in a bad marriage by her religion, confined within the dirty beige walls of her small home, raising five children. Every day, she wore a dingy white apron, her prematurely gray hair pulled into a bun, resignation in her eyes, and her arthritic hands to the bone cooking and cleaning and tending to the needs of her children, whose singular dreams were to leave that house, that town, that country, as soon as they could. They all left her.

Karina swore she wouldn't repeat her mother's life. As much as Karina loved being Grace's mother, she would not bear child after child, adding brick after brick to the wall of her maternal prison. Grace would be her only child. One and done. But Richard wanted many children, a big family.

Her carefully buried deception peeks out from its hiding space for the briefest moment, long enough for shame to seep through the walls of her stomach, sickening her. She drains her martini, distracting her tortured, guilty mind with the cozy warmth of booze.

When Grace turned five and went to kindergarten, Karina would have the time to pursue jazz. That was the plan. But then Grace went to school, and Karina's excuse migrated back to Richard. She discovered charges for an expensive dinner and drinks for two on his credit-card bill; salacious text messages from some woman named Rosa on his phone; a pair of black lace panties in his suitcase, not a gift for her. At first, these betrayals shattered Karina's heart. She felt stunned, gutted, humiliated, dishonored. She wept and raged and threatened divorce. And then, after a few days of wild emotion, she would feel wrung out, calm and strangely satisfied. Over time, her heart hardened to it all. She almost craved the detective work, the thrill of finding the next damning text message, the momentary drama it awakened in her and ultimately, the narrative it supplied.

Grace was in first grade, eighth grade, a sophomore in high school, and Karina painted herself the victim, trapped in a bad marriage by the rules of a church she no longer believed in but still obeyed and the barbed-wire reasons of her own making. She carefully constructed her life, creating a predictable stability in her safe career as a teacher, teaching students to play classical piano in the private confines of her suburban living room, where her students have always been too young, unformed, and musically naïve to question her, stretch her, or push her outside her comfort zone.

And she could blame Richard and his affairs for holding her back. He was wrong and bad, and she was right and good, and she could resent him for her unfulfilled dreams of playing jazz, and this was the perfect excuse, the brilliant smoke screen deflecting anyone who might inspect the situation for the truth. The truth is, she was terrified of failing, of not making it, of never being as recognized and loved as an artist as Richard is.

But then she got divorced and Grace went to college, her excuses literally out the door. With seemingly no one left to blame, she pointed her finger at the hands of time. Too much had passed. Her chance had passed. It was too late.

She watches Alexander on the stage, new to the jazz scene, about her age, and that last pin falls. She can now see that every collapsed excuse she abided to like God's commandments existed only in her mind. Her unfulfilled life has always been a prison of her own making, the thoughts she chose and believed, the fear and blame, paralyzing her in her unhappiness, telling her that her dreams were too big, too impractical, too unlikely, too hard to achieve, that she didn't deserve them, that she shouldn't want them, that she didn't need them. These dreams of playing jazz piano were for someone else, someone like Alexander Lynch. Not for her.

As she listens to Alexander play, she steps out of the carefully constructed, now-unlocked cage in her mind. She hears him messing with the melody, accenting the ascending chords and varying the phrasing, and she feels the exuberant curiosity in his improvisation, searching for something new, unafraid, and his freedom becomes hers. She sees what's possible for her if she dares to claim it.

The trio finish their final piece of the night, stand, and bow. The audience is on its feet, applauding, begging for more as the musicians humbly exit the stage. Karina wipes the tears from her eyes in between claps, feeling breathless, cracked open, pulsing with desire, and, although she's not quite sure how, ready to live.

CHAPTER TWENTY-SEVEN

Richard wakes from having dozed off, parked upright in his wheelchair in front of the TV, wishing he could be reclined. Although the TV has been on since this morning when Bill set him up here, he stopped watching it at least a couple of hours ago. His heavy head has tipped down, chin to chest, and rolled right, and he doesn't have the neck-muscle strength to correct it. His towel bib has fallen off his chest, and the front of his shirt is soaked with drool. His eyeballs are still tired from straining to look up and left to see the TV. So he stares at the floor, where his eyes and head are pointed, and listens to *Judge Judy*, surrendering to what is.

He's in the Maserati of power wheelchairs. Front-wheel drive with two motors, it's tricked out with mag wheels, eight-inch casters, a tilt-in-space reclining feature, and a hand-operated joystick that comes standard with this model. But because he has no hands, he has no way to control it. He ordered it so long ago, when he still had the use of his left hand, when he could still play the piano, when he could still hope that he'd never actually need the chair. He's in the driver's seat of a sexy sports car, unable to place his hands on the steering wheel or step his foot on the gas, forever parked in the garage.

There are tech devices that would allow him to control the wheelchair with his chin or tongue or even his breath, but Karina and Richard haven't ordered anything. The activation energy is a mountain precipice—too many insurance forms, the astronomical cost despite any coverage, the wait to receive the device. It's probably hard for anyone associated with Richard to invest time or money in his ability to move his chin or tongue. How much longer will he be able to breathe? Ordering a wheelchair-operating device powered by breath begs an answer to that question, and Richard would rather not ask it. So he's trapped wherever someone parks him, mostly here in front of the TV or in the living room. He can't leave the house until the ramp is completed because his chair doesn't fit through the door to the garage.

For some absurd reason, the loss of his legs took him and Karina by surprise. It shouldn't have. Bill and the other home health aides from Caring Health, his physical therapist, Kathy DeVillo, and his neurologist all told them, warned them, practically begged them to build the ramp sooner rather than later. Don't wait. They both blew it off. Richard truly believed he might never need the damn chair. He'd been wearing the ankle foot orthotic on his right foot quite comfortably for so long, and his left leg seemed to be in good shape. He formulated his own highly unscientific, clinically unproven theory that the disease had arrested, rendered permanently dormant in his legs, and threw his faith into this theory like a religious zealot. He would never lose his legs. Amen and hallelujah.

Shortly after ALS severed his right leg from his control, his left leg threw up its white flag. Paralysis settled in rapidly, as if someone had pulled the stopper at his ankle and all the sand came pouring out. Sitting in his wheelchair, staring at the floor and unable to leave the house, it's clear now. No part of him is safe from this disease.

He hoped they wouldn't have to spend any money on an unwanted construction project, an ugly, utilitarian ramp extending from the front door to the driveway, announcing his handicap to the world. Thankfully, his condo finally sold last week, so he can afford the ramp. He'd much rather leave that money to Grace.

So here he sits, Mr. Potato Head without arms or legs, a bobblehead on a breathing torso. His neck is too weak to hold his head up reliably, especially later in the day—making use of the Head Mouse, even when he's wearing a neck collar, an exercise in frustrating madness, so he's disconnected from his computer until they get the Tobii eye-tracking-technology device. It's been ordered. He's down to 120 pounds from 170, physically

♪

disappearing, and yet he's taking up more and more space—this wheelchair, the hospital bed, the BiPAP machine, the shower chair, the Hoyer lift that should arrive any day now.

Transferring him from the bed into the chair in the morning and from the chair into bed in the evening is a massive chore that requires great strength and trained technique. Despite how slight and fragile his mass is, he's deadweight, like a sleeping child. Karina can't do it. Bill has been coming for two shifts since Richard lost his legs, morning and evening, using all his muscle and height and a gait belt to lift Richard's body safely from point A to point B. The Hoyer lift, which looks like a cross between an exercise machine and a hammock swing, will make it possible for anyone to safely move him in and out of bed.

He hears the doorbell ring. Just weeks ago, this might've been the sound of him stepping on the call button taped to the floor by his bed, but now, it can only be the actual doorbell at the front door. He hears men's voices and the sound of something being rolled into the living room. It must be the lift.

A few minutes later, Bill's legs and feet appear before Richard.

"Hey, Ricardo, let's get you out here. Karina has something for you." Bill says this with unbridled exuberance, like a parent about to present a small child with a special gift. *Oh, goody! A Hoyer lift! Just want I've always wanted!*

Bill rights Richard's head back into position against

the headrest, and an enormous relief washes through Richard like warm water. Bill wheels him out into the living room. Richard stares at a grand piano in front of the bay windows facing the street where the couch should be. Karina is beaming.

"Wha?"

"I saved it," says Karina.

"Is-tha-mi?"

"I couldn't let someone else own your piano."

He can't believe she did this. It's incredibly thoughtful and sweet and well-intentioned, but seeing his piano again, after he'd already said good-bye and made peace with never seeing or touching or hearing it again, turns him inside out, as if he's just unexpectedly bumped into an ex-lover in the living room, still not over her. He's all emotion and no words, choked up.

Karina and Bill stare at him, expectant, hoping for joy. He wants to give it to them, searching for a way. He looks at his piano, his beloved, from across the room. He can't bear for them both to be paralyzed, still, silenced.

"Wi-you play-fo-me?"

"It'll need to be tuned."

"Tha-so-kay."

Karina hesitates. She's never played his piano. His piano was his. He smiles and sends her a long blink, his version of permission and please. She acquiesces, sits at the bench, hands poised over the keys, and pauses.

She twists around to face him. "What do you want me to play?"

He thinks, his favorites all raising their hands emphat-

♪

ically like eager students who know the answer. Mozart, Beethoven, Chopin, Debussy, Liszt. Pick me! Pick me! Too many choices crowd his head. Karina, sitting at his piano, waits for an answer. She's waiting to play. She's been waiting for twenty years.

"Play-me soh-jazz."

This time, Karina smiles and slow blinks, her version of a nod, a thank-you, and the energy in her gesture is passed between them, a moment of invisible yet palpable connection. She breaks the spell, thinking now, deciding what to play, her eyes scanning upward, as if reading her own mind.

She grins. "I'll do 'Somewhere over the Rainbow.' Bill, you want to sing?"

"Do happy little bluebirds fly? Hell yeah, I'm singing."

Bill scooches next to Karina on Richard's bench. Karina begins to play, setting the mood in a prelude before the lyrics begin. Richard expected her rendition to be loungy, predictably ragtime, upbeat and swingy, but she slows it all down instead, dwelling on the notes, adding interesting chords and embellishments, and he's genuinely surprised. Impressed. Enjoying it. She's into the melody now, and Bill is singing. Their rendition is restrained and romantic. It evokes a gentle sadness, a fond memory of a lost love. It's a dreamy lullaby, easily the most beautiful song Bill has ever sung.

Richard listens to Karina play and Bill sing, and instead of feeling grief stricken or jealous that he'll never play his piano again, he feels strangely happy. He's setting his piano free, letting it go, sending it off on its next journey without him. Then, as Karina plays the final phrasings and his heart moves with the notes, it occurs to him that it's not his piano he's letting go of, setting free.

It's Karina.

CHAPTER TWENTY-EIGHT

The Hoyer lift still hasn't been delivered, and until it gets here, Bill is the lift. He's singing Madonna's "Like a Prayer" while securing a gait belt around Richard's legs, just above the ankle. It's evening, and Bill has already brushed Richard's teeth and washed his face. Even though Richard won't go to sleep for another five hours, it's time to get him from the wheelchair to the bed. Richard is Bill's last patient of his shift, and Bill is Richard's last hired help of the day, and Karina can't get him out of the chair. So to bed he goes.

Bill weaves a second gait belt around Richard's torso and secures it snug around him while Karina looks on. Bill grabs the suction wand from the rolling cart next to him, flicks the machine on, and vacuums out the saliva pooled in Richard's mouth. Bill has learned through experience to do this prior to moving Richard, otherwise the puddle of saliva waiting in Richard's mouth tips forward when he's vertical, spilling out and onto Bill. His job is not for the squeamish. He then fits a soft cervical collar around Richard's reclined neck so his head won't flop forward. He arranges Richard's socked, belted feet parallel on the pivot disc, a human-size lazy Susan placed at the base of his chair, adjacent to his destination, the bed. It takes a grown man and all this time and equipment to move him a few inches. Bill squats in front of Richard like an Olympic skier.

"One, two, three."

Bill pulls on the gait belt around Richard's chest with his right hand while lifting him under the shoulder with his left, and in a forceful snap, Richard is standing on his paralyzed legs.

The extensor muscles in his legs are spastic and rigid, making it possible for him to bear his own weight. While completely unresponsive to any voluntary command, like a child's plastic action-hero figure, he can be stood up if balanced properly. Bill lifts and rests Richard's arms atop each of Bill's shoulders to keep them from hanging down and pulling painfully on Richard's shoulder sockets. Bill's biceps are positioned under Richard's armpits, his hands clasped around Richard's back. Richard stands slightly taller, but they're pretty much eye to eye.

"My friend David would be so jealy if he knew I got to slow dance with you like this every night. He has such a crush on you."

Richard raises his eyebrows, requesting more information.

"He saw you play at BSO three years ago. I almost went with him. Isn't that funny? I almost knew you before I knew you."

The belt around the bottom of Richard's legs keeps his ankles from rolling out. Without it, he'd be standing on top of his anklebones instead of the bottom of his feet. Bill keeps him balanced on his feet for at a least a minute before moving him along, somehow intuiting how delicious this feels, to be stretched out and vertical, his bones stacked and bearing weight, like finally standing after a transatlantic flight in a cramped plane seat. Richard's been sitting in this chair, in the same position, for eight hours. Richard sighs, enjoying the sweet relief of being an erect structure, visiting the memory of being an upright man.

Their slow dance ends when Bill spins Richard ninety degrees on the pivot disc, so that his butt is now up against the bed. Using the gait belt around Richard's middle, Bill lowers him carefully onto the mattress. As always, Bill sticks the landing.

"I still think I could do that," says Karina.

"I've been doing this a long time, honey. I make it look a lot easier than it is. Believe me. You don't want to drop him. You could both get hurt. Wait for the Hoyer. It should be here any day."

Bill tugs on each side of the slide sheet, squaring Richard's body in the center of the bed, and arranges Richard's arms and legs like flowers in a vase. Reaching over to the bedside table, Bill grabs what looks like a one-liter clear-plastic water bottle. He reaches under Richard's boxer shorts, pulls out his penis, inserts it into the bottle, and waits a few seconds. As usual, nothing happens. The waiting was just a courtesy. Bill then pushes down on Richard's abdomen with the heel of his hand, pressing firmly on his bladder over and over, as if he were pumping water from a well. It works, and the bottle slowly fills with urine.

Karina looks away, trying to offer a sense of privacy, a strange and futile gesture. Richard's body parts are in varying states of nudity and being handled all day long. He is showered, toileted, wiped, washed, dressed, and undressed. His body is simply another task to complete, a job to do. His naked body is treated neutrally by every home health aide, every visiting nurse and physical therapist, a thin layer of a latex glove between his skin and actual contact with another human being. His is just another penis, just another saggy ass, just another patient's decrepit body. So Karina doesn't need to look away. He's just another ex-husband with ALS.

When his bladder is emptied, Bill tucks Richard's penis back into his boxers and leaves the den to wash the bottle in the bathroom. Now Karina takes over. She lifts Richard's T-shirt, attaches a syringe of water to his MIC-KEY button, and flushes the line. Normally refreshing, the water feels alarmingly cold in his belly. She then switches to a pouch of Liquid Gold.

"Okay you two." Bill is now wearing his hat and coat. "I'm off like a slutty prom dress." He gives Karina a one-armed hug and a kiss on the cheek. "Be good," he says to Richard. "See you tomorrow."

"Thank you, Bill," says Karina.

Richard slow-blinks. It's the end of the day. He's too tired to form words.

Karina presses slowly and steadily on the syringe plunger, delivering Richard's liquid dinner into this stomach. The entire meal takes about a half hour, and they usually have the TV on to keep them company, occupied, and safely distracted, but today, the TV is off. Bill's singing must've snagged a circuit in Karina's brain. She's humming "Like a Prayer" while she stares vaguely at the wall, a slight smile on her lips. He wonders what she's thinking about.

She's had a lightness about her since she returned from New Orleans. He hears her singing pop songs while cooking in the kitchen and noodling jazz riffs on her piano in the mornings. He's been catching her face enjoying distant daydreams. Her energy has changed. Her presence feels less heavy, less oppressive, happier, hopeful even, and while he can't put his paralyzed finger on the reason for it, this unexplained shift in her has provoked a corresponding shift in him. He watches her face, and he recognizes her again, the woman he fell in love with so long ago. She's feeding him, taking care of him, and what he'd been selfishly viewing as an act of martyrdom or duty, he suddenly sees as an act of love.

His heart swells, overwhelmed, and as she hums Madonna, he remembers the first time he heard Karina's voice, her Polish accent, how desperate he felt to hear her speak to him, his delight when she finally did. He stares at

LISA GENOVA

her green eyes, her amused mouth, and hopes she catches him looking at her.

Just like all those years ago, he aches for her to speak to him. He's never told her that he's sorry for cheating on her, for hurting her, for stealing that smile from her lips for so long. But he is sorry and hopes that she somehow knows this, that she can sense the regret and apology in him the way he can sense this new joy in her. He wants to hear her voice tell him that she's okay. He wants to be forgiven. He wants.

The syringe is emptied. Karina refills it with a second helping. As she's reattaching it, her warm, gloveless hands touch his bare, concave stomach, and although from her perspective, her hands are in the business of feeding her ex-husband through a PEG tube, for Richard, the touch feels intimate, personal, human.

At first, embarrassed, he hopes she doesn't notice that he's hard beneath the bedsheet and his boxers, but then he hopes she does. Every day he wakes to morning wood and can do nothing but wait it out. He hasn't masturbated since his left hand left him in October. He purposefully no longer imagines anything sexually desirable during this daily rise and fall. But now, as he's unexpectedly turned on, he imagines Karina touching it, touching him, and his desire is excruciatingly urgent, building in his penis, his heart, and his mind, silently begging for her to notice. He wants her to lie down next to him, to kiss him while stroking him. He wants to be a man and not a failing body in a bed. He wants to be touched, to be loved, to come. It's been so long. He wants.

She finishes the syringe, flushes the tubing with water, and caps the MIC-KEY button. She lowers his shirt, pulls the covers up to his chest, and stands.

"Okay, you're good until ten. You want the TV on?"

He stares at her, unblinking.

"You want anything?"

He smiles. If only he had the strength to tell her.

She hesitates, eyeing him quizzically. "Okay, I'll check on you in a bit."

She leaves the door to the den cracked open. He sits in bed and stares at the open door, listening to the sounds of her making her own dinner in the kitchen, wanting.

CHAPTER TWENTY-NINE

Richard sits in his wheelchair in the living room where Karina left him about a half hour ago, where he'll stay until Karina or the next home health aide moves him. She parked him in a rectangular patch of sunlight, angled toward the windows, as if a warm and sunny view of Walnut Street is supposed to make him feel more optimistic, less trapped. He knows she's well-intentioned. He watches the blithe movement of squirrels and birds. Everything alive moves.

He hears Karina sneeze three times. She's been fighting a cold for the past week, staying away from him as much as possible so as not to infect him. She's in the kitchen, cooking breakfast. Triggered by the torturously delicious smells of coffee and bacon, saliva pools in his mouth. He gurgles on it and swallows over and over, trying to push the gluey liquid down, struggling not to choke. A string of sticky drool descends over his bottom lip and lands on the cotton towel draped over his chest like a bib for this very reason. He turns his head left and right, but the spiderweb of drool won't break. He gives up.

He shifts his focus away from the sun and animated existence and instead looks upon his Steinway. Eighty-eight glossy black and white keys. God, what he wouldn't give to touch them.

Ten feet in front of him.

A million miles.

He stares at it with agonizing desire and apology, as if he's broken a sacred promise, a marriage vow. He imagines the action of each key, the blending colors of sound, music coming into existence, birthed through his body. He imagines a series of ascending arpeggios, and they become the sound of Karina's laugh.

His piano. The relationship is over. He's still working on letting it go. *It's not you, it's me.* Taking the blame doesn't change a thing. They are divorced, rejected and abandoned, reduced to pitiful statues collecting dust in the living room.

Careful not to tip his head even slightly downward else it flops forward, chin to chest, unable to right itself, he stares at his legs, his feet angled toward each other, pigeon-toed, and he suddenly resents Bill for arranging his feet in this unmanly way, a body position that speaks uncertainty, meekness, submission. Then he laughs at himself, as if anything about an emaciated man dying of ALS in a wheelchair could possibly communicate machismo, as if anyone but his piano were in the room to judge him. Bill dressed Richard's feet this morning in thin wool socks and black loafers. Shoes on a man whose feet will never again walk this earth. The irony and tragedy of wearing shoes make him want to cry. He can't stand to look at his feet. Literally.

Instead, he studies the rubber flesh of his flat right hand, limp and lifeless; his curled, distorted left hand, no longer possessed by him; both placed on pillows over the arms of his wheelchair in exactly this position by Bill over an hour ago. Richard's entire body is a costume discarded, the party over. He returns to what used to be his elegant left hand and commands the fingers to straighten, knowing they won't. He changes tack. *Please*. His limbs are petulant children, unreachable through begging, bribery, ultimatums, or sweet talk.

He tries to imagine the war beneath his skin; the invaded countries of his neurons and muscles overwhelmed, decimated; the neutral territories of bone, ligament, and tendon rendered useless by the horrific destruction surrounding them. His entire body is detaching, unzipping from his soul.

He turns his head ninety degrees left, then right, testing himself, relieved that he can still do this. Once his neck and voice are paralyzed, he'll be reduced to eye-gaze technology and a computer-generated voice for communicating. He opens his eyes wide and pinches them shut tight. Good. When he can no longer blink, he'll be locked in. He doesn't want to die, but he hopes he dies before that happens. Maybe that won't happen.

He can feel his tongue wriggling inside his mouth, undulating as if a family of earthworms were dancing within it, celebrating a rainstorm. When he speaks, his tongue feels thick, the volume thinned and barely audible. His words, once a finely detailed painting, are painfully slow to produce and almost impossible to comprehend, strangled and lacking consonants. A Pollock piece. Free jazz.

Already compromised to what Dr. Goldstein says is now 39 percent forced vital capacity, every single inhale is a struggle. Every exhale is incomplete. He's forced to sip air a teaspoon at a time when he's desperate to gulp it down by the gallon, each taste an agonizing disappointment, evidence of the withering muscles surrounding his ribs, his abdomen, his diaphragm. Pulling in enough air to simply sit motionless in the wheelchair is conscious, draining work.

He's probably close to needing the BiPAP 24-7 but won't admit this aloud or even request it for purposes of a temporary rest during the day. He won't let anyone advance his wheelchair one inch onto the handicapped ramp of that slippery slope. Even now, every single night, he still can't believe this is his reality. He's traded bed partners, beautiful women for a BiPAP. It's the worst monogamous relationship of his life. And they can never break up. Without the BiPAP at night, he might retain too much carbon dioxide in his sleep and suffer brain damage or suffocate and die.

He doesn't want to die.

He opens his mouth wide and closes it several times, regrettably sensing a new and unmistakable slackness in

LISA GENOVA

his jaw. And so it begins. Once the weakness ensues, there is no abortion, no retreating, only a relentless, insidious icy downward luge into paralysis. Soon, his jaw will hang open, ribbons of saliva will continually stream over his bottom lip, and he won't be able to talk. He frowns as he imagines this likely development, the impossible-to-mask spectrum from pity to disgust in Karina's and Bill's and every stranger's eyes when they look at him. He doesn't even want to face his piano like that.

When will this next irreversible insult be inflicted? To-morrow? Next week? End of the month? This summer? The answer is yes.

He studies his hands that will never again look familiar to him, fingers that used to carry exquisite strength and agility, that a year and a half ago played eighty-seven pages of Brahms I without error. He misses playing Brahms, feeding himself lunch, scratching his nose, touching a woman, making Karina laugh. He apologizes to his be-loved piano for abandoning it, to Karina for abandoning her, and he suddenly feels the cumulative weight of every single loss all at once like a concrete slab dropped onto his chest.

And he can't breath. Without the slab on his chest, every inhale was already an intended dive into open ocean, stopped dead in ankle-deep water. Now, suddenly, the tide has gone out. He's gasping, drowning on dry land. He can feel the adrenaline kick, the fight-or-flight animal instinct. This is life threatening. *More air now.* Yet, he can't run, and he can't fight, and he can't get more air now. He tries to use his next exhale to call for help, but he succeeds only in

E V E R Y   N O T E   P L A Y E D

♪

265

spitting. Karina's in the kitchen drinking coffee, and he's dying in the living room without notice.

Inhale. Exhale.

His body is seized, the tendons and muscles of his neck squeezing, shaking violently with effort. Each breath feels like drawing air through a thin, clogged straw. It feels like suffocating. Fear rises in his throat where oxygen should flow. He swallows, choking on it.

Breathe in. Breathe out.

Shallow sips. He's so hungry for air. His cells are literally starving for oxygen. Keep breathing.

He calls up what it took to master Rachmaninoff's Piano Concerto no. 3. Ten grueling hours every day, relentlessly focused, playing each movement over and over, fighting through excruciating physical pain and mental exhaustion until he could play the entire piece by memory and without error. Now his tenacity, his will, his purpose, is trained on breathing.

In. Out.

This is now his song to play. He is not this paralyzed body, these screaming lungs, this primal fear. He will be an instrument of breathing.

Breathe.

Again. Pull the air in. Push it out. Again. It's not enough. He's fatigued, strangled, starving for air, failing.

A few short and long months ago, playing piano was like breathing to him. Now breathing is breathing to him. His work. His purpose. His passion. His existence. He has to keep breathing.

He doesn't want to die.

CHAPTER THIRTY

Karina panicked and called 911. Richard was intubated in the ambulance by a woman with intensely focused blue eyes and a raised coffee-bean-brown mole above her right brow. He never lost consciousness and kept his eyes on hers while she worked on him. Insertion of the endotracheal tube was violently swift and invasive, and the gagging, discomforting pressure of the first few moments was quickly eclipsed by the massive relief of air moving in and out through his windpipe. Once in the ER at Mass General Hospital, someone drew blood, and he had a chest X-ray, which revealed pneumonia. A nurse ran an intravenous line of antibiotics, and he's now in the ICU with Karina, waiting for Kathy DeVillo.

Karina is standing next to him, over him, her arms crossed as if hugging herself, watching him intently, studying him, which worries him because he's not doing anything. He wonders what she's seeing. She looks scared.

The antibiotic fluid running through his veins is ice-cold. Despite staring at him like a specimen under a microscope, Karina doesn't seem to notice that his skin is covered in goose bumps. He wishes she'd lay a heavy blanket over him. His face itches where the tube is taped across his mouth, and he wants to ask Karina to scratch it for him. He tries to talk, but his effort is smothered, blotted out when it hits the impenetrable wall of hard plastic running the length of his throat. He cannot speak. He stares wide-eyed at Karina, sharing her fear.

With the BiPAP, he was still in charge of breathing. He initiated the inhales, and the machine assisted him, ensuring that the draws were deep, the exhales complete. As he watches his chest rise and fall, he realizes he's no longer involved. The ventilator is doing 100 percent of the work. He is being breathed. His fear dials up. His heart pounds as if running for its life. Yet his breathing is steady, untethered from his terrified heart and the blood accelerating through his cold veins.

Kathy DeVillo enters the room, wearing black yoga pants, a frumpy oversize gray sweater, a soft pink scarf, no jewelry, and no makeup. It's Sunday. He imagines her at home on her couch, watching a movie on Netflix when she was paged. He wishes he could apologize for bothering her like this. She stands on the other side of the bed, opposite Karina, and takes a noticeable moment before speaking. Her mouth is somber. Her eyes look into Richard's like peaceful warriors.

"Hi, Richard. Hi, Karina. So." Kathy sighs. "Here we are. I'm going to do a lot of talking. You ready?"

No one answers.

"Yes," says Karina.

Kathy gives Karina a close-lipped smile and then looks straight down into Richard's eyes, waiting a moment. He's afraid of what she's about to say. Although he's never heard the speech she's about to deliver, he knows what's coming. This train has been barreling toward him on a one-way track for fifteen months. And he's still not ready for it.

"So you know you've been emergently intubated, and you're in the ICU. My purpose today is to give you all the information I know. I'm your GPS, but you're still the driver of the bus, okay? I'm here to tell you, if you go right, this will happen. If you go left, that will happen. You make the decision, but here are the consequences, okay? Blink once for yes. Keep your eyes open for no."

Richard blinks.

"If you hadn't been intubated and put on a ventilator, you would've died. Falls, significant weight loss, and pneumonia, these are the three red flags of ALS. They signify the disease escalating and failure to thrive. When these happen, it tips you over the cliff. About a month ago, your FVC was around thirty-nine percent. The pneumonia tipped you over. You weren't getting sufficient oxygen, and you don't have enough reserve. The choices now are to have the tracheostomy surgery and stay on a vent or to be extubated and terminally weaned."

She pauses. No one says anything. *Terminally weaned.* Does that mean what he thinks it means? He can't ask.

♪

269

"So let's look at the first choice. The surgery. The general surgeon will say, 'Trach surgery is no big deal,' and he's right. It's a straightforward procedure. That's his tribe's language, but it's not the language of ALS. In terms of your psychological well-being, this choice will change your life. It's a very big deal. If you get the surgery, you will need *a lot* of infrastructure to care for you."

She points her gaze at Karina, and Kathy's expression is high-definition clear. Karina would be the infrastructure.

"In theory, you can get trached and vented and live a normal life span. But you're going to need twenty-four-hour, seven-days-a-week, three-hundred-sixty-five-days-a-year ICU-level care. You either need to pay about four hundred thousand dollars a year for private nursing care, or you'll need at least two people willing to do this for you at home. This is required. You're in the ICU. Only certain specialized docs and nurses can care for you now. Unless a minimum of two people get extensive training to be your ICU nurses, we cannot let you go home because it wouldn't be safe. It's a 24-7-365, no-vacation job."

"What about long-term-care facilities? Could he go there?" asks Karina.

"There are three places in Massachusetts equipped to care for people with a tracheostomy on a ventilator, but there's about a one-year waiting list for a bed in any of these, and it's extremely expensive. Most insurances won't cover it. Yours doesn't cover it."

Richard watches Karina's face pale as she begins to absorb the dreadful ramifications of this choice.

"A trach is not a silver bullet. If you get this surgery and go on a vent, you are trading one can of worms for another. You're still getting a can of worms. This is not a cure, okay? It's important you understand this. The disease will continue to progress. You might eventually be locked in. All you're doing is protecting the airway."

"What happens if he doesn't get the surgery?"

Although Karina asked the question, Kathy delivers her answer to Richard. She never breaks eye contact.

"If you choose not to do the surgery, we'll either order a palliative-care consult here or you'll go home to Hospice. You'll be extubated to a BiPAP. They'll give you medication to keep you comfortable, and they'll slowly bring down the BiPAP machine. Your breathing will get shallower and shallower, and eventually you'll stop breathing on your own. You'll die of respiratory failure."

Death by suffocation. He's avoided imagining this in any detail, what the actual end of ALS might look like for him. Even with the need for the PEG tube and the BiPAP and the paralysis of his legs, despite every escalating loss in ability, thoughts of his death continued to be blurry and remote like a car racing by on a road in the distance, the make and model impossible to describe. Now the damn thing is parked right in front of him, and his heart is screaming, pounding, panicked. Again, his breathing remains calm, dictated by the ventilator, and the mismatch in physiology feels like a shattering earthquake in the foundation of his being. Like he's coming apart.

"Could the antibiotics clear the pneumonia and then

he'd be like he was before this happened and breathe on his own?"

"This isn't a spinal-cord or lung injury. This is his diaphragm no longer working. It can't heal."

"But he was breathing earlier today. Couldn't this be just a momentary crisis and he could come off the vent and still breathe?"

"That's very unlikely. I see about three hundred people in your position every year. And in the twelve years I've been doing this, I've only seen that happen one time."

So there's a chance. But it's remote. And Kathy has had this horrific conversation over three thousand times. Richard wants to cry for both of them.

"If you were us, what would you do?"

"I'm not you, and even though I'm around it every day, I'll never know what it's like to have ALS. I don't know your finances or your relationship, so I really can't answer that. I will say this. If you choose the trach, every six months I'll ask you, 'When is enough enough for you?' In our experience, patients who go on the vent typically get pneumonia after pneumonia. The disease doesn't stop. Eye movements can be good for many years, but like I said, eventually he might be locked in."

"What do most people do?"

"About seven percent get vented."

"Why so few?"

"This is a very difficult, intimate decision. If Richard gets this surgery, assuming you're his caregiver, your quality of life is going to go way down. I don't care how kind or tough you are, you'll end up getting something called compassion fatigue. It's essentially PTSD."

Kathy waits, perhaps thinking that Karina will have another question. She's silenced. Kathy turns her attention back to Richard.

"In Massachusetts, if you decide to get the trach and later change your mind, you can elect to go off the ventilator in the hospital or at home with Hospice. How old is Grace again?"

"She's twenty," says Karina.

"She's in college, right?"

"Yes."

Richard blinks.

"If you wanted to see her graduate or get married, if you wanted to stick around a bit longer, some people choose to go on the vent for this one last thing and then elect to go off it."

Grace graduates in a little over two years. He'd like to see that. He'd like to see her get married. He'd like to meet his grandchildren. He'd like to live.

Kathy sits on the edge of his bed so she's now closer to eye level and puts her hand on his. Her eyes are the color of deeply steeped black tea, tired and kind. Her hand is so blessedly warm and human.

"Are you afraid to die?"

He blinks.

"I'm sorry to be so blunt. Are you afraid of suffering at death?"

He blinks.

"What else are you afraid of?"

Letting go. Disappearing. Not existing. There is another fear, lurking in the shadows of his consciousness, but he can't identify it.

"I'm going to leave you and Karina with some information and a letter board. I know you haven't had to use one of these yet, and it'll be slow and frustrating, but it'll give you a way to express whatever you need to ask or say."

"How quickly do we have to make this decision?"

"I don't want you to make this decision today. Think on it and think of questions, and I'll be back tomorrow. He can't be intubated like this for very long. This decision can't happen over a week's time. It can't wait too long."

Kathy goes over how to use the letter board. Richard only half listens. He's more captured by the steady, rhythmic sounds of the ventilator, the push and pull of air forced in and out of him, the percussive music of his body being breathed. In. Out. In. Out. A clock ticking. Kathy finishes her tutorial.

"Okay, I'll be back tomorrow. So we're one hundred percent clear on the choices. Your choice is either to be extubated and most likely die, or you're getting the surgery and asking Karina to take care of you twenty-four/seven. You understand that these are your choices and the consequences of each?"

Richard blinks and doesn't look at Karina. He assumes she understands as well.

It's either his life or hers.

CHAPTER THIRTY-ONE

Standing at the end of a long line in the hospital cafeteria, Karina waits to pay for her second cup of coffee. She's in no hurry. The man in front of her is dressed in blue scrubs, carrying a tray of yogurt, granola, fruit, and orange juice. She's hungry, but the thought of food makes her nervous stomach turn. More coffee won't sit well in her either, but she needed something else to purchase, a reason to stay in the cafeteria, and coffee seemed like the simplest choice. She left Richard's room in the ICU yesterday evening and hasn't drummed up the nerve yet to return. She hasn't picked up that letter board. She doesn't know what he's thinking, what he wants to do. She hasn't asked him. She knows she has to. One more cup of coffee first.

If this were a movie, she'd have her hands over her eyes, her breath held, silently begging the woman waiting in line to pay for coffee not to go up to the ICU. If this were a book, she'd close it without turning the page. She doesn't want to know his decision.

She's such a coward. She didn't used to be. She used to be fearless. She left her family, her home, her country, when she was eighteen and never looked back. Where did that woman go? She wishes she could reclaim that courageous spirit who graduated with honors from a college in a foreign country and played piano in New York with the best jazz musicians in the city. Maybe she could start by being a woman who finishes her coffee, takes the elevator to the ICU, picks up that letter board, and finds out what happens next.

What if he wants the surgery?

She can't be his 24-7 caregiver. But there's no one else. His parents are dead. His brothers have jobs and wives and kids to raise. Private help is insanely expensive, and Richard's money is gone, already sunk into his care, the wheelchair, the lift, Grace's college. He can't ask Grace to do this for him. Karina won't let him.

He's not her husband anymore. She doesn't have to do this. He's not her burden to bear. She thinks of his affairs, of all the women he's slept with. Where are all these women now? Not in the hospital cafeteria. Not in the ICU. Not in her den every day for the rest of his life.

She thinks of the decade she spent lying to him, pretending to want more children, feigning disappointment every month, feeding him medically plausible reasons for her fictitious infertility, pretending to go to doctor appointments. The first coffee sours in her stomach, and she feels as if she could throw up.

He wanted more children. He especially wanted a son. Every month for years, he thought they were trying to conceive. She got an IUD when Grace was three and never told him. She was afraid to tell him the truth, that he wouldn't want her anymore, that he'd divorce her. And then where would she be? Disgraced and alone, a single mother to a preschooler, divorced and unemployed in a foreign country.

When Grace was thirteen, Karina went to her ob-gyn to have the IUD replaced. But it wouldn't come out. It had embedded in the wall of her uterus, and she needed surgery to remove it. Petrified of surgery, she confessed everything to Richard. Her decade of deception.

When she allows herself to remember that day, she's still haunted by the reaction on his face, his expression evolving from shock to grief to rage. The rage remained, burned into his features and probably his heart. It took them a year to separate and another two to get officially divorced, but their marriage was over the day she told him what she'd done.

He's never forgiven her. She doesn't blame him. Whatever his sins were, this one was entirely hers. Maybe caring for him on a vent for the next decade is what she deserves, penance for this unforgivable sin. Maybe that would finally absolve her.

If he says he wants the surgery, can she refuse to be his caregiver? She'd essentially be sentencing him to death. If he wants to live, who is she to say that he should die? Should she shut up and do whatever he wants, whatever it takes to keep him alive? An old but familiar resentment flares. Twenty years ago, he accepted that teaching position at New England Conservatory, made the decision to move them from New York to Boston without regard for her happiness, her freedom, her career. He stole the life she wanted from her. And here she is, all these years later, considering the real possibility of playing jazz again, and Richard still has the power to stop her.

She doesn't want to be sentenced to life as his caregiver, a prisoner chained to his paralyzed body. What will he do? It's going to be a death sentence for one of them.

"Is that it?"

"Huh?" Karina looks up, baffled.

"Is it just the coffee?" asks the cashier.

"Oh, yeah. Sorry."

Karina pays and finds an empty seat at a table for two. She wraps her hands around the paper cup and brings her nose to the lip, inhaling the smell instead of drinking. She checks her phone, hoping for a text or email that will keep her busy. She has nothing.

She tries to imagine where Richard's head is at, to gamble on his decision. While his body is useless and essentially dead already, his mind, his intellect, his personality, are still perfectly intact. What would she do? She takes a sip of the coffee she doesn't want and knows her answer before she swallows. She wouldn't get the surgery. She wouldn't go on a vent. She wouldn't want anyone giving up his or her life to keep her alive. She wouldn't want to linger on like that, locked in, totally dependent on others for everything.

But Grace. She wouldn't want to leave her yet. What will Grace do after college? Who will she marry? What will her life look like? Who is she going to be? Karina wants to know, to be here to see it all.

What if it's not forever? What if he chooses the surgery so he can see Grace graduate in two years, or he only needs caregiving for one more year until a bed becomes available in a facility? Could she do that? She stayed married to him, trapped in their broken relationship, persevering for at least ten years for the sake of Grace, appearances, her religion, and security. So she could do this for one or two years. But what if it's more? What if he wants to go on living at any cost?

She closes her eyes and prays, searching for the right thing to do. She opens her eyes and stares into her coffee, at the doctor reading his phone at the table across from her, at the cashier ringing up the next customer. No one and nothing have an answer for her.

Even Kathy couldn't tell them what to do. *The trach surgery is a horrible choice. I would never do that. I recommend extubation and death by suffocation at home with Hospice. That's the only way to go.* Karina wishes the decision were black-and-white like this. Instead, she and Richard have been thrown into the deep end of a gray ocean. There is no horizon, no North Star visible in the gray sky, only these impossible choices before them.

She sits until her coffee is stone cold, the cup still full. It's almost eleven o'clock. Time to face the music. She tosses her cup in the trash, rides the elevator to the ICU, and takes a deep breath before entering Richard's room.

The back of his bed is partially reclined, so he's sitting up. He's awake, looking at her with round, alert eyes. He looks smaller than he did yesterday, his emaciated body disappearing beneath the hospital sheets like a magic trick, the breathing tube and ventilation machine overwhelming his modest mass. The machine clicks and whirs, and Richard's chest forcefully rises and falls about every three seconds. She eyes the letter board on the table next to his bed and then quickly returns her gaze to Richard's chest, pretending she didn't notice it.

She tries to smile. "Has Kathy been here yet?"

He does nothing but stare wide-eyed back at her, and she wonders whether his lack of response means no, he didn't hear her, or he's ignoring her.

"Are you still waiting for Kathy?"

He blinks.

"Okay."

She could wait for Kathy to find out if he's made a decision. She doesn't have to ask him. Kathy can do it. That's Karina's plan. She sits in the visitor's chair next to his bed and intends to stay busy on her phone until Kathy appears. Karina scrolls through her newsfeed on Facebook without interest. She's sitting to his right, and Richard can't turn his head, but she can feel his eyes on her. She glances up, and his eyes lock onto hers, desperate, begging for communication.

"We're going to wait for Kathy, okay?"

He stares at her, unblinking.

"Do you want to tell me something before she gets here?"

He blinks.

Shit.

"Do you know what you want to do?"

He blinks.

Her stomach hollows out, and her heart beats in her throat. Reluctantly, slowly, she picks up the letter board. She turns back toward the door, trying to will Kathy's appearance. No one is there. She turns back to face Richard and holds up the letter board.

"Is the first letter in the first row?"

She waits. Nothing.

"Second row?"

He blinks.

"Is it *E*?"

"*F*?"

"*G*?"

"*H*?"

He blinks.

"*H*."

"Is the second letter in the first row? . . . Second? . . . Third? . . . Fourth?"

He blinks.

"Fourth?"

He blinks.

"Is it *O*?"

He blinks.

"Okay, *H-O*. Is the third letter in the first row? . . . Second? . . . Third?"

He blinks.

"*M*?"

He blinks.

"*Home*?"

He blinks. A tear falls from his right eye. She pulls a tissue from her coat pocket and blots his face.

"You want to go home?"

He blinks.

But does that mean he wants to have the surgery and go home on a vent or be extubated and go home?

"Do you want the surgery?" she hears herself ask.

He stares at her, eyes wide, tears welling out of both now. He doesn't blink them away.

"You want them to take the tube out and go home?"

He blinks through wet eyes.

"My God, Richard. You understand what that means, right?"

He blinks, and she is simultaneously relieved and devastated. She bursts into tears, crying hard, alternately mopping his face and hers with the same pathetic tissue.

"I'm so sorry, Richard." She searches her pockets for another tissue, not finding one. "I'm so sorry. Do you want me to call Grace?"

He blinks.

"Okay. She'll be here. Who else? Your brothers?"

His eyes remain steady.

"Bill?"

He blinks.

"Trevor?"

He doesn't blink.

"Okay. Me, Grace, and Bill. Anyone else?"

He stares through his shiny, wet eyes straight into hers. She wipes her nose with the damp tissue and sniffs.

"Are you scared?"

He blinks.

"I am, too."

She sits on the edge of his bed and holds his bony, lifeless hand in hers. She pulls out her shirtsleeve and gently wipes the tears from his eyes and cheeks and then does the same to hers.

"Thank you," she whispers.

He blinks.

CHAPTER THIRTY-TWO

Grace still hasn't taken her coat off. She's standing at a remove from the end of his bed, her suitcase by her side. She arrived about an hour ago, coming straight from the airport. Her face is drawn, her eyes steeled, her expression flat and unfamiliar to him. She feels so far away. This is not her normal face. He wants to tell her to come closer and smile, an absurd request even if he could make it given the circumstances, but he wants to see her face the way he loves it most—bright eyes, rosy cheekbones perched high atop each side of an easy smile, happy. He supposes his face, unshaven with a tube inserted into his mouth and taped to his cheek, looks unfamiliar to her, as well.

Karina asked her many questions about classes and her boyfriend when Grace first arrived, but they've run out of conversation. Everyone in the room is quiet. Karina is sitting in the chair next to him, her arms crossed tight in front of her chest as if she's cold. She looks tired, serious, vaguely alert. Kathy is standing by the ventilator, reading something on her phone. Bill sits at the foot of the bed, rubbing Richard's feet and calves with his warm, strong hands. God bless Bill.

The sense of waiting is fog-thick, ominous, surreal. The moment feels important, urgent, yet absolutely nothing is happening. It's absurdly mundane.

A slender woman with a boyish haircut and many silver-studded earrings enters the room.

"Hello. Is this Richard?"

"Hi, Ginny," says Kathy. "Yes, this is Richard Evans. And this is his ex-wife, Karina; their daughter, Grace; and home health aide extraordinaire Bill. This is Ginny from Hospice."

Instead of shaking hands, she hugs everyone. She stands over Richard and places a hand on his shoulder. Her eyes are brown and without makeup, clear and calmly confident. She smiles in a way that feels natural and not at all inappropriate for the situation. There is no joy, no pity, no forced falseness in her gesture, and without words she communicates, *I'm here with you.* Richard wishes he could thank her.

"I'll let the doctor know that you're here," says Kathy, excusing herself from the room.

"Let's talk about a few things before the doctor comes. Our goal today is to get you comfortably home. The doctor is going to remove the endotracheal tube and switch you over to a BiPAP. We won't know until he does this, but if your breathing muscles are totally gone, the BiPAP won't be able to sustain your breathing. If that should happen, I'll administer morphine and a sedative through the IV line, so they'll take effect immediately. I'll be here to make sure that you feel calm. You won't struggle, and you won't feel like you're suffocating. And everyone will be right here with you. Does that sound okay?"

The mechanical ventilator breathes air into Richard's lungs. Then it draws air out. Absolutely nothing about what she just said sounds okay. He blinks. Karina holds his hand in hers. Bill squeezes his foot. Ginny, whom Richard had never seen before a minute ago, keeps her hand on his shoulder, and he's grateful, reassured by her presence and touch. This isn't her first rodeo.

Kathy DeVillo returns with Dr. Connors, a blue tie peeking out from beneath his buttoned white lab coat, a pen and a phone tucked in the front pocket, a stethoscope around his neck. He was clean shaven when Richard was first admitted to the ICU but now has the beginnings of a beard. He's been in and out, checking on Richard many times over the past three days.

"How we doing?" asks Dr. Connors.

Richard's trachea feels bruised, dry, and brutalized. His lips are painfully chapped. He's fixated on an obsessive desire to clear his throat and struggling to ignore an intense itch on the top of his head that seems intent on burrowing into his brain. And if things go sideways, he's going to die today.

"Are we waiting on anyone else?" asks Kathy.

Everyone looks to Richard. He doesn't blink.

"No," says Karina.

"Yes," says Ginny. "I've called for a music therapist."

"A what?" asks Karina.

"Someone to come and play guitar, something relaxing to keep Richard calm."

Richard raises his eyebrows in alarm, hoping Karina sees him.

"God no," says Karina. "No. Call him off."

"Are you sure?" asks Ginny.

"Positive. He'd detest that."

Richard blinks several times.

"I'll play something from my iPhone." Karina looks to Richard. "Mozart?"

He thinks. *No. Keep going.*

"Bach?"

He stares, unblinking.

"Schumann?"

He blinks.

"Okay."

She doesn't ask him which piece. He trusts that she knows. He watches her search. Then the music begins.

Of course, she knew. It's Schumann's Fantasie in C Major, op. 17, his greatest masterpiece, and Richard's favorite piece to play. He listens to the first few measures of the first movement and wonders.

"Yes, this is you, playing at Carnegie Hall," says Karina.

His mouth is immobilized, but his eyes are smiling. He blinks.

The serious business of what awaits them pauses as everyone listens. The first movement of this fantasy is dense and dreamy, a passionate lamentation, Schumann expressing his longing for his beloved Clara, separated from him by her father. Richard locks his eyes with Karina's as they listen, knowing she knows the meaning behind the composition, and his heart aches for her to know how grateful he is to her and how sorry he is. Even if he didn't have a tube in his throat, even if he weren't too tired and scared to use the letter board, even if it weren't too late and he could speak, he's not sure he could find the words big and true enough to heal what he's done to her.

He keeps his eyes with hers alone, willing the notes to speak for him, and he's swaddled in her gaze. Tears spill down his face. Karina squeezes his hand and nods.

The second movement changes mood abruptly. It's a majestic march, powerful, extroverted, bombastic, fast, and extremely difficult to play. Richard's professional career passes through his consciousness. Curtis, New England Conservatory, the prestigious concert halls and symphonies, the world-renowned conductors, the orchestras, the festivals, the solo recitals, the audiences, the standing ovations, the press and accolades. It was a beautiful life. It all went by so fast.

Dr. Connors checks Richard's vitals and explains what he's about to do.

"Are you ready?"

Richard looks to Grace. Bill notices and extends an arm, inviting her closer, inside their circle. She edges next to her mother.

"I'm here, Dad." Grace looks terrified. "I love you."

Richard blinks, loving her back. He prays this isn't the last time he hears her say those words.

Dr. Connors positions himself over Richard's face and peels back the tape.

"Okay, on three. One, two, three."

Dr. Connors yanks hard on the end of the tube, and it slides up from inside Richard for a surprising length, a procedure as brutishly physical and indelicate as the tube's insertion. The tube is out, and everyone looks at Richard, waiting. No one, including Richard, is breathing.

He's playing the third movement now. The melody is solemn, a reconciliation. The BiPAP mask is placed over his face, and still there is no air. The ventilator is quiet. There is no sound but for Richard playing Schumann. His head begins to tingle as the room narrows. He stays focused on Grace and Karina and Bill and the music, and suddenly there are no boundaries between the vibrations of the notes and the people in this room. He doesn't want to leave them. He wants to keep listening, vibrating, breathing, being.

He wants a few more notes. Another movement. Just a bit longer. He doesn't want to die in the ICU.

His lungs call out to his diaphragm and the muscles of his abdomen, searching, pleading. He plays the final notes of Schumann's Fantasie, slower, softer, hopeful, a whispered prayer to God. Everyone in the room and Richard's lungs wait in stillness for an answer.

CHAPTER THIRTY-THREE

They've been home for three days now. With Richard's consent, Ginny weaned him off the BiPAP two days ago. His breathing is extremely shallow, but he's still going. Despite the shortness of his breath, he doesn't seem to be agitated or struggling. Ginny has him on regularly scheduled doses of morphine for any discomfort and Ativan for anxiety. He's sedated, in and out of consciousness, sleeping most of the time. Karina knows it's not right to think this way, but she keeps wondering how long he can go on.

When they arrived safely home, she and Bill rolled Richard's hospital bed into the living room so he could be next to his piano. Grace is camped on the couch with her bedding and pillow, still in her pajamas at dinnertime, typing a paper for school on her laptop. She's been sleeping on the couch, watching over her father day and night, waiting for the end. They're all waiting.

The house is eerily quiet. They haven't turned on the TV. Karina canceled her piano lessons for the week. She hasn't left the house in three days. They're existing outside of time, cocooned in the living room, unaware of world events, ears tuned in to the faint, intermittent sound of Richard still breathing.

It's not that Karina's needed at home. There's not much to do now. She's got cabin fever and would love to go for a morning walk with Elise, but she can't risk leaving the house. He might not even be conscious when it happens, but she feels she should be here. She owes that much to him. To both of them, maybe.

Ginny comes for a couple of hours each day to oversee things, to monitor Richard and administer his meds while she's here. She just left a few minutes ago. Bill comes in the evenings. He tends to Richard's body and keeps Karina company. He should be here in a couple of hours.

She checks the time. She'd normally feed Richard now. Instead, she delivers a syringe of water through Richard's PEG tube, then caps the MIC-KEY button. Two days ago, Richard was awake when Ginny was here. She asked him if he wanted to discontinue nutrition. He blinked. She asked him if he wanted to discontinue the BiPAP. He blinked.

He has pneumonia and is no longer being treated for it. His 110-pound, paralyzed body is pumped full of morphine and Ativan. He hasn't eaten in two days. Yet, part of him is still holding on.

"I'm going to take a shower," says Grace.

"Okay, honey."

Karina sits in the wing chair positioned next to Richard's bed. She studies his face while he sleeps. His cheeks are sunken beneath his speckled beard. No one has shaved him since he was rushed to the hospital six days ago. His lips are cracked and scabbed. His hair and eyelashes are black and beautiful.

He exhales. She waits and waits. She wonders and leans in. He inhales. How does he still have the strength to keep breathing?

She puts her hand on top of his. His hand is bony and cold, unresponsive to her touch, the skin mottled, pooling with blood. This disease is hideous. No one should have to go through this.

"I'm so sorry, Richard. I'm so sorry." She starts crying. "I'm so sorry."

At first, her apology is purely about the unfairness and horror of having ALS, but as she keeps crying and repeating herself, the meaning of her apology changes. She moves to the edge of the wing chair and lowers her head closer to his ear.

"I'm sorry, Richard. I'm sorry I denied you the family you wanted. I'm sorry I deceived you. I should've had the courage to tell you the truth. I should've set you free to live the life you wanted with someone else. I'm sorry I stopped being the woman you fell in love with. I pushed you away. I know I did. I'm sorry."

She watches his face as she thinks, searching the darkened hallways of their history for any more boxed-up, unspoken words. She finds none. Her tears subside. She pulls

LISA GENOVA

a tissue from the box on the side table, wipes her eyes, and blows her nose. She takes a deep breath and sighs, and the unexpected noise that leaves her is low and anguished, a howl. She inhales again and feels twenty years lighter.

"We did the best we could, right?"

She waits, listening to him breathe. She returns her hand to his and scans his face for any sign of responsiveness. She can't know if he's asleep or knocked unconscious on high doses of Ativan or in a coma. He doesn't open his eyes. She searches for even an incidental, involuntary twitch in a facial muscle that she can interpret. He's still. He can't squeeze her hand. She can't know if he heard her.

"I wish I'd done better."

"Everything okay?" asks Grace.

Karina turns around. Grace is standing at the bottom of the stairs in a maroon University of Chicago sweatshirt, black leggings, and slippers, wet hair pulled up in a ponytail. Karina can't tell by her posture or expression if Grace heard any of Karina's confessions or crying.

"Everything's the same. You hungry?"

"No."

As if in solidarity with her father, Grace hasn't eaten anything since yesterday. Grace settles herself back on the couch. The day is fast turning to night, and darkness invades the living room. Grace's face is illuminated by her laptop screen like a flashlight. Karina stands, intending to turn on a lamp, but, once up, walks over to the piano instead.

She sits down and places her fingers on the keys. Without thinking, she begins playing Chopin's Nocturne in E-flat Major, op. 9, no. 2. The melody is gentle, relatively easy, and delicious to play, like comfort food. She loves the freedom the piece gives her with the tempo, the glassy trills, the decorative tones. The melody evokes sense memories of her mother's pierogi, a gentle rain outside her dorm window at Curtis, dancing a waltz with Richard in New York. The piece builds, its crescendo a passionate embrace, then tumbles into trickling water, thrown confetti, a return home, safe, held.

She plays the final tender note, and the sound floats throughout the room before disappearing, a sweet memory. She turns around and is surprised to see Grace up from the couch, sitting in the wing chair. Her eyes are glossy, wet with tears. At first, Karina assumes Grace was moved by Chopin's nocturne. But then Karina listens.

She keeps listening. She waits and holds her breath, straining to hear an inhale. The room remains quiet. She waits past the point of knowing, to be sure.

He's gone.

EPILOGUE

Karina's standing in the den, an empty cardboard box in her hands. It's been eight days since Richard died. She's been avoiding this room.

Bill brought boxes for Richard's clothes. She's donating them to Goodwill. She stands without moving, observing all the equipment that was part of her every day for months, now abandoned, historical relics. The hospital bed, the wheelchair, the Hoyer lift, the suction machine, the cough-assist machine, the BiPAP, the piss bottle, the pivot disc. She's offering those and anything she might be forgetting to Caring Health.

She places the box on the floor but doesn't know where to begin. The room feels strange without Richard in it. She supposes it will go back to being the den after she clears everything out, but she can't imagine that. He lived in this room for only four months, but it no longer feels like her den. Richard had ALS in this room. She looks at his empty bed, the wheelchair, his desk chair, and feels his energetic impression everywhere, this room still thick with intense memories of Richard and his ALS. Her eyes well, and she rubs the goose bumps on her arms. Or he's decided to haunt her.

She sits down at his desk and swivels in the chair. Maybe Grace will want his computer. She went back to school yesterday. She seems to be doing okay. It's good she has classes and her friends and a demanding schedule to give her life structure, to keep her moving forward.

The house is quiet again. No more whirring of the BiPAP, no alarms sounding when the mask goes askew, no more coughing, gagging, choking. Those sounds are done and gone. Richard is gone.

What will she do now? She feels the familiar void, like something heavy and queasy sinking in her stomach, as if she's eaten something gone bad. Should she resume her piano lessons? Or should she pack up the entire house and move to New York? Her heart races, nervous at the daring thought of it. She swivels in her chair, not settling on an answer.

Maybe packing up Richard's clothes is enough for right now. She sighs and doesn't move off the chair. Instead, she checks her email on her phone. At the top of her inbox is an email from Dr. George. She opens it.

Dear Karina,

I'm so sorry about Richard. I enjoyed getting to know him, if only briefly. I know you said he decided on using a computer-synthesized voice when the time came instead of banking his own. Well, I double-checked the recorder I lent you before wiping it and giving it to another patient, and there was a single legacy message on it that you'll want. I've attached it for you here.

Be well,

Dr. George

She hesitates, then taps on the attached MP3 file.

"Hi, Ka-ri-na. I-like-tha Doc-to-Geor calls-thi-sa le-ga-cy me-ssa. I-been-thi-king a-lot a-bou wha-my le-ga-cy will-be. Will-i-be-my pi-a-no ca-reer? Or-Grace? Tha-sa-be-tter one.

"May-be-iss this. Wha-I-have to-say to-you.

"Ka-ri-na. I'm-sor-ry. I'm-sor-ry I-chea-ted o-nyou. I'm-sor-ry I'm-the-rea-son you-sto-pla-ying jazz. I-was-a te-rri-ble hus-ba to-you. You de-ser be-tter.

"If-I-ha-da wish fo-my-le-ga-cy, ih-wou-be this. You-are-so ta-len-ted. You-are-sti-young. You-are-hea-thy. You-have e-ve-ry-thing you-nee.

"Go-to New-York. Play-jazz. Live-your-life. Be-ha-ppy."

She sits still in the chair, amazed to be hearing Richard's voice again, stunned by his message, these words she's always wanted, needed. She plays it again, and the sick feeling in her stomach dissipates. Her heart is pounding, awake, excited. She plays it again, and his words release the last of her grip on twenty years of

♪

blame and resentment, of being right at any cost. The cost has been astronomical.

A plan for her future forms as she listens, determined thoughts that sound pitch-perfect in her mind's ear, a composition of notes she's been wanting to play her whole life. She's going to pack up this room, and then she's going to need more boxes. But first, she plays his message again, grateful to hear the sound of his voice, forgiving him, feeling his presence in this room and in his words, knowing she, too, is forgiven, free.

LISA'S CALL TO ACTION

Dear Reader,

Thank you for reading *Every Note Played*. Maybe prior to reading this book you read *Tuesdays with Morrie*, watched *The Theory of Everything*, or dumped a bucket of ice water over your head. You probably had some awareness of ALS. I hope you now have a deeper understanding of what it feels like to live with this disease.

I also hope you'll join me in putting that empathy into action. By making a donation to ALS care and research, *you* can be part of the progress that will lead to treatments and a cure and help provide proper care to the people who desperately need it now.

Please take a moment, go to www.LisaGenova.com, and click on the "Readers in Action: ALS" button to make a donation to ALS ONE, an extraordinary organization determined to deliver a treatment or cure for ALS and dedicated to offering improved care now. For more information on ALS ONE, go to www.ALSONE.org.

Thank you for taking the time to get involved, for turning your compassionate awareness into action. Let's see how amazingly generous and powerful this readership can be!

With love,
Lisa Genova

ACKNOWLEDGMENTS

This book began with Richard Glatzer, who, along with his husband, Wash Westmoreland, wrote and directed the film *Still Alice*. Richard had bulbar ALS, which means that his symptoms began in the muscles of his head and neck. I never heard the sound of Richard's voice. He brilliantly codirected *Still Alice* by typing with one finger on an iPad.

Richard, I am forever grateful to you for all you gave to the creation of the film *Still Alice*, for sharing with me what it feels like to live with ALS, for showing us all what grace and courage look like, for not giving up on your dreams. Richard died on March 10, 2015, shortly after Julianne Moore won the Oscar for Best Actress for her role in the film.

I met Kevin Gosnell, his wife, Kathy, and his sons, Jake

and Joey (and later Scott), shortly after Kevin was diagnosed with ALS. Within minutes of knowing him, I knew three things:

1. Before ALS takes him, Kevin is going to change the world.

2. He's also going to change me.

3. I love this man and his family.

Right after Kevin's devastating diagnosis, he framed his terrifying situation in the most selfless way I can imagine. He thought, "How can what I'm about to go through serve others?" He then gathered the best people in medicine, science, and care and formed ALS ONE, an extraordinary collaboration determined to discover a treatment or cure for ALS while promising the best possible care to people living with ALS now. I invite you all to learn more about Kevin's important legacy at ALSONE.org and get involved. Kevin passed away on August 8, 2016.

Thank you, Kevin, for inviting me into your home, for sharing your life and family with me. I owe so much of my understanding of ALS to you. But beyond that, you were simply one of the best human beings I've ever known—your generosity and grace; your loving leadership; your unwavering sense of purpose, of contribution to the world beyond yourself; the life lessons you gave to your boys, which I now give to my children; the enormous love you shared with your family and everyone who came into your life. I always felt like part of your family in your home. I love and miss you. I hope I've made you proud.

I met Chris Connors at the ALS clinic at Massachusetts General Hospital six days after his ALS diagnosis. I was struck by how calm and laugh-out-loud funny he was given his situation. I adored him immediately and asked if we could stay in touch. We spent the next many months corresponding by email. His "ALS Diary" was intimate, vulnerable, heartbreaking, and hilarious. I laughed and cried through most of his emails.

Chris, thank you for sharing your humor, how much you loved Emily and your boys, your fears, your courage, and so many specifics of dealing with the losses that come with ALS. I feel incredibly lucky to have known and loved you. Chris died on December 9, 2016. I encourage you all to Google his obituary.

I met Chris Engstrom at his parents' house on Cape Cod. He was my age, handsome, scrawny, his strangled voice mostly unintelligible. He was an artist educated at Yale and loved hiking in the woods, but he could no longer walk or hold a paintbrush in his hands. The hiking boots on his paralyzed feet broke my heart. But he could raise his eyebrows to say yes, and he could still communicate—at first using a rollerboard strapped to his arm, his hand placed by someone else onto a computer mouse, later with only his eyes using a Tobii. He had a beautiful smile and a twinkle in his eyes—I'm pretty sure he was flirting with me.

Chris became my dear friend. Thank you, Chris, for sharing your fears and frustrations and anger, your hopes and beliefs and love. I'm in awe of your artwork and poetry. I'm still envious of your writing! Thank you for reading the first many chapters of this book, for offering me insights and spot-on feedback, for not letting me get lazy with even one word. I love and miss you. Chris Engstrom died on May 7, 2017.

Enormous gratitude also goes to Bobby Forster, Steve Saling, Sue Wells, Janet Suydam, David Garber, Arthur Cohen, Chip Fanelli, and Lawrence Jamison Hudson. Thank you for your generosity and trust, for sharing your experiences and perspectives, for helping me understand ALS for this book, and for sharing wisdom beyond the pages of this story.

Thank you, Kathy Gosnell, Rebecca Brown George, Casey Forster, Ginny Gifford, Joyce Siberling, Jamie Heywood, Ben Heywood, and Sue Latimer, for so generously sharing your experiences with ALS. Your love and support for your husbands, brother, and friend are extraordinary and inspiring.

Thank you, Dr. Merit Cudkowicz, Dr. James Berry, and Darlene Sawicki, NP, for allowing me to shadow you at the ALS clinic at Massachusetts General Hospital, for answering every question I asked, for helping me understand the clinical picture of ALS. It would be easy to imagine a team such as yours needing to build emotional walls. There is no cure for this disease. You witness too much heartbreak, loss, and death. I'm utterly amazed by all of you, so grateful for the kindness, dignity, and humanity you give to every patient, every day, above and beyond the call of pure medical care. You are all heroes.

And then there is Ron Hoffman. Ron is the founder and executive director of Compassionate Care ALS, an organization that provides much-needed guidance, equipment, and comfort to overwhelmed families traveling this unfamiliar, complex, difficult journey. He is an angel and a hero, and I'm beyond grateful to call him my dear friend. He is also the author of *Sacred Bullet*. Everyone should read this important book. Ron, thank you for inviting me into your world, for the many road trips and house calls, for showing me this beautiful work that you do, for teaching me so much about ALS, living, and dying. You are a gift to every person who is lucky enough to know you, including me. For more information on Compassionate Care ALS, go to www.ccals.org.

Thank you to Erin MacDonald Lajeunesse, Kristine Copley, and Julie Brown Yau of Compassionate Care ALS and Rob Goldstein of ALS TDI for sharing what you know about caring for people with ALS and for introducing me to people who have it. Thank you to John Costello for showing me all the fascinating, creative tools people with ALS can use to continue communicating as they become increasingly paralyzed. Thank you for all that you do to help people with ALS stay connected, for preserving their voices. Thank you to Kathy Bliss for helping me understand the important role of Hospice and palliative care.

Thank you, Abigail Field and Monica Rizzio for the wonderful piano lessons. For insights into classical piano, jazz piano, and life as a concert pianist, enormous thanks to Abigail Field, David Kuehn, Dianne Goolkasian Rahbee, Jesse Lynch, and Simon Tedeschi.

Thanks and love to Anabel Pandiella, John Genova, Louise Schneider, and Joe Deitch for taking me to piano concerts; to Gosia Mentzer and Anna O'Grady for answering many questions about Poland; to Jen Bergstrom, Alison Callahan, and Vicky Bijur for your insightful edits and for championing this story.

Love and gratitude to my team of early readers: Anne Carey, Laurel Daly, Mary MacGregor, Kim Howland, Kate Racette, and Danny Wallace. Thank you for reading the chapters as I wrote them, for going on this ALS journey with me, for your unwavering love and support.

Thanks and so much love to Sarah Swain, James Brown, Joe Deitch, Merit Cudkowicz, Ron Hoffman, and Kathy Gosnell for reading the manuscript and offering invaluable feedback.

AUTHOR'S NOTE

In May 2017, about the same time that I finished the final draft of this book, the FDA approved a new drug for the treatment of ALS. Radicava became available by prescription to patients in August 2017, as this book goes to press. Administration will be by intravenous infusion in twenty-eight-day cycles and cost $1,000 per infusion. We don't yet know whether insurance will cover this. In a trial in Japan, Radicava slowed a decline in physical symptoms by 33 percent.